NOBODY LIVES FOREVER

Doc Ganson's career has bottomed out, but he has a plan for the perfect con—a rich widow, ripe for the plucking. All he has to do is convince the big guy, Jim Farrar, to take her on. But Farrar is growing tired of the grifter's life. And he certainly doesn't want to have anything to do with a lowlife like Doc. He misses his life back in Florida, and crazy redhead Tony. But his lawyer, Johnny Doyle, talks him into it. Then Farrar meets the mark, Mrs. Halversen, and old habits take over. He charms her in spite of himself. Meanwhile, Doc is growing impatient. He doesn't trust Farrar. And when Doc doesn't trust someone, there's hell to pay.

TOMORROW'S ANOTHER DAY

Everyone admires Lonnie and his carefree attitude. He seems to be born lucky, particularly at cards. He even wins Ballard's restaurant in a card game. Which is where he meets Mary. She's with the Greek, the only one of the gamblers who doesn't admire Lonnie. In fact, the Greek resents him. And when Lonnie snatches Mary away from him—and marries her, no less!—his resentment turns to plans of revenge. Lonnie used to be quite a risk-taker, but under Mary's influence, he puts all that behind him. Until the perfect scheme arrives. How could he know that behind this gamble is the Greek's vindictive retribution?

Nobody Lives Forever

Tomorrow's Another Day

W. R. BURNETT

Introduction by Nicholas Litchfield

STARK
HOUSE

Stark House Press • Eureka California

NOBODY LIVES FOREVER / TOMORROW'S ANOTHER DAY

Published by Stark House Press
1315 H Street
Eureka, CA 95501, USA
griffinskye3@sbcglobal.net
www.starkhousepress.com

NOBODY LIVES FOREVER
Published by Alfred A. Knopf Inc., New York,
and copyright © 1943 by W. R. Burnett.

TOMORROW'S ANOTHER DAY
Published by Alfred A. Knopf Inc., New York,
and copyright © 1945 by W. R. Burnett.

"The Gangster Novel Writer Who Was Shot with Luck"
copyright © 2024 by Nicholas Litchfield

ISBN: 979-8-88601-077-0

Book design by Mark Shepard, shepgraphics.com
Proofreading by Bill Kelly

First Stark House Press Edition: March 2024

THE GANGSTER NOVEL WRITER
WHO WAS SHOT WITH LUCK

by Nicholas Litchfield

The highly adept and versatile William Riley Burnett (1899–1982), unafraid to pursue new varieties of genre and invest his considerable talents in articulating the crudites of iniquitous killers and con men, pounded out thirty-nine novels and collaborated on sixty motion pictures, including the quintessential war movie *The Great Escape.* It's no exaggeration to say that Burnett's literature significantly impacted the film world. The mood and tone of his work inspired heavyweight Hollywood producers and directors like Darryl F. Zanuck and John Huston, and his formidable characterizations and dialogue helped shape the careers of iconic movie stars like Edward G. Robinson and Humphrey Bogart.

During the 1930s, while still fresh-faced on the writing scene, he headed to California to work as a screenwriter, remaining there for the rest of his life. He devoted much of his time to film and television scripts, either adapting his novels and short stories or enriching the cinematic luster of other works. By 1941, "he had become one of Hollywood's highest-paid screenwriters" (Fowler, 1982). In 1943, he received an Academy Award nomination for Best Original Screenplay for *Wake Island*, fashioned from one of his stories. He also wrote scripts for popular television series in the 1950s and 1960s, including *The Untouchables* and *Naked City. The Great Escape* earned him a Writers Guild Award nomination in 1964 for Best Written American Drama.

His success gives the outward appearance of a man shot with luck who found himself at the right place at the right time and was sharp enough to capitalize on a series of good hands until he broke the bank. Maybe there's a bit of truth in that, but most of all, Burnett was an imaginative and industrious writer who wrote for fun rather than profit and persevered despite rejection.

Interestingly, he had no formal training as a writer, although he did attend the School of Journalism at Ohio State University. Curiously, he dropped out after one semester.

He married soon after, at age twenty-one, and worked a succession of unfulfilling jobs, including factory work, selling insurance, and as a statistician for local government. He found time in his evenings and weekends to write fiction, producing "a hundred short stories, a half-dozen plays, and five novels" (Barry, 1981). Like most aspiring writers, he sent his fiction to a slew of editors and received generic rejection letters in return. According to Burnett, a personalized rejection slip from Maxwell Perkins, a well-regarded editor at Scribner's, offered encouragement and made the would-be author persist with his writing endeavors. Perkins subsequently rejected another of Burnett's manuscripts, leading the unpublished writer to temporarily shelve his literary aspirations.

A dispiriting stint as a night clerk in a sleazy hotel made him reevaluate his career and start pitching the novel to other publishers. His luck changed when The Dial Press accepted *Little Caesar* for publication. That acceptance marked the turning point in his life.

The book was published in June 1929, becoming a global hit, and proved to be his masterwork. It was translated into at least twelve languages, and Warner Brothers acquired the movie rights. The 1931 movie became a highly revered blockbuster, considered one of the defining movies of the early period of talkies, a prototype for the gangster movies that followed.

Burnett's good fortune continued with his second novel, *Iron Man*, a Book-Of-The-Month Club selection (Patterson, 1929). It was released on Jan 1, 1930, just seven months after his debut as a published author. Having written to no avail for almost a decade, he achieved unparalleled success by the time he reached thirty years of age. It is a testament to persistence and never allowing a good story to die in vain.

Surprisingly, despite writing many short stories, Burnett rarely placed his fiction in magazines. *Saturday Evening Post* and *Collier's* are among his list of publications, but, by and large, the slicks published serializations of his novels rather than original stories. His best success came in November 1929, months after his debut novel hit bookstore shelves. "Dressing Up," published in *Harper's Magazine*, is a wry tale about predatory department store clerks taking advantage of an uncouth gangster who has come into money. It's not your usual literary awards contender, but interestingly, the story shared joint first place for the prestigious O. Henry Award (*New York Herald Tribune*, 1929).

Placing work in magazines probably meant little to Burnett. He found more lucrative markets for his short fiction—case in point, "Red's Café," a murder mystery. Though never published, film actor Jack Carson read it and purchased it with hopes of hawking it to film executive Jack L. Warner and landing the starring role (Citizen-News, 1945). In fact, Jack Warner acquired numerous stories penned by Burnett, including *Nobody Lives Forever* and *Tomorrow's Another Day* (The Seattle Star, 1945; The Salt Lake Tribune, 1945), the two novels collected in this volume.

Originally a 1943 *Collier's* serial (Harper, 2000), and published in book form by Alfred A. Knopf soon after, *Nobody Lives Forever*, Burnett's thirteenth novel, is a tough-guy tale about a motley gang of derelict swindlers looking to fleece a naïve millionaire. The shady group is led by Dr. William Ganson (alias Bill Watts or Dr. Walter Harris Bright). Although he has a legitimate medical degree, he's a dangerous, disloyal, scumbag junkie whose license to practice medicine was revoked. His dilapidated fellow conmen include Windy Mather, an old strongarm man who was once a professional wrestler; the erudite ex-con Shake Thomas (nicknamed "Shakespeare" because of his reading habits); and elderly ex-con Pop Gruber, an astronomy-loving rogue, referred to as "a clearinghouse for criminal information."

When Doc's college friend, Charley Evans, the manager of the Marwood Arms (a fancy hotel), sings the praises of one of his guests—the lonely, widowed millionaire Mrs. Gladys Halvorsen—Doc schemes to swindle the trusting woman out of her money. He enlists the services of James "Jim" Lloyd (alias Jim Farrar, alias Reed Wallace, alias James Driscoll), a small-time crook who happens to be a great operator with women. Although Jim is smitten with a stunning floozy, Miss Antonia Blackburn, his love for money persuades him to go along with Doc's scheme. Greed, deceit, and just plain folly scupper the gang's plans and turn their promising con into a big, bloody catastrophe.

Bolstered by strong characterization and first-rate dialogue, *Nobody Lives Forever* is an absorbing drama with an inspired assortment of peculiar eccentrics. If the plot lacks complexity, Burnett makes up for it with carefully crafted suspense and authentic portrayals of despairing people searching for happiness and a change of circumstance. As John Selby of the *Rocky Mount Telegram* wisely noted, this is a story "stuffed with characters quite out of the ordinary" but which "have lungs that pump, hearts that beat, and emotions that fluctuate" (Selby, 1944). Tense, lively scenes involving the Doc are nicely balanced with sensitive, touching conversations between Jim and Gladys. However despicable these grasping characters are, ultimately, you find yourself invested in the gang's pursuit of money and committed to staying for the climactic outcome.

According to newspaper reports, Warner Brothers bought the author's pitch in late July 1941 and hired Burnett to develop the screenplay, with Ann Sheridan and Humphrey Bogart slated to costar (R.W.D., 1941). Purportedly, Oscar-nominated screenwriter Dale Van Every, who adapted the famed 1937 movie *Captains Courageous*, was attached to the project (Mines, 1941). There's no record of his involvement in the finished product, though. Postponed for years, the movie, adapted by Burnett, eventually hit screens in 1946 and featured three impressive actors: John Garfield and Geraldine Fitzgerald (both Oscar nominees) and three-time Oscar-winner Walter Brennan.

His next novel, *Tomorrow's Another Day*, also issued first as a magazine serial and then published by Alfred A Knopf, was purchased by Warner Brothers. This was an era where a book seldom sold "for more (and usually for much less) than $50,000," whereas a play, "even a flop, can earn six high figures" (Wright, 1946). The savvy Burnett, a prosperous screenwriter-producer since 1929, added a stipulation to his contract that put him in a mighty position and made him wealthier than any of his peers. Typically, he would have his novel serialized in a magazine, published as a novel, and acquired by a film studio. Often, he was contracted to write the screenplay. At some point, after MGM acquired the rights to one of his stories, Burnett negotiated a ten-week hiatus in which to write a novel, offering screen rights for $100,000 and collecting ten percent of the film profits. Later, he negotiated a contract where the studio granted him a ten-week salary to write a novel, with a five-day option to buy the story at a stipulated price (Wright, 1946).

It was a profitable ploy, and Warner Brothers exercised its option on multiple occasions, including *High Sierra*, *Nobody Lives Forever*, and *Tomorrow's Another Day*. The latter, published in 1945, was assigned to the production slate of Robert Buckner (Hanna, 1945), an outstanding screenwriter with a background in journalism and Broadway plays. Alas, neither he nor whoever took over from him at Warner Brothers when the much-in-demand Buckner moved to Universal had success with the project. More than $100,000 was spent trying to develop it into a movie starring Erroll Flynn, but ultimately it became the episode, "Thanks for Tomorrow", in Season 2 of the *77 Sunset Strip* television series (Skolski, 1959).

Phil Strong of the *New York Herald Tribune* once observed: "The reader can always depend on one thing in W.R. Burnett's books and that is action which is almost cinematic. Mr. Burnett tells and runs" (Strong, 1938). While this may be true of much of Burnett's work, truth be told, little about *Tomorrow's Another Day* indicates it would translate well to the big screen. The story moves through gambling rooms and the racecourse, but the clipped action is sparse, and the plot points thin. Chiefly, it's a straightforward, character-driven drama heavily focused on burgeoning romance and spiteful retribution. Affluent businessmen like Benny Hayt, Jack "The Greek" Pool, and W. W. Keller, all members of the big gambling syndicates, and the much-feared mobster Gus Borgia, populate the pages, helping make sure the story "lingers in the purlieus of gangsterdom" (Burke, 1945).

Front and center is Lonnie Drew, a handsome, cavalier gambler who has won and lost half a million dollars in his lifetime but continues to stop fear from interfering with his game. When a winning hand of cards lands him Lake Shore Inn, one of the most fashionable restaurants in town, he decides to curb his betting instincts and try his hand at being a businessman. Although his hard work pays off, a constant fear of failure and of disappointing Mary Donnell, the beautiful local model he falls in love with, lures him back to the gambling world. Despite his savvy, the odds are stacked against him—Jack Pool, sour at Lonnie for stealing his girlfriend, baits him with a good race tip, secretly wanting to bring Lonnie down. The smooth, conniving, professional gambler is willing to jeopardize a hefty payout and, potentially, a brutal reprisal just to see Lonnie suffer.

"However shallow the mind of a gambler may be, W.R. Burnett reaches the bottom of it," writes a book critic at the *New York Herald Tribune* (Conrad, 1945). From a writing standpoint, the premise that grips the second half of the book might otherwise feel contrived and asinine, but Burnett is sufficiently persuasive to make Jack Pool's hatred convincing and his bold actions conceivable.

Although not as affecting as *Nobody Lives Forever*, Burnett's expert pacing and vivid storytelling enhance his novel. Relationships blossom, hatred sizzles and hopes and fears turn on the flip of a coin.

Journalist Lawrence Witte once said: "I can, without contradiction, state that Burnett has never turned out a 'bad' novel. He is a superb storyteller, with a pen that captures dialogue so readable that he could be writing with a tape recorder—it's that natural." Without question, Burnett had a great understanding of the characters he presented, exposing their strengths and foibles and the complexities of personality. It wasn't luck, timing, or advantageous contacts that brought him success but shrewdness and hard graft. His adaptability and refusal to give up ensured his many works found a foothold. The movie adaptations left a lasting impression, but so did his novels.

—December 2023
Rochester, NY

··

Nicholas Litchfield is the founder of the literary magazine *Lowestoft Chronicle*, author of the suspense novel *Swampjack Virus*, and editor of ten literary anthologies. His stories, essays, and book reviews appear in many magazines and newspapers, including *Colorado Review*, *Daily Press*, *Pennsylvania Literary Journal*, *Shotgun Honey*, *The Adroit Journal*, and *The Virginian-Pilot*. He has contributed introductions to numerous books, including seventeen Stark House Press reprints of long-forgotten noir and mystery novels. Formerly a book critic for the *Lancashire Post*, syndicated to twenty-five newspapers across the U.K., he now writes for *Publishers Weekly*. You can find him online at nicholaslitchfield.com and on Twitter: @N_Litchfield.

Works cited:

Barry, Daniel. "W. R. Burnett (Nov 25 1899-)." American Novelists, 1910-1945, edited by James J. Martine, vol. 9, Gale, 1981, pp. 103-107. Dictionary of Literary Biography Vol. 9. Gale Literature: Dictionary of Literary Biography, link.gale.com/apps/doc/ETPTWF285492141/DLBC?u=nysl_ro_rchstpro&sid=bookmark-DLBC.

Burke, Harry R. (Nov 18, 1945). "Books." St. Louis Globe-Democrat, p.41.

Citizen-News (May 3, 1945). "The Hollywood Scene." Citizen-News, p.8.

Conrad, George (Nov 25, 1945). "Tomorrow's Another Day, by W.R. Burnett." New York Herald Tribune, p.F14.

Dinerstein, Joel and Anna Schuleit Haber (2017). American Cool: W. R. Burnett and the Rise of Literary Noir. Virginia Quarterly Review 93(3), 174-181. https://www.muse.jhu.edu/article/714624.

Fowler, Glenn (Apr 29, 1982). "W.R. Burnett, 82, The Author of 'Little Caesar' and 40 Films." New York Times, p. D23.

Hanna, David (Feb 2, 1945). "Week's film news in review." Daily News, p.30.

Harper, Katherine. "W. R. Burnett (Nov 25 1899-Apr 25 1982)." American Hard-Boiled Crime Writers, edited by George Parker Anderson and Julie B. Anderson, vol. 226, Gale, 2000, pp. 31-47. Dictionary of Literary Biography Vol. 226. Gale Literature: Dictionary of Literary Biography, link.gale.com/apps/doc/TTRMZC576389690/DLBC?u=nysl_ro_rchstpro&sid=bookmark-DLBC.

Mines, Harry (Oct 24, 1941). "Ann Sheridan with Bogart." Daily News, p.30.

New York Herald Tribune (Nov 7, 1929). "W.M. John Ties W.R. Burnett in O. Henry Award." New York Herald Tribune, p.18.

Paterson, Isabel (Dec 31, 1929). "BOOKS and OTHER THINGS." New York Herald Tribune, p.12.

R.W.D. (Aug 6, 1941). "Hollywood News and New York Screen Notes." New York Herald Tribune, p.12.

Selby, John. (Jan 26, 1944). "The Literary Guidepost." Rocky Mount Telegram, p.4.

Skolski, Sidney (Sep 1, 1959). "Hollywood Is My Beat." Citizen-News, p.9.

Strong, Phil (Apr 17, 1938). "On the Kansas-Missouri Border." New York Herald Tribune, p. H4.

The Salt Lake Tribune (Feb 18, 1945). "Film Prospects." The Salt Lake Tribune, p.45.

The Seattle Star (Apr 11, 1945). "Picture Is Taken From Stage Play." The Seattle Star, p.7.

Witte, Lawrence (May 16, 1962). "The World Of Television." The Evening Independent, p.6.

Wright, Virginia (Jan 11, 1946). "World Collection." Daily News, p.23.

Nobody Lives Forever

W. R. BURNETT

To Whitney

BOOK ONE

A cynic is a person who knows the price of
everything and the value of nothing.
                                                    OSCAR WILDE

I

Doc Ganson was a slender, little man of about forty-five. His hair was Indian-black and his narrow, bony face was pale. Although there was nothing actually wrong with him, he gave at first glance the appearance of deformity; sometimes men referred to him as a hunchback. His mouth was thin-lipped and grim; and his eyes looked startlingly black and bright owing to his pallor.

Doc was standing at the window of his shabby Los Angeles hotel room, staring morosely down into the street below. A thick June fog blurred the lights and moved slowly between the buildings, urged on by a gentle, variable wind. Beyond the rooftops he could see the golden glow of Chinatown; a tourists' Chinatown full of Chop Suey joints and phony oriental shops.

Behind him, Shake Thomas rustled his Racing Form. Doc turned in irritation.

"Got a good one, I'll bet," he sneered.

"Yeah," said Shake, pushing back his hat which he rarely removed. "Got what looks like a good one in the third at Aqueduct. All I need now is a stake."

"All any of us needs is a square meal," said Doc. "Where's Windy? Where did he say he was going? I don't like the idea of him wandering around alone. He might stick somebody up. When he gets hungry he's hard to handle."

"If he does and gets away with it, it's all right with me," said Shake. "It's like them Romans. It ain't being crooked that counts; it's getting caught. Like when the boy hid the badger in his shirt and it et his guts ..."

"It was a fox," said Doc, "and the boy was a Spartan, not a Roman. Don't you ever get anything right?"

"Five dollars says it was a badger," said Shake, outraged by Doc's offhand superiority. Shake had spent twelve of his forty years in various prisons and had read hundreds of books; so he considered himself quite an authority. He was known in the profession as "Shakespeare," because of his wide reading, and he took the nickname seriously.

He was a big, placid man with a dewlap and a stomach. Owing to the strain of prison fare and confinement, he was old for his age. He was bald, wore glasses, and all his upper teeth were false. He puffed at the slightest exertion and slept over twelve hours a day; when he was awake he was either studying a Racing Form or reading a book—any book. Print was print to him. He'd pore for hours over an antiquated history of the city of Los Angeles he'd picked up in a secondhand bookstore for ten cents. With him, reading was a substitute for vice.

At one time he'd been high up in the ranks of con men. He had a fine personality for the trade; he looked good-natured, honest and dependable; and he was very handy at steering a sucker. He'd made quite a few good takes. But a combination of heedlessness and apathy led to his downfall; he was arrested again and again; finally, he began to lose cases. A stretch in a tough Southern prison completed his ruin. Now he was not only outmoded, but broke. However, it didn't worry him much.

"So you want to bet five dollars!" sneered Doc. "Stop clowning."

"I'll have five bucks someday, won't I? What's the matter—don't you trust me, Doc?"

Doc flung himself into a chair and stared sulkily at the floor, ignoring Shake's remarks. There was a long pause and the room was so quiet that the night noises from the huge, sprawling city gradually grew more and more audible.

Finally Doc observed, as if talking to himself: "If we could only figure an angle on that rich dame."

Shake stirred, looked up from the Racing Form, and sighed.

"Yeah," he said, nodding his head slowly, "a dame with over a million dollars. Can you imagine! I get gooseflesh just thinking about it."

Doc puckered up his face and stared at the dirty, ragged carpet. This rich dame was to Shake and their other pal, Windy, no more than a rosy, impossible dream. But to Doc she was an actual bright hope. When the world looked blackest he would sit down and quietly force himself to think about her; he would turn over and over in his mind schemes to relieve her of enough sugar to buy himself security against the dark future which he always felt was menacing him. At times he hated her— this fortunate woman who had everything he wanted: money and the respect of her fellows. It seemed unfair to Doc that she should walk about with a tranquil mind, enjoying the present, able to ignore the future, while he could just barely get enough to eat and was headed, unless checked, for the charity ward and, ultimately, the potter's field.

He didn't even know the woman personally: he had only heard about her. In the whole country Doc had only one respectable acquaintance left: this man lived in Los Angeles, was fairly prosperous, and was managing the swankiest apartment hotel in the Wilshire District. Doc ran into him one day on the street; in fact the man had accosted him. They had gone to college together. He bought Doc a drink and they talked over old times. They had lost track of each other years ago, and the man—Charley Evans—knew nothing whatever about Doc's running fight with the law. Doc told him that he had given up his practice due to ill health and was now dabbling in California real estate; he intimated that business was terrible. In the old days Evans had been known as the tightest bird in the school; Doc saw him shying off from a touch and it amused him. However, Doc finally did put the bite on him for a twenty and laughed to himself when he saw how relieved Evans was that the sum wanted had been so modest.

He saw Evans from time to time. It always cost Evans money, but the amounts were so trifling that it made no difference to him. He liked to talk to Doc about the past. One night, after a couple of tall beers, feeling slightly mellow, Evans told Doc about Mrs. Halvorsen, his star boarder. A lonely widow—forty—very nice-looking, and with a million and a half dollars.

"If I was a handsome man I'd certainly try to marry her," he said, laughing. "She's a real lady—so polite and considerate. Doesn't know a soul out here. Her husband died in Minneapolis and left her all this money—he was in the flour business: must've cornered it, considering what he made out of it. He was a lot older than she was—a kind of invalid; she looked after him, stayed with him; one of those kind of women."

Doc grinned cynically.

"Yeah," he said. "I'd look after a man with that kind of money myself—and would I stay with him!"

Evans laughed appreciatively, but shook his head.

"I see what you mean. But I don't think that was it. She's just a wonderful woman—and lonesome! Goes to movies by herself—eats by herself. It's sort of pathetic in a way. I introduced her to a couple of nice men I've got staying with me—you know: solid fellows in their fifties. But she didn't seem to care much about them. I often invite her to my table. Once in a while she eats with me in the evening. She never has much to say. To tell you the truth I'm afraid I don't interest her at all." Evans sighed. "I don't know," he added, as if summing the whole thing up.

Doc grinned.

"Maybe you and these other solid men are not what she's looking for. Why not try me?"

Evans laughed, hitting Doc on the back. Doc drew away sharply—he hated easy familiarity—but recovered so quickly that Evans, who was a little obtuse anyway, didn't notice the movement. Doc had been known as a "devil with the women" in college. Evans thought his remark very funny.

"I couldn't do that," said Evans. "I've got the poor lady's best interests at heart."

Doc laughed it off. Although he spent half his time trying to delude himself, he still had a pretty good idea of his own limitations: he wouldn't have a Chinaman's chance with the elegant Mrs. Halvorsen.

But she was seldom far from his thoughts. He sought Evans out so often that the hotel manager began to shy off. There was something about Doc's interest in Mrs. Halvorsen that puzzled and worried him.

Besides, his friend, Doc, who used to be such a card, had changed. The more Evans saw of him the less he liked and trusted him. He began to avoid Doc—saw him only when he couldn't decently put him off.

Doc sat up so suddenly that Shake jumped. Doc was always startling him by abrupt, unexpected movements.

"Look at my clothes," said Doc, bitterly. "How could I get in with a dame like that?"

Shake stared—then understood. Funny about Doc—always thinking up schemes to take that luscious million-dollar sucker.

"It wouldn't help," said Shake, tactlessly. "She wouldn't go for you."

"Plenty have."

"I ain't seen any flocking around, Doc. Quit kidding me."

Doc burned in silence. The ambition of his life was to shine in the eyes of women; in fact, a woman had started him on the road down. He could have killed Shake with pleasure. He threw a look at him which made the big man very uneasy. Shake was a coward and at times very much afraid of Doc.

"I didn't mean nothing, Doc," he said, smiling placatingly. "Just kidding."

Doc gritted his teeth but said nothing, and Shake sat shaking his head slowly.

"No use, Doc. We might as well forget it."

There was a long pause. Taxis hooted in the stillness. Finally Doc got up and began to pace the floor. He spoke bitterly.

"It's enough to make a man want to go out and hang himself. A sucker like that flying around, and us without a dime. No front. Nothing."

Doc went back to the window and stood staring out at the fog. A black depression settled over him. He began to tremble. With a curt exclamation, he went hurriedly into the bathroom and locked the door.

Shake shook his head sadly.

"At it again," he told himself. "If he was wise, he'd leave that stuff alone. It's a bum idea. You'd think a doctor would know better."

Making a clucking noise with his tongue, he picked up the Racing Form and began to study it.

"He's running out of stuff, too," Shake said, half aloud. "When he gets clear out, there'll be hell to pay. He'll be out prowling the drug stores."

In a little while Doc came out of the bathroom and went back to the window. His cheeks were flushed. He looked better.

"I'm not going to give this one up," he said, without turning. "Not if I have to get in touch with a couple of the boys and split with them to strongarm her for the diamonds and the fur coats."

Shake dropped the Racing Form.

"Take it easy, Doc."

"I'm tired of living like this. You've got to take the plunge sometime."

"Stick to your own racket."

Doc turned. His eyes were glittering. Shake felt very uneasy when Doc was like this; he looked and was dangerous.

"We're in a nice fix," he cried. "If we lose this dame ..."

"Relax, Doc. We never had a chance to do anything but lose her."

Doc sat down, but jumped up immediately and began to pace the floor.

"I won't give up. I'll figure an angle if it kills me."

Just as Shake was about to speak soothingly, the door opened and Windy Mather came in. He was a huge man with powerful shoulders and a look of stupid immovability. Ordinarily he was good-natured enough, but he took careful handling. He was an old strongarm man and had worked for various mobs in the East. As a young man, he'd wrestled professionally, had his nose broken, acquired a slightly cauliflowered ear. Now in his forties he was running to fat, but he was still strong enough to handle six ordinary men.

He shut the door behind him, then without a word walked to the middle of the room and stood grinning at them.

"Well?" said Doc, impatiently. When Windy grinned like that he knew something was up. Doc felt vaguely hopeful.

Still grinning, Windy took a small roll of bills out of his pocket and waved it.

"See?"

"How much?" asked Doc.

"Thirty-three dollars."

"Where'd you get it?"

Windy grinned widely. He always had a hard time expressing himself and usually spoke in monosyllables. His bashful silence had earned him his nickname.

"This dame—I helped her."

"What dame?"

"She wanted to roll this guy, see?"

"What guy?"

"The guy with the dame. He put up a howl, see? I saw her come out of the joint with him."

"What joint?"

"Where they was."

"Oh, hell," said Doc. "Give me the money."

Windy was going to protest, but Doc pulled the roll away from him and stuffed it into his pocket. Windy frowned, then grinned. Doc studied his face for a moment.

"How much did you hold out?"

Windy flushed.

"Me?"

"Yes—you."

"I got maybe a couple of bucks stashed."

Shake got up and put his hand on Windy's shoulder. "Listen, Windy. Will there be a beef?"

"No beef. It was easy. Nice dame. She wanted me to go home with her."

Doc laughed.

"Probably wanted to roll you for your share. You're going to get yourself in a jam some night."

"I'm careful," said Windy, grinning.

None of them spoke until they'd finished eating. They sat stowing the food away, ignoring each other. Long thick strands of fog were gliding past the misted windows of the restaurant. In the bar a jukebox was playing a sad, sentimental, little tune.

Pretty soon Doc pushed back his chair and sighed.

"I feel better."

"Yeah," said Shake, wiping his mouth elaborately with a napkin and pushing his empty plate away. "I'll say."

Windy went on eating in stolid silence.

"Look at him," said Doc. "It's his second shot at it, too, you can bet. He grabbed a meal before he brought us the money. Didn't you, Windy?"

"Just a sandwich, Doc. Well—two sandwiches. I was so hungry I couldn't stand it when I passed one of them joints—heard 'em sizzling."

Doc took out a couple of cigars, handed Shake one; they lit up and sat smoking in silence. Finally, Windy finished eating and sighed loudly, then he snapped his fingers.

"Doc."

"Yeah?"

"There was a thing I wanted to tell you."

"Think hard."

"I got it. I run into Gyp Connors. Remember him?"

"A guy to avoid—a rat."

"I don't know. Well—I run into him. He told me something. That big guy's in town."

"What big guy?"

"The top guy. The Florida fellow ..."

Doc started.

"Who—Jim Farrar?"

"That's the one. Gyp says he swears he seen him in a car." Doc and Shake exchanged a glance. They had both worked with Jim Farrar in the old days. Shake laughed good-naturedly. "What do you think of that? He's Doc's pet hate."

"Who?" Windy demanded, looking from one to the other. "The top guy?"

"Top guy, my foot!" said Doc, bitterly. "He's just had a run of luck, that's all. He'll get caught up with."

"Never yet," said Shake. He laughed. "Regular Casanova, Jim is. The babes really go for him—and does he work at it. Murder!"

"Murder is right. What they see in that big, swell-headed phony ...!" Doc hesitated, and sat thinking.

"Remember the little blonde singer, Doc?" asked Shake. "The one who was going to marry that New York millionaire till she met Jim Farrar?"

Doc flushed slightly. The prettiest girl he'd ever seen in his life and she wouldn't so much as look at him; and he'd been in the money at the time; white tie and tails, the works! He nodded without looking at Shake, lost in bitter reflections.

"What happened?" Windy demanded, staring.

Shake laughed.

"Well, Jim not only copped the guy's girl, he beat the guy for fifty grand and made him like it."

Windy guffawed.

"Yeah," said Doc, "but the girl tried to turn Jim in later."

"That was after he gave her the brush-off."

"Big stiff!"

Doc sat suffering. Imagine a guy so lucky or so well-endowed or so something that he actually brushes off a gorgeous babe like Rita, that singer! At the time Doc would have given his right arm for her. Even now, ten years later, he could see her plain as day—so pretty and desirable.

"What do you suppose the top guy's doing out here?" Shake demanded. "He was killing 'em in Florida. The fix must be in here. Jim wouldn't work without a fix. It's like Napoleon said...."

"The hell with Napoleon," Doc broke out. "Whatever it was he said you wouldn't get it right. Maybe Jim's on the lam."

"From what?"

"You never know." Doc hesitated, sat lost in thought, then he gave a start. His eyes flashed so wildly that for a moment Shake imagined that Doc had gone berserk at last, as he had always feared he would. "He's our man," cried Doc.

"What are you talking about?" Shake demanded.

Doc snorted impatiently.

"Don't you see? Jim's the very guy to beat this rich widow. It's his kind of stuff."

Shake blinked, then a smile spread over his slack face. "What do you know ...!"

"I'm not so sold on Jim as some people," said Doc. "But this is his meat. He's got a way with women; no doubt about it." Doc rubbed his hands together and smiled grimly. "I don't like the big guy; but we need him on this one, and I'd split with Hitler if I couldn't work it any other way."

"What's going on here?" asked Windy, looking from one to the other.

They ignored him. Doc, preoccupied, was already working on the idea. Shake sat staring. At last his smile faded; he shook his head.

"No, Doc. You're just kidding yourself like you been all along on this deal. Jim wouldn't work with us. He'd have us kicked out if we located him."

"Oh, yeah? What's the matter with us?"

"Use your eyes. We look like bums. We haven't got any dough. What's your proposition? Jim furnishes the front money; makes the take and splits with us. It ain't reasonable."

"How many million-dollar suckers do you find? A dame at that. All we've got to do is locate Jim. I'll sell him."

"I'm not even going to think about it. With the kind of luck I been having, it just couldn't happen."

"Let's go hunt Pop Gruber. If anybody knows where Jim is, he will." Doc jumped up, his eyes glittering with excitement.

"You birds going to try to work with the top guy?" Windy demanded, staring.

"Sure."

Windy guffawed.

"That's just plain nuts—us tramps!"

"We'll see," said Doc.

II

Pop Gruber was what is known as a "character." He was a thin, wiry, little man in his late sixties; his color was good, his eyes sparkled, and he looked as if he'd last forever. You would take him for a small-town bookkeeper, and yet, aside from the strongarm rackets, he had run the gamut of crime. As a newsboy in Indianapolis he'd learned to pickpockets; then, always rising in his profession, he'd turned sneakthief, shoplifter, small time grifter, and at last he'd got in with a big con mob and prospered to such an extent that for two years he retired from the rackets. But he came to grief when Denver was cleaned up by Van Cise; he was tried, convicted, and sent to prison for a long stretch. When he got out he was an old man, and was smart enough to realize it. The big dough was now out of his reach. He got a little stake together and went to California, where he became a familiar sight on the streets of Los Angeles.

Every clear night he appeared on some downtown corner with his tripod and telescope. For one thin dime he would show you the moon, or Saturn, or some other celestial object of interest. People liked this pleasant, innocent-seeming old fellow. Occasionally he picked a drunk's pocket, but nobody knew that except the cop on the beat, who split with him. And he had another way of making money. He was a clearing house for criminal information. This was something even the cop on the beat didn't know; Pop was no informer; he worked only with the racket men. Every out-of-town pickpocket, shoplifter, or con man who wanted his presence known to his Los Angeles coworkers got in touch with Pop. For a small fee he obliged. He had enough on half a dozen big-timers to hang them, but he was absolutely trustworthy, and everybody knew it.

Children liked Pop. He'd show them the moon through the telescope and talk to them in a way they could understand. Mothers referred to him as "that nice old man." While Pop was engaged with the children, some dubious individual, wanted for anything from safe blowing to rape, would be standing in the background, pretending to read a newspaper, waiting for a word with Pop. Where was Chicago Louie, the lamster, holing up? Where could New York Blondie be found? Smiling, Pop would give out the information. Money would be slipped into his hand, and maybe the mug would even look through the telescope for the benefit of the tame citizens.

While Pop was long on information regarding others, he was short on information dealing with himself. When he wasn't on one of the downtown corners, he was very hard to find. He moved frequently. He never ate in the same restaurant or drank in the same bar two days running. There was really no reason for him to be so extremely cautious. He was just cagey by nature and the older he got the cagier he became.

It took Doc four days to find him. Every night Doc cursed the fog which rolled in about sundown, making it impossible for Pop to get any customers for his telescope. On the fourth night a strong wind blew the fog away before nine o'clock. Doc hurried downtown. There was Pop on one of the busiest corners, blandly explaining all about the moon to a young couple. The girl kept giggling and asking questions. Doc could have throttled her. What the hell did she expect for a dime!

Pop knew that Doc was behind him, but gave no sign. While answering the girl's inane questions, he proceeded mentally to catalogue Doc as follows: Dr. William Ganson, alias Bill Watts; alias Walter Bright. Legit. M.D., but barred. On the junk. Broke. Small-time con man. Untrustworthy, even dangerous.

Finally the young man dragged the girl away from the telescope, gave Pop a quarter and told him to keep the change.

"Thank you, sir," said Pop, touching his hat and bowing slightly. "That's very kind of you."

Doc stepped up hurriedly and handed Pop a dime.

"You look right in here, sir," said Pop. "The moon's full tonight. Pretty, ain't it?"

Doc pretended to look.

"I understand the top guy's in town."

"Is he?" said Pop innocently.

"Are you kidding?"

"No."

"It's worth a lot."

"How much?"

"We've located a million-dollar sucker."

Pop adjusted the telescope, getting closer to Doc. "No use, Doc."

"Why?"

"He's quit. All washed up."

"Is he in town?"

"I'm giving out the information. He made a big take and quit."

"This is the biggest thing yet—and a dame. Easy touch for him."

"No use. Come on, Doc. That's all."

"Tell me one thing: is he in town?"

Pop said nothing. Doc raised up and moved back from the telescope. A woman was waiting to look at the moon. Doc slipped Pop a dollar.

"Okay. He's in town," said Doc. "I got a pretty straight talk on that. This is worth a lot to you, Pop."

Pop adjusted the telescope for the woman.

"You see? The moon's full tonight. Pretty, ain't it?" Pop smiled at the woman, who looked and cried: "Oooo! Seems scary when you see it so plain." Then he moved back.

"No use, Doc. Run along. The copper's due. Call box right over there."

"Where'll you be later?"

Pop hesitated.

"I might have a drink at Maxie's around midnight."

Doc turned and walked away.

"What are all those big, funny-looking dimples?" the woman demanded.

"Mountains and valleys, ma'am, just like we have; only the moon's dead; nothing lives on it."

The woman shuddered and drew back.

"I don't like it," she said. "It makes me feel funny to see it away out there in space all by itself."

Pop nodded understandingly. He'd felt that way, too, at first. But now the moon was as familiar to him as Maxie's Bar; it was like an old friend.

When the woman had gone, Pop stood wondering why he'd considered having anything to do with Doc Ganson. Was it the phrase, "a million-dollar sucker"? Even a hopped-up small-time con man would think twice before saying such a thing? No use anybody trying to kid Jim Farrar. Doc either had hold of a big one or he was crazy. Anyway, Jim had quit cold. Pop sighed, and stood thinking about how the top guy had suddenly loomed up out of the fog.

"It was just like I was seeing things," mused Pop.

The night had been clear and he'd been doing a pretty good business. All of a sudden, it seemed like, the air got full of dampness, the neon signs looked blurred, then the fog came down. Pop was just packing up when—round the corner came the top guy, looking as big and husky as ever, followed by Doyle, his mouthpiece.

"Hello, Pop," he'd said. "How is it?"

"Fine. And you?"

While they talked, Pop's shrewd eyes had detected that something was seriously wrong with the big fellow; he wasn't sure just what. The fact that he was quitting, however, was a tip-off in a way. A guy going strong like Jim Farrar doesn't just up and quit.

The little Irish lawyer had acted funny, too—like he was embarrassed or something. The big fellow had said:

"If Ray Slavens happens to show, tell him where to find me. Nobody else. I'm holing up."

Then he winked at Pop; but it wasn't a light-hearted wink, the old man decided: Jim's eyes looked sad; then he'd turned and the fog had almost immediately swallowed him up. Pop saw him dimly as he swung his heavy shoulders round a corner.

"All the same," Pop mused, "a million-dollar sucker might interest him—a dame at that."

III

Jim Farrar was sitting in a swanky Los Angeles hotel room with his lawyer, John Stanislaus Doyle, better known as Johnny the Priest. The big fellow was drunk and Johnny grimaced as he watched him pour himself another long shot of bourbon. He had been worried about the big fellow for quite a while: something was biting him and he sat searching his face, as he had been doing off and on for months, for a key to his changed behavior. Some of the Florida guys—Abe Cole, for instance—shrugged it off with the remark that Jim had finally tangled with a dame who had his number. But that was too easy and too commonplace. Johnny was pretty sure it went deeper than that.

Johnny was considered the "cultured" one of the boys; principally because he'd graduated in law from a good Midwestern university, but also because he wore glasses with a cord to them and had an ascetic, priest-like air. He was under medium height, but looked taller owing to his leanness. His blue eyes seemed cold and aloof behind the thick lenses of his glasses. He was a great guy for putting the chill on some bumptious sucker.

He had been disbarred in Illinois for an alleged jury manipulation; but after a decent interval some of his political friends had managed to get him reinstated. However, things didn't go too well for him so he moved to Florida where he met Jim Farrar and prospered. He was in his late forties, but didn't look within ten years of his age.

Jim stirred uneasily in his chair and sat staring morosely at the floor, drink in hand. Johnny regarded him nervously. He'd certainly been pulling some funny ones lately. Getting bugs over that chiseling Chicago dame; letting her make a slob out of him in front of his friends; taking it on the lam when she finally decided to brush him off. Imagine, her brushing off Jim Farrar! It seemed incredible. And then this silly trip to California. Johnny had gone through hell trying to get tickets for the jump. You couldn't make Jim understand about the war. The hell with the war, he said. To him it was just a minor irritation. Not only that. It was dangerous for guys like them to go jumping around outside their own bailiwick; especially so as Jim was carrying a wad: nearly a hundred thousand G's he'd chiseled out of the Florida suckers. Of course—he wasn't wanted. In fact, in spite of everything, he'd had a big season the winter before and no squawks. What an operator!

Jim was a funny guy. Almost always willing to talk—on any subject he understood: he was far from silent. And yet he could clam up like a Yankee farmer if he got an idea you were trying to find out something.

Take the California trip. No sense to it at all by any rational standards. Abe Cole had said flatly that Jim was crazy for taking such a chance—and predicted a jam. Johnny taxed Jim with it—but Jim clammed up. He wouldn't even intimate why he wanted to go to the West Coast. He just did—that was all.

He sat studying Jim in silence, noting the bloodshot eyes, the graying hair, the evidences of strain in the face, the restlessness—in short, the great change which had taken place in the big fellow in the last few months.

"Jim," he said, finally, "what's biting you?" The big fellow shifted in his chair uncomfortably but said nothing. Johnny removed his glasses, and cleaned them energetically, turning a vague, nearsighted glance on Jim. "The boys've been talking about you a good deal lately."

"When didn't they?"

"That's not what I mean."

"What *do* you mean?"

"Oh, I don't know," said Johnny, evasively, sorry now he'd brought the matter up. After a moment he took the plunge. "They say you just don't give a good goddamn any more. Ray Slavens told me you almost blew the big one just because you got sore at the sucker. Fine thing, getting sore at the sucker!"

"He was such a dumb quail. Anyway, I had my own troubles, and this guy wanted to be with me every damn minute. I couldn't shake the so-and-so off. I began to think the poor stiff was in love with me."

"It's your winning personality."

"I got fed up. One night I told the guy to get the hell out and leave me alone. Roy almost fainted. But the guy liked it."

Johnny looked at Jim for a long time in silence. He had always envied him and had always been puzzled by him. He just seemed to hypnotize people. There'd never been another con man like him. Some of his victims didn't even get sore at him after the touch. Several came back for more, believe it or not!

Jim sighed and ran his hand over his face wearily. "I was having trouble with Tony."

"How that little bum ever got such a hold over you I'll never know."

"She was no bum to me, Johnny. I know what the guys thought of her. But it was mostly talk. None of them knew her."

Johnny turned away and clamped his mouth shut. Half of Jim's Florida pals had known Tony only too well. But bringing it up now would lead to nothing but trouble.

"Funny!" Johnny laughed. "A guy with a reputation like yours—well, you don't expect him to go berserk over a babe like Tony. She's been on the merry-go-round for some time."

"Not long. She's only twenty-one right now."

"When did she stop having birthdays?"

"Okay! I'll admit I didn't see her birth certificate."

Johnny stared at Jim, and shook his head. "I don't get it!"

Jim winced faintly, remembering something. "It was just one of those things. Oh, well. I'm getting along. I'll be forty-two my next birthday. It's not like I was twenty-five."

He got up and stood looking vaguely off across the room. "Johnny, I pulled my last touch."

The lawyer started. "What's that?"

"I'm done. No more."

"Oh, you're drunk."

"No. I'm all through. That's why I'm here in California. I'm going to lay back and relax."

Johnny smiled.

"You're crazy. Okay, so you've got a hundred grand. It won't last you two years and you know it."

"Two years is long enough."

"Then what?"

"I'll tell you a story," said Jim. "It won't take long."

Jim hesitated, ran his hand across his face.

"All right. Go ahead," said Johnny with a touch of impatience.

"Remember hearing about the King—Tom Rodney?"

"Sure."

"He was the greatest con man that ever lived. He took some English Duke for a hundred thousand pounds. That's a take! He was a great operator with women...."

"Like yourself."

"Not me. I'm a rank amateur compared to the King. I proved it."

"We all get in too deep once in a while."

"Pass it. So I'd been hearing about the King ever since I was in knee pants. My old man knew the King, thought he was wonderful. One day he pointed him out to me at a race meeting. Great big, broad-shouldered guy—good-looking—and he had a babe on each arm. The kind I'd've given years off my life for then; I was a punk kid, about fourteen. What a guy—he owned the world!

"Well, about twenty years later I got picked up in Toledo and thrown in the can for investigation. The King was in there, too. He was a filthy, stinking old man, arrested for molesting a young girl. He had cataracts on his eyes and sores all over his face. He sort of drooled when he talked. Jesus!"

Jim put down his drink and stared at the floor. Johnny looked at him with his mouth slightly open, seeing a Jim Farrar he had never seen before and couldn't have imagined for himself.

"After I blew my top over Tony," Jim went on, as if talking to himself, "I figured my time was getting short ..."

Johnny was somewhat appalled. "Wait a minute. You're just tired, Jim. Been drinking too much. A couple months in California and you'll be right back where you started."

"No. When I get rid of this wad, I'm done."

"What do you mean? A guy just can't stop living because he wants to."

Jim glanced up. His eyes were steady.

"Why can't he?"

Johnny stared. "Come on, Jim. Cut it out. I know you better than that. It's that damn bourbon. You'll be seeing little men with long beards next. Let's play rummy, forget our troubles. Everybody gets depressed once in a while. It's natural."

Johnny got up and began to rummage feverishly through his suitcase, searching for a deck of cards.

"Sometimes at night," said Jim, "I wake up in a cold sweat. I been dreaming about the King and how he looked in that Toledo jail. Only it's always me, not the King. I mean I'm mixed up with him. He's half me and I'm half him."

"Where did I put those damned cards?" said Johnny, talking loudly as if to drown out Jim's words. "I saw them this morning. Now how in hell could they get out of this suitcase without...."

A glass fell with a crash. Johnny turned. Jim was leaning over the table with his head buried in his arms.

Johnny was scared. It looked like the big guy really was nuts. Here he was only forty-two, not wanted by the law, and with a cool hundred grand to play with. It didn't make any kind of sense at all.

"It's that damn liquor and that damn impudent little twist," he told himself. "He'll get straightened out and we'll both be laughing about this in a couple of months."

Jim raised his head and looked foggily at the little lawyer.

"I feel better," he said. "Man, have I slipped! I break down like an old whore." He laughed, but his laughter grated on Johnny's nerves.

There was a long pause. Johnny finally found the cards and they began to play rummy. Johnny lost steadily, squirming; Jim played imperturbably; after a while he spoke.

"Just forget I ever said anything, Johnny. I've been drinking too much and not eating enough."

Johnny smiled with relief.

"That's what I thought." There was a pause, then Johnny burst out. "Wait a minute. Stop picking up two cards at a time and looking at my draw. What a crook!"

Then they played in silence for a long time. Finally Johnny blitzed Jim, who threw down his cards indifferently, and got up, yawning, haggard with boredom.

"What I don't get," said Johnny, "is what you dragged me all the way out here for—if you're strictly out of the racket."

Jim reddened slightly.

"Figuring you might like the ride. Lam back whenever you get good and ready. I'll pay your fare."

Johnny was just on the point of making some retort but caught himself in time. Jim went into the bathroom and slammed the door violently. The little lawyer lit a cigarette and smoked slowly and thoughtfully.

"Lonesome, that's what he is," he told himself, between drags.

"Lonesome—just like any plain chump."

Johnny smiled. In spite of himself, it pleased him to see the big fellow—
for a change—reacting just like anybody else.

IV

Doc was sitting in a booth waiting, when Pop walked into Maxie's Bar.
Without a word, Pop sat down opposite him and ordered a glass of
draught beer.

"Well?" Doc demanded, his eyes glittering eagerly.

"Hold your horses. I told you it was no use."

"He's here and I know it. All I want to know is: how do I find him?"

Pop got up deliberately and put a nickel in the battered old electric
piano. It began to play a ten-year-old tune, honky-tonk style, grindingly
discordant. He sat down.

"When you get excited, Doc, you talk too loud," said Pop, mildly. "Tell
me about the sucker."

Doc did so, omitting her name. Pop was silent for a long time. The
piano stopped playing and a drunk staggered over to start it again, but
couldn't get his nickel in the slot. Pop got up and helped him, then he
sat down and lit his pipe.

"As a rule," said Pop, "a smart guy don't try to beat a woman. At least not
with the old-line gags. Women are smarter than men and they yell louder."

"We'll put it up to Jim. He can handle it any way he likes."

Pop considered.

"Dig up five hundred and I'll go to the top guy's mouthpiece for you."

"You're crazy," cried Doc. "We haven't got it. We haven't got fifty dollars."

"That's what I thought."

"All I want to know is: where is he? Is that worth five hundred?"

"Yes. Because he's quit. He don't want no part of anything. Last thing
of all he wants is to be buzzed by a broken-down con outfit."

"I was pretty big once."

"Once don't count."

Doc ran his hand nervously through his lank black hair. His face got
very pale. An almost unbearable depression settled over him. He needed
a whack of the stuff. A sudden murderous impulse made him stiffen; he
lightly touched the small automatic in his coat pocket. He glanced up.
Pop was studying him.

"Don't do nothing rash, Doc," said the old man, mildly.

"It's enough to make a man hang himself," Doc exclaimed.

There was a long pause. Doc put his hands on the table and stared at
them. He felt like yelling with misery. Too many things had happened
to him in the last few years. It seemed that life had but one purpose: to
make a stinking bum out of Dr. Walter Harris Bright, M.D.

Pop ordered another glass of beer.

"Doc," he said, "tell me about that sucker again."

V

Jim felt restless and uneasy. He'd been sitting in the sun for nearly an hour and it was beginning to bother his eyes. He looked about for his sunglasses but couldn't find them; then he remembered he'd left them in the glove compartment of the second-hand Cadillac he'd just bought. He turned to call the Filipino houseboy, then changed his mind.

"The devil with it," he said, and moved his beach backrest to another angle, trying to avoid the direct glare of the sun on the water.

In this position he could see far up the beach. The sky was pale blue, the air crystal clear. White gulls flew lazily above the breakers, crying harshly; from time to time a heavy pelican dove at the green water like a small dive-bomber. The sun beat down mercilessly, and heat shimmers rose from the ridge of rocks just north of Jim's beach house.

Physically, Jim had improved. He had already lost nearly ten pounds and had acquired a suntan. His eye was clearer, his step firmer; due not only to the sun and sea air, but also to the fact that he'd cut down his liquor consumption. He'd seen too many of the boys end up as dismal rummies, avoided by everybody. Feeling as he did, always either depressed, irritated or bored, it took a great effort of the will for him to stay away from the bottle.

"I'm not ready for that yet," he told himself, laughing harshly.

For months Jim had humored himself, let things slide. Nothing interested him: he was absentminded, apathetic, off-hand with everybody. Now the time had come to do one of two things: either he must call a halt and try to get himself in hand, or he must say the hell with it and walk out into the ocean till his hat floated.

He sat staring at the curving crescent of beach, idly raking up small piles of sand and flattening them again, repeating this process over and over. Suddenly he became aware of what he was doing, laughed harshly, smashed his hand into the sand, then jumped up and started for the beach house. Through the living room window he could see the Filipino houseboy running the vacuum cleaner.

A character—that boy! Eating like a horse because he was underweight and couldn't get in the army. His home village in Luzon was in the hands of the Japs—he was dying for a crack at them. Jim thought he was very funny, but he liked him and had a certain respect for his sentiments.

"Me—playing in the sand," Jim jeered. "Too bad I didn't bring my little bucket and spade."

Why kid himself? He knew what he wanted: Tony! Goddamn it: pride was pride, but a guy could overdo it; no use cutting off your nose to spite your face. Tony had a mind of her own. But was that wrong? So had he and, on top of it, he'd had his way with women so long that he was spoiled. Tony wouldn't take it. And then—just at the wrong time—that actor friend of hers had to turn up. "I'll show you," said Tony. "I didn't know you went for 4-Fs," Jim sneered. "I don't see any gun on your shoulder," Tony replied with a cutting laugh. He slammed the door in her face—then waited for her to phone him. He waited for weeks. One day he ran into her. She was with her actor friend: a big effeminate-looking hamola with dyed blonde hair. Tony looked the other way when he started to speak to her.

Telesfero shut off the vacuum cleaner as Jim entered the room. Jim was living under the name of Lloyd and gave out that he was an oil man. Telesfero, who had been a lowly busboy three months before, was in awe of this big, husky, serious-looking man, who towered above him; he thought that he must be very powerful, very rich.

"Heard anything from Mr. Doyle?" asked Jim.

"No sah," said Telesfero, his flat brown face wrinkling into a sad grin.

"It's a wonder he couldn't hang around once in a while," Jim muttered to himself as he crossed the living room and went into his bedroom.

Telesfero felt a slight tremor. He was very sensitive and knew that the boss was in a bad humor. He bowed in Jim's direction, then hurried out into the kitchen with the vacuum cleaner.

Jim sat staring at the telephone on the night table for a long time. Then, hating himself for it but feeling a marked exhilaration, he put in a call for Miss Antonia Blackburn in Miami, Florida.

When Johnny came in toward evening, Jim was walking up and down the living room in blue denims and an old sweater, smoking a cigar.

"Hello, Jim," Johnny said, taking off his coat quickly and going to the improvised bar to mix himself a drink. "Boy, am I thirsty. Hot in the city."

"What do you go there for, then? Why don't you stay here where it's cool?"

Jim spoke peevishly and Johnny turned to look at him.

"If you want the truth, I get tired of those goddamn waves pounding away all day long. I get enough of them at night. They shake the joint."

Jim grunted.

"Pour me one," he said.

"Besides," said Johnny, mixing the drinks, "I had some business to look after."

Jim turned away, making no comment. He wouldn't admit to himself that he'd been lonesome all afternoon and was sore at Johnny for staying away so long.

"What!" said Johnny, "no ice? A fine place this is getting to be with you practically on the wagon."

"Telesfero," called Jim in a loud voice.

Just as he called, the phone rang. Jim made a sudden move to answer it, then checked himself. Johnny glanced at him shrewdly, knowing something was up. They heard the murmur of Telesfero's high-pitched voice as he answered the phone in the hall; then the little Filipino came in.

"On your call to Miami, sah ..."

Jim threw a quick look at Johnny, who turned away with a smile.

"Yeah?" Jim demanded.

"They cannot locate Miss Blackburn, sah."

Jim compressed his lips, then smiled slightly. With Johnny present, he didn't feel so alone. The hell with Tony! She never need know that he'd tried to get in touch with her.

"Cancel the call. Then get some ice."

Telesfero bowed and went out, shutting the door.

Jim turned, and stared hard at Johnny, daring him to say something. But Johnny made no comment and in a moment sat down and lit a cigarette. Jim sat across from him. They smoked in silence. Telesfero came in with the ice, then he lit the lights and went out. Dusk was falling over the sea and in the hush of early evening the roar of the waves grew louder and louder. Johnny finished mixing the drinks and handed Jim one.

"Here's looking," said Johnny. They drank.

"What's this business you had in town?" Jim asked finally.

"Pop Gruber got in touch with me. Wanted to see me."

"Pop ! What about?"

"Just a little private matter." Johnny finished his drink, and began to mix another one. "No kidding, Jim," he said, "don't this place give you the willies? I mean, don't you want to get out once in a while to a night spot and see the babes, hear some music? Bright lights—you know."

"I've had my share of that."

"Sure. But a guy can run anything in the ground. Even this kind of stuff. Okay. It's nice. You get all tanned, you get nice and healthy. But so what? The sun gives you wrinkles and pretty soon your tan peels off. And at night the waves bang away without a letup; soldiers and sailors and Christ-knows-who-all patrol the roads with loaded guns and if a guy makes a crooked move he's liable to stop lead; and the dimout— brother!—if you drive any place you do it by instinct. Wait till gas rationing comes in—then you'll be marooned out here."

"Stop hunting for something to worry about."

"As a matter of fact, Jim, I'm worrying mostly about you. Look. You can't spend the rest of your life like this. Hell, you're not old. You can't just up and quit. It's not natural."

"Oh—drink your drink."

"No kidding. You're just in a state, and you've got to snap out of it." Johnny hesitated as Jim shifted about, irritated; then he held up his hands as if to ward off a blow. "All right. All right. Have it your way."

"I cut down on my drinking, didn't I?"

"Yeah, and none too soon."

"Look—you can't have it both ways, Johnny. You yell about my drinking—I cut it down. Now you're yelling because I don't want to go running around night clubs like a hick tourist on a bender."

Johnny sat thoughtfully sipping his drink before replying.

"Maybe it's something you've just got to work out for yourself," he said at last with a sigh. "On the square—would you get back to normal if Tony was here?"

Jim thought for a moment, then he got up and stood looking at Johnny so long in silence that the little lawyer got uneasy.

"About that phone call," said Jim. "I just got to worrying about her. She's got no dough. And it's a cinch the actor's strictly from hunger. Tony likes nice things—good living. Tough for her not to have dough."

"Oh, I don't know," said Johnny. "You don't believe all that stuff she gives out—do you? About how her old man used to own horses. If he had any horses, it's even money they were hitched to a beer wagon."

"She acts to me like she's used to dough."

"She was certainly getting used to yours."

"Dough's not the answer with Tony. We fought like wildcats."

"And you lost for once. That's about the size of it, isn't it, Jim?"

"I don't know."

Jim sat down. There was a long silence. In the midst of it Telesfero called them to dinner. Johnny ate with gusto, but Jim seemed to have no appetite at all. When they were having their coffee, Johnny said:

"I understand there are some beautiful suckers in this man's town at the present time."

Jim made no reply.

"I heard about a dame today with nearly two million. A widow."

Jim got up, then he yawned and stretched.

"Think I'll listen to the news. Want to hear it, Johnny?"

Johnny said nothing, but gritted his teeth in irritation, and stared angrily at the big fellow as he went back into the living room, then he poured himself a stiff drink of brandy. In the living room the radio came on with a violent blaring, then a suave, patronizing voice began to give the war news. Johnny got up and went out onto the dining room balcony for some fresh air. The sea was black as ink—along the shoreline only a few dim lights showed. But toward the east, searchlights raked the darkness, moving slowly, crisscrossing, then going out one by one.

Johnny was still trembling slightly from his attempt to interest Jim in the million-dollar babe. Maybe he'd spoken too soon; maybe he hadn't spoken soon enough. With Jim in his present state of mind, it was hard to figure out just what course to pursue. Johnny was a little awed by the thought of all that money lying around waiting to be plucked. The setup was perfect for him. A push. He couldn't miss. Money from home. Of course the big fellow would pick this time to sulk—and over a promiscuous little twist with a line a half-wit could see through.

"Only that's not all of it," Johnny mused as he sipped his brandy. "Tony just caused the blow-off. It's been coming on. Jim hates the thought of getting old. But hell, he's five or six years younger than I am. He's not old."

Johnny thought about Tom Rodney and shuddered slightly. That was the sort of thing that was worrying the big fellow and he'd just have to get it off his mind some way. How?

The little lawyer stood shaking his head in the darkness. A prize take just around the corner, and the best operator in the business—the one man for the job—had to get temperamental like a hammy motion picture actor! A sucker like that wouldn't be around forever. Sooner or later some wise boy would take her for a jolt—and spoil the play for everybody else. Now she was virgin territory.

The cool sea breeze slightly stirred the little lawyer's thinning hair. Eastward, the searchlights had been switched on again. But this time Johnny didn't see them. He was painfully trying to make up his mind what to do. He'd got a letter from Roy Slavens, which he hadn't shown to Jim. Among other things it stated that Jim's girl had gone West with Austen, the actor, and had got stranded in Phoenix. It would be a cinch to get her to come on to L.A. No matter what Jim said, she was strictly on the chisel.

But Johnny was leery. Tony might be a help and again she might not. It was possible she'd get Jim so upset that he'd never get himself straightened out again.... On the other hand ...!

VI

The five men sat in a semicircle in the smoke-filled room, looking like a group of conspirators in a bad play. They had talked themselves out and got nowhere. They were all irritated and kept glancing at one another with mild hostility.

Windy was the first to regain his normal frame of mind. He tipped back his chair and rolled a cigarette and when he caught Johnny's eye he grinned ingratiatingly. After all, Mr. Doyle was a gent, educated, well dressed, and the big fellow's lawyer: quite a guy.

Shake was depressed. When he'd heard that Johnny the Priest had come in on the thing he'd considered it in the bag. The bad news Johnny brought had deflated him. Sighing, he picked up a newspaper and began to glance absently through it.

Old Pop smoked stolidly but he was terribly disappointed. For years he'd accepted his lot with resignation and had expected to do so till he died. But that was all over now. He'd caught a faint glimpse of El Dorado and it had turned his head. He hated the thought of going back to his narrow way of life. A man needed something to look forward to.

Doc was the most deeply affected. He was so nervous that his face was twitching. He kept clenching and unclenching his small, ugly hands. Once more life had struck him a stinging, unexpected blow. It was more than a man could bear. He wanted to do something violent. He wanted to knock somebody down and trample them. He felt cruel and vicious, like a cornered rat. Most of all, he wanted to confront Jim Farrar, the man responsible for this unbearable disappointment, and tell him in a loud voice what a stupid, lucky, swell-headed, blundering fool he'd always been!

Johnny took off his glasses and cleaned them energetically, meanwhile peering about him with a vague, apologetic look. He felt very uneasy. He'd lost touch with this kind of men. He feared and resented their shabbiness and their greed. He was used to operating with a careless big-timer. He felt somewhat degraded.

Doc jumped up abruptly, startling them, and went to the window. Searchlights were raking the sky. Doc hoped the Jap bombers would come over and blast the hell out of this sprawling, overgrown hick town where he'd suffered so much and so fruitlessly. Images of destruction passed before his eyes: he saw jets of flame as the bombs exploded, he saw buildings crumble, and men hurrying ant-like from walls which fell and crushed them. He turned; his face was pale and his eyes flashed wildly.

"I've got to talk to him," he said, addressing Johnny, "and you're going to tell me where he is."

Johnny put on his glasses quickly. His face hardened, lost its priest-like look. His eyes narrowed and his glance was cold. The nerve of this two-bit bum!

"I'll tell you what you're going to do, Doc," he said slowly, "you're going to keep that dirty shirt of yours on."

Pop, Windy and Shake waited in trepidation, glancing furtively at Doc. Johnny got up and put on his hat. Doc hesitated, looking murder at Johnny, then he began to tremble. Without another word he went into the bathroom abruptly and slammed the door. They heard a key turn.

"Someday he's going to hurt somebody," said Pop, mildly.

Shake shook his big head slowly from side to side.

"I wish I could get him off that junk. Wouldn't you think a doctor'd know better? That's what I'm always saying."

Johnny walked to the door.

"Guys, I'm doing the best I can. If I pull it at all—it's going to take time. But if Doc ever gets to the big fellow it'll all be over. He'll throw Doc right out on his neck. You guys have got to keep him quiet."

Johnny's hand was on the doorknob when Shake stammered, then spoke.

"Mr. Doyle—we was figuring you might ..." Shake grinned sheepishly.

"Oh," said Johnny, and taking a ten-dollar bill out of his pocket he put it on the table. "Stretch it. It's my own dough, and I may never get it back."

"Thanks, Mr. Doyle," said Shake.

"Yeah, thanks," Windy echoed, grinning widely.

"Goodbye, Pop," called Johnny, as he went out.

There was a pause. Pop was just getting up to go when they heard Doc fall in the bathroom. Shake ran to the door, shook the knob, called to Doc distractedly. Silence. Shake was unnerved. Doc was his only bulwark against nothingness; without him he'd be like a kid lost in a big city. Windy brushed Shake aside and put his shoulder to the door, which opened with a crash.

Doc was lying on the floor, pale as death, and twitching. He was having some kind of fit. They picked him up and carried him to the bed, where he lay staring at them with unseeing eyes, gasping violently for breath. In a little while he began to revive. He turned to Shake.

"This is it, I guess."

"No, Doc," said Shake, patting him. "You'll be all right."

A few minutes later Doc fell asleep. His snores reassured them.

VII

The Biltmore lobby was jammed with people: soldiers and women everywhere—a wartime crowd. Johnny shoved his way through the press toward the elevators. He was forced to wait, and as he stood before the huge bronze elevator grills, looking about him absentmindedly at the busy, laughing crowd, he kept turning over and over in his mind the various approaches he had worked out during an almost sleepless night. Tony was a handful. Jim's experience had proved that. If he took one false step he might ruin everything. It wasn't that Tony was so smart: she wasn't. But she was abnormally headstrong and touchy. Very easy to insult.

Johnny pushed his way into the elevator: a guy could wait around all night being polite. People were packed into it like chickens in a crate, and it smelt of perfume and liquor. Next to Johnny a grinning infantry lieutenant was cuddling a little blonde.

Johnny smiled grimly to himself.

"Go to it, bud," he thought. "You're sure entitled to it. But can't you wait till you get her up to your room?"

At Tony's door, Johnny knocked, then waited for a long time. He shifted from foot to foot. She knew he was on his way up. What was the idea? With an effort of the will Johnny quelled his impatience. This damn thing was getting everybody jittery. If they weren't careful, pretty soon they'd all be as unstrung as Doc.

Finally the door was opened. There was Tony, her bushy dark-red hair hanging to her shoulders, her greenish-grey eyes heavily rimmed with mascara, her high cheek-boned face a mask of indifference. She had hastily flung on a black velvet dressing gown, which she was holding about her carelessly.

"Hello," she said, coldly.

Johnny compressed his lips, then forced a smile. A fine greeting! He'd got her out of hock to the tune of three Cs, and she acted as if she wasn't sure whether she'd let him in or not.

"Hi, Tony."

He stepped in and she shut the door. The place stank like a French brothel; clothes were scattered all around, there was an open box of chocolate creams on the table, and a few movie magazines.

"The place's a wreck," said Tony. "I hope you don't mind, Mr. Doyle." She smiled ironically—or at least it seemed so to Johnny. A very irritating broad.

He sat down. She lit a cigarette and flung herself on the couch, her dressing gown flying. Her long, slim, well-shaped legs were bare almost to the hip for a moment. Johnny stared openly. What a dish this wacky red-headed babe was! Not the kind, of course, you'd expect to get a guy like Jim behind the eight ball, but, nevertheless.... Johnny'd had a yen for her ever since the first time he'd seen her swinging her hips through the lobby of a Miami hotel. But the big fellow had beaten him to the punch—so, hands off. He wasn't like some of Jim's other pals. Not that it was a matter of principle. He just wasn't going to let a broad break him up with the big fellow. Plenty of broads around—but only one Jim.

"How's my big boy?" asked Tony. "Too proud to come down himself, eh?"

Johnny shook his head.

"He doesn't know a thing. Thinks you're in Florida."

"Now I'll tell one."

"Take it from me. It was my idea and—not that I want to be nasty about it—my dough."

Tony studied Johnny's face suspiciously.

"I don't believe you," she said finally.

Johnny's irritation got the best of him for a moment. "The big fellow doesn't need anybody to pimp for him. You know that."

Tony drew back sharply.

"Don't talk like that to me. Nobody talks like that to me and gets away with it."

"All right," said Johnny grudgingly. Who did she think she was, this dame—Lady Astor? "But you've got the wrong slant."

"What's your angle, then?" she demanded. "Are you an old friend of the family? Or do you go about helping poor, defenseless women?"

"I was figuring you might be a little help in the biggest thing that's been around since Ringling Brothers. But I don't know."

"Nothing personal, eh? That's good. Those thick glasses of yours are hard to take."

Johnny reddened slightly.

"Did I ever throw a pass at you?"

"Only with your eyes, Mr. Doyle. I stayed at arm's length."

"I guess you get a lot of passes thrown at you at that. No wonder. Sitting around with your dress up."

Tony shifted her position calmly. And Johnny sat biting his lip, trying to reorganize himself. This babe threw him off key.

"I still think my big boy's behind this," said Tony. "His face looked awfully long the last time I saw him."

"Things didn't work out so well with Austen, I take it."

"How could they? He needs a mama. That's what he's looking for.

Wanted to cry on my shoulder. I'm not the type."

"I'll bet you didn't get anything like that from the big fellow."

"It would've been a nice change. He's got a disposition I wouldn't wish on my worst enemy. He walks over you or else. Nobody walks over me."

"He's spoiled. Had things too easy."

"Rancid, is the word."

Johnny shook his head dubiously.

"I guess it's no use."

Tony glanced at him quickly.

"What's no use?"

"Trying to get you to control yourself. There's a fortune in it."

Tony sat up.

"At least I'm listening."

Johnny asked her for a drink and she got a quart of Scotch out of her suitcase. After he'd taken a long pull he went over and sat on the couch with Tony and told her carefully and at great length as much as he wanted her to know about the business in hand. She listened attentively.

The one thing, aside from the red hair and the lovely slim figure, that made Tony so attractive was the look of sensuality her face had in repose. Johnny had noticed it many times, envying Jim. But now she was all business. Her face was devoid of any suggestion of sensuality; her look was serious, intent, sexless. As he talked, Johnny sat mentally patting himself on the back for his astuteness. Strictly on the chisel—this girl. With the right kind of handling, she'd be a big help. All they needed was to get Jim over the first hurdle. Once he got rolling they could all sit back and relax.

"Well?" said Johnny, finally; considering the question a mere formality.

Tony nodded without a word. They exchanged a look. Johnny felt a slight chill go down his spine and got up hastily.

"How about lunch?"

"Let's have it here," said Tony, stretching lazily. "I don't feel like getting dressed."

Johnny called room service and ordered, then he crossed the room and sat on a straight chair a long ways from Tony, who studied him for a moment, then burst out laughing.

VIII

Jim had been in swimming and was just putting on his clothes when he heard Johnny's car drive up. About time that little mick was showing! During Johnny's absence Jim had been getting more and more irritated with him. After all, the guy might hang around once in a while. It wasn't too much to expect. He walked over and hastily kicked the bedroom door shut. But almost immediately Johnny knocked on it.

"Jim."

"Yeah?" called Jim, sulkily, after a pause.

"Can I see you a minute?"

"What's the rush all of a sudden? You saw me this morning, didn't you?"

Johnny opened the door and came in. Jim was just pulling on a fisherman's jersey. His arms and torso were tanned a deep brown and looked powerful. He was losing a lot of the loose fat he'd been accumulating in Florida cocktail bars.

"You're sure getting in shape, Jim," said Johnny. "Maybe you're right about this place. You look ten years younger already."

"I don't feel younger."

Johnny hesitated. He wasn't quite sure how to break the news. He was afraid he'd get Jim and Tony started off wrong.

Jim finally got the jersey set to suit him, then he turned and glanced at Johnny.

"Well? What are you staring at?"

"I ran into a friend of yours downtown."

"Yeah? I hope you didn't tell him where I am. I don't want to see anybody."

"Well," said Johnny, "I had a feeling you'd want to see this party." Jim opened his mouth to speak but Johnny beat him to it. "So I brought her along. I'll take her right away if you say so."

Jim grabbed Johnny by the arm and held him so tight it hurt.

"Not Tony!"

Johnny nodded, wanting to break into song. A wide grin had spread over Jim's rather solemn face, making him look like a mischievous kid. Was he pleased! It was going to be all right—very all right.

"Where is she?" Jim demanded.

Johnny jerked his thumb toward the living room and Jim rushed out. Johnny followed leisurely and when he got there Jim was sitting in one of the big chintz-covered armchairs with Tony on his lap. They held a kiss so long that Johnny shook his head in admiration, then called:

"Break."

Jim looked at him, grinning.

"When I want him he's never here—when I don't want him ..."

"I was just getting around to that. Look, folks. I'm going to drive down to Santa Monica for dinner. May stay all night at the hotel. See you later."

"You don't need to overdo it," said Jim.

"Oh, I'll be back eventually. I'm figuring you and Tony have got a couple things to talk over. So get at it."

Jim and Tony exchanged a long look, then they both burst out laughing. Johnny laughed, too, but they ignored him. He stood for a moment watching them, then he turned and left the room, glad that everything had worked out so nicely, but feeling hollow and lonesome and envious of Jim. Just as he shut the front door Jim called:

"Bye, Johnny."

The little lawyer grimaced and didn't reply. He walked thoughtfully to his car, got in and drove off. It was nice to be a prima donna and have things your own way; of course, you had to deliver; that was the tough part of it. Most guys had no particular gifts of any kind; they just had to knock out a living as best they could. Nothing was handed to them on a silver platter. They had to sweat and connive for what they got. But take a guy like Jim. Looks, brains, ability; the works; a lucky stiff!

After a moment Johnny began to laugh at himself.

"It's funny what a little twist will do to a guy. Cut it out, John Stanislaus. If you got it you wouldn't think it was worth the trouble."

Later that night, Johnny met a couple of soldiers in a beach cocktail bar and got tight with them. One was a Boston Irishman with a fine tenor voice. He sang "Kathleen Mavourneen" and "Mother Machree" to loud applause. Johnny cried into his highball. He was a sucker for an Irish tenor.

IX

The clock struck midnight hollowly and Tony started. She had been dozing on the big living room divan, wrapped up in a heavy ulster of Jim's. It was a cool night, a strong wind was blowing, and a heavy surf was pounding at the beach and sending long shudders through the house. She got upon one elbow. Jim was putting more wood on the fire. The radio turned way down, was playing dance music softly. The room looked wonderful lit only by the flickering flames on the hearth. Tony lay back with a sigh. Jim looked so big and powerful, silhouetted against the firelight. She hugged herself under the ulster. Too bad it couldn't always be like this with them.

Jim worked at the fire languidly, smoking a cigarette, and humming with the radio. He felt perfectly contented. The fog had lifted. The past seemed like a nightmare. He shook his head in perplexity. Could that actually have been him quarreling peevishly day after day with Johnny, and sulking like a grammar school kid?

He flushed with shame as he remembered his first night in Los Angeles. He'd broken down, actually broken down, like a cheap junky in the hands of the coppers—and right in front of Johnny. It was incredible. "No wonder the little mick thinks I'm ready for the man in the white coat," he told himself grimly.

"Hello," called Tony softly.

"Hello," said Jim, turning and smiling at her. "Nice tune, eh?" He jerked a thumb at the radio. "How about a dance?"

"Sorry to refuse. I think I'll lie this one out. God, I'm tired."

"Little girl, you've had a busy day."

"You can say that again. Say—Jim. What about that Filipino boy? Who am I supposed to be?"

"Why—Mrs. Lloyd. You just got in from Florida."

"He gave me a fishy look."

"Don't worry about him. All he thinks about is his relatives in the Islands—and getting in the army. He promised to send me back some Jap ears—if he ever gets across."

"This war is certainly getting to be a nuisance," said Tony, yawning. "I wish they'd get it over with. What the hell are they fighting about, anyway?"

"That I don't know. It happens every so often. I remember the last one. I was a senior in high school the year it was over."

"My God—are you that old?" Tony burst out laughing.

There was a short silence, then Jim laughed, too; but he was forcing it. No use kidding himself. Tony was a very irritating girl.

"Yeah," he said, "look how gray I'm getting."

Tony got up quickly and flung herself into his arms, kissing him repeatedly.

"I'm kidding, Jim. You're young enough. Plenty young enough. On you gray hair looks good."

Tony spoke softly, placatingly; she was sweet and yielding. A sudden suspicion crossed Jim's mind. Tony was out of character and he wondered why.

"How did you happen to run into Johnny?" he asked, taking her arms from around his neck.

Tony sat down on the divan and Jim sat beside her.

"I was just going into the Biltmore. I looked up and there he was. Was I surprised!"

"Then what?"

"We had lunch together."

"Was it his idea for you to come out to the beach?"

"No," said Tony, shaking her head vigorously. "I asked him to bring me."

"What did he tell you about me?"

"Nothing much. Said you weren't feeling so good, and that you were practically on the wagon."

Jim hesitated for a long time, then he got up and lit a cigarette.

"You know, Tony," he said, "you haven't even told me how you happened to be out in this neck of the woods. This is no third degree—but ..."

"I was looking for you."

Jim was unable to resist the glow of pleasure this simple statement gave him.

"How come?"

"That's obvious."

"What happened to whosis—the ham?"

Tony hesitated, lit a cigarette, then stalled around making herself more comfortable on the couch.

"I guess I might as well tell you, Jim," she said, shrugging. "I went broke in Florida. He paid my way out."

"He didn't come along by any chance—did he?"

"As far as Phoenix."

Jim shook his head in irritation.

"How you could put up with that big fag …!"

"I had to get here—that's all."

"Why?" asked Jim.

Tony smiled up at him. She looked beautiful, actually beautiful, Jim decided, in the firelight. She was very tired and this gave her a certain languor she didn't ordinarily possess, and there were faint blue shadows of fatigue under her eyes, softening her face and making her look younger, less self-assured.

Jim felt a sudden pang, and bent down toward her.

"You know why?" said Tony, softly and seductively. "I said I'd never chase you—not in a thousand years," she went on, reaching up and putting her arms around Jim's neck. "But here I am."

He was completely won over. All his suspicions had disappeared. He felt like the old Jim Farrar. Now things were on the proper footing.

"And am I glad to see you," he said, magnanimously, kissing Tony, then picking her up in his arms. "How about calling it a night?"

"Yes," said Tony, sighing wearily and settling her head against his shoulder. As he carried her into the bedroom, she murmured: "And so to sleep." Then added: "And I do mean sleep."

Jim laughed appreciatively.

X

Jim's eyes had been bothering him a little lately, so Johnny drove. It was a moonless night, and the beach road which followed an eccentric course between the headlands on one side and the ocean on the other was dark as a pocket. The parking, lights were hardly any help at all. If it hadn't been for the white line, driving would have been impossible.

"Damn the Japs," said Johnny. "If this is a dimout, I want to see a blackout sometime."

"Look there," said Jim, jerking his thumb at the ocean.

Johnny took a quick glance, then swung the wheel over suddenly; he'd almost gone into the sand.

"Stop bothering me," he said peevishly. "You look at the wonders of nature; I'll drive."

Huge waves glittering eerily with phosphorescence were rolling into the pitch-black beach under the dark sky. A faint ghostly light trembled over the sea. It looked unreal and somewhat frightening. Jim felt very uneasy as he watched the waves break with a resounding crash and send up an evil-looking green spray.

"This sure looks like the jumping-off place tonight," he said, but Johnny made no reply.

A nervous fidgety little man, the unremitting strain of the last few weeks had him badly on edge. The nearer the big deal moved toward its consummation the more jittery he became and it could still go wrong, damn it!

Johnny had given the meeting between Jim, Doc, and the others a lot of thought. Doc's hotel room was impossible; Jim wouldn't be seen in a joint like that. A downtown bar was no good; some noisy member of the bunco squad might blunder in. He finally decided on a big cocktail bar at the beach, owned by an Irishman he'd made friends with and could trust; it had a private room, just right for his purpose. He and Jim were to meet the others there.

Johnny smiled to himself at his own astuteness. After a few days of Tony's company, Jim was ready to listen to reason. Apparently he'd forgotten all that nonsense about quitting the racket, spending what money he had, and then fluffing off. Silly idea, anyway. He only made one objection. "You know, Johnny," he said, "I've never tried to beat a woman yet."

"Yeah," said Johnny; "but this woman's got around two million dollars."

Later the lawyer had a little trouble with Tony.

"Look," she said, "this dame's loaded with money, and Jim's quite an operator. Suppose he marries her—then what?"

Johnny snorted.

"He wouldn't marry a Rockefeller—that guy!"

"I don't know," said Tony, dubiously. "It's worth a thought."

"Take my word for it," said Johnny, dismissing the subject with a decided gesture.

As Johnny drove up in front of the cocktail bar, which was known as the Ship and had a façade tricked out with portholes, ropes and anchors, he said:

"They're a sad-looking lot, Jim. Windy and Shake are has-beens of the worst kind; and Doc's on the junk."

"I know them," said Jim, impatiently. "None of them was ever too much."

Johnny glanced at Jim out of the corner of his eye. No doubt about it: Jim was at the top of his profession: he was the best. Still—there were a few other guys around who knew their business, too; but you'd never think so to hear Jim tell it. Johnny considered this a bad weakness. It was foolish and dangerous to underestimate everybody.

"Doc was pretty big at one time," he couldn't help saying, at the risk of irritating Jim. "So was Shake. Of course, poor old punchy Mather never used anything for brains but muscle."

"Pop's got more sense than the three of them rolled into one," said Jim, mildly. "Always did have. And that," he added, "is not saying much."

They got out of the car and went into the cocktail bar. It was Monday, an off night. There was nobody at the bar except a couple of lonesome-looking buck privates, drinking beer. The bartender grinned at Johnny.

"Them guys you're expecting are here," he said.

"Thanks," said Johnny, and went through the bar and out a door at the back, which led, by way of a passage resembling a ship's corridor, to an arched entryway, beyond which was a stateroom door. Jim followed him, calmly smoking a cigar.

The soldiers stared after them.

"Who's that big guy?" one of them asked the bartender.

"I wouldn't know, pal."

"Ain't I seen him in pictures?"

"There you got me," said the bartender, polishing a glass.

The other soldier grinned apologetically.

"My pal—here. He's queer for movie actors."

"Where do they hang out? I walked up and down Hollywood Boulevard all one afternoon and never seen a one."

"That's tough," said the bartender.

Pop, Windy, Shake and Doc were sitting around a table, drinking beer. When Jim came in, they all got up but Doc, who sat staring—his face pale, his eyes glittering. Johnny groaned inwardly. Doc was loaded to the ears. Jim shook hands all around, smiling pleasantly, and exuding that goodwill which was his stock in trade. Johnny studied him covertly. It was amazing. Even Doc thawed a little and managed a smile which was almost good-natured.

Jim sat down and refused a drink. Johnny buzzed the waiter and ordered another round of beer for the four men and a highball for himself. Jim leaned his elbows on the table and talked calmly about Florida and how things had gone to hell since the Army took over. It was a dead spot now.

"I hear you done all right," said Windy so obsequiously that Doc threw him a sharp glance. Doc was used to being the big guy to Windy. At the moment he was less than nothing and it griped him.

"Pretty fair," said Jim, grinning. "Pretty fair."

Johnny glanced about him. They were all grinning in sympathy with Jim—all but Doc. He had tipped his chair back into the shadows, effacing himself, and he sat looking on enigmatically—like the skeleton at the feast. Johnny thought that Doc was not long for this world. He looked white and spent.

"You like it out here, Mr. Farrar?" asked Shake politely.

"Yeah," said Jim. "It ought to be a great spot after the war."

The waiter came with the drinks, put them on the table and went out.

Shake and Windy sipped their beer, smiling happily, basking in Jim's presence. To them it was too good to be true. But Doc, sitting back in the shadows, his hat pulled down almost to his nose, let his beer get flat as he studied Jim—a man he had always hated and envied. He noted the tanned, virile face; the steady, dark eyes; the curly dark hair, streaked with gray—the look of unshakable self-assurance. He took in the expensive clothes, the careful grooming—the air of money-in-the-bank. Doc hated and envied Jim not only for his easy successes with both men and women, but for his health and strength—his essential normality. In his whole life nothing had ever come easily to Doc! He'd worked his way through school only to run into disaster when he came to practice. Later, going off at a tangent, he had prospered as a racket man, but his nerves had gone back on him and he'd had to resort to drugs. No matter which way he turned, his path was ultimately blocked. He was like an experimental rat in a labyrinth which had no outlet.

Doc restrained himself with an effort. It was nauseating the way Windy and Shake were fawning on Jim. He wanted to jump up and say: "We don't need you as much as you think, you big bastard! We've got a proposition to make. Take it or leave it."

Shake began a long-winded story about a big take he'd made in the old days. When Shake once got off on one of those stories he was oblivious to those around him; he talked for his own benefit. Doc noticed the look of boredom and indifference which the big fellow made no attempt to hide. In fact, nobody listened to the story except Windy, who guffawed in the right places—thinking Shake must have been quite a guy in the old days.

Jim finally cut Shake off in the middle of his story with a curt but good-natured "Yeah—I remember all about that."

But Shake was hard to stop. Mentally, he lived in the past as all men without hope do. At times he almost drove Doc frantic by persisting in telling him a story he'd already told him fifty times. Something would remind Shake of a certain episode in his past. He'd say: "Did I ever tell you about that time I was broke in Cheyenne, Wyoming?" and, no matter what your reply was, he told the story. Either you had to listen or leave the room.

"I'll bet you never got the right slant on the girl angle, Mr. Farrar," Shake persisted. "She was from Wilkes Barre, P. A. I run into her one night in the hotel...."

"Why don't we get down to business?" Jim demanded, turning to Johnny.

"I've been thinking the same thing for a long time," said Doc irritably.

"... she looked like a million," said Shake, "but she didn't have a dime ..."

Doc turned and shouted contemptuously at Shake: "Will you shut up with your goddamn silly stories!"

Shake turned and looked mildly at Doc.

"I was figuring Mr. Farrar would like to know the inside on that one. We ..."

"Some other time," said Jim.

"Remember to tell me, will you, Shake?" Windy pleaded. "That's sure a mighty interesting story."

Johnny groaned inwardly. What a crew! It was a wonder Jim didn't walk out on them. A sudden premonition of disaster flashed through Johnny's mind. Nothing good could come of an association with a knocked-out bunch like this. He glanced at Jim. But the big fellow's air reassured him. He looked calm, competent, all business.

"We know there's no doubt about Mrs. Halvorsen," said Jim. "Johnny looked her up. She's got millions. In fact there's no doubt about anything at all except this: I operate alone without interference of any kind."

Pop took his pipe out of his mouth long enough to speak. "Naturally," he said.

"Wait a minute, Pop," Doc cut in. "You've got no say-so in this. You contacted Johnny, that's all. I promised you five hundred—and that's it. Mrs. Halvorsen belongs to us"—he indicated Shake, Windy and himself— "we located her."

Johnny saw that Jim was getting annoyed.

"What's your point, Doc?" Johnny interposed hastily.

"I'm just settling Pop—that's all. So we'll know where we stand."

"I was figuring I ought to have a cut," said Pop, his heart sinking.

Jim glanced at him quickly.

"I'll take care of you. Forget it."

Pop smiled, but said nothing. His worries were over on that score. The big fellow was not given to idle talk. Pop couldn't resist throwing a triumphant glance in Doc's direction.

Doc boiled and tipping his chair forward got to his feet.

"That means we don't owe you a thing, is that it, Pop?" he asked, his voice trembling slightly.

"How do you figure?" Johnny cut in.

"You keep out of this," said Doc. "Listen ..."

Jim slapped his hand down on the table, and they all looked at him.

"Wait a minute, you guys. Now look. Either you stop this penny ante squabbling, or I'm out."

There was a long pause. Pop smiled to himself in grim satisfaction. Doc's face twitched violently and he got paler than ever, but he compressed his lips and said nothing. Windy and Shake held their breath, scared half out of their wits by this sudden, unfavorable turn.

"Pop gets his five hundred," said Jim. "Is that understood?"

Nobody said anything. Johnny glanced at Doc, who after a long pause, nodded.

"All right," said Jim. "Now about the rest of the setup. You guys found the sucker—fine. But I've got to finance the job, do all the work, and take the risks. I want two-thirds. It's the only way I'll operate."

"That only leaves us a third between us," said Doc. "That's highway robbery."

"Wait a minute, Doc," said Shake. "A third of something is better than all of nothing. That's plain arithmetic."

"Suits me," Windy put in; but everybody ignored him.

"I got to think this over," said Doc.

Jim got up abruptly. "Take it or leave it right now," he said as he put on his hat. "It's all one to me. I won't starve."

Doc winced slightly but stubbornly held his ground. What a spot to be in! He didn't have a leg to stand on and knew it. And yet something inside him resisted. He'd been pretty big once, himself. He was no small-timer anybody could push around.

Jim turned and walked to the door. Johnny got up slowly and followed him. He wasn't worried because he could tell Jim was merely putting on an act—the clincher. The big fellow wasn't really annoyed at all. He was merely operating automatically, as he had done on their arrival with his goodwill act.

Just as Jim started out the door, Doc called in a harsh voice.

"All right, Farrar. That's it. But let me ask you a question?"

Jim turned.

"Yeah?"

"How big do you figure the take will be?"

Without hesitation Jim said:

"With that kind of money—a hundred Gs."

"Will you guarantee us thirty thousand dollars?"

"Yes," said Jim, "if I make the take."

"Okay," said Doc.

Jim said goodbye to the others offhandedly and went out, followed by Johnny. When the door shut, Doc said:

"He'll probably blow it. He's beginning to look old. A guy can't go on forever."

Pop glanced at Doc with a smile of amusement, but made no comment.

"Ten grand," cried Windy. "I get ten grand. I just figured it out."

"If and when," said Doc.

"Cut it out, Doc," Shake put in; "you know the big fellow don't blow them."

Doc sat down and drummed on the table. His ego had got a bad jarring. He was used to Windy and Shake, both inferiors, and to the riffraff he met in the cheap bars he frequented. He was not in any way prepared for a clash with a man like Jim Farrar. It had been a physical shock, as if he'd been whipped. He felt exhausted and ashamed. He smiled ironically for the benefit of the others.

"Every time I see Jim Farrar I'm surprised how much bumpkin he's got in him."

Nobody said anything. They all knew Doc better than he realized.

On the way home Jim was silent for such a length of time that finally Johnny took his eyes off the white line long enough to throw him a glance of inquiry. The big fellow's face looked slack and sad in the dim light from the dash.

"The nerve of that coked-up ex-croaker," said Johnny, trying to draw Jim out.

"What a bunch!" said Jim, then lapsed into silence again. Although Jim said nothing about it, the old disquiet had returned. The sight of those four has-beens, in that dismal backroom, had driven all thoughts of Tony from his mind; he felt depressed and alone. No matter how you tried to gloss it over, fundamentally things were mighty ugly; a man had nothing to look forward to but decrepitude. Jim tried to picture himself as he would be at Pop's age; an old bore, probably buttonholing any guy in sight so he could talk about himself and what he used to be. His hair white, no teeth, no manhood; no nothing. What was the sense in hanging on? Jim had a sudden impulse to call the whole deal off. It was absurd, this rushing around, trying to make a fortune. In fact didn't all activity seem futile? Everything led to old age and ultimately the grave. He groaned inwardly, hoping that Johnny would not notice his mood.

But when they got to the beach house, Tony had a fire going and the big room was so cheerful and Tony looked so damned good in a dark-green hostess gown that Jim gradually recovered his spirits. She kissed him and said:

"How about some scrambled eggs? Say the word—and I'll fix them with my own lily-white hands."

"Sounds fine," said Jim, hugging her. "Eh, Johnny?"

Johnny shrugged.

"I think I'll drink my sustenance—if you don't mind."

Behind Jim's back he winked and nodded at Tony, who made a quick gesture with thumb and forefinger which said: "Nice work, kid."

While Tony was in the kitchen, Jim sat staring into the fire which was leaping on the hearth and giving off a fine, clean odor.

Johnny came over from the bar and stood beside him with a highball in his hand.

"This should be a record one," he observed.

"Yeah," said Jim. "I'll really fix myself for life with this one. Only thing is—I don't like giving a woman the business."

Johnny snorted.

"With her money, she can stand it."

XI

Charley Evans, Doc's college friend and manager of the Marwood Arms, was very much taken with his new "guest," Mr. James Lloyd, the oil man from Houston, Texas. "He's got wealth written all over him," he told his sister who lived with him, "but he's so democratic. His business manager, a lawyer by the name of Riley, made all the arrangements for him and took our most expensive suite without a quibble. I expected to see some very snooty person—after all, most of our guests—and many of them very exclusive people—make their own arrangements. I was very surprised when Mr. Lloyd turned up. He's so friendly I felt at home with him right away. Every employee in the place thinks he's wonderful. He's a good tipper, of course, and that helps with the employees; but that's not everything by any means. As you know, darling. Remember the trouble I had with that Russian prince? He was a big tipper, but in spite of that, every employee in the place wanted to drop something on him. He was insufferable. So nasty—even to me. I'm glad he left. He'd eventually got arsenic in his soup. That crazy Italian chef—well...." His sister nodded to show that she was listening. Charley was always talking about his "guests"; especially the wealthy ones. She thought that her brother was a very nice man, but at times his snobbery jarred her sensibilities.

During Jim's first week at the Marwood he was seldom around the place. He left about ten in the morning and went to his beach house where he spent the day with Tony, lolling about in the sand. Johnny would turn up late in the afternoon and they'd all have dinner together. Jim usually got back to the Marwood early in the evening and went immediately to his suite. He was a slow and calculating operator. He knew it would be remarked that he was seldom around; and that was exactly what he wanted.

Johnny had moved to a Santa Monica hotel in spite of protests from both Jim and Tony. It looked better, he insisted. "To who?" Jim demanded, jeering at Johnny. "To Telesfero—if nobody else," Johnny said and was howled at. All the same, he had his reasons. Tony made him uneasy. She was just the kind of dame who would get herself into a jam out of boredom. She was on the chisel—true; but she was not smart and strong-willed enough to control her nature for any length of time— even to encompass an important end. She'd got Jim back into the saddle—and as far as Johnny was concerned, she'd served her purpose. Besides, she was extremely attractive to him and he knew that if he hung around while Jim was away it was only a question of time till he'd be in bed with her. He'd heard a lot about her and her appetites from some of Jim's Florida pals. She was a very casual babe; completely without scruples.

He had a beef with Jim about leaving the beach house, and Jim, by some of his remarks, almost goaded him into stating his real reasons for leaving. At times Jim amazed him by his obtuseness. Johnny had never kidded himself about his personal appearance—he was far from handsome and admitted it. All the same, he'd never lacked for women. What made Jim so certain Tony wouldn't give him a tumble? Didn't he know that looks and size weren't everything? Hadn't he yet got wised up to the fact that to some women—especially women like Tony—a little homely man on the spot was better than three far-away Adonises?

Later, he had another beef, and a more serious one, with Jim. There was around seventy-five thousand dollars in cash hidden in the beach house, and Johnny was the only one who knew where it was with the exception of Jim. Johnny insisted that it be moved to a safety-deposit box. And when Jim demanded to know why, Johnny said:

"In the first place: I know where it is. In the second place: Tony."

"You're not insinuating she'd jump with it, are you?"

"She's human."

"And so are you."

Johnny kept his temper with difficulty.

"That's what I mean."

"That's not what you mean. You just don't want to be blamed in case it disappears."

"Right," said Johnny.

"It's not going to disappear." Jim studied Johnny for a moment, then said patiently: "I want it where I can get my hands on it. In this business you never know. I might have to lam quick. I shouldn't have to tell you this."

There was a certain coolness between them most of one afternoon due to the second beef. Johnny thought Jim was acting like a pigheaded fool; and Jim thought Johnny was acting like a petty larceny jerk. Things were finally smoothed over, and they all had dinner together, Tony getting a little tight and amusing them by smoking a cigar and doing an exaggerated Conga at the same time.

At the beginning of his second week at the Marwood, Jim decided it was time to show himself at dinner. He put on a tuxedo which had set him back two hundred dollars in Florida and went down to the bar at a quarter till eight. He made a fine appearance with his curly, graying hair carefully brushed, and his tanned face looking very dark above his immaculate white shirtfront. He drank two sidecars, talked amiably with the bartender, and ignored the other people in the bar. A couple of women made complimentary remarks about him to their escorts, who made cracks at his expense in reply.

At a little after eight, he entered the dining room. Andre, the headwaiter, who hadn't seen Jim before but had heard all about him along the hotel grapevine, recognized him at once, and conducted him to the best available table. Jim had no sooner been seated than Charley Evans came over to him, beaming.

"Good evening, Mr. Lloyd," he said, bowing politely. "Happy to see you here. I think you'll find our cuisine above reproach—in spite of the trouble we're having due to the war. If not, please tell me."

"Thank you, Mr. Evans. Won't you sit down?"

Charley sat down quickly, smirking.

"Just for a moment."

"I like the Marwood," said Jim. "Very comfortable. I've been so busy lately I haven't been able to see much of it. But things will slack off soon, then I'll be here more. I need a rest."

"We'll see that you get it. The Marwood is a quiet, restful place. I want to keep it that way, so I'm careful about my guests. Hollywood just around the corner, you know." Charley raised his eyes and shook his head, conveying that compared to Hollywood, Sodom and Gomorrah were resorts for aging Methodist ministers.

Encouraged by Jim's polite interest, Evans chatted on. Jim thought the little manager was an eight-cylinder bore and a jerk, but you'd never have guessed it from his manner. Evans glowed with pleasure as he sat hobnobbing on an equal footing with this obviously rich and able man; so democratic, so easy of approach, so unlike many of his rich guests, who seemed to think that a hotel manager was some sort of servant.

Evans suddenly realized that he was taking up a lot of Jim's time and reluctantly got up. Just as he was saying goodbye a tall woman in a white dinner gown was escorted to a nearby table by Andre, who was all smiles and bows.

"Good evening, Mrs. Halvorsen," said Evans, bowing. "It's nice to see you."

"Good evening, Mr. Evans," said the woman, in a pleasant voice.

Jim paid no attention. Evans turned to him.

"A charming woman, Mr. Lloyd. One of our most valued clients."

"Really," said Jim without turning.

Evans went over to Mrs. Halvorsen's table, a little annoyed by Mr. Lloyd's lack of interest in his pet guest.

Jim ordered, then sat smoking a cigarette and calmly looking about the dining room, which was gradually filling up. Out of the corner of his eye he saw Evans leave Mrs. Halvorsen's table. Little by little, he moved his chair so that without seeming to, he could get a good look at his "sucker." He was surprised. He'd heard only that she was a rich widow— forty. He'd expected her to be dowdy; or fat and kittenish; and an easy touch. She was neither fat, kittenish, nor dowdy, and she looked like anything but a pushover. She was tall and slender, with a trim figure; her hair was dark and abundant, and she wore it up; her face was narrow, sensitive, and patrician-looking. She had fine dark eyes under arched black brows. She looked poised and self-assured. She was dressed simply and wore no jewelry except a wedding ring. Aside from a slightly worn look and a certain tiredness about the eyes, she might have been a woman of thirty, or less.

Jim was slightly annoyed. If he knew anything at all about people, she was going to be a problem. He'd expected something much easier. This would take careful and astute managing. He felt suddenly tired. Here he was on the same old merry-go-round again; the thing he'd run away from. Groaning inwardly, he saw the whole boring comedy, step by step; the approach, the buildup, the clincher, the take, the brush-off. It might be a matter of weeks—months even; when all he wanted to do was lie in the sun and enjoy Tony's company. Hell, he had plenty of money. Damn Johnny for getting him into this; damn them all—the jackals, waiting around while he made the kill for them.

Turning to the waiter, he ordered a bottle of wine. He needed something to pick him up and he didn't want to order liquor in the middle of a meal—it would be noted as an eccentricity, and commented on. He wanted to keep his conduct as conventional as possible; this had a tendency to allay any suspicions that might arise.

He finished his dinner before Mrs. Halvorsen, and left without a look in her direction.

The next afternoon he ran into the manager in the lobby and stopped to talk with him. The manager commented on the coolness of the summer weather, and assured Jim that ordinarily California summers were not nearly so cool. "Not that they are ever hot, in the Midwestern sense," he added hastily. Then he said with an obsequious smile: "The charming lady I was telling you about—Mrs. Halvorsen—asked me who you were. She was surprised when I told her you were an oil man. She said you looked more like a doctor."

"A horse doctor?" Jim asked, playing it straight. Evans was a little bewildered by this comment.

"No. No," he said. "A real doctor—a scientist."

"She's a nice-looking woman," said Jim. "Seems to be. I didn't get a very good look at her."

He turned away as if to go to the elevator. Evans detained him.

"I hope you don't misunderstand my talking about Mrs. Halvorsen," he said, feeling that Jim was being somewhat offhand and wondering why. "She's one of my favorite people. I thought you'd be pleased to know she asked about you."

"Thanks—I am," said Jim, thinking: "If I didn't know better, I'd be pretty sure dear little Mr. Evans was a pimp."

"She's a very cultivated woman," said Evans. "Very wealthy."

"I'm sure she is," said Jim, and turning away again, went to the elevator.

Evans bit his lip in annoyance. He had wanted to arrange an introduction. He'd expected it to be easy, Mr. Lloyd had seemed so approachable; but in this matter, well—he felt a certain constraint in the oil man's attitude. "Oh, well—rich men," he soothed himself, "they have to be so careful. It's too bad. He's the most presentable and suitable man that's been here since Mrs. Halvorsen arrived. I do hope she doesn't get bored with the Marwood Arms—after all, it is a little quiet here; pretty staid." Being a worrier by nature, Evans felt somewhat upset— it was his business, as manager, to keep the Marwood Arms filled with rich and respectable people—Mrs. Halvorsen was both to a marked degree. Now if she were to get bored....

The elevator door opened and Mrs. Halvorsen got out. Jim stood aside to let her pass. She was wearing a dark blue suit and a very attractive large hat. Her eyes rested on his face for a moment—her glance was pleasant, neither distant nor provocative; and yet there was a certain shyness about it that made it very attractive to Jim. He smiled in a friendly way, and bowed slightly as she passed; then he got into the elevator and went up to his room.

While he was shaving he talked to his image in the glass.

"I won't have any trouble meeting her—that's a cinch. In fact that damned little clunk of a manager's trying to make it too easy—like a hostess in some clip joint. It's funny. Why a dame with that kind of money and class is lonesome beats me. That's one for the book!"

Two days later Jim went into the bar at cocktail time. He was feeling a little weary. Tony had been wild as a hawk all afternoon; he had never known her to be so lascivious before—she'd surprised him; then her mood had changed so quickly he was dumbfounded—she had insisted on having a violent row with him over nothing; and then, just as he was on the point of telling her to shut her big mouth, she'd become very apologetic—almost groveling in fact; then before he'd got accustomed to this new mood, she was amorous again. "Well," Jim told himself, "at least she's not boring."

The bar was very restful, with its subdued air, and its scattering of polite people, talking in low voices. He sat at the bar, sipped a highball, and meditated.

In a moment, he heard a pleasant voice behind him and turned. It was Mrs. Halvorsen and she was accompanied by a tall man about fifty, very well dressed, and with a languid, well-satisfied air, which annoyed Jim. Mrs. Halvorsen's shy, pleasant glance rested on his face for a moment. He smiled.

"Good evening," he said.

"Good evening, Mr. Lloyd," she replied, and went on.

She and the man sat at a table some distance from the bar, and Jim couldn't observe them without craning his neck. He paid for his drink and went out. It was time he did something. This big guy with her looked like dough and also like a guy who'd been around.

Shortly before he went into dinner, he managed to run into Evans as if it were an accident. He spoke to him in such a friendly way, that Mr. Evans responded, glowing, and asked him to dinner. Jim accepted.

Mrs. Halvorsen had dinner with the big guy, but Jim could see that she wasn't much interested in what he had to say. Her eyes kept wandering about the room. Finally she looked at him and he smiled and nodded. Evans smiled and nodded, too.

"Who's the man with Mrs. Halvorsen?" Jim asked.

"Mr. W. W. Manning," said Evans, promptly, "a big corporation lawyer—retired. He's been one of my valued clients for years."

"He looked familiar to me. But I guess I'm wrong."

"Would you like to meet him?"

"Yes," said Jim. "It's possible I've met him before. I'd just like to know."

When they'd finished dinner, they stopped at Mrs. Halvorsen's table. Evans introduced Jim to both Manning and Mrs. Halvorsen. They talked for a moment, then Jim said he'd have to go, that he wanted to get a good night's sleep, as he was going to the beach for a swim. He glanced at Mrs. Halvorsen.

"It's nice at the beach now," he said, talking directly to her.

"I haven't been to the beach since I've been here—not to swim, that is."

"You can have my share of that," said Manning. "I don't trust the Pacific—it's grossly misnamed. Riptides: I don't know what all."

You big cluck, Jim thought. It was obvious the lady wanted to go for a swim.

"Well, goodnight," said Jim. "It's nice to have seen you."

He smiled at Mrs. Halvorsen, who smiled, very friendly, but with a slight touch of disappointment—which Jim didn't miss.

As soon as Jim got to the lobby he shook off Evans by telling him he was going to take a walk before turning in. He went to a drugstore down the street and called Johnny on the pay phone, telling him what arrangements to make: Tony was to spend the whole day at Johnny's hotel or anywhere else she could think of: Johnny was to come to the beach house, and be the host.

"I'll do the rest," said Jim.

"Nice work," said Johnny.

That night Jim slept fitfully. His nerves were on edge, as they always were at the beginning of the long process which led eventually to separating a sucker from his bankroll. At dawn he got up and looked out the window. Along the wide boulevard tall palm trees stood rigid in the pale morning light. The air was crystal clear, promising a hot day; perfect for the beach.

"She likes me, that woman," he observed as he got back into bed. "Yep: I could see it in her eyes. But with her I've got to go slow—she's a new one on me!"

XII

Jim called Mrs. Halvorsen at ten the next morning. He apologized for phoning so early but she said she'd been up for hours; her voice sounded very pleasant and friendly; Jim thought he noticed a faint note of eagerness even. He told her his business manager, Mr. Riley, had a beach house and he often went down for a swim. It was such a beautiful day, he said, he was wondering if she'd like to go along. They could be back at the Marwood for dinner—if she preferred.

"I'd like it very much," said Mrs. Halvorsen.

"Could you leave in an hour?" Jim asked, politely.

"Half an hour, if that suits you better."

Forty-five minutes later they were in Jim's Cadillac on their way to La Junta Beach. Mrs. Halvorsen had on a navy-blue sweater, and a white coat and skirt, and seemed quite youthful, not only because of her slim figure, but also because of her expression—she looked eager and expectant, like a kid going to a picnic.

"Damn nice-looking woman—and a lady," Jim told himself, glancing respectfully at Mrs. Halvorsen from time to time. "Not my type—but I'm a so-and-so if I can see why she's running around loose; even if she didn't have a plugged dime. With all that loot—well, the boys are sure missing a bet."

"I understand you're in the oil business," said Mrs. Halvorsen, politely.

"More or less," said Jim.

"In Texas?"

Jim nodded.

"At one time my husband had quite a large interest in the Santa Ana field—it didn't pan out."

Jim glanced at her covertly and was reassured. She wasn't trying to pump him; she was just making conversation.

"We all lost a little in that field," he said, with just the right degree of carelessness. "As a matter of fact I made most of my money in the oil refining business. What I made there, I dropped in the fields. Now with the government taking it all—well, I'm lucky to eat." He turned and when their eyes met, he laughed. She laughed also. "But I eat pretty well."

"The Marwood's rather nice, don't you think?"

"Yes," said Jim. "Nice place."

"A little quiet for you, perhaps."

Jim glanced at her. There was a slight degree of irony in her smile. What the hell, he thought.

"At times," he conceded.

"You mustn't misunderstand me, Mr. Lloyd. I'm not implying that you're fast. You just don't seem quite as—well, ossified as some of the men I've met there."

Jim laughed. He was genuinely amused. He hadn't heard the word "fast" used in that sense since he was a boy. In the old days his mother had always been condemning somebody as "fast."

"The Marwood's very respectable," said Jim, and then in an apparent burst of candor he went on: "Personally, I like to get drunk once in a while. Not too drunk and not too often. But don't tell on me. Mr. Evans wouldn't like it."

Mrs. Halvorsen had quite a laugh over this. It's not that funny, thought Jim. But he laughed, too—at length. By the time they got to the beach road, he had Mrs. Halvorsen gasping for breath with remarks which to him were only mildly funny; in fact, many of them were more than a little on the corny side. Well, Jim thought, maybe that's what living in Minneapolis does for you.

When they got to the beach house, Johnny was so punctilious that Jim was afraid he was overdoing it. As a matter of fact, Johnny, somewhat overwhelmed by Mrs. Halvorsen, was nervous. He envied Jim his ease of manner, his entire lack of self-consciousness. What a guy! Give him a week and he'd date up any dame in the country.

After a little conversation, Jim suggested that they go in swimming. Johnny was talking too much; and Jim was afraid he'd make a slip of some kind. From time to time he glanced at Mrs. Halvorsen. Her attitude reassured him; she seemed to accept everything without question, and to be completely at ease.

Johnny showed her to a bedroom, carrying her little beach bag for her—as obsequious as a red cap working for a big tip.

"My wife's out of town, Mrs. Halvorsen," he said. "This is her room. Everything all right?"

"Perfect—thank you."

Johnny bowed slightly, shut the door, then hurried down to the locker-room below stairs, where Jim undressed for the beach.

"You mean to tell me that dame's lonesome?" he demanded of Jim, who was leisurely taking off his clothes.

Jim nodded.

"I'd say so."

"Why? I don't get it. Good-looking—and with all that dough. Has she got an air! Brother! She looks like a queen ought to look."

"Oh—don't overdo it."

"How did you make the connection? If you're not the damnedest guy!"

"Are you surprised? I've been doing all right for fifteen years or so."

Johnny stared at Jim with awe and admiration. The big fellow was an irritating so-and-so, and at times seemed very obtuse and pigheaded, but he certainly knew how to deliver the goods. No wonder he was the top man.

"Look, Johnny," said Jim, struggling into his trunks, "don't talk so much—just relax. If she asks you a question, answer it, and let it go at that. Leave the rest to me."

"I thought I was doing all right," said Johnny. "Naturally I was a little jittery." He threw a reproachful glance at Jim, who ignored it.

"Where's Tony?"

"She went into Los Angeles on a bus."

"What time will Telesfero be back?"

"Not till late."

"Look—I don't want her here for dinner this time. That'll come later. Make some excuse about the Filipino boy."

Johnny nodded.

"Want me to stick around?"

"Yes," said Jim, "and close. I'm going to play this one smooth."

Johnny grinned and nodded, then stood studying Jim, who was now ready for the beach. He looked much bigger and huskier without his clothes; although he was fatter than he should have been, he was deeply tanned and had shoulders and legs like a blocking half; his body didn't look forty-two years old.

"Okay! Okay!" said Jim, misinterpreting Johnny's stare. "So I'm fat. But I'll get it off."

"I wish I was fat like that," said Johnny, wincing slightly as he thought of his own meagre, flat-chested body.

Johnny whistled under his breath when Mrs. Halvorsen came down the stairs to the beach, carrying her robe; she had on a white one-piece bathing suit which set off her slender figure to perfection. Jim held his hand out to her and helped her down the last few steps. Johnny saw her give Jim a quick admiring glance, then lower her eyes modestly. Jim grinned at her.

"My name's Jim," he said.

"Mine's Gladys," she replied, and they both laughed.

They went over and sat down under the beach umbrella. It was a beautiful day with a delicate blue sky and huge masses of white cottony clouds at the sea horizon. There were gulls everywhere.

"It seems strange without the boats, doesn't it, Jim?" said Mrs.

Halvorsen, hesitating for a moment over his name in a way that pleased him.

"Yeah," said Jim; "that ocean looks mighty lonesome at times. You never see anything now but a few fishing boats. At night it's worse, Gladys." He brought her name out as if he'd known her for years.

Johnny watched them for a minute, then he cleared his throat and said:

"Excuse me. I'll be right back."

Jim glanced up in annoyance. But Johnny hurried into the beach house, ignoring him.

"I like Mr. Riley," said Mrs. Halvorsen. "He's so friendly and considerate."

"He's a nice fellow—a little talkative at times."

"Oh, I don't mind that. As a rule I haven't much to say myself. I like to listen."

"I like to hear myself talk," said Jim. "We ought to get along all right."

Mrs. Halvorsen smiled and her eyes lingered on Jim's face. "I'm sure of that," she said after a moment.

What the hell, thought Jim; and glanced at her guardedly. Then he relaxed. It wasn't a feminine lead, or "come on." It was just a nice remark. This dame was all right.

They talked about California for a few minutes, then Johnny came out. He'd changed his clothes. He was now dressed in a blue and white polo shirt, white ducks, and a yachting cap. Jim thought he looked ridiculous and wanted to laugh, but restrained himself. Mrs. Halvorsen turned and said:

"Why, Mr. Riley—how nice you look."

Jim saw Johnny's puny chest expand.

They stopped on the way home and had dinner at a little fish place on a pier. As they ate they could hear the water washing under them and feel the shock as the waves broke against the pilings. They'd had two cocktails before dinner. Mrs. Halvorsen had protested that one was her limit, but had a second one anyway. Much to Jim's amusement she got a little tight and very talkative without the slightest idea that she was either.

Jim had a brandy after the dessert and she had one, too. "Just to keep you company," she said.

Night had fallen. A stiff breeze began to blow and they heard it moaning about the little frame restaurant. At sea, a boat whistle sounded, mournful in the darkness. The proprietor built a fire in the small stone fireplace and soon the flames were leaping and crackling.

"This is nice—very nice," said Mrs. Halvorsen. "I don't know when I've had such fun."

"I'm glad to hear that," said Jim.

"I've gone about hardly at all for years. Mr. Halvorsen was never in really good health; besides, he hated traveling—didn't like people either.

He liked to sit at home and read, and listen to the radio." She hesitated and glanced down at her brandy glass. "Not that I minded. In fact—I was happy to do whatever he wanted me to do."

"That's mighty unusual," said Jim.

"Is it?" asked Mrs. Halvorsen in mild surprise. "I never thought of it that way. You see—I owed everything to Mr. Halvorsen. I was his secretary."

Jim was a little surprised at this. She was not his idea of the secretary who marries the boss; she was not his idea of a secretary—period.

"I worked for him for nearly ten years," she went on. "He was the loneliest man I'd ever seen in my life—I felt so sorry for him."

Jim murmured politely and she looked up quickly.

"I don't know why I'm telling you all this," she said. "Please let me know if I'm boring you—but it's been so long since I've met someone I could talk to."

"You're not boring me at all."

She hesitated, sipped her drink, then smiled at Jim. "I'm afraid I am—you're just tolerating me."

She said nothing more about her private life, and Jim didn't press her. On the way back to town he suggested a movie. "If you're not too tired," he added.

"I'm not tired at all," she said. Movies bored Jim; he seldom went and then only to kill time, or duck somebody. But Mrs. Halvorsen was a fan; knew all about the stars. Later, on the way home, she told Jim that movies and radio were wonderful for people, particularly lonely people.

Jim thought she was a queer bird, but liked her. There was a certain honesty about her he couldn't help admiring. Honesty was a quality he didn't expect in a woman—or in hardly anybody for that matter; but in his experience it was less likely in a woman. By honesty he meant "rightness." A right guy doesn't rat on his pals, or double-cross them, or welch on a debt. Plenty of people considered absolutely honest by society could not be classed so according to Jim's standards; they lacked "rightness" and in many cases throve financially on this lack. Mrs. Halvorsen did not belong with such people, Jim felt. She was "right."

XIII

For two days, Jim stayed away from the Marwood as much as possible. He didn't want Mrs. Halvorsen to get any idea he was rushing her; and, besides, certain that she liked him, he thought it would do her good to get a little impatient and begin to wonder why he hadn't called.

The evening of the second day he had a brawl with Tony at the beach. It started at dinner. Tony took a drink or so too many and began to make remarks that Jim resented. Johnny tried to quiet her, knowing that Jim would only stand so much. But Tony was in one of her headstrong moods and persisted. Finally, Jim spoke to her so sharply and contemptuously that she jumped up, flung a plate at him, then burst into tears.

The plate missed Jim, and crashed against the wall just as Telesfero came in with the coffee. The little Filipino put the coffee down hastily on the serving table, and went back to the kitchen, where he stood trembling. Johnny took his head between his hands and groaned.

Jim sat staring at Tony with distaste.

"Why don't you grow up?" he demanded finally, in a cold contemptuous tone. "Always yelling and throwing things!"

Tony turned and ran into the bedroom, slamming the door. There was a long silence. Johnny sighed and lit a cigar, glancing at Jim, who was calmly pouring the coffee.

"Getting fed up with her?" asked Johnny, cautiously.

"I don't know," said Jim. "We had a row like this the second day I was out with her. I wish she'd relax a little—for Christ's sake."

"If she's around she drives you nuts—if she isn't, you wish she was. Is that it, Jim?"

Jim turned and studied Johnny.

"Something like that. Why?"

"Well—I found her; brought her out here. I can always take her back."

Jim got up with his coffee cup in his hand and began to pace the floor.

"It's a thing that's hard to explain," he said. "I don't get it myself."

"Someday, you're going to stop one of those missiles," said Johnny. "I hope it's a tomato and not a flat-iron."

"Her aim's bad," said Jim, then suddenly he burst out laughing.

Johnny stared.

"What's funny?"

"I was thinking about one night in Miami. We were in a joint. Some guy sitting at the next table kept staring at Tony. He was a stuffed shirt from New York on the loose—slumming, you know. Tony got so sore at me she tried to hit me over the head with her purse. It slipped out of her hand just as this guy was crooking his elbow and he got a high-ball and Tony's purse right in his smug kisser." Jim leaned on the back of a chair to laugh and almost spilled his coffee. "I never saw such a look on a guy's face in my life. One of these pompous, dignified birds. Oh, brother!"

The bedroom door opened and Tony came out, looking very contrite.

"What's so funny?" she asked in a mild, apologetic voice.

"You," said Jim. "I was telling Johnny about that time at the Moulin Rouge."

"My God," Tony exclaimed. "The guy I hit had ten million bucks. But was it funny."

She and Jim both roared with laughter. Johnny stood looking at the pair of them, wondering. Tony had a very strong hold over the big fellow; no doubt about it. He'd take things from her he wouldn't take from anybody else.

Tony glanced at Jim, then she put her arm around his waist and her head on his shoulder.

"I'm sorry I was bad," she said.

"Oh—cut the baby talk."

Tony drew back from him.

"I'm trying to make up," she exclaimed, her voice rising, "and look how you act."

Jim opened his mouth to speak, but Johnny beat him to it.

"Sit down, Tony. I'll pour you some coffee. Let's all relax."

Tony sat down, sulking. Jim stared thoughtfully at the floor, sipping his coffee.

"Look," said Johnny, "why don't you two try to get along better—you're wearing me out."

Tony and Jim glanced at each other, then laughed. Jim came over and bending down, kissed her on the mouth. She turned quickly and put her arms around his neck.

"No million-dollar widow's going to get you," she said. "Don't ever think she is."

"What Jim likes is her bankroll, darling," said Johnny. "Please—for God's sake—relax."

Half an hour later, Johnny left for Santa Monica, thankful to get away. Not only because he was tired of the constant bickering, but also because Tony was becoming more and more attractive to him. A crazy dame, who would never get a man in anything but trouble—headstrong, self-willed, violent; and yet....

"I'd sure take a chance—if the setup was different," Johnny told himself. "But I got to ease things along till the take. Maybe Jim'll be so sick of her by that time, he'll tell me to cart her off. And will I!"

Not long after Johnny left, Jim got up to go, but Tony protested.

"It's only eight-thirty," she said.

"I want to get back around ten. Business reasons."

"What does this woman look like?"

"She's tall—forty years old," said Jim, indifferently.

"You better make this take without any monkey business or I'm going to be very, very annoyed."

"She's a nice woman. No nonsense."

"Oh, yeah?" said Tony. "I know all about those forty-year-old widows. A cripple's not safe."

Jim shrugged. In comparison with Mrs. Halvorsen, Tony at times seemed pretty gross. He was anxious to get away.

But suddenly Tony flung herself into his arms, kissed him violently, bit him, but drew back and laughed at him as soon as she felt his arms tightening.

"I guess you're not in such a hurry," she jeered.

Jim tried to pull her to him, but she broke away and shoved a chair in between them.

"Come and get me," she cried, then she dashed past him, ran into the bedroom, and held the door shut.

Jim finally managed to force it open. Tony stood in the middle of the room, laughing at him. Just as Jim started toward her she turned out the light. He caught her after a struggle.

"Tony," he said, "you know what you are? You're nothing but an animal."

"Is that bad?" cried Tony.

Jim didn't get back to the Marwood Arms till after three in the morning.

XIV

It was a hot night in town and Pop was sitting by an open window in Maxie's Bar, drinking a cold stein of beer, fanning himself, and praying for a breeze. The narrow street looked dingy and forbidding in the dimout. The bar was crowded with sailors, who bickered drunkenly, and kept the battered old automatic piano going without a letup.

Pop felt a little weary and defeated. He wasn't the man he'd been a few short weeks ago and knew it. The brief glimpse he'd got of El Dorado had unsettled him. He'd come to hate standing on a corner with his telescope, cadging for dimes; worse still, his memory had begun to fail him, he'd lost his alertness, and his underworld clients, who had always praised him before, and said he was one hundred per cent, were beginning to wonder about him.

Pop was always dreaming now. Doc had promised him five hundred; that wasn't a fortune by any means; but all in a hunk, it wasn't to be sneered at. The big fellow had said he'd take care of him. Pop would speculate for hours over just what the big fellow meant. Was Jim implying that he'd get a full share—ten grand? It could hardly be that and yet it was nice to think about. Or did he mean that he'd just take care of him personally for—say: a couple thousand bucks. Either way, he'd have a nice roll in his kick and could take it easy for a while. Maybe long enough.

Pop ordered another beer. Two sailors were dancing together to the piano, clowning, and they got annoyed when the bartender asked them to cut it out. Pop looked for something to get behind in case a fight started. But one of the sailors, older than the rest, smoothed things over.

The waiter came with Pop's beer and he sat sipping it and looking out the window. God, it was hot. Nice to be out in the country on a night like this. But Pop wasn't thinking about the California countryside. He'd been born in Indiana and the older he got the more he thought about his home state. He was thinking about a flat farm country, bathed in soft moonlight, with crickets chirping in the tall grass, frogs croaking in the ponds, and cows standing along the fences chewing their cuds in the darkness. Dogs barked, answering each other from farm to farm, and lightning bugs flew among the big trees, giving off a faint, intermittent green glow. Summer smells were everywhere, and the air was damply cool—delicious.

Pop started. Somebody was touching him on the shoulder. It was Doc, smiling ironically, and not looking quite so seedy as usual. He had on a new shirt and tie, and his clothes had been brushed; he was even freshly shaved.

"Hello, Doc," said Pop, returning from a dream-Indiana with an effort. "Sit down."

Doc sat opposite Pop and ordered a highball with a flourish. The waiter threw him a satirical glance, but made no comment.

"I was looking for you, Pop," said Doc. "Missed you—so I thought I'd try here."

"Yeah?"

"Nothing important. I was just wondering if you'd heard anything."

"Not a thing."

"You wouldn't hold out on me, would you?"

"Why should I?"

"Well—I figure you're pretty thick with Johnny and Jim."

"I'm waiting—the same as you fellows are."

"He better make this one, because I'm counting on it. Counting on it big."

Pop thought that Doc's eyes didn't look right. It was probably the junk.

"If he can't make this one, nobody can," said Pop. "Just keep your pants on, Doc."

"I wish I knew what was going on. I got a good notion to buzz my friend, Charley Evans. I don't like to be in the dark—especially with a deal this big."

Pop meditated, then spoke mildly.

"It's all right to talk to me that way, Doc, but not to anybody else. If the big fellow hears about it, you might get in trouble. You're not insinuating he'd try to gyp us, are you?"

"He's not the man he used to be."

"Are you? Am I? Who is?" Pop sipped his beer philosophically, and wished that Doc would go away and leave him alone. There was something very disquieting about the restless, soured little doctor. An inhuman quality hard to describe. Pop was reminded of what he'd once heard a judge say: "A man desperate through lack of hope." That was Doc in a way. "Be sensible," Pop went on. "Don't go buzzing nobody. You might cause trouble—a beef. Leave it to the big fellow. He's been making record scores for years."

"Yes—and taking advantage of small guys working with him. Two-thirds! Robbery—that's what it is."

Pop finished the rest of his beer and stood up.

"I'm sleepy."

"Sit down. I'll buy you a drink."

"No thanks. Doc—if my advice is worth anything, listen; don't tangle with the big fellow. Keep your nose clean. He's a good-natured guy but he's no one to cross. Goodnight."

He went out hurriedly. Doc sat watching him go.

"We'll see who's tough to cross," said Doc, half-aloud, then he turned and called for another drink.

Shake was sitting with his chair tipped back and his feet on the window sill, talking to Windy, and looking out across the dingy rooftops of the dimmed-out city.

"With that kind of dough," said Shake, "I'll retire. If a guy's careful he can get by—and get by good—on eight—nine hundred bucks a year. Just think of that, Windy. Once I get my hands on that dough, I'm a cinch to live easy without a worry for ten-eleven years. I'll just sit in my room and read all day long. Reading maketh a full man," he added, glancing at Windy.

Windy looked thoughtfully at the floor.

"What's that 'maketh' business?" he asked finally.

"It's the same as 'makes'," Shake explained.

"Why don't you say so then?"

"It's a quotation from old-time writing. That's the way they used to say 'makes' in them days."

"Why?"

"Because that's the way they said it."

Windy pondered.

"Why does reading make a man full?" he inquired.

"A full man," said Shake. "Not a man full."

"You sure you got that right? It sounds kind of silly."

"Certainly I've got it right," said Shake indignantly. "Are you trying to tell me about reading and things like that? I've read over a thousand books, and I'll bet I read two thousand more before I kick off."

Windy looked at Shake for a moment with awe.

"I wish I could read a book once," he said. "But I always fall asleep."

There was a short silence, then Shake asked:

"What you going to do with *your* dough, Windy?"

Windy scratched his head.

"I ain't decided—I got so many things I'd like to do. At first, I figured I'd get me a young babe. With that kind of dough a guy can get any kind of doll he wants. But I don't know. Then I figured I'd stash my dough and join the army."

"They wouldn't take you. You're too old."

"Too old—hell. I can lick any six guys you name." Windy trembled with indignation. "I'm strong as an ox. I'd take a Heinie in each hand and knock their dumb square heads together. Then when the war was over I'd come back with a medal. I'd unstash my dough and I'd be somebody."

"Suppose you get shot."

"Yeah," said Windy. "I thought about that."

After a while, Windy got up, yawned and stretched, then lay down on the couch. Silence settled over them and the street noises came in through the open window and filled the hot, smoky little room. Windy fell asleep, and dreamed that he was a hero and a general was pinning a medal on his chest. Shake sat on, staring out across the rooftops of the dark, sweltering city, and thinking how nice it would be to have his own room, his own books, plenty to eat, and nothing to bother him.

XV

Jim found Mrs. Halvorsen in the bar. She was sitting on a stool sipping a brandy. She turned just as he came in as if she had expected him. Jim noticed that there was a certain constraint in her greeting, and wondered. Had she decided she'd been too friendly? Or was she a little put out that she hadn't heard from him? He smiled wearily, sat down beside her, and ordered a double brandy.

"I'm worn out," he said.

"What's the matter, Mr. Lloyd?" she enquired, very formal.

"I've really been working hard the last few days."

She turned to look at him.

"Business?"

"Yes. Things just kept coming up—and Riley couldn't handle them alone. The war's knocked the devil out of everything. A man doesn't know if he's going or coming." He took a long sip of brandy and shuddered. "This is the first drink I've had in two days. I'll probably get tight and obnoxious."

Mrs. Halvorsen smiled faintly.

"I was wondering why I hadn't seen you in the dining room."

She was still rather formal and Jim decided it was time to put on a little pressure.

"I was going to call you. I wanted to ask you to dinner. I know a place at Palos Verdes I think you'd like. But I just couldn't get away—so I decided not to bother you." Mrs. Halvorsen said nothing but sat staring thoughtfully at her drink so Jim went on: "Would you like to go to Palos Verdes tonight?"

Mrs. Halvorsen bit her lip.

"I'm sorry—I can't tonight. I'm to have dinner with Mr. Manning."

"Couldn't you put it off?"

"I don't think I should. He's been very nice to me."

"Well," said Jim, "I don't want to insist. I've just sort of been looking forward to ..." He paused, glancing at her, and noticing again that strange mixture of eagerness and restraint in her attitude. He had no doubt that she'd prefer having dinner with him, but on the other hand, she was not the type of woman who goes around standing guys up. "Oh, well," he said, "maybe some other time."

Mrs. Halvorsen took a sip from her glass.

"Perhaps we could make it tomorrow night," she said, her manner rather cool.

"Tomorrow night will be fine," said Jim, grinning. "Shall I meet you here at eight?"

"I'd rather you came up after me."

"I'll be there."

The little restaurant at Palos Verdes was in the midst of eucalyptus trees on the top of a hill, overlooking the ocean. They had a table at a big window. It was a clear night and far below them the dimmed-out shoreline stretched for miles. Jim could see that Mrs. Halvorsen was very happy. They had two cocktails before dinner.

"I'm getting to be quite a toper," she said. "I'll tell you a secret. I never had a drink of brandy before—till the other night. My—but it's strong."

"It should be taken in small doses," said Jim. "Otherwise somebody touches you on the shoulder and you turn around and nobody's there."

She puzzled over this for a moment, then smiled. She was very charming when she smiled and Jim looked at her with a certain amount of admiration.

"I've never heard anybody talk like you," she said. "Sometimes I have to stop and figure it out."

"I've spent a lot of time with rough guys—in oil towns," said Jim. "I don't talk as well as I should."

"Oh, it's not that. I like the way you talk. Only it sort of bewilders me at times."

On the way back to the hotel, Mrs. Halvorsen was silent for so long that Jim began to look at her out of the corner of his eye. But her face seemed so tranquil in the light of the dash that he felt pretty sure nothing was wrong.

As he was leaving her at the door of her apartment, she held out her hand to him. It was cool and firm: Jim liked the feel of it.

"I'm afraid I'm not very good company," she said with one of her charming smiles. "But I really had a nice time."

"What do you mean you're not good company?" said Jim. "I don't know when I've had more fun."

"You wouldn't just be saying that, would you?" said Mrs. Halvorsen, putting her head on one side, and smiling up at Jim. In spite of her poise, there was at times a certain over-archness in her manner; probably, Jim thought, due to awkwardness. The little lady just hadn't been around very much.

And as he was saying good night he noticed again in her attitude that strange mixture of eagerness and restraint.

Jim unlocked the door of his apartment thoughtfully. Care was necessary with Mrs. Halvorsen. She was a new breed to him.

After the dinner at Palos Verdes, they went out together almost every night. They went to movies and regular theatres: and they made all the tourist joints, including Olvera Street, Chinatown, and even Earl

Carroll's, where Jim saw a tall blonde girl in the chorus he decided to check on for future reference—but changed his mind, figuring he had his hands full at the moment.

Mrs. Halvorsen was so dainty, and moved about with such an air, that Jim got so he took a definite pride in her company. They were a fine-looking couple and people stared at them.

She enjoyed herself quietly. At times Jim worried about her, wondering if she wasn't bored. But when he left her she always told him what a wonderful time she'd had and there was something about the way she said it that convinced him of her sincerity.

They became more and more friendly, but in spite of this Jim still felt a certain constraint in her attitude toward him: as if he were on trial. At times it made him somewhat awkward in manner.

Jim was more than a little puzzled. He just wasn't sure of his approach.

XVI

They were sitting in a Hollywood Boulevard movie theatre. There was a double bill and one of the pictures was a gangster thriller. Much to Jim's amazement Mrs. Halvorsen got so excited during a chase sequence, when a car plunged over an embankment, that she gave a faint scream and took hold of his arm. He turned to look at her. She was intent on the picture, her eyes wide, her lips parted; but in a moment she sensed his scrutiny and looked at him.

"Exciting, isn't it?"

"Yeah," Jim replied, wanting to laugh. Imagine a woman her age getting that excited about a gangster chase. Kids slept through them now. All the same, it gave him a nice feeling which he didn't understand at all. "It's just that she's been cooped up so long, I guess," he told himself. "Been sitting around the house for ten years listening to the radio with a guy old enough to be her grandfather—almost. It's like a guy coming out of stir after a long jolt. Everything you see hits you harder than it did before. Like when Pete Weston was let out of Joliet: a little dog barked at him and he almost had a fit."

Jim thought the show would never be over; he crossed and uncrossed his legs fifty times; but Mrs. Halvorsen seemed perfectly contented. They saw two full-length pictures, a newsreel, an animated cartoon, an educational film dealing with what to do in an air raid, and an Army short. It was nearly one o'clock when they came out of the theatre and they'd gone in fairly early.

"I liked both pictures, didn't you?" said Mrs. Halvorsen as they walked up Hollywood Boulevard toward the parking lot.

"Yeah," said Jim.

It was a warm summer night and there were a lot of people on the streets, considering how late it was. Earlier in the evening there'd been a mist, but now the atmosphere was clear and stars were twinkling brightly all over the sky.

Mrs. Halvorsen took Jim's arm at an intersection. A couple of passing girls looked at him, then made some remark. He glanced at Mrs. Halvorsen; she was frowning slightly.

"What's the matter?" he asked.

"Nothing."

"You're frowning."

"Those girls," said Mrs. Halvorsen.

"What about them?"

"They were looking at you. One of them said: 'Look at that guy, honey.'"

"Maybe they meant somebody else. Or suppose they didn't?"

"I've seen women in the hotel staring at you."

"It's the way I wear my neckties," said Jim with a laugh, wondering what in the devil she was getting at.

There was a pause. They crossed the street and entered the parking lot. Jim handed the attendant his ticket, then gave him a big tip. The man grinned and ran off after the car.

"It's strange," said Mrs. Halvorsen, "but the minute I saw you I knew you weren't married."

"You mean I don't look sad?"

"Is that how you feel about marriage? That's a purely impersonal question, you understand. I'm so curious about you, Jim. I've never met anybody like you before."

"Well," said Jim, "I never gave it much thought. It just didn't occur to me to get married."

The attendant came with the car. Jim helped Mrs. Halvorsen in, then he got in, and drove off.

"Why not?" asked Mrs. Halvorsen.

"Oh, I don't know. I've got nothing against it particularly. I guess I'm not the type."

Mrs. Halvorsen was silent for so long that Jim turned to look at her. What the hell, he thought. Then he started slightly. This million-dollar baby was toying with the idea of marrying him; no doubt about it. The thought jarred him for a moment out of his oilman role. He shoved his hat back and ran his hand nervously over his face. Pleasant vistas opened out before him. Marrying a dame with nearly two million was something to think about. But in a minute he recoiled from the idea, remembering what he'd said for years: "A guy who marries for money is getting it the hard way." Still ...

Mrs. Halvorsen repeated his name several times before she brought him back to earth.

"Yeah?" he said, coming to suddenly.

"You're acting very strangely."

"I was just thinking," said Jim.

Mrs. Halvorsen sat lost in meditation. Jim could think of nothing to say. They drove to the Marwood in silence. The doorman opened the car door and Mrs. Halvorsen got out. Jim was just about to follow her when he noticed a little man standing at the corner under a partially dimmed-out streetlight. It was Doc.

"Shall I put it in the garage for you?" asked the doorman.

"No," said Jim. "I want to see the garageman." He leaned out of the car and spoke to Mrs. Halvorsen. "Shall we have a cocktail, or is it too late?"

"I'd love a cocktail. I'll wait for you in the lobby."

The doorman escorted Mrs. Halvorsen into the hotel. Jim drove off. At the corner, he slowed down. The little man turned.

"Doc?"

"Yeah—it's me."

"Looking for somebody?"

"Not in particular," said Doc, insolently.

"Oh—just looking for trouble."

"If you want to put it that way."

Jim controlled himself with difficulty. It was obvious that Doc was loaded; with liquor, junk or both.

"Look, Doc. Be a good boy. Go home. Relax. Everything's going to be all right."

"It better be."

"Don't try to be funny. Who do you think you're talking to—Windy? Now get the hell out of here before the hotel manager sees you. One more dumb play like this and I'll turn the sucker back to you. As a matter of fact—it's not a bad idea to do it right now."

Jim started to shift gears. Doc recognized the "Clincher" but couldn't resist it. There was always the possibility with a big-timer like Jim that he wasn't kidding.

"I'm going," said Doc, and turning abruptly, he hurried across the street and disappeared into the shadows.

Jim drove into the hotel garage, muttering to himself. Why didn't Doc drop dead and save everybody a lot of trouble? He was just living on borrowed time as it was; anybody could see that.

"Check the oil, gas and water," Jim said to the garageman.

"Yes sir, Mr. Lloyd."

They had a drink at the bar, which was deserted except for a couple of dignified-looking gray-haired men, patrons of the hotel, who were stewed to the ears. Both talked at once; neither listened. It got funnier and funnier. Mrs. Halvorsen struggled with her laughter. Shaking his head solemnly, Jim said:

"Mr. Evans isn't going to like this. Gives the place a bad name."

They went up in the elevator together and Jim took Mrs. Halvorsen to the door of her apartment.

"It's nearly two o'clock," said Jim, glancing at his watch. "I didn't know it was that late."

"Is it—really? I was going to ask you if you'd like to drop in for a moment. But since it's so late...."

"Yeah," said Jim. "I'd better go and get some beauty sleep."

But he hesitated. He was studying Gladys closely and it seemed that the slight suggestion of constraint, always so noticeable in her attitude, had vanished. She looked eager and hopeful. There was a sweetness and charm about her at this moment which made Jim feel very strange. Her dark eyes, usually bright and alert, were soft, almost pleading. He felt that she had finally accepted him—at least in an emotional sense. If he knew anything, this was the time to blow. Let her think about him for a while.

"Goodnight," he said. "Will I see you tomorrow?"

"If you like."

"Dinner?"

"Yes, Jim."

She said this so compliantly that Jim was touched. Grinning, he reached out and patted her arm, then he turned and hurried down the hall to his apartment. At the door he turned. Gladys was watching him. He waved and she waved back.

Sitting at the dressing table in a negligee, combing her thick dark hair, Mrs. Halvorsen was trying to explain to herself her attitude toward Jim Farrar: but finally, with a sigh, she gave it up. It was no use. Nothing in her life had prepared her for an encounter with a man like him. Instinctively she knew that he was not the kind you built your future around: there was nothing comfortable about his presence: the effect he had on her was too powerful. Actually—although she would hardly admit it to herself—this mattered very little.

She leaned forward and stared closely at her image in the mirror. There were wrinkles about her eyes that worried her, and a couple of days before, she had discovered a few gray hairs. Funny! Until lately, she hadn't paid much attention to such things. Now....

Combing her hair slowly, she thought about the past, which, as she lived it, had seemed so right, so inevitable. She hadn't merely acquiesced—accepted her fate because of an inability to alter it: she was contented. She hadn't been too sorry when she was forced to withdraw from the University because her father had lost his money. The death of her father, after a long illness, had seemed right to her: anything to ease his suffering. And she had considered herself very lucky, penniless as she was, to land an office job with Halvorsen and Company, one of the biggest firms in the Middle West. In the eyes of the other employees, her rise was phenomenal: in two short years she had moved from the personnel department into the sanctum of sanctums— Mr. Halvorsen's office. The "old man," as he was called all over the plant—behind his back—frightened her at first, he looked so grim and remote. But when she got to know him better, she realized that this was a front: actually he was extremely lonesome, trusted no one, and feared people for this reason. Besides, he was a semi-invalid, always in the hands of the doctors. She became his confidential secretary; and for eight years not only took care of all his personal affairs, but nursed him, humored him, and, as far as possible, made him happy. No one was more surprised than she, when the "old man" asked her to marry him. She was barely thirty: he fifty-five and ailing. She hesitated: but he gruffly explained to her that he didn't mean he wanted "any nonsense" with her: he merely wanted to be sure she got his money when he died. After the marriage, the "old man" took a new lease on life, his grim face smoothed out and he was heard to laugh at the plant, shocking many old employees. He lived for nearly ten years longer and died in his sleep with a smile on his face. Mrs. Halvorsen still missed him: in his way he'd been a fine man: but she'd only had the mildest, most comfortable feelings in regard to him. She realized that more than ever, now that she'd met Jim, who made her pulses jump, and had changed the face of the world for her, merely by his presence.

Mrs. Halvorsen leaned forward still farther toward the mirror and pursing her pretty lips, carefully plucked out three new gray hairs. Then she studied her face for a long time, and finally smiled. No doubt about it, she didn't look her age. The result, perhaps, of the long calm years with Carl. All of a sudden she felt young, fluttery, restless.

She got up and danced a few dainty waltz steps with an imaginary partner, watching herself in the full-length mirror: then she flung off her negligee, jumped into bed, turned off the lights and lay in the warm summer darkness—expectant, hopeful: hardly able to wait for the dawn of a new day.

XVII

They were sitting in Johnny's Santa Monica Hotel room. The windows were wide open and a stiff breeze was blowing in from the sea, bellying the curtains.

Jim had told Johnny as much about the setup as he wanted him to know; never mentioning the marriage angle, of course. The little lawyer sat thinking it over, staring out at the harbor on which the bright sunlight was glinting.

"It's almost time for the plunge," said Jim. "But I'm in no hurry."

"What angle you going to use?"

"I haven't made up my mind. Anything will do—take it from me. I could even borrow a big wad from her with a little buildup. But I don't like that; the brush-off would be tougher unless I left town. I think oil investment's the best. I've already told her I'm in the oil refining business. That doesn't sound like wildcat stuff. She's a cinch for a hundred G's; maybe more."

Johnny nodded thoughtfully. He'd been in on take after take with Jim and the big fellow always operated in this apparently careless, unorthodox manner. In the old days he'd been an expert at the Big Store and the wire game; but he'd given them up, except for an occasional beat, because he said they were played out, and, besides, they bored him. He'd work carefully at the buildup until the sucker was ready to swear that the big fellow's word was good as his bond, then he'd quickly figure an angle and before you could realize it—the sucker was taken, the dough divided, and everybody happy; even sometimes the sucker, who didn't know he'd been taken.

"I'll let you know when to vacate the beach house," said Jim. "No use to leave till we have to. Tony likes it there."

Johnny showed a flicker of interest, then restrained himself.

"You and Tony getting along all right?" he asked after a pause.

"One day it's okay—the next day it isn't. It's not as bad as it used to be at that. I'm wearing her down, or vice versa."

Johnny lit a cigarette and made no comment. Two days ago Tony had turned up at his hotel, saying she was bored to death staying at the beach alone, and that if he didn't buy her a drink and talk to her she'd go out and pick up the first soldier she saw—just for laughs. Johnny got her out of the hotel and over to the Ship as fast as possible. It wasn't healthy fooling with Jim's women—if he caught you. He took her into the private room, bought her a few drinks, and gave her a talking to, warning her to be careful. She laughed at him. She wasn't afraid of Jim, she said, boasting that she had him where she wanted him.

"Just like I could have you where I wanted you—if I wanted you," she added, laughing at Johnny.

They got a little tight before they were through and Tony sat on his lap, clowning, but getting him into such a state that he tried to talk her into going back to the hotel with him. After this show of power, Tony abruptly told him goodbye and left. Johnny had felt a little uneasy ever since. A bad dame, Tony. She'd get you into a jam out of boredom.

Just as Jim got up to go, the phone rang and Johnny answered it. He recoiled slightly, then recovered.

"Jim's right here," he said.

"Who is it?" asked Jim, surprised.

Johnny handed him the receiver.

"It's Tony."

"Hello," said Jim, annoyed. "How did you know I was here?"

"I didn't," said Tony. "I wanted to make a date with Johnny."

Jim grimaced.

"Cut the comedy. What is this—a routine check-up?"

"Wise guy! You know everything."

"What are you trying to do—put Johnny over a barrel?"

Johnny glanced up uneasily. Jim looked at him and shrugged as if to say: "She's nuts—this dame." Johnny sighed with relief.

"I think he'd look cute over a barrel—but you'd look better. Jim—if you don't spend more time with me I'll do something desperate."

"Such as?"

"You worry about that."

"Look—I've got work to do. Relax."

"Coming down this afternoon?"

"I'll drop by. But I can't stay. Got to be in town for dinner."

"What—again? Don't that woman do anything but eat? On the other hand, I hope that's all she does."

"I'll be there in a few minutes. Goodbye."

Jim looked at Johnny and shrugged.

"When they passed out the brains—she got slighted."

"If she was as smart as she is good-looking, it'd be too much," said Johnny.

As soon as Jim left, Johnny called Tony.

"Hello, honey," she said lazily. "I thought you'd be calling. Did I scare you?" she laughed softly, but there was a jeering note in it.

"Jim just left."

"So I see."

"Take it easy, Tony, will you? For the love of Pete!"

"How did I know His Nibs would be there? I was going to drop by and see you."

"Don't come here anymore, Tony. You'll get both of us in trouble."

"Okay. I'll be over at the Ship as soon as Jim leaves."

Johnny hesitated, hating himself.

"What time?"

"How do I know what time? You wait."

She hung up. Johnny rose and began to pace the floor. The nerve of that broad, ordering him around. Who did she think she was, anyway? Johnny fumed and fretted, then he got out a bottle and took a stiff drink. What made him so furious was that he knew he'd be at the Ship as soon as he could get there, and that he'd wait around till she came— no matter how long it took her.

XVIII

It was Saturday night and the fashionable little nightspot was crowded. Jim and Mrs. Halvorsen were in evening clothes and that, together with the fact that they were a fine-looking couple, made them more than a little conspicuous. The people around them, for the most part connected in some way with the movie industry, were dressed anyhow; there was only one other couple in evening clothes.

A Los Angeles columnist went from table to table, talking to acquaintances, and trying to find out who Jim and Mrs. Halvorsen were. They both looked like money; and they both looked out of the ordinary. Nobody had ever seen them before so the columnist gave up with a sigh: if all these bright boys and sharp girls didn't know anything about them—well, they couldn't possibly be "anybody."

A rhumba and conga band alternated with another outfit. Jim wouldn't and Mrs. Halvorsen couldn't dance to the South American music. They sat sipping their drinks, watching the dancers on the crowded little floor, and waiting for the straight band to take over.

"I wish I could rhumba," said Mrs. Halvorsen, glancing at Jim.

"I don't," said Jim with a grin. "I'd have to get out there if you did. A man looks silly doing that dance. For a woman, it's all right."

"As a matter of fact, I haven't danced in ten years."

"I used to dance quite a bit in Florida," said Jim. "In a weak moment, I let a woman teach me the rhumba—then I was stuck with it. She wanted to rhumba all the time."

"What happened to her?"

Jim looked up in surprise.

"The rhumba dancer? Oh, she's in New York, I guess. Why?"

"I just wondered." Mrs. Halvorsen lowered her eyes and took a sip from her glass.

Jim studied her briefly. For the first time since he'd known her he felt a marked sexual attraction. She was wearing a yellow evening-gown, her thick, wavy, dark hair was set off with a couple of flowers, her dark eyes were shining with excitement: she looked very striking and unusual. Jim couldn't get over it, and kept glancing at her. It couldn't be the alcohol; he'd only had a couple of drinks. He'd always liked her looks which were of a delicate, aquiline, patrician order; but, in spite of her obvious interest in him, she had always struck him before as being withdrawn and over-lady-like. Now it was different, quite different.

"Shall we have another drink?" asked Jim. "I think this spilt band's going to play forever."

"This 'what' band?"

Jim was puzzled, then he understood. "Oh—this South American band, or whatever it is."

"At times you talk so strangely," said Mrs. Halvorsen, smiling.

"Sorry. I've met all kinds in the oil fields. I'm not as careful about the way I talk as I should be."

"Please don't be careful. I like it." She lifted her glass and finished off her drink. "I'm ready for another one now. It will be my third and that's two above my limit—so ..."

"I'll see that you get home safe and sound."

Jim turned and ordered. The South American band concluded its number, then left the stand.

The waiter brought their drinks and they sat sipping them, waiting for the second band to get started.

"Gladys," said Jim, "you certainly look beautiful tonight."

"Thank you. And you look very handsome. As a matter of fact, I wish that little blonde over there would stop staring at you."

Jim smiled but did not look in the direction of the blonde. He didn't need to; he'd already noticed her, catalogued her, and dismissed her. He'd seen hundreds like her in New York and Florida; an affected dame with a line of some kind—strictly on the chisel. The guy with her looked like he had everything but good sense. A perfect combination.

"Do you think she's pretty?" Mrs. Halvorsen persisted.

Jim glanced at the blonde.

"Depends on what you mean."

"Do you like that artificial type?"

"I don't think of women as types, mostly," said Jim; "at least not after I know them."

"And you've known quite a few, haven't you?"

"No more than average."

Mrs. Halvorsen gave him a look of disbelief, then laughed, and drank almost half her drink in one swallow. Jim sat trying to figure out what she was getting at. Several times now she'd tried to lead him into talking about the women he'd known. What was the idea?

"She's still staring at you," said Mrs. Halvorsen, who was beginning to show the effect of her drinks.

"She probably thinks I look like money in the bank."

"You're too modest."

The band leader waved his hands in a bored and languid manner and the band began to play a popular tune in slow tempo.

"Let's dance," said Jim, rising.

Mrs. Halvorsen smiled and got up. Her smile was a little uncertain and Jim took her arm and helped her onto the dance floor. People were already crowding in from all sides. Jim and Mrs. Halvorsen began to dance. After a few steps they collided with a couple. It was the blonde and her escort, a sour-looking middle-aged man, rather fat.

"Sorry," said Jim, smiling.

The man compressed his lips and said nothing, but the little blonde smiled up at Jim and in a sweet voice said:

"Oh—that's all right."

Her eyes lingered on him. She turned to look after him as the crowd separated them. Jim heard the man say angrily:

"Eloise, if you don't...."

Jim grinned.

"That man's got his troubles." He glanced at Mrs. Halvorsen, who was looking at him fixedly with an expression he couldn't make out.

"I want to go home," she said.

Jim's grin faded.

"Why, what's wrong?"

"I don't feel well—anyway, it's too crowded in here. Hot. I can't breathe. I can't stand crowds. They make me nervous."

Her voice rose. Jim glanced about them in embarrassment as he escorted her from the floor.

Mrs. Halvorsen sat without speaking while he paid the check, and waited for his change. As soon as the waiter returned, Jim got up and helped her into her wrap. She rose quickly and hurried out between the closely-packed tables, never looking back at him once.

They stood in silence, waiting for their car to be brought around. The stars were shining, a gentle breeze was blowing from the south.

"Nice night, isn't it?" said Jim, glancing at her curiously—feeling a little uneasy.

She looked round her like a sleepwalker.

"I suppose it is."

They drove back toward the Marwood in silence. Jim kept glancing at her out of the corner of his eye. Finally he asked: "Something wrong?"

"No," said Mrs. Halvorsen mildly.

"Don't you feel well?"

"I shouldn't have drunk that third drink."

She spoke remotely, almost harshly.

Jim began to get annoyed. Why should she talk this way to him? He'd done nothing.

"I'm sorry," he temporized.

She settled herself more comfortably, sighed, and stared straight ahead.

As they got close to the Marwood, Jim said:

"Feeling better?"

She nodded slightly.

Jim was more than a little annoyed now. He had to keep reminding himself that this was strictly business, and that Mrs. Halvorsen, for all practical purposes, wasn't an individual at all—she was merely an impersonal problem. He had a strong desire to give some kind of expression to his irritation.

He took a corner sharply, throwing the wheel over. Mrs. Halvorsen, unprepared for it, fell up against him. He glanced at her. Her face looked pale and drawn in the soft glow of a dimmed-out streetlight. She stared directly into his eyes with an expression he couldn't fathom, then she drew away.

"Sorry I cut that one so short," said Jim, trying to make his voice sound apologetic.

They crossed the lobby in silence and went up in the elevator. They both spoke nicely to the elevator boy, but ignored each other. What the hell, Jim thought, trying to control his irritation.

As they walked down the corridor toward her apartment, she got out her key. Jim expected her to hand it to him as she always did, but as soon as they reached her door she unlocked it, opened it, and went in. Just as she was shutting the door behind her she said in a strange voice:

"Good night."

The door shut. Jim stood there staring at it, then he turned and walked down the hall, irritated and puzzled.

As he opened his door, he said aloud:

"Is she nuts, or am I?"

He took off his dinner coat and flung it on a chair, then he tore off his collar and tie, and unbuttoned his shirt; then he kicked off his patent leather shoes. Yawning widely, he got out a pint of bourbon and poured himself a drink which he took at a gulp.

"Let her sweat," he said, pouring himself another drink. "I don't know what's wrong with her, but whatever it is—she'll get over it. They always do."

It was nice to relax—get out of character. He was tired of being the conventional oil man. He wanted to be himself. A thought struck him, and he sat up suddenly. Tony! That's what he needed.

"She's crazy," sighed Jim. "But what a dame!"

He'd known a lot of women in the last twenty years, but none as exciting as Tony. He'd felt that way about her since the first time he'd seen her at the Casino. She had on a green evening gown covered with sequins; it looked great with her red hair. She was at the roulette table, smoking a cigarette, and staring intently at the spinning wheel. When she lost she groaned; when she won she cried out with pleasure.

He was with Roy Slavens. Indicating Tony, Jim said:

"That's for me."

Roy gave Tony the once-over, then glanced at Jim.

"Just another redhead, pal."

"That's one man's opinion. Find out who she is."

From that night on he'd hardly had a peaceful moment. At least not until he'd finally taken it on the lam; even then he wasn't free of her; he carried her image with him everywhere. At times she irritated him almost beyond endurance; they'd quarrel bitterly, hating each other; little by little the hatred would recede, but the emotional violence, brought on by their quarrel, would increase, if anything, and, carrying over into their love making, would finally exhaust them.

Jumping up, Jim began to change his clothes, throwing his discarded shirt and pants on the floor. Just as he was tying his tie, the phone rang. To his surprise it was Mr. Evans, who seemed upset.

"Mr. Lloyd?"

"Yes."

"I hate to trouble you, sir. But—if I may ask you this question—wasn't Mrs. Halvorsen out with you this evening?"

"Yes. We had dinner, then went to a club."

"Anything wrong? I mean, did Mrs. Halvorsen seem upset?"

Jim hesitated. He didn't like the sound of this. What the hell had happened? No doubt about it—the woman had been in a peculiar state of mind. Jim got cold at a sudden premonition. She'd knocked herself off! Several times she'd told him how lonely she'd always been. No relatives; no close friends; nobody.

"I didn't notice anything in particular."

There was a pause. Then Mr. Evans went on:

"Sorry to trouble you, sir. But did you know that Mrs. Halvorsen was checking out?"

"What?"

"She's packing. I've called a taxi for her—it will be along in half an hour—and I'm now making out her bill. I just wondered if you...."

"It's news to me," said Jim. "Thanks."

"I feel so badly about it," said the little manager. "I can't imagine what...."

Absentmindedly, Jim hung up, then he stood in the middle of the room, staring at the carpet, thunderstruck. This unaccountable turn of events drove every thought of Tony from his mind. All his instincts rebelled at the idea of a million-dollar sucker running out on him. What a chump that would make of him!

He hesitated, then reached for the phone. It rang sharply, startling him. He answered.

"Jim?" It was Mrs. Halvorsen. She spoke timidly. "Yes, Gladys."

"Your voice sounds nice, Jim. I'm surprised that you don't hang up in my ear."

"Why should I? I just figured you didn't feel well."

"I acted like the dope I am. A fine way to behave when you've been so nice to me; and we've had such fun; the loveliest time I've ever had in my life."

Jim sighed with relief. Dames!

"Oh, that's all right."

"No. I want to apologize—abjectly."

"Forget it." He almost added "sister"; and smiled to himself, wondering what her reaction to that would be. She'd probably laugh, and like it.

"I almost left without talking to you, I was so ashamed."

"You almost what?"

"I'm leaving, Jim."

"Why?"

"I've got my reasons."

"What are they?"

"I don't think you would be interested."

"Try me."

"No—really ..."

"I'll be right there."

She began to protest, but he hung up, dashed out of his apartment, and down the hall. He knocked at her door. After a long pause, she opened it. She was dressed for the street in a tailored suit. Her eyes were red; she'd been crying. Aside from that, she looked wonderful—trim, smartly dressed, aristocratic, markedly individual. Jim felt a little clumsy and inadequate for a brief moment. As Doc would have said: "The bumpkin in him came to the surface."

"What's this all about, Gladys?" Jim asked. "I don't understand."

"Come in." Jim entered and she shut the door behind him. "Sit down, Jim. Let's talk this over calmly."

Jim sat down and lit a cigarette. He noticed that his hands were shaking and lowered them quickly. She sat opposite him.

For a moment she couldn't bring herself to speak. Jim glanced at her. She looked sad but determined, as if she'd made up her mind to a certain course of action in spite of everything.

"I've decided not to see you anymore, Jim."

"What have I done?"

"You haven't done anything but make me happy—and show me the best time I've ever had."

Jim smiled slightly.

"You'll have to make it clearer than that."

"I intend to." She got up and stood looking directly at Jim, making him a little uneasy. "It's this—if we keep on this way, Jim, you're going to become indispensable to me. In fact—you are. I'm happy only when I'm with you. But it hasn't been going on very long. So tonight I made up my mind I'd go away and never see you again—that way I'd get over it. If I stay much longer—I'll never get over it."

Jim glanced at her guardedly. He could see that her calm was deceptive; she was holding herself in with a great effort.

"I see."

"You're not very communicative, you know," she went on. "But I think I've been able to figure out the kind of man you are. The fact that you've never been married is proof of what I mean."

"I don't get it."

"At least a dozen women must have tried to marry you—obviously without success. You're just not the kind of man who marries and settles down."

"You're more or less right."

"If you would happen to, by some accident—your wife would have very little peace of mind."

"Why do you say that?"

"Tonight that blonde girl was the prettiest woman in the place. She singled you out. That decided me."

"She probably thought I looked in the money."

"You've said that. I just don't believe it."

"As for her being the prettiest woman—she's not even in your class."

Jim felt much better. Mrs. Halvorsen wanted to marry him, but was afraid of it. All she needed was a little careful handling. It was too bad in a way that things had got into this state. Any sort of take was obviously out now. Marriage was something else. He saw difficulties ahead. Tony; Doc; the boys. But what a way to sign off from the racket for good: with a cool million!

Mrs. Halvorsen had sat down again. She was obviously nervous and at a loss what to say next.

Smiling to himself, Jim said slowly:

"I'm still not sure what this is all about. But I'm going to make a guess. Either I'm crazy—or we've both got marriage on our minds."

"I certainly have," said Mrs. Halvorsen, sadly.

"That makes two of us. It's up to you."

She sat as if glued to her chair and began to twist her handkerchief into a ball. Jim studied her, wondering what his next move should be; he didn't want to overdo it.

"You mean it—seriously. Don't you, Jim?"

"Sure."

"Why me?"

"I might ask you the same. It's just one of those things." He hesitated and crushed out his cigarette. "If you're dubious about it, think it over; take your time. If you're not, let's jump down to Mexico. Get it over with."

She got up and began to pace the floor nervously.

"I don't think it will work out, Jim."

"I'll do my best to make it work out—that's all I can say. I'm not going to promise miracles." She stood looking at him in silence, her face drawn with indecision. "There's only one thing I don't like about it," Jim added. "You've got more money than I have."

"How do you know?"

"Mr. Evans was bragging about you. Said you were very rich."

"I'm supposed to be. I've got money—quite a bit. But taxes ate up most of my husband's estate."

Jim laughed.

"Taxes have practically eaten me up. I'm the next thing to a pauper."

Mrs. Halvorsen shrugged impatiently.

"That's not important."

"It is to me. Wait till I start borrowing money from you—you won't like it."

"I tell you that's not important. We'll never starve—if that's what's worrying you."

She spoke so sharply, that Jim got up as if annoyed. Inwardly he was applauding himself, for playing it so cagily.

"It's the kind of thing a man thinks about," he said with some dignity.

"Oh, Jim," she cried.

He took her in his arms. She began to sob. He could feel her shaking.

"I think Mexico's our best bet," he said calmly.

"You take charge, Jim. I'm tired of worrying about everything. I want to relax." She hugged him fiercely as if she was afraid he'd get away. "Think for me, Jim. Tell me what to do."

Jim held her tenderly, and stood wondering just how he was going to handle Tony and the rest. In a way, it wasn't any bed of roses he was getting himself into.

BOOK TWO

But at my back I alwaeis hear
Time's winged chariot hurrying near
And yonder all before us lye
Desarts of vast Eternity.
ANDREW MARVELL

I

The Mexican town sweltered under the mid-afternoon sun. Dogs lay panting in whatever shade they could find, and along the side streets men, dressed in nothing but shirts, pants, and straw hats, were sitting on the pavement with their backs to the adobe walls of their houses, drowsing or languidly smoking. An occasional battered Ford bumped over the rutty streets, honking at the goats and chickens which moved lazily out of the way.

Beyond the town, the mountains rose steeply, looking stark and forbidding in the clear, dry light. The sky was very blue and almost cloudless; a few wispy white strands of vapor clung to the highest peaks. High up, an eagle circled, intently watching something below him.

Jim, in his shirt sleeves, walked slowly down the main street, hot and thirsty. He was sweating profusely and from time to time he took out his handkerchief and mopped his brow. With a sigh of relief he turned into a little corner cantina. The shutters were up and it was damp and cool inside, smelling of beer. Nobody was about. Jim tapped on the bar with a fifty-cent piece and waited. He tapped again, impatiently. These spigs—they'd never look after business. They hoped that if they ignored you, you'd go away. In a few minutes a fat Mexican woman waddled in from the back with a baby in her arms. She smiled pleasantly.

"Good day," she said.

"Hello," said Jim. "How's chances of getting a bottle of beer—cerveza? A quart." He pantomimed a big bottle.

The woman nodded, reached under the bar, and brought up a pint, then another one.

"Only pints," she said, grinning. "How do you like my son?"

"Nice-looking kid," said Jim, hurriedly. "Look—this beer's warm. now about cold beer?"

"Sorry. No cold beer. Nobody's got cold beer except the hotel." She grinned and chucked the baby under the chin. "Isn't he cute—my son? Very big and strong."

"Very cute," said Jim, morosely. "How about opening those bottles for me?"

The woman giggled.

"Oh—I forget. Usually my husband he looks after things. Last night he took sick. Won't get up. I think he was drinking—myself."

While she was trying to open the bottles the baby crowed loudly and began to kick his mother with his brown bare feet. She laughed, turning to the baby and forgetting all about the bottles.

"You better stop that, Antonio," she said. "I'll get mad." She turned to Jim. "He kicks like a mule—he's so strong."

Jim opened the bottles and paid the woman, who grinned and bowed slightly. Jim went over to a table near the door, took off his hat, and sat down.

"Make yourself comfortable, sir," said the woman. "I have work to do." She went out cooing to the baby, who was still kicking at her vigorously.

The beer wasn't quite as warm as Jim had feared. In fact, it was much cooler than that he'd tried to drink at the hotel. What a place! Nothing worked and nobody gave a damn. The electric refrigerators at the hotel had broken down the night before, and were still out of order. The dark little manager rushed around busily, reassuring everybody—but nothing was done. There probably wouldn't be any ice for a week.

Jim felt somewhat ashamed as he sat drinking his beer slowly and enjoying himself in the damply cool little cantina. Gladys, who hadn't got up due to the heat, had wanted him to stay with her; she had never been in a foreign country before, and the strangeness of it made her somewhat ill-at-ease. She hadn't asked him to stay, but it was obvious to Jim that she didn't want to be left alone in that hot, dingy, box-like hotel room.

But he couldn't help it. He had to get away. For over a week he'd had scarcely a minute to himself. For the first time in his life he'd been cooped up, day and night, with another human being, and the confinement made him irritable and jumpy. Later, he'd do as he pleased; go and come when he felt like it; but this was supposed to be a honeymoon and he was trying to play it straight.

Gladys was not only nervous and touchy, but extremely affectionate. She treated him as if he were a big, blundering, kindly St. Bernard dog. She stroked him, patted him, talked baby talk to him, and didn't want him out of her sight over a minute at a time. Two things about her surprised him very much: the violence of her emotions, and her simplicity. She seemed like a school girl when it came to love. He found it hard to believe that she'd ever had any experience at all.

She was a light sleeper; he was not. If he turned over abruptly or talked or groaned in his sleep, she woke immediately, thought there was something wrong with him, and wasn't satisfied till he'd opened his eyes and assured her that he was all right.

Finally he said:

"Honey, I hate to bring it up—but you're used to an invalid. I never have anything wrong with me. Stop worrying."

He'd spoken more sharply than he'd intended, and she'd been so hurt and affronted that she was unable to sleep the rest of the night. As soon as he woke in the morning, she began to tell him how rude he'd been in the night, and he was forced to apologize two or three times, before he could get her to drop the subject. He found her too sensitive for her own good; in this respect she certainly didn't belie her appearance. There was something very finely-drawn, and highbred looking about her, like a thoroughbred filly.

If things had been on a different footing, Jim wouldn't have been so patient. As with Tony—for instance. It wasn't that Gladys was now his wife, however, that caused him to restrain his difficult nature. In spite of their intimacy, he still thought of Gladys impersonally: she was a business problem and, as such, deserved careful and patient handling.

Jim finished the first bottle of beer and started on the second. He didn't want to rush things with Gladys, but in a few days he'd have to be getting back. He'd communicated with nobody but Johnny. And even the little lawyer didn't know that he was getting married. Jim felt a bit strange about that phase of the setup. It was going to cause trouble, plenty of it—no doubt about it. First—Tony was going to throw a tantrum. Second—he'd have a row with Johnny who would warn him that he was skating on thin ice—and that he might have a brush with the law. Third—Doc would probably take it into his addled head to make difficulties.

Jim had no doubt whatever of his ability to cope with all the various problems raised by his marriage—still, it was going to take a little doing.

Tony would cause him the most trouble. Even now she was probably raising hell with Johnny, trying to find out where he was. He'd given Johnny the unpleasant task of telling her that he'd been called away on a very important matter. He hadn't wanted to tell her himself and be forced to go through the usual silly, pointless, inevitable row.

Tony!

Her image rose before him, seductive and mocking: her bushy red hair wild, her grey-green eyes narrowed with laughter, her full lips parted, showing her strong white animal teeth. The image was so vivid it was almost like a hallucination, and Jim ran his hand nervously across his eyes. Damn his eyes, anyway—they'd been giving him a lot of trouble lately. He winced away from the idea of getting glasses—he wasn't that old yet, by God!

He finished his second bottle of beer and got up. Through the open door, he could see the blinding sunlight. He wanted to stay in this cool, restful little place and drink a couple more bottles of beer. But he knew that Gladys would be wondering where he'd got to.

"Oh, hell," he said, "I'll be getting back."

He went out into the heat and glare of the deserted street.

Gladys was lying back in the big chair, looking very pretty in her negligee, but rather pale. Jim had just had a bath and was sitting on the bed in a dressing gown, his powerful, hairy legs stretched out.

Night had fallen. Music drifted up from the street: Mexican music, corny and sad.

"How do you feel?" Jim asked, finally.

"Oh, I feel all right," said Gladys, but he knew she didn't.

"Look—I think we ought to be getting back."

Gladys glanced at him, smiling slightly.

"Fed up already?"

Jim shrugged impatiently.

"Of course not. I'm worrying about you. You haven't been up to par since we got here. It's too hot; it's too dry; you can't get anything you want. It's like living in Alaska or some place."

"We could go on to Mexico City."

"Yeah—we could. But why? What's wrong with Southern California?"

"Nothing." She gave Jim a quick, penetrating glance.

He noticed it and looked at her thoughtfully, wondering what she meant by it.

"Anyway," he said, "there's a war on. It's not a bad idea to be in your own country."

"I suppose that's true. What about the war, Jim? How do you stand— I forgot to ask." She looked at him anxiously, trying to keep her face composed.

Jim was a little surprised by the question.

"Me? Oh, I registered in Florida. Far as I know, I haven't been classified. No reason why I shouldn't be 1A."

"You're married now."

"Just," said Jim.

Gladys smiled faintly.

"We might adopt a few children."

"I'd rather join the army."

"Do you really feel that way, Jim?"

"No—just clowning."

"Sometimes it's very hard to know what you think or feel. I often wonder if you ever say what you mean."

"Oh—once in a while I slip up." Jim laughed to himself at this strictly private joke.

"When I first knew you, I thought you were one of the most forthright men I'd ever met. Now I think you're one of the least."

"Is that bad?"

"It makes me a little uneasy at times."

"Why should you be uneasy?"

Gladys hesitated. Looking down at her hands she said abruptly.

"Jim—who's Tony?"

He didn't move a muscle—if anything he sat too still—but he felt a slight quiver in his stomach.

"Tony?" He stalled, glanced at his wife. "Why—I used to know a girl in Florida named Tony."

"You knew her pretty well—didn't you?"

"Yes."

"Last night you were turning and twisting in your sleep. I thought you were in pain or something. So I tried to wake you. You pushed me away and said: 'My God, Tony; can't you let me alone!'"

Jim burst out laughing.

"That's a hot one."

Gladys turned and smiled at him, trying to appear amused, but there was a hurt look in her eyes. Jim smothered his irritation and went over to her. She reached up and took hold of his hand.

"Jim," said Gladys, looking up at him, "be honest with me—that's all I ask."

"Sure," said Jim. "Why shouldn't I be?"

"At times I feel that you're not. I can't explain it. I try to talk myself out of it. But it's no use. I feel that you're hiding something from me—I don't know what. Gradually the feeling goes away. But it comes back."

Jim grinned carelessly, and Gladys' heart contracted. How could she think such things about him? Ridiculous! No man with a grin like that could be anything but honest and aboveboard. It was only when she was lying awake in the darkness while he slept—or when he was away from her—that she distrusted him.

"I'm sorry you're not happy," said Jim. "Maybe this wasn't such a good idea for you."

"I *am* happy," Gladys declared with a vehemence that surprised him. "I've never been so happy in my whole life. I'm so happy it makes me uneasy."

"Uneasy about what, honey?"

"Oh—it just seems too good to last."

Jim patted her shoulder.

"Come on, honey. That's no way to feel. Let's have dinner. That's what you need—something to eat."

"Will you call room service?"

"Sure—only why don't we go down and eat in the dining room?"

She looked at him softly.

"No. I want to eat up here alone with you. And listen to the music, and maybe go out on the balcony, and look at the stars ..."

Jim bent down and kissed her; he was highly irritated but determined not to show it. He wanted to dress up in his best and swell around the hotel; maybe order champagne in the dining room and take a gander at the upper-class chilis—some of them weren't bad, though a little dark for his taste.

"Just as you say, honey. Good idea. Why don't we have some champagne? Celebrate a little."

"Oh, fine. Shall we dress?"

"No. Let's eat this way. It's a hot night."

Later, they went out on the balcony to look at the stars. Due to the champagne, Gladys was feeling rather gay. She stood pressed up against

Jim with her arms around him, listening to the Mexican music which drifted up to them lazily from a big cantina across the street.

It was a moonless night but so clear that the mountains could be seen beyond the town, looming up huge and hulking under the glittering diamond-points of the stars. A warm breeze was blowing, carrying the smell of dry vegetation.

"I love you, Jim," said Gladys.

"Same here, honey."

A high-pitched melancholy tenor voice, accompanied by guitars, began to sing a Mexican love song.

"I always dreamed about something like this," said Gladys. "I never had any idea it would really happen."

Jim was going to make a crack about the tenor, but wisely refrained.

II

Jim was so preoccupied that from time to time Gladys asked him if there was anything worrying him. He kept answering her in the negative, but as this did no good, he finally told her that his eyes were bothering him.

"Yes," said Gladys, "I've noticed you frowning, as if your eyes hurt you, especially in the sun. I think you should have your eyes examined, Jim. That's something you shouldn't take any chances with."

"Oh—they'll be all right," said Jim offhandedly. "I can see fine."

"Eyestrain can cause a lot of trouble. I know. I suffered from it for years without realizing it."

She turned and put her head on Jim's shoulder. They were driving through burnt-up country, toward the border. It was a very hot day with an almost metallic blue sky and a dazzling sun. Heat waves danced over the flat land, which was empty except for boulders, mesquite, and giant Saguaro cactuses. On the road ahead of them they saw, from time to time, quickly-vanishing mirages which resembled shallow pools of water, as if it had rained recently. As they crossed one desert sink the mirage moved ahead of them for miles, then disappeared at a turn. Gladys remarked how awful it would be to be lost in a place like this, then shuddered. Jim agreed with her. In the desert a man was nothing: he was less than the lizard, the coyote, or the black ominous buzzard.

"My eyes never bother me except in the sun," said Jim.

Gladys laughed. She was feeling much better, and was more herself. She looked so young at times that Jim had to keep reminding himself that she was forty years old.

"You know what I think," she said. "I think you're too vain to wear glasses."

Jim glanced at her, slightly annoyed.

"Could be."

"*I* am."

He glanced at her again, grinning.

"Do you need them?"

"Need them! I wear them all the time for reading. That's my deep dark secret."

"You do? I never saw you with them on."

"You never saw me reading. As soon as the honeymoon's over—in nine or ten years—I'll start using them again."

Jim laughed, then fell into a long silence. Gladys kept glancing at him, but said nothing. His preoccupied silences always worried her and she wanted to bring him out of them, chiefly because she'd come to feel that when he wasn't noticing her in one way or another she was only half alive. It was a trying state of mind, and she fought against it; especially so as she realized that it was growing on her. It explained so many things about her that Jim couldn't comprehend: her lack of ease, her sudden hurt withdrawals.

Jim wasn't worrying about his eyes. He had other problems which seemed to him at the moment much more important. He was worrying chiefly about Doc: as soon as that little chiseler found out he had married Mrs. Halvorsen, he was going to regret having agreed to the thirty grand guarantee. A junky is always unpredictable, but especially one like Doc: smart to start out with, educated, soured, beaten, but not resigned. "Oh, well," Jim told himself, "maybe I'm looking for something to worry about. Ten G's ought to quiet a guy with the seat out of his pants."

Naturally he had no intention of telling Doc, Shake and Windy that he'd married the sucker. But Doc had run her down in the first place through Evans, the manager, and eventually he'd find out. If he could only figure some way to persuade Gladys to keep the thing a secret.

Jim started slightly. It seemed to him that Gladys was reading his mind because she was saying:

"I can hardly wait to see Mr. Evans' face when we tell him, Jim. What will he think of me? Knowing you such a short time: running off and marrying you like this."

"I'm not looking forward to it," said Jim. "He's such a nosy little guy."

"I know he's going to be shocked. But it's sort of fun in a way. It will be the first time I've ever shocked anybody in my whole life."

Jim couldn't help laughing at this, because it sounded so juvenile: you'd never think it was a responsible forty-year-old woman talking. All the same, he was laughing only superficially. He was pretty sure if he suggested keeping their marriage a secret Gladys might suspect something; and it was much too early for that. Later, when he'd got some of her money nicely cornered, it wouldn't matter so much.

Jim suddenly made up his mind: he'd play it straight in regard to Gladys, ignoring Doc. Now he felt better. Settling down in the seat more comfortably he began to talk to Gladys, telling her about horse racing in Florida and its many ramifications, which he knew only too well. Gladys was delighted; and sighed with relief. He was talking to her, paying attention to her, being interesting for her benefit; his preoccupation had entirely disappeared.

But while they were going through the boring customs routine at the border, Jim lapsed into silence again, thinking about Tony. Another headache! If he wasn't such a chump over her this would be the time for the brush-off. He was fixed for life, providing he wanted to play it that way. With a little effort he could make himself indispensable to Gladys, a lonely, credulous, inexperienced woman. But there were other things in the world besides security: something which had never been much in Jim's thoughts. He needed Tony. Why—was another matter, and he didn't go into it very deeply. He only knew that for the first time in his whole life he actually needed a specific human being. In spite of the fact that he had many times defended Tony against Johnny's slurs, he knew in his heart that she was a wrong one, that she didn't love him in the accepted sense of that term, and that if the going got too tough it was possible she'd sell him out. He wasn't a self-deluded chump. He was just up against something that was too much for him.

"It must be my age," Jim mused. "This would never've happened to me at twenty-five."

"They certainly take their time, don't they, dear?" Gladys observed, trying to bring Jim out of his preoccupation again.

"What?" mumbled Jim, coming to slowly.

"The officials—they take their time."

"Sure. They love it. Put a uniform on a guy and he starts shoving everybody around. Oh, well."

He seemed in an ill humor. Gladys felt uneasy when he was that way. She put her hand on his arm, patted him. He turned and gave her that grin, which always soothed and disarmed her.

"I guess we can stand it," he said. "We're not going any place in particular—and we're in no hurry to get there."

Gladys laughed.

"You say things in such a funny way," she said, patting him.

Jim pondered. This little lady certainly must have known some dull citizens in her day.

III

Johnny was standing at the bar, having a drink, when Jim came in. The little lawyer looked pale and jittery, and when he turned, his smile seemed forced.

"They here?" asked Jim, jerking his head toward the private room.

"Yeah," said Johnny, "and they've all got the jim-jams. I'm getting so I can't stand hungry guys. You've spoiled me."

"You don't look so good yourself."

"Why should I? Carrying over thirty G's in cash around with me. I almost brought along a heater—but talked myself out of it."

"That would've been bright."

"I can't help it. I'm nervous. Say—for God's sake, Jim—wise me up. What's happening?"

"How's Tony?"

Johnny hesitated for a split second, shifted his weight, then took a sip from his drink.

"She's all right. But I've been having trouble with her."

"What kind?"

"I had to pull a frame so I could get my hands on this dough without her being around. I asked her to come in town and have a drink with me. Then I stood her up. I called the place where I was to meet her, but she'd already left. Damned if she don't waltz back to the beach before I can get out. Thank God I had the dough in my pocket. But I sure had some explaining to do. She didn't believe a word I said."

"Is she on the warpath?"

"About you? Yes."

"I'll drive down after a while."

The bar was deserted except for the bartender and a couple sitting in a dark corner booth. Jim ordered a shot of bourbon, and threw it down with a quick movement.

Johnny kept staring at him anxiously.

"Please, Jim. Let me in on the play. I haven't had a decent night's sleep in a week."

"Brace yourself," said Jim. "Don't yell. Mrs. Halvorsen is now Mrs. Jim Lloyd."

Johnny's hand gave a jerk. His highball glass slipped from his fingers and smashed on the floor. The bartender glanced up from the end of the bar, grinned.

"Bring him another drink," said Jim, "and put the glass on my bill. I'll have another one, too."

When the bartender came with the drinks, Johnny said:

"My hands are sweaty. It slipped. Lord, it's a hot night."

"I didn't know my liquor had that kind of kick," laughed the bartender, a big tough-looking Irishman, "jumping out of a guy's hand."

He went back to his newspaper, chuckling at his own wit.

"On the square?" Johnny demanded, as soon as the bartender was out of earshot.

"Yeah," said Jim. "On the square. I'm going to pay these has-beens off with my own dough. It's too early yet for me to make any kind of a take; and I want them out of the way."

Johnny pondered.

"Doc won't like it. He'll try to cut in if he finds out you married her."

"We'll worry about that when we get to it. I may get rid of him before he finds out."

"You'll never get rid of him. I know that guy," said Johnny, taking a long pull from his glass. "He's an A-Number-One bastard."

"A lot of guys used to be afraid of Doc. I never was. He knows it and it gripes him. If he's wise, he won't push me."

Johnny turned to look at Jim. The big fellow's habitual expression of lazy good nature had disappeared: his face looked leaner, harder—dangerous. It was the face of the Jim Farrar, who, that night in the crowded Casino, had taken the gun away from Fargo—a coked-up Chicago hoodlum; not only that: he'd further humiliated him by walking him Spanish through the jammed nightclub and throwing him out in the alley. Fargo went around telling the boys that either Jim left town or he'd kill him. But Fargo cracked under the strain and ended in the cooler, raving.

It was only at times that Johnny remembered what a tough boy Jim actually was. He was too used to him; too conscious of the big fellow's weaknesses. The little lawyer was like an animal trainer who yawns in the face of a panther: not out of bravery, merely out of over-familiarity. Johnny paled slightly—thinking about Tony. Damned little bum. God, how he wished he'd never brought her on from Phoenix.

"Come on," said Jim. "Let's pay off the jackals."

Jim turned and started back toward the private room. Johnny grinned weakly at the bartender.

"Send us back a round, Clancy. It's all to go on Mr. Lloyd's bill."

When Jim opened the door of the private room, he found Shake, Windy, Pop, and Doc sitting around the table in tense silence. They all looked up eagerly, almost pleadingly—except Doc. He was sitting with his arms folded, his hat tilted over his eyes, and a thin smile of superiority on his grim mouth.

"Hello, boys," said Jim, taking off his hat and sitting down.

Shake, Windy and Pop nodded and smiled and spoke to him all together, like a bunch of school kids greeting the teacher. Doc merely pushed his hat back and put a cigarette in his mouth. His eyes had an unnatural brightness. Johnny glanced at him uneasily.

"Well, Mr. Farrar," said Shake with a placid smile, "I understand you scored."

Johnny held up his hand.

"Hold it. Some drinks coming."

In a few minutes a waiter brought their drinks. As soon as he'd gone, Jim said:

"Yes, boys: I scored. Now Mr. Doyle's going to pay you off according to my instructions."

"I believe we've got an agreement," said Doc, mildly.

"We have," said Jim, "and I'm abiding by it—naturally."

"A guy can always trust you," said Doc with gentle irony, which was missed by Shake, Windy and Pop, who were hungry for their cuts. But Johnny glanced at Jim in trepidation. Why was it that junkies were never satisfied till they got their ears slapped down? Jim ignored Doc.

Johnny took out four packages of bank notes, consulted the notation on each wrapper, then distributed them. Pop's old hands were shaking so that he could just barely control them. For a moment his cut lay before him on the table, untouched. Windy seized his at once and tore off the wrapper with a yell of triumph. Shake sat holding his package carefully before him, staring at it incredulously; two tears sprang to his eyes and ran slowly down his pale, fat cheeks; he took out a dirty handkerchief and blew his nose as if it were a bugle. Doc picked up his money without looking at it and slipped it carefully into his coat pocket.

"Pop," said Jim, "you'll find twenty-five hundred dollars in your package. I told you I'd take care of you. The rest of you'll find ten G's each, minus one third of five hundred. The cut you promised Pop. Everybody satisfied?"

"You bet," said Shake in a stifled voice, then he blew his nose again.

"Thanks, Mr. Farrar, thanks," faltered Pop, happy in a way: but also, now that he knew the exact amount, a little disappointed. In his daydreams he'd convinced himself that he'd get a full share: ten G's. After all, twenty-five hundred really wasn't very much dough. He looked at the others with envy.

Windy was wildly counting his money, riffling it with a dirty forefinger which he kept moistening with his tongue. Suddenly he glanced up, coming to himself. He thought the big fellow was looking at him with marked disapproval.

"It's not that I think it ain't all here," he stammered, grinning ingratiatingly at Jim. "It's just that I like to count it. I never seen so much money all in one hunk before. Excuse me, Mr. Farrar."

Jim glanced around at them, fighting down a growing distaste, then he got up. Johnny quickly followed suit, anxious to be gone.

"You satisfied, too, Doc?" asked Jim.

"Certainly, certainly," said Doc, readily. "An agreement's an agreement. Only I'd like to see you for a minute alone, Farrar. Just a little private matter. Nothing to do with this dough."

Shake, Windy and Pop all turned to look at Doc, wondering what was up. Johnny glanced at Jim, saw his face harden, knocked wood unobtrusively, and hoped for the best.

Jim glanced at his watch.

"All right, Doc. I got a couple of minutes."

"Thanks," said the little Doctor, with mock graciousness. The others started to file out, looking back.

"We'll wait outside, Doc," said Shake.

Doc nodded. Johnny herded them out, then turned to Jim.

"I'll look after them."

"Okay," said Jim. "I'll be right with you."

Johnny glanced from Jim to Doc, then hesitated, swallowed, and went out, shutting the door softly.

"Pretty smooth," said Doc.

"You think so?" asked Jim with narrowed eyes.

"Yeah. That just goes to show what a bankroll means. It takes capital to operate. Maybe a guy does have to lay out thirty grand or so; if he's got it—fine. I never saw the guy yet who wouldn't lay out thirty grand to net a million."

"Get to the point."

"The point is: Pop, Shake, and Windy are two-bit crooks. You can push them around all you please. That's your business. But you can't push me around."

"I just handed you ten grand. Is that what you call getting pushed around?"

"In a way—yes."

"Not in my language."

Jim put on his hat and turned to go.

"Look—Farrar," said Doc, "I don't want any trouble with you. I know you're a bad boy to monkey with. But so am I."

"I'm going to get sore in a minute," said Jim mildly.

"I wouldn't advise it. First place, I got a rod in my coat pocket. Second place, I can spoil your nice little setup in five minutes. All I have to do is sing, and you're out over thirty grand for nothing: strictly for nothing." Doc laughed sardonically. "It was a good idea to marry the dame. But I got a better idea. Cut Doc in—that will make it much cozier."

Jim controlled himself. This took a little finagling. He didn't want a coked-up small-time bad man running loose, gumming the works; on the other hand, at the moment he didn't want to strongarm Doc—that could come later.

"The trouble with you is, Doc," he said quietly but bitingly, "you're neither a crook nor an honest man. You've never yet made up your mind which you are. You're inclined to be a rat on both sides of the fence. Now that's bad."

Doc smiled calmly.

"All right, call me names."

"A guy's got to pick out a set of rules and stick to 'em; he just can't make 'em up as he goes along. At least it's not healthy."

"I feel all right."

"What I'm getting at is: an agreement's an agreement."

"Exactly, and thirty percent of a million—we'll say just one million to be fair—is three hundred thousand dollars. But—I'm not crazy. I'm not asking for anything like that. I just want in on the play—that's all."

"I'll have to think it over, Doc," said Jim, looking at Doc judiciously and rubbing his chin as if he actually was thinking it over. In reality, he was wondering if Doc could be stopped any way short of a rubout.

"Don't think it over too long."

"You can always call Johnny. He's at the Ocean View Hotel, Santa Monica."

"And you and the missus are at the Marwood, where my big-mouthed friend, Charley Evans, is the manager. He thinks you're a wonderful couple. Told me all about it without prompting."

Jim turned.

"Goodnight, Doc. Take a tip. Get off the junk for a while. Maybe you'll see things differently."

"I doubt it. Goodnight, Mr. Farrar."

While Jim was talking to Doc, Johnny finally managed to get Tony on the phone.

"Look—Tony. Jim's here. He'll be down to see you soon. Watch your step."

"Well—that's news," said Tony, lazily. "How is my big boy? Was he glad to see you—his only friend and pal?"

"Cut it out, Tony."

"Did you let him know how society was getting along at La Junta Beach? The prize social note is as follows: Mr. John Doyle of Florida is now taking his siestas with Miss Antonia Blackburn, also of Florida by way of Chicago and the Holland Tunnel."

"Here comes Jim."

Johnny hung up abruptly, and got out of the phone booth without Jim seeing him.

IV

Tony's attitude puzzled Jim. When he came in she was lying on the divan, reading a magazine. She looked up, her face calm, and said off-handedly:

"Hello, Jim. Did you have a nice trip?"

"Yeah," he said, glancing at her, surprised.

He'd expected a violent reaction of some kind, and in a way he'd looked forward to it. No matter how angry Tony became—sometimes she lost all control of herself almost to the point of hysteria—she got over it quickly; and her emotions, just as violent as before, veered in another direction: she either burst into tears or cried as if she'd lost everything in the world, or she became wildly amorous. Jim often wondered if this extreme emotionality didn't explain the hold she had over him.

Puzzled, Jim reacted in a characteristic way. He stalled. He took off his coat and put it with his hat in the hall closet, then he loosened his tie, lit a cigarette, and sat down opposite Tony, who lay looking at him with what seemed like complete indifference.

There was a long pause. Tony tossed her magazine aside and lit a cigarette. Her bushy red hair was going every which way—she had no makeup on except lipstick, and, across the bridge of her nose and on her prominent cheekbones, her freckles were visible, making her seem younger, more wholesome, less artificial. Even so—compared to Gladys she looked like a theatrical trollop: promiscuous, greedy, and treacherous.

"I understand from your pal, Johnny, that you had to go to Mexico on business," she said. There was something in her tone that made Jim sore, something cold and jeering.

He decided he'd give her a jolt.

"Yes," he said, bracing himself for what he was certain would follow, "big business. I married a million dollars."

Tony laughed and puffed on her cigarette.

"I expected that."

"Smart girl—aren't you?" said Jim, annoyed by her attitude.

"Sort of. Well—it's all right by me. With little Tony on your hands, you're going to need a million dollars."

"I was getting by with less."

"But things are different now."

Jim got up, came over to Tony, and stood looking down at her.

"Listen, honey. Maybe I didn't hear right, but it sounded like you were threatening me. Don't get too big for your pants. It's not healthy."

Tony studied Jim's face, more than a little upset by a feeling she'd never experienced with him before. She was afraid. To her, Jim had always seemed lazy and good-natured, smart in his way, all right, but very susceptible to women, and not too hard to manage. Now in his face, which usually had a certain softness about it but at the moment looked lean and hard, and in his narrowed dark eyes, she sensed, for the first time, a bleak quality, an inhumanity, a mercilessness, which filled her with uneasiness.

Her attitude changed completely. She looked up at Jim with a soft, compliant expression.

"Are you in love with her, Jim?"

"Of course not. What the hell are you talking about!" Jim spoke harshly, sensing a victory.

Tony turned away from him suddenly and burst into tears.

V

When Doc came in, Shake was sitting at the table leisurely shuffling through a stack of books he'd just bought at a second-hand bookstore. He glanced up at Doc briefly, then looked again. He hardly knew the little doctor, who was wearing an expensive double-breasted blue suit, new black shoes, a black Homburg hat, a white shirt with a fashionable low collar, and a dark blue tie. A white handkerchief with a light blue border was carefully arranged in his breast pocket. Doc had been to the barber's where he'd had a massage and a close shave; and his coarse black hair, which almost always looked shaggy, was nicely trimmed and pomaded.

"Well—for God's sake," said Shake, genuinely startled. "You look like Chi in the old days, Doc."

Doc studied himself in the mirror complacently.

"Just shows you what a little capital will do. The guy downstairs didn't know me. Now I'm ready for business."

"What business?"

"Any that comes along. I've got that front I've been talking about."

"Yeah," said Shake, "but.... Look. We just made a big score. Why don't you relax, Doc?"

Doc laughed sardonically and sat down, carefully pulling up his trousers to preserve the crease.

"Shake," he said, "I just moved into the Marwood Arms."

"What?" cried Shake, then he laughed. "Stop kidding."

"I'm not kidding."

Shake stared at Doc for a moment, puzzled, then he realized that the little doctor meant it.

"But—Doc: I can't live there. Too expensive."

"Who said anything about you living there?"

"But I thought we...." Shake's face fell. He looked like a kid ready to burst into tears. The flaccid dewlap under his chin trembled slightly

"No," said Doc, lighting a cigar. "Doc's on his own from here on in. You should have seen the face on my old inseparable pal and companion—Charley Evans." Doc laughed scornfully. "He didn't want me, but what could he do? I had the dough to pay in advance—two hundred and fifty bucks for one month: robbery! And I knew he had some vacancies. He's always shooting off his big mouth. Besides, we went to college together. He was stuck." Doc laughed again.

Shake's mouth dropped open.

"But—Doc; that's where the big fellow beat the sucker." His eyes narrowed suddenly; and his sheep-like face took on a look of exaggerated cunning. "What are you pulling, Doc?"

"Nothing. Nothing. Any place that's good enough for Jim Farrar's almost good enough for me." He laughed and slapped his thigh. "I figured it might be a good hunting ground since we did so well there once."

"You're going to get in a jam. Why don't you relax for a while—enjoy your dough?"

"This is just petty larceny to what I'm going to have." Doc puffed on his cigar meditatively, then got up. "Well, I guess I'll be on my way. I got to go over to a luggage store and pick up a couple of bags I bought, then I'll drop by Oviatt's and pick up the rest of my new clothes; grab a taxi and I'm all set." He turned and walked toward the door.

Shake was hurt. It seemed mighty heartless of Doc to walk out—just like that—after all they'd been through together. A vague uneasiness began to grow on him. It was going to seem awful lonely without Doc.

As the little doctor reached the door, Shake got up. His hands were trembling and he had an all-gone feeling in the pit of his stomach.

"You can take my old clothes and throw them in the sewer—or sell them if you like," said Doc. "I'm brand new from the hide out. And, Shake, I'll make you a present of that Gladstone bag of mine: it cost me seventy-five dollars in Chicago."

"Thanks, Doc," Shake faltered. "It's going to seem mighty funny around here without you and Windy."

"Windy! Where the hell is he?"

"Frisco. Left at noon."

"What's he going up there for?"

"Remember that dame he rolled drunks with? He took her on a trip. Says she's a hell of a nice woman."

"I'll bet!" said Doc, laughing. "Two bits Windy turns up in a couple of days, broke. He would pick a drunk-roller! A dame like that'd kill a guy for ten bucks—let alone ten G's!"

Shake hesitated, then said in an unnatural voice:

"Give me a ring once in a while, will you, Doc? I might get sick or something, and I got nobody. I don't want to be dumped in no hospital."

"Oh, relax, you big chump," said Doc, scornfully. "Nothing'll ever happen to you. You'll dry up and blow away at the age of ninety. If you were like me, you'd have something to worry about. So long."

Shake took a step forward toward Doc and made a move to shake hands with him, but Doc, with one of his abrupt movements, was out of the door, which shut with a bang.

"That Doc!" said Shake, aloud. "He's a queer one. You'd think he'd only met me yesterday." Shake was deeply wounded. He sat down and began to look listlessly through the books he'd had so much fun buying: they didn't mean much at the moment. "And that damned dirty Gladstone bag," said Shake, outraged. "That's a hell of a present!"

VI

When Pop came out of the pawnshop where he'd been forced to stay longer than he'd intended, he noticed by a street clock that his watch was slow. He immediately got very much upset and ran off, looking for a taxi. The old Pop would not have become so flustered over the possibility of missing a train: another one always came along sooner or later. But Pop was confused. Now he did not live according to plan. He merely acted on impulse.

He realized dimly that he'd not shown his usual acumen in dealing with the pawnbroker. The so-and-so had robbed him. His old pal, the telescope, had been worth a lot more than the pawnbroker had allowed him on it. Pop hated to part with it, but resisted this feeling, considering it weakly sentimental. After all—what was a telescope? Nothing but a metal tube with some glass in it. It was silly to attach any value, aside from a monetary one, to it. And yet—it had been through rough times with him; and on many occasions had provided him with a much-needed meal.

Pop hesitated and seriously considered going back for the telescope. But a taxi came along and he got into it. As they drove through a crowded Los Angeles street on the way to the station, Pop looked about him like one in a dream. He actually had nearly three thousand dollars in cash; he actually was leaving the big California city where he'd been a familiar figure for years; and he actually was going back to his birthplace, that small Indiana town where he could live out the rest of his life in peace.

"Hot, ain't it?" said the taxi driver, turning and grinning.

"Yep," said Pop. "I'm sort of glad I'm getting out. It's not the kind of heat I like."

"Going back East?"

"As far as Indiana—that's my home state."

"I'm from Illinois myself," said the driver. "But I'll take California every time. All I wish is—they'd let me stay here. But I'll be in Iceland or Ireland or God-knows-where pretty soon. I'm being inducted a week from today."

"That's tough."

"Yeah," said the driver, sadly. "Damn it; I wish I'd never got divorced now. There I was with a wife and two kids. I didn't know when I was well off. But a guy can't foresee a thing like that." The driver pushed his cap back and meditated. "At that—I don't know. My wife was hell to live with. And them kids—boy!"

"Maybe the war won't last," said Pop indifferently. "Maybe they'll get it over quick."

"Not the way we're going. Oh, well. My old man went through a war. I guess I can do it." The driver turned and looked at Pop. "Them trains are mighty crowded right now and you never know whether you're going to eat or not. They feed the soldiers first. Better pick up something in the station; take it with you; then you don't have to worry."

"Thanks for the tip," said Pop.

Toward one o'clock that night, Pop woke with a start. He was riding in a tip-back chair in the tourist sleeper. He stared up in bewilderment at the dimly-lit ceiling of the car. He couldn't orient himself; the slight swaying of the train and the lickety-lick of the wheels puzzled him. He felt terrible. Pains were shooting all through him.

Suddenly he sat up—realizing where he was: an old man starting out alone on a wild goose chase. And for a second he saw himself and the world with startling clearness: his dream blew up like a punctured tire.

"I'm a goddamned old fool," groaned Pop. "I should have put my money in the bank and stayed right in L.A. Kept my telescope, raked in the dimes and whatever else I could get my hands on. Hell, I never did like Indiana—even when I was a kid."

The pains grew worse. Pop was wide awake now. He began to shake. With an effort he pulled himself out of the chair and got unsteadily to his feet. A sudden animal fear of death took hold of him: he began to sweat—a cold clammy sweat that chilled him to the bone. The train swayed round a bend. Pop made a grab for the chair, missed it, and fell.

The next thing he knew he was lying with his head propped up on a stranger's knee. The stranger had on a uniform.

"Is he all right?" a woman's voice asked anxiously.

"Yeah," said the soldier. "I think he just fainted. Poor old guy."

Pop resented the soldier's tone. He struggled to get up.

"Let me alone," he said, weakly. "I'm okay."

Several men came hurriedly down the aisle.

"Here's the doctor," said somebody.

Pop protested, but the doctor bent down and gave him a cursory examination, then he used his stethoscope.

"Ever had any trouble with your heart before?" asked the doctor, a sleepy, solemn-looking man with a too-perfectly trimmed slight mustache.

"It's not my heart," said Pop, indignantly. "I lost my balance and fell."

They took Pop off the train at Phoenix and he went to the hospital under the care of a doctor, who met the train. The other doctor had made all the arrangements about Pop's luggage and tickets. He wasn't a bad guy at that, Pop decided, in spite of the cookie-duster.

Pop didn't mind the ride in the ambulance. He was sweating from weakness, but outside of that he felt all right.

Later in the day he said to the doctor who dropped in to see him:

"Listen, Doc—when can I go back to L.A.?"

The doctor, a young man with a strong, healthy, red face, rubbed his chin and smiled. He liked this old bird.

"I thought you were on the way to Indiana."

"Changed my mind."

"Your people will be disappointed."

"What people?"

"Oh," said the doctor, then he bent down and felt Pop's pulse. "Young man," he went on, "haven't you ever been told it's dangerous to go around in this wicked world carrying a roll like that?"

Pop started.

"Where is it?"

"In the hospital safe. You'll never see it again. That's going to be the amount of my bill."

Pop grinned feebly.

"How about L.A., Doc?"

"We'll talk about that later."

"I'll make it, won't I?"

"Sure." The big young doctor grinned and Pop lay back, feeling very contented.

On the way to his office the doctor met Pop's nurse.

"Funny old fellow, isn't he?" she said.

"An old reprobate—or I don't know anything," said the doctor, grinning. "I like him."

"So do I. He's so anxious to get back to L.A. You'd think the rainbow came down there."

"I hope he makes it," said the doctor, shrugging, his face falling slightly.

VII

Charley Evans, who was standing near the reception desk, whistled softly to himself as Mr. and Mrs. James Lloyd got out of the elevator—thinking what a fine-looking couple they were. It was a pleasure to have people like that at the Marwood. Charley swelled with pride: after all he was responsible, in a way, for getting them together. And yet—sometimes he had vague misgivings. It seemed very strange to him that quiet, retiring Mrs. Halvorsen would suddenly elope to Mexico with a man she hardly knew—like a susceptible and romantic boarding school girl. And besides at times there was something about handsome Mr. Lloyd—he didn't quite know what—that made him slightly uneasy.

He recalled a little episode of last week. Mr. Lloyd was at the desk talking to the clerk when he came up. Mr. Lloyd concluded his business with the clerk, then he turned and said:

"That was a fine dinner we had tonight, Mr. Evans. Excellent."

Mr. Lloyd was smiling and looked very pleasant and good-natured as he always did. Of a sudden—for a brief moment—his expression changed. His face lengthened, his eyes narrowed, his lips were compressed into a grim line: he looked hard; actually hard like a—well, like a tough customer of some kind. In an instant he was smiling again, and Charley stared, unable to adjust himself to the swift change of expression. Mr. Lloyd had glanced momentarily off across the lobby. Charley turned. His old friend—his college chum—Dr. Walter Bright was going into the dining room.

Later, Charley recalled little Doc Bright's peculiar interest in Mrs. Halvorsen. There was something there maybe ... But after a while, Charley dismissed the thing from his mind with a sudden effort. His sister was always telling him that if he wasn't careful he'd get to be an old fuddy-duddy: fussy and abnormally suspicious.

In the dining room that night Andre seated Mr. and Mrs. Lloyd at a table near Dr. Bright. Evans watched carefully. The men ignored each other; ate calmly. Oh, well, Charley thought, I guess I'm just imagining things.

The next day he was certain of it. He had quite a talk with Mr. Lloyd; and in the middle of it he introduced Doc Bright's name into the conversation. Mr. Lloyd showed nothing but a polite interest and finally said:

"It's nice having a doctor handy. A person never knows when he might need one."

"He doesn't practice anymore. Retired, I think," Charley explained.

... yes; they were a fine-looking couple, Charley told himself, as the Lloyds walked toward him across the long lobby; and it was silly of him to have any second thoughts about them. They were rich, presentable people; the kind anybody would be glad to have for friends.

Just as they neared the desk and were smiling at him, Dr. Bright came in the front door and hurried over to the clerk to ask after his mail. He never got any, but he always asked.

There they were, the Lloyds, and there was Doc—the bane of Charley's life now. The Lloyds spoke to Charley and so did Doc. There was nothing he could do. He introduced them. The men shook hands, murmuring the usual polite and meaningless phrases. But Doc bowed to Mrs. Lloyd and said—in a voice Charley thought was overdone and in very bad taste—that he was proud to meet such a beautiful woman.

Mr. Lloyd thanked Doc, then the Lloyds went into the dining room. Charley thought it was pretty evident that the Lloyds didn't want anything to do with Doc—and he didn't blame them.

"Nice people," said Doc with a grin.

"Yes," said Charley, stiffly, "extremely nice."

Doc turned away abruptly with a laugh and walked toward the elevators.

A damned irritating little man, Charley decided. He fervently wished that he could find a way to eject him from the exclusive Marwood.

VIII

Jim managed to control the outward signs of his restlessness, but he found it more and more difficult to stifle the yawns he felt coming on every minute or so. He was playing casino with his wife, and being badly beaten, owing to his lack of interest. Gladys was happy. Her dark eyes were dancing, and she was getting a big kick out of the game, playing for all she was worth. There was something markedly girlish about this forty-year-old woman that was very puzzling to Jim, who often studied her covertly. Except for a slightly worn look she showed scarcely any signs of age at all. And then she was so enthusiastic, so easily entertained; not in the least blasé.

Jim turned his head away slightly and stifled a yawn. Gladys gave a triumphant cry; she had taken his built-up tens with big casino. Jim didn't get a point.

"And I thought you knew so much about gambling," Gladys crowed, laughing delightedly. "It's a good thing you don't depend on it for a living."

She gathered up the cards and got ready to shuffle them. But Jim got up and, turning away, yawned widely. "What's the matter, darling?"

Jim stalled, then said:

"My eyes—they hurt."

Gladys hurriedly put down the cards.

"You see, Jim? Why won't you listen to me? You've just got to go and get your eyes examined. You've probably had eyestrain for years without knowing it."

Jim controlled his irritation with difficulty. She was always harping on this subject. They were his eyes, weren't they? What the hell did she care how he treated them?

"Oh, I don't know." He flung himself into a chair and picked up the evening paper. But the print swam before him: not because of his eyes but because he wasn't interested in anything at the moment—least of all a newspaper—except getting out of the apartment, away from Gladys's over-solicitousness: he wanted to spend a rowdy evening with Tony, who had become so loving and reasonable of late that he hardly knew what to make of it.

Gladys came over, took the paper from him, and sat on the arm of his chair.

"I'll read it to you, darling. What shall we start with?" Jim groaned inwardly and said:

"Let's just start on page one and work our way through it." He spoke more ironically than he'd intended. Gladys glanced at him.

"You feel jittery, don't you?"

"I don't know," said Jim, "just sort of restless, I guess."

She studied him anxiously.

"Are you bored, Jim? If so—please tell me."

"Of course I'm not bored."

"I'm afraid I'm not very stimulating company. Are you sorry?"

"Sorry about what?"

"That you married me."

"Oh—Gladys !" Jim exclaimed impatiently.

She glanced at him, noted his irritation, then she said quickly:

"Would you like me to mix you a drink?"

"Yes," said Jim, brightening slightly, "bourbon and soda."

Gladys got up and went to the little bar just beyond the living room: He heard the pleasant clink of bottles. He got up and went to look out the window. It was a warm summer night. A lukewarm breeze was stirring the tops of the tall royal palms just below him. The moon had not yet risen and the dimmed-out city looked a little dismal.

Gladys spoke from the bar.

"That doctor we met's a strange little man, isn't he?"

"Yes," said Jim, "very strange."

Doc—that dirty little vermin! What did he think he had to gain by moving into the Marwood? Did he have any idea he was going to make somebody nervous? What a damn fool trick. Jim laughed curtly and unpleasantly, feeling for a moment that same cold anger he'd felt when he saw Doc crossing the lobby. Doc might have to be dealt with eventually; but there was no real hurry; maybe time would take care of that.

"He's sort of interesting-looking in a way," called Gladys.

Jim grunted. A woman's viewpoint. Doc—interesting-looking! He was about as interesting as a bad case of small-pox. Women never knew. Where men were concerned, they went around in a state of befuddlement; especially a woman like Gladys. He'd married her—

hadn't he?— With no trouble at all. Not that that was so hard to understand. But he'd deluded her without the slightest difficulty. Doc— interesting!

"He doesn't look like much of a doctor to me," said Jim, chuckling to himself.

"He looks like a hypnotist I saw in Chicago once," called Gladys; "his eyes—I mean."

Jim shrugged and turned away from the window, yawning. Gladys came in with his drink. It had too much soda in it, but he said nothing.

"Aren't you having one?" he asked.

"No. I don't like it much."

"You used to pour it down a little."

"That was only on your account," said his wife with a laugh. "I've caught you now. I'm not going to poison myself anymore."

"Fine thing," said Jim, laughing good-naturedly. "So that's the way you got me—plying me with liquor."

"It's the only way I could think of."

Jim laughed and put his arm around her. She immediately hugged him and reached up for a kiss. Jim kissed her. Then he raised his glass to his lips, but she took his head between her hands, turned his face away from the glass, and kissed him repeatedly.

She wanted him badly at the moment and he knew it, but the prospect didn't please him: he felt too dissatisfied and restless. He also knew that if he turned her advances aside, although she wouldn't say anything, she'd feel hurt and begin to worry about him being bored.

He put his glass down and took her in his arms.

"A man can drink any time," he said.

Gladys laughed delightedly.

Jim woke with a start. He was sweating and felt jittery and all at sea. But finally he got himself in hand. Gladys was breathing evenly beside him, fast asleep. Although he was in a cramped position, he refrained from turning over, afraid he'd wake her. He didn't want her worrying about him. He moved gently in the bed, easing his legs and arms. Gladys murmured in her sleep. He froze and waited. Nothing happened, and he sighed with relief.

He'd dreamed the old dream again, and he felt so low that he could hardly keep from hurrying out to the bar and throwing down a few quick ones. But that would entail explanations—for it would wake Gladys and she probably wouldn't get back to sleep the rest of the night. He stifled a groan. There he was in jail—half Tom Rodney, half himself—a disreputable, sick, and dirty old man, pulled in for molesting a little girl. Even the turnkeys—those chiseling rats—looked upon him with pained disgust. The judge was stern and unbending—it was a dream so he was an honest judge—and not only sentenced Jim-Rodney to life imprisonment, but berated him as a disgrace to the human race. Jim-Rodney wept and said: "My only disgrace is—I'm poor and old."

Jim groaned, thinking about this recurrent dream; it had a certain prophetic quality that disturbed him very much. Gladys stirred in her sleep. Jim froze again. She reached over and touched him and whispered: "Jim—are you all right?"

He lay motionless, scarcely breathing. Gladys waited, then she cuddled up to his back and put her arm over him. After a moment, she pressed her lips gently to the nape of his neck, and settled herself for sleep again.

Jim couldn't get back to sleep. All night long he heard taxis hooting on the boulevard and the occasional distant whine of a police car siren. A belated drunk sang a popular love song, giving it an ironical intonation, as he passed in front of the hotel, his footsteps echoing hollowly along the deserted street. Mocking-birds chirped and twittered in the palm trees just below the bedroom window.

Jim lay hating himself and the world. He felt old and spent and nothing seemed worth the effort. He wondered if he'd ever sleep again and as he wondered, he began to speculate vaguely on the nature of sleep. You lie down, shut your eyes, and lose consciousness. It was a sort of temporary death—disturbed by dreams. Maybe actual death was like that, too: maybe heaven and hell and all other such stuff that people believed in existed only in dreams.

Just as it began to get light, Jim fell into an exhausted sleep. Gladys woke about nine and tiptoed around the bedroom so as not to disturb her husband. He'd looked tired the night before and she was a little worried about him.

At noon she woke him and asked if he was hungry.

Jim sat up and stared about him. Sunlight was streaming in the windows and a fresh breeze was blowing out the curtains. Gladys stood beside the bed, smiling, and looking so pretty and sweet in her long, flowered dressing-gown! Jim felt fine. He grinned.

"I'll say I'm hungry.

Gladys disappeared into the living room and came back at once, carrying a tray loaded with food: bacon and eggs, fried potatoes, a stack of buttered toast, a jar of jam, and a pot of coffee.

"Here you are," she cried, triumphantly. "All ready to eat."

"Oh, boy!" Jim exclaimed, his mouth watering. "Let me at it."

She settled the tray for him then stood watching him with a smile as he began to eat. After a few mouthfuls he looked up at her.

"Say—how about you?"

"I ate two hours ago."

"You shouldn't ply me like this. First it's liquor. Now it's food. If I'm not careful I'll get fat as a pig."

"I don't care if you do."

"Oh, no? You'd soon start looking around if I got fat."

Gladys frowned indignantly.

"Don't talk like that, Jim. I wouldn't care if you weighed two hundred and fifty pounds. You'd still be you."

"There'd be more of me to love—eh?"

He grinned, meaning it. The breakfast was great. Jim loved to eat: all his life he'd been forced to restrain his almost abnormal appetite.

Gladys stood watching him eat, smiling contentedly.

IX

Jim hadn't intended to surprise Tony by going to the beach to see her without calling up first. He'd been so anxious to get there that he'd forgotten all about it. Unable to stay away another night, he'd told Gladys that some important business had come up and he'd have to spend quite a bit of time with Mr. Riley—his business manager. Gladys asked him when he'd be back. He told her he wasn't sure; but he probably wouldn't be home till about ten. Anyway—he'd call and let her know. "I'm going to be awfully lonesome," Gladys said.

Impatient to get away, Jim kissed her hurriedly.

"'By, honey. I'll be seeing you."

He went out the door quickly without looking back. Her heart contracted slightly; she turned away, miserable. She knew she was being silly and foolish, but when Jim was away from her she felt lost— it was awful, but wonderful, too.

No—he hadn't intended to surprise Tony. But she seemed almost stunned. She was standing in the middle of the living room with nothing on but an unfastened bathrobe: not even shoes. Her hair was all wild, and there was a sleepy, drugged look in her eyes. She stared at him, open-mouthed, as if he were a ghost.

Jim was so glad to see her that things registered slowly. He assumed she'd been taking a nap on the divan and that he'd startled her out of it. He took her in his arms.

"Sorry, Tony—if I scared you. I forgot to call."

"Oh, that's all right," said Tony, giving him a strange, weak smile.

He heard a car start up and hurriedly drive off. A sudden suspicion stabbed at him. He held Tony off and looked at her, then he turned and went into the bedroom, switching on the lights. The bed was tumbled and the back window which opened onto the beach road was wide open. Tony came and stood in the doorway.

"What's the matter, Jim?" she asked, calmer now.

"Nothing, nothing," said Jim, trying to control himself.

"Just thought I heard something."

"Really, Jim—no kidding: you shouldn't come busting in here like this. You almost frightened the daylights out of me."

"Were you in bed?"

"Sure I was."

"How come all the lights were on in the living room?"

"Because I'm scared at night—all alone down here. It's spooky with the dimout and everything."

Jim stood looking at her. She shoved her hair back over her ears with a graceful gesture, then she shuddered delicately.

"I'm cold. I'm going back to bed."

Turning away slightly, she dropped her robe, hesitated briefly in order to allow her nakedness to have its effect, then she slipped into bed and pulled the covers up to her chin.

"What's wrong with you, honey?" she demanded. "You look haunted."

Jim made no reply. But already he felt much better. It would be damned silly of Tony to double-cross him; she had nothing to gain except momentary pleasure and everything to lose. It was probably just his damned suspicious nature. He trusted nobody.

Jim turned out the lights and began to undress.

"How's the missus?" asked Tony, feeling more and more sure of herself as time passed.

"Okay," said Jim curtly, thinking how strange it was that every time Tony mentioned Gladys's name he resented it. "Good Lord," he told himself, "I'm getting so used to playing the straight man—I'm starting to feel like one." He decided to end that silliness. "She's just too goddamned nice for my taste," he said, brutally.

Excited now, Tony giggled.

"In bed you mean?"

"Mind your own business," said Jim, harshly, in spite of himself— then he laughed to show that he was only kidding.

Down the road fifty feet or so from Jim's beach house Doc was sitting in a parked car with the motor running—so pleased with himself and the world for the time being that he could hardly refrain from shooting off the small automatic which felt so heavy and reassuring in his coat pocket.

Jim Farrar—the wise guy, the big fellow, the top man! He'd show him. What did the guy take him for—a clunk? It was a simple matter to follow any one. Didn't Jim know that? Of course he did. The answer was that the big fellow just didn't care. He'd been blundering around with his head in the clouds for years. But no man's luck holds forever.

Doc chuckled delightedly. The big fellow not only had a broad stashed— he was getting the same merry old runaround that most guys got.

"Oh, boy," crowed Doc, "did that baby come out of that window! Just like he was shot out of a cannon."

Doc leisurely lit a cigar and took a few puffs on it, then he put the car in gear, turned it around, and started back toward town.

"Now I'm ready to talk to that cluck," he thought. "I'll bet his snooty missus would give her right eye to know about Jim's broad and where she's stashed. But maybe I better hold that back. Yeah. I'll hold it back. I got plenty to make a start with—without that."

Doc drove along in the dimout, whistling an old tune of his Chicago days—"I Can't Give You Anything But Love, Baby"—and puffing contentedly on his cigar. He hadn't felt in such good health and spirits for years.

"Tough luck it was too dark for me to get a good look at the guy who came out of the window," Doc mused. "Might've been somebody I know." Doc laughed loudly at his own wit.

At a turn of the road, he saw a cocktail bar.

"I think, Doctor," he said, "I'll treat you to a couple of drinks. You've earned them tonight."

Jim had temporarily lost all sense of time. Wrapped up in an old bathrobe he was sitting on the dressing table bench with his feet on the bed and a drink in his hand, talking about the past. Tony, in her dressing gown, was standing beside him with one hand on his shoulder, looking at herself in the mirror as she listened.

"... that was long before your time in Florida," Jim was saying. "If you think it was wide-open when you got there—you should've been there in the twenties."

"It's nothing now," said Tony with a trace of bitterness.

"Soldiers all over the place. Say—I'm getting hungry, Jim. Why don't I whip up some scrambled eggs or something?"

"It's not a bad idea. But wait a minute." Jim suddenly became conscious of the passage of time. "Got a clock around here?"

"It's stopped," said Tony. "I don't like to know what time it is—anyway, the ticking bothers me."

Jim picked up his vest and fumbled for his watch.

"It's not late," said Tony. "The missus is probably fast asleep. She sounds like the type who goes to bed at nine o'clock."

"Good Lord," Jim exclaimed, looking at his watch. "It's nearly midnight."

Tony burst out laughing, pointing at Jim in her mirth. "The way you said that! A person'd think you never stayed out that late before."

"Yeah," said Jim, "but I told her I'd be home by ten. She worries."

"Let her worry. Do her good. What does she expect you to do—punch in? Come on. Let's get something to eat."

"I'm sure I told her ten," said Jim, trying to remember. He glanced up; Tony was giving him a pitying look. "Oh, the hell with it!" he cried, rising. "Let's go see what's in the kitchen."

"Atta boy," shouted Tony. "Stand up for your rights."

As Jim turned away she flung her arms around his neck from behind and he carried her piggy-back through the living room and into the kitchen.

As Jim was driving through Westwood Village he glanced at his watch: ten minutes after three. Suddenly he remembered that he'd told Gladys he'd call her.

"Good Lord!" he cried and stepped on the gas.

There were very few cars out. The street lights were dimmed and the big sprawling community looked dark and deserted as Jim drove east at a high rate of speed toward the faint glow of downtown Los Angeles.

In all his life he'd never felt so upset about keeping somebody waiting. In fact he'd hardly given it a thought before. If you were hours late or didn't turn up at all—what did it matter? Whoever was waiting could do as they liked: ignore it, get sore about it, or go away. But this was different. Gladys would be terribly worried; no doubt about it—and for some reason he didn't think it was fair that she should be. This feeling surprised him till he found an explanation for it. Hell—he was no heel. A man in his position ought to make a few concessions. Damn Tony; the little bum!

He passed an all-night restaurant which cast a pool of light at a corner where a few men were congregated: a newsboy, a taxi driver, and a couple of motorcycle cops. He slowed down at the sight of the cops. All he needed now was to get stopped for speeding.

One of the cops snapped his fingers as Jim's Cadillac rolled by, kicked the stand from under his motorcycle, and started off with a roar. He caught up with Jim two blocks beyond the corner and forced him into the curb. Jim sat swearing to himself, waiting for the cop.

"Hello," said the cop, smiling, as he came up to Jim. "Stepping on it—wasn't you?"

"Was I?"

"Yeah." The cop took out a notebook, riffled the pages with a thick forefinger, found what he was looking for, and putting the book away, pushed back his cap and stared at Jim. "Mister—are you James Lloyd?"

Jim hesitated. Damned if this wasn't a funny one.

"Why?"

The cop studied him.

"Let me see your driver's license."

Jim gave it to him. The cop glanced at it and handed it back. "Okay, Mr. Lloyd. Get home as fast as you can. Your wife's looking for you."

"No kidding?"

"No kidding, Mr. Lloyd." The cop laughed. "And if I know women—you're in trouble."

Jim shook his head slowly from side to side, very much annoyed. Fine thing!

"And by the way," the cop said, "better see about getting a California driver's license if you're going to stay here. Save you trouble. Just a tip."

When Jim entered the dimly-lit lobby, Charley Evans, looking pale and anxious, hurried up to him at once.

"Little late for you, isn't it?" Jim demanded, surprised.

"Oh, I'm so glad you're all right," said Evans. "Mrs. Lloyd—well, we've had quite a time with her. My sister's up with her now."

"I had to go to San Diego on business," said Jim, saying the first thing that popped into his head.

"Your wife was so worried."

"Thanks for your trouble," said Jim. "I'm sorry she's so upset."

They went up together in the elevator, the nightman staring at Jim curiously out of the corner of his eye. What an uproar that big guy had caused!

Jim was so nervous that for a moment he couldn't unlock the door of his suite. Evans, as shaky as Jim, watched Jim fumble with the key, a look of acute anxiety on his usually composed, conventional face. Finally Jim got the door open and rushed in. Gladys was lying on the divan, fully dressed, with a cold towel on her forehead. Evans's sister, a fattish, kindly-looking woman of fifty, was sitting nearby, glancing at a newspaper.

Gladys gave a cry, threw the towel off, then jumped up and rushed into Jim's arms.

"There!" said Miss Evans. "I told you, dear."

Jim, feeling very much embarrassed, stroked Gladys's hair awkwardly, and glanced at the Evanses as if to say: "Too bad she got so excited over nothing."

"We'll be going," said Miss Evans. "Come on, Charles."

"Thanks," said Jim. "Thanks very much."

Gladys seemed unable to speak. She nodded at the Evanses and smiled weakly and distractedly.

When they had gone, Jim said:

"I'm sorry, Gladys. I should've sent you a telegram."

"I was sure you'd been killed or badly hurt in an automobile accident." She looked at him with an expression of acute distress. "What happened, Jim, darling? Where were you?"

"Let's get comfortable," said Jim, "and I'll tell you all about it."

He was appalled by Gladys's appearance. She seemed to have aged ten years. Her face was pale, there were dark circles under her eyes, and the lines about her mouth looked much deeper. There was a hurt, bewildered expression in her eyes that was painful to see. Jim was puzzled. This was a new one. Nobody had ever felt that way about him before. In fact the feeling in itself was incomprehensible to him. How could one person mean that much to another? He often berated himself for needing Tony—but God knows he didn't need her that bad!

He got Gladys to sit on the divan and he sat beside her, holding her hand.

"I had to go to San Diego on business, darling," he said, smiling at her, and speaking soothingly. "Riley said we'd jump down and come right back. I'm a stranger here. I didn't know it was such a trip."

"You promised to call me."

"I know. I tried to—from San Diego. But that place's like a camp—it belongs to the Army and the Navy. A civilian's got no show at all." Jim hesitated for a moment in his ad libbing. Lucky he'd read a lot of stuff about San Diego in a newspaper! "You practically can't make a long-distance call. Priorities. So that was that. Then when it got so late I didn't want to call and disturb you—on the way up, I mean. I figured you'd go to bed when I didn't show up...."

"How could you think that, Jim?"

"Well—why not?" Jim laughed. "I'm no kid. I can look after myself."

"I can't help it. When you're not here I just...." Gladys lowered her head and began to cry. Jim put his arms around her and held her tight.

"There, there," he said, feeling like a damned fool. "Now, now."

"Please," sobbed Gladys, "never, never do that again."

Jim woke up just before sunrise and couldn't get back to sleep. Gladys, absolutely exhausted was sleeping heavily, and to Jim's amusement, snoring slightly. It seemed like such an incongruous thing for so ladylike a person to do.

He lay for a while staring at the dim, reflected light on the ceiling, then he wanted a cigarette. He eased himself slowly out of bed. Ordinarily this would have awakened Gladys but not tonight: she was too worn out.

Jim went into the bathroom, shut the door softly, lit a cigarette and sat on the edge of the tub to smoke.

Suddenly he heard a cry, followed by frantic, scurrying footsteps. Startled, he jumped up and flung open the bathroom door just in time to see Gladys go hurrying past, her hair flying, her eyes heavy with sleep.

"Jim! Jim!" she cried.

He caught her in the living room and hugged her to him, overcome by a strong but ambiguous emotion.

"Here I am, honey. Here I am. What's wrong?"

"Oh, God," cried Gladys. "I thought you'd gone." She clung to him like a drowning woman.

X

Johnny seemed fidgety and inattentive and Jim glanced at him several times speculatively, wondering what was on the little lawyer's mind. He wasn't looking too well either: his face was paler than usual and seemed drawn.

They were sitting in the Marwood Arms bar. It was the middle of the afternoon and the place was deserted except for a bored, white-coated bartender and a waiter, both of whom were reading a newspaper at the corner of the bar, looking about furtively from time to time for fear Mr. Evans, who was a stickler, would come in and catch them at it. But they weren't too worried. Times were changing. Now—nobody needed to take any punishment in order to keep a job with men pouring into the Army and the defense plants the way they were! Able-bodied, overage men were at a premium: they could pick and choose. The bar waiter and the bartender had talked it over several times: it was a very pleasant state of affairs.

Johnny had called Jim: told him he'd have to see him. Gladys heard the phone conversation and got so upset—fearing another trip to San

Diego—that Jim had asked Johnny to meet him in the Marwood Arms bar. Before the little lawyer could state his business Jim told him how Gladys had got so upset about him staying out late, then he prompted Johnny what to say in case she came down later to have a drink with them.

"Tony was just full of the devil that night," said Jim, laughing. "I couldn't get away."

Johnny lowered his eyes and made no comment. He seemed so preoccupied that Jim looked at him quizzically, then asked:

"Say—what's wrong with you, Johnny? Been sick?"

Johnny roused himself and forced a smile.

"Me? I never get sick. I just haven't been getting enough sleep. Besides—I got bad news for you. Of course—I think I can handle it— but...."

"Well, come on. What is it?"

"Windy got in a jam up in Frisco. He was in jail a couple of days before he could get word to Shake. Poor old Shake. He was so damned upset, he cried when he was telling me about it. I wonder what's eating the big slob?"

"Never mind about Shake."

"Well—Windy took a dame to Frisco. I guess he got to bragging about all the dough he had on him and he wakes up one night and the dame's going through his clothes, looking for the roll. Windy gets so sore he belts his girlfriend a couple and knocks her out—he claims he just slapped her. Well, before she goes out she yells bloody murder and somebody calls a cop and Windy's taken down. They find the roll on him and figure he's bumped somebody off for it. He claims it's his own dough—which it is. But he's being held for investigation—aside from assault and battery."

"Damn," said Jim. "Those cheap bums never turn out to be anything but cheap bums. You jump up to Frisco and straighten it out." Jim thought for a moment. "Has he talked—about the money, I mean? Did he give 'em a story?"

"No. I'll say that for him. He insisted it was his and clean—then clammed up."

"Good. You get up there right away and tell the police you owed Windy that money: a gambling debt; and you just got around to paying it. See what you can do about the other charge. Get him off; then tell him if he gets in any more trouble you'll have him beaten up by a couple of strongarm boys: tell him I said so."

Johnny hesitated, lowering his eyes.

"I was figuring maybe we could telegraph Joe Welch, Jim. He'd handle it for us. Save a trip."

Jim leaned back to stare at Johnny. What was the matter with the little Irishman?

"Are you crazy? This one's got to be handled right. Might get us all in a jam—if Windy'd happen to crack."

"All right, Jim," said Johnny, resignedly.

"And don't waste any time. Start now."

Johnny finished off his drink and got up. He hated to leave Tony—even for a day. He was so jealous of her he couldn't think of anything else. He'd spent one sleepless night after another, thinking about her and Jim. It was as if he'd suddenly gone insane: he wasn't like himself at all. It was ridiculous and pathetic that a thing like this could happen to him at his age—after all he'd been through.

"Jim—having any trouble with Doc?"

"Yes," said Jim, his mouth looking a little grim as he said it. "He's braced me a couple of times—but I've put him off. He's a problem."

"Is he trying to put on the old bite?"

"That's the general idea. He knows Gladys now—to speak to. Every time he gets a chance he tries to talk to me when I'm with her."

"That's bad. Doc's game. Don't scare easy."

"If he wasn't a junky it would be simpler. But junkies are like women—you never know what they'll do."

"Go slow, Jim; please," begged Johnny. "I know you—you're all right up to a certain point; then you blow up. If you blow up with Doc you'll have to complete your play—because he'll stand fire. He has. Remember the Willy Johnson business? And Willy was a bad boy."

"You worry about Windy—I'll look after Doc." Jim spoke sharply. He didn't like advice from anybody. He'd been getting along all right for years, handling situations just as dangerous as this one.

"Well, don't get sore," said Johnny, trying to laugh placatingly; he didn't want to get Jim all upset as he had to hit him for dough. "I'm not trying to tell you how to run your business. You know what you're doing—always have."

Jim was mollified. He glanced up at the little lawyer with a smile.

"I really pulled one this time, didn't I? I even went Tom Rodney one better. He never married over a million bucks."

"Who did? No racket man that I ever heard of. You're sure up there." Johnny smiled to himself as Jim glowed. Flattery was one thing you couldn't overdo! "Jim," he said, "I hate to bring this up—but I need a little dough."

Jim stared.

"What happened to that twelve hundred?"

Johnny hesitated. He couldn't tell Jim that Tony had borrowed nearly eight hundred of it.

"Well," he said, "I didn't tell you at the time—but I owed most of it: had to send it to Florida. Keep my credit good in case we might have to jump back."

"How dough gets away!" said Jim, slowly shaking his head. Extravagance was a fault he understood. He'd run through close to half a million himself in the last fifteen years. "Okay, Johnny. I got four hundred on me. Make it do till you get back."

"Thanks, Jim," said Johnny, taking the money and carelessly stuffing it into his pocket. "I'll call you long distance as soon as I get it straightened out."

They shook hands. Just as Johnny turned to go Doc came into the bar, looking very spruce in a new gray suit. He had a lightweight gray hat at an angle and he was swinging a cane. Johnny glanced at Jim and shrugged. Doc spotted them and came over at once.

"Hello, Johnny," he said, smiling.

"I'm just going," said the little lawyer, in a hurry to be off.

"Don't let me chase you away," said Doc, sitting down at the table with Jim. "I'll buy you a drink if you'll stay."

"Be seeing you," said Johnny, going out quickly.

Jim started to get up, but Doc put a hand on his arm. "Too bad about Windy, wasn't it?"

Jim sank back into his chair.

"Was it?"

"In a way. Shake got in touch with me. I told him to contact Johnny at Santa Monica. After all, it's your headache; not mine. Of course if the take had been bona fide...."

"Listen, Doc," said Jim, slowly, "you're either just naturally nuts, or that junk's got you. Take my advice; get out of this hotel. Mind your own business. Keep away from me. I'm getting a little fed up with this."

"I was hoping you were. So I figured maybe we could get down to business today. Your wife told me where to find you."

"My wife! Where did you see her?"

"I went up to your apartment. She was very nice to me—very polite."

"You keep away from my apartment. Evans is just looking for an excuse to throw you out of here. Maybe I'll give him one."

"If you do—I'll see that you're kicked out right behind me."

There was a pause. Jim sat staring at the table, trying to control the fury that was rising within him.

"Doc," he said, in a voice that shook slightly, "I don't know what to say to you. I've never been up against anything like this before. I always worked with right ones. Rats are a little scarce in this profession."

Doc smiled easily and flicked at his well-pressed trousers with his cane.

"You're just wasting your time trying to make me sore. I know what I want and I know how to get it. No matter what you say I'm not going to blow my top. So you might just as well talk business."

"You'll never get a cent, Doc. Do you think I'm a chump? Once I start paying you—I'm stuck. I'll have you on pension the rest of your life. Of course—maybe that won't be very long."

Doc laughed.

"Still trying to scare me, eh? I'm disappointed in you, Farrar."

"I wish you'd stop asking for it, Doc."

Doc's eyes narrowed, his smile disappeared. He leaned forward tensely.

"Maybe you're the one who's asking for it," he said, "and I've got it right here in my pocket."

Jim glanced at Doc, then laughed.

"A two-bit bad man full of junk. No, Doc. Not a dime—never." He turned and called the waiter, who came over hurriedly, smiling. The waiter liked Mr. Lloyd: he was a good guy and a big tipper: not like this little frozen-faced weasel with him, who never tipped at all. "Bourbon and soda," said Jim to the waiter, who bowed slightly, then turned to Doc.

"And you, sir?"

"I'll pass this one."

The waiter left, and returned in a minute or so with Jim's drink. He wondered what was wrong with the two men: they were sitting in stony silence, neither looking at the other. The waiter picked up Jim's tip, grinned, and went back to the bar where he was having a heated but whispered discussion with the bartender about the projected gas rationing.

"I'm a reasonable man," said Doc, finally. "And I'm no blackmailer. I don't want to bleed you, Farrar. Hand me a hundred grand and that will be the end of it."

Jim merely laughed. Doc sat very still for a moment, wondering if it was time to indicate that he had an ace in the hole. He decided against it.

"All right," he said slowly. "You know best. But I never figured you'd turn out to be a clunk. A man who won't spend a hundred G's to protect a million—well ..."

"How do you figure to cut in, Doc?" asked Jim in a mild voice.

"That's easy. A word to the little woman—letting her know what kind of a guy she's mixed up with."

"She wouldn't believe you. It's your word against mine."

"When I got through she'd believe me—all right. I'm a great convincer. She could get her marriage annulled like that." He snapped his fingers.

Jim leaned forward and spoke in a low but cutting voice. "Doc—I'm going to warn you for the last time: if you so much as say a word out of the way to my wife—I'll kill you."

Doc shook his head slowly.

"You can't scare me, Farrar."

Jim opened his mouth to speak further, but hesitated. Gladys was in the doorway, glancing in his direction timidly. She had on a tailored suit and a small hat: she looked wonderful.

"Doc," said Jim, "here's my wife. You can speak your piece right now. Either that—or get on your feet and get out of here."

Jim got up and motioned for Gladys to come over. Doc rose also. When Gladys got to the table, he bowed slightly, and said:

"I found him, Mrs. Lloyd. Now I'll run along. I might be in the way."

Gladys looked from Jim to Doc.

"I hope I'm not intruding. Did you finish your business?" She looked about her. "Where's Mr. Riley? I wanted to say 'hello' to him."

"He's gone, honey," said Jim. Then he turned to Doc, who was hesitating, and said curtly: "Goodbye, Doctor."

"Goodbye," said Doc. "I'll see you later."

He walked off abruptly.

Jim and Gladys sat down.

"I hope I didn't interrupt anything," she said, looking at Jim lovingly; and when he merely smiled and shook his head, she went on: "That little doctor—he's the strangest man. When he looks at you his eyes seem to bore right through you."

"He's a bore, all right," said Jim.

Gladys laughed as she always did at his jokes.

"Darling—I think I'll have a drink. I feel sort of festive in my new suit."

"That's fine," said Jim. "I'll have one with you."

He ordered. Gladys leaned toward him and patted his arm. "Do you mind me following you around?"

"Not at all."

"To tell the truth—I just couldn't sit up there any longer. I wanted to be with you, Jim."

"Glad to have you."

"I was afraid you might have to go off some place again with Mr. Riley."

"He has to go to Frisco on business."

She sat up and looked at Jim anxiously.

"You're not going, are you, darling?"

"No. He can handle it."

"Oh, I'm so happy. Will you take me to see Bob Hope tonight?"

Jim nodded slowly. He'd promised Tony he'd come to the beach but he wasn't nearly as anxious to go as he thought he'd be. Another night would do just as well.

"Oh, fine," said Gladys. "And Jim—will you take me to the Vine Street Derby for dinner so I can look for movie stars!"

"Yes. But why you want to see them is what I can't figure out!"

"You don't understand. When I was living in Minneapolis, going to movies was one of the few pleasures I had. Carl was ill most of the time and—well, I could forget myself at a movie. Those people meant a lot to me."

"It's all right with me," said Jim, "just so I don't have to get autographs for you."

Gladys laughed appreciatively. The waiter came with their drinks. Jim sat sipping his highball and thinking about Tony. She was gradually losing her power over him. He was getting used to Gladys, and compared to her Tony was coarse and common. As soon as he got Gladys settled in the movie he'd tell her he had to go out to the men's room: from there he could call Tony on a pay phone so she wouldn't sit around wondering what had happened to him.

XI

Jim was sitting in the living room waiting for Johnny's long-distance call and swearing at himself beneath his breath for having allowed Gladys to inveigle him into that damned eye examination. When he'd got back from the eye doctor's, there'd been a note for him at the desk: Mr. Riley had called from San Francisco; would call again.

He heard Gladys humming a popular tune in the bar where she was mixing a drink. He relaxed slightly, stopped swearing and smiled to himself. It was nice to have a woman like Gladys around. He'd known a lot of women but none like her. She seemed to think more about his comfort and well-being than she did about her own. And that was one for the book! In a career ranging over twenty years and at least that many states, Jim had never encountered anything resembling it— except in his mother. Of course, it had its drawbacks—she could hardly stand him out of her sight, and at times her over-solicitousness was trying—but it gave him a very comfortable feeling. He had always been so self-sufficient that he hadn't given a damn how anybody felt about him. He had never actually needed anybody: not even Johnny, who had been closest to him for a long time. Tony was another matter—but he needed her in a different sense; and that need, much to his relief, was now passing.

Jim laughed to himself. Was he changing? Imagine him allowing a woman to drag him to an eye doctor? Even Gladys. There was nothing wrong with his eyes—or very little; half the time he merely pretended that they were bothering him to explain his restlessness and boredom. Making sardonic comments to himself, he'd been ushered into a series of little rooms where he was forced to sit in front of machines that looked like complicated instruments of torture and peer through one lens after another. That wasn't so bad. But the croaker's nurse had filled his eyes with some kind of drops and for a couple of hours he'd been practically blind, and Gladys had had to lead him around.

"Yeah," he said to himself scornfully, "all I needed was a seeing-eye dog and a tin cup. Like old Gig Black in Chicago. Gig—what a character! Best cannon in the Middle West—and he had to go blind. Oh, well. That's the breaks."

Just as Gladys came in with his drink, humming happily, the phone rang. It was Johnny, calling from Frisco.

"Yeah?" said Jim.

"It's okay," said Johnny's voice. "I sprung the big punk. I also put the fear of God in him." Johnny laughed curtly. "I gave him such a scare that he begged me to hold on to his money for him. I found out he wanted to stay in Frisco, so I opened an account for him at a bank: he's going to draw his money out weekly—fifty at a time."

"Nice work." Jim glanced up. Gladys was standing across the room, pretending to read a magazine, but she was listening so hard that she was almost rigid. Jim smiled.

"I had to oil the police department a little," Johnny went on. "I'll get back in town without a dime."

"I'll look after you," said Jim. "Goodbye."

He hung up and Gladys came over with his drink. Jim pulled her down on his lap and kissed her. She ran her hand lightly across his forehead and said:

"How are your eyes, darling?"

"Great. I can almost see. I go to a doctor to get examined and he blinds me."

"I can hardly wait to see you in glasses. You'll look so distinguished."

"They'll go with my gray hair, all right, and my paunch."

"What paunch! I never saw a man with a better build than yours."

"Why—darling! I didn't know you went around staring at men's builds."

He frowned. She studied his face, unable to make up her mind whether he was joking or not.

"Well, a woman just can't help...."

Jim laughed and kissed her.

"If I didn't know you better," he said, "I'd think you had a guilty conscience."

"You don't know me at all—and I have," said Gladys, laughing.

While they were eating dinner, Jim began to wonder about Doc; he hadn't seen him for a couple of days. It was possible, of course, that Doc had decided to give up after their talk in the bar: possible, but rather unlikely. Jim just couldn't make up his mind what to do about the little doctor. It was a ticklish proposition.

After dinner they went to a movie and Jim slipped away to the men's room and called Tony. It was the third time this had happened in a week. Tony sounded sleepy and sullen; also rather indifferent Jim thought, wondering. In a short time now he'd have to make some plans in regard to Tony: Florida was the place for her. But it might take a little finagling. Before Tony said goodbye she told Jim she needed money and would he send her some. "Of course," she said, "I can't expect you to bring it—now that you're in high society." She laughed unpleasantly. Jim curtly promised her the money and hung up.

They ran into Mr. Evans in the lobby when they got back to the hotel and stopped to talk with him for a moment.

"What's happened to our little friend—the doctor?" Jim inquired.

"He's left," said Evans with a rather strange expression, Jim thought.

"Sudden, wasn't it?"

"Yes, rather. You see he became very ill the other night. Fainted. The house doctor went up to attend him. He—uh—the doctor, I mean, thought it might be better if Dr. Bright went away some place for his health."

On their way up in the elevator Jim was very thoughtful. There was something funny going on. For years, Doc had had seizures of one kind or another: Ray Slavens had always insisted that Doc was an epileptic. Jim wasn't sure; but he did know that the junk wasn't helping him any.

Jim came to himself. Gladys was squeezing his arm and looking up at him, a little worried because he was so preoccupied. But she smiled at once when he winked at her.

That night in bed Gladys said:

"Sometimes I just can't believe it."

"Believe what?"

"Well," said Gladys, "it seems like it was meant to be—us, I mean. Otherwise, I can't understand it at all. Things like this just don't happen by accident."

Jim, who had engineered the "accident," didn't know quite what to say.

"The first time I saw you—I knew," said Gladys. "You looked so big and strong and handsome. My heart almost stopped. And I knew— instantly."

"I felt almost the same," said Jim, going along with the play.

"You did not. You hardly looked at me. But I don't care. That's all over with now—that anxiety, I mean. Just think—I almost ran away from you."

"Why?"

"I was afraid."

"Of what?"

"I know other women would want you—like the blonde at the nightclub. I was afraid I couldn't stand the strain."

"Aren't we getting along all right?"

Gladys sighed deeply.

"I'm so happy I don't know what I'm doing half the time."

After a moment, Jim fell asleep. Gladys lay beside him, making no attempt to sleep, happy to be close to him, watching over him as a mother watches over a child.

XII

Jim was in the barbershop when Shake got him on the telephone. Shake was crying and was so terribly agitated that Jim couldn't make any sense out of what he was saying and, besides, Jim thought the barber was looking at him strangely. He told Shake he'd call him back and abruptly hung up.

As soon as the barber finished shaving him, he went across the street to a drugstore and used a pay phone.

"My God, what took you so long, Mr. Farrar?" Shake demanded. "It's goddamned serious. Honestly, I...."

"Is it about Doc?"

"Yes. Doc, he ..."

"All right. Give it to me fast."

"Doc worked himself into a bad jam, Mr. Farrar. He got in a row with a couple of guys and a woman in a beer joint. Just plain citizens—see? You know—softies. I guess Doc got nasty. One of the guys didn't like it so he clipped Doc on the jaw. Doc won't stand for nothing from nobody— least of all a softy. He had a cane with him—so he beats the hell out of those two guys with it. He even hit the woman—though I don't suppose he meant to...."

"Wait a minute, Shake. If you want me to get Doc out of a jam, the answer is: no."

"Don't hang up. It ain't that, Mr. Farrar. The coppers're after Doc and he's got to lam, but he says you're going to pay him first. That's what I wanted to tell you. He's looking for you right now—and Mr. Farrar: he's in a mighty bad humor. He's been feeling bad lately—and since they throwed him out of that hotel because the doctor seen all the junk he had around, he's been like a crazy man. Lucky he didn't take a fall on account of that junk. I tried to get Johnny Doyle on the phone and couldn't reach him. I tried and tried...."

"Thanks, Shake." Jim hung up, and stood for a moment meditating. What a fine bunch of no-good so-and-sos he'd got himself mixed up with. He must have been crazy to think anything good would come of mixing in with scum like Doc and his broken-down mob.

He hurried out of the drugstore and started across the street. He had gone about ten paces when he saw Doc. The little doctor, looking as seedy and shaggy as he had in the past, had seen him and was coming at him undeviatingly, his face set and white. They met at the curb just in front of the Marwood Arms.

"Farrar—I want to see you."

"All right," said Jim. "Here I am. Take a good look."

"I'm leaving town," said Doc, "and ..."

"That's fine."

"Yeah—but it's not that easy. Before I leave we got to settle that little proposition we talked over."

"This is no place to talk."

"There's a little bar right back of the hotel. We can talk there. Come on."

Doc was loaded to such an extent that Jim was surprised that people on the street didn't turn to look at him. His eyeballs were yellowish, his face was white, and the right corner of his mouth moved slowly with a slight spasmodic twitch. Jim walked along beside Doc, watching him out of the corner of his eye, trying to figure out what it was best to do. Any man in such a condition is dangerous; Doc was doubly so being a bad one to start with. Jim couldn't see what alternative he had; for the moment he'd be forced to humor Doc.

One side of Jim's nature was patient and calculating: this, together with his personality and looks, had made him a success; but there was a quick-acting, impulsive side, too, which occasionally got the upper hand, and almost always landed him in trouble. As he walked beside the little doctor, he had a sudden impulse to clip him on the jaw, take his gun away from him, and beat him unmercifully. Maybe that would take the steam out of him. The calculating side of Jim's nature held him back. But all the same a cold rage was growing inside him. Doc had to be stopped, one way or another.

They went into the dark little bar side by side, and for some reason Jim took a good look at it, noting the cheap woodwork, the dismal indirect lighting, the garishly-colored jukebox near the door; its gloomy and clandestine atmosphere. He had a strange sensation that he'd seen the little joint before—although he was certain he'd never crossed its threshold. He felt somewhat uneasy and glanced at Doc, who, looking neither to right nor left, stalked up to the bar and asked the bartender if there was a room where they could talk business. The bartender nodded.

"Straight back through that doorway. Room on the left."

"Bring us back a couple of bourbon and sodas," said Doc.

Jim, still feeling strange, followed Doc back through a narrow passageway, and into a little room in which there was a table for two, a leather couch, and a slot for the jukebox.

Doc sat down abruptly and tilted his hat over his eyes. Jim sat opposite him.

"I got myself in a little trouble," said Doc, "so I'm leaving this fair city before some stupid flatfoot catches up with me. There's an out for you— you can always yell copper."

"You're the rat in this outfit," said Jim calmly. "I never yelled copper in my life, and never will."

"Well—I was figuring maybe you were getting so respectable: married to this rich dame and all." Doc chuckled mirthlessly.

The bartender brought their drinks and as Doc made no move to pay, Jim tossed some money on the table, and told the bartender to keep the change. The bartender went out grinning.

"Always the big shot," jeered Doc. "Can't help trying to impress the yokels." Doc compressed his lips and leaned toward Jim. "A guy who does that is nothing but a yokel himself. And that's what you've always been to me, Mr. Jim Farrar—a big yokel."

Jim's fingers had begun to twitch. His cold rage was growing. In a little while, if something wasn't done, he was going to twist this damned junky's head off.

"Doc," he said, "you're a little, sick guy. But you presume on it too much. Now moderate your tone and speak your piece, before I forget myself."

"If you forget yourself, Farrar, it'll be the last thing you ever do. I got a gun on you under the table and I'll blow your guts out."

"I sometimes wonder about you, Doc. You make a lot of shooting talk. Did you ever shoot anybody?"

Doc smiled grimly.

"You got guts anyway—that's something. Look, Farrar; nobody's going to shoot anybody, as long as our play is completed. I want my dough."

Doc sounded more reasonable now. Jim decided to stall.

"How much?"

"All you can get your mitts on. I was asking a hundred grand. But that's silly at the moment. I know it takes time to raise that kind of dough."

"I got maybe three hundred bucks on me."

Doc laughed.

"That won't do. Don't you get it? I want real money—five figures."

"No," said Jim.

"All right," said Doc, decisively. "I'll go up and get it from the missus."

"Are you crazy, Doc?"

"No. Are you? I think maybe the missus might pay off. That is, when she finds out what kind of information I've got about you."

"Go ahead. There's the door. It's your word against mine—and you wouldn't stand a chance."

"I might—if I told her about the broad you got stashed at the beach."

Jim didn't move a muscle. There was a long pause. The little room became so still that the creaking of Doc's shoes as he shifted uneasily sounded loud and startling. Jim's face was grim and rigid. Doc watched him warily, gradually losing most of his cockiness. There was something extremely disquieting about the big fellow's immobility.

"That's a horse of another color," said Jim, speaking in a hollow voice, and moving his lips with an effort as if they were almost too stiff for him to handle. "I guess I better go get you some money."

Jim stood up. He had reached his limit and he wanted to get out of this dismal place, this trap, this cheap, sad little joint which had stabbed him with a premonitory fear the moment he'd stepped into it. He didn't know exactly what he was going to do. He wanted to hurry back to the hotel and see Gladys; he wanted to stall until things blew over; most of all he wanted to erase Doc from the human scene—Doc, the stinking rat; Doc, the abortionist, the junky, the disappointed big shot, who couldn't make the grade, no matter which way he tried it; Doc, the evil little man, eaten up with envy and greed: Doc, at the end of his rope, striving furiously to cause as much trouble as possible before his last long jump into oblivion.

"I don't trust you, Farrar," said Doc, a little undecided.

"You'll have to."

"Wait," said Doc. "I didn't tell you you could leave. I'm still holding a rod on you."

"It's not going to do you any good to shoot me," said Jim coldly.

"If you double-cross me...." Doc began, then paused uncertainly for a moment, "I can see a double-cross in your eyes, Farrar." Doc laughed with a touch of hysteria. "Don't do it—you'll regret it."

Jim opened the door. At that moment somebody put a nickel in the jukebox; it began to play a hot swing tune, the small loudspeaker overhead filling the little room with jumping rhythm. Doc winced at the sudden sound and got half off his chair.

"Wait here," said Jim. "I'll get you all the money I can lay my mitts on."

Doc rubbed his hand over his face; a look of bewilderment showed in his black eyes: for a moment he stared like a somnambulist. He shook his head slowly.

"I'll never see that money," he said, his voice rising shrill above the jump music. "This is it, Farrar."

Jim stared. Doc was talking wild.

"Wait for me, Doc," he said. "I'll be back."

Jim went out, closing the door behind him. He hurried through the bar and out into the sunshine. He felt sick. A minute more and he'd've killed Doc or been killed by him. He was so upset that he hardly knew where he was or what he was doing.

He walked mechanically into the lobby of the Marwood and stood waiting for the slow-moving elevator. It seemed hours before the grilled doors opened and admitted him. The elevator boy grinned and said:

"Good afternoon, Mr. Lloyd. Nice day, isn't it?"

Jim mumbled something and the boy glanced at him, wondering what was wrong.

A stranger met him when he opened the door of his suite. The stranger looked like Gladys; but obviously wasn't. He'd never imagined that Gladys could look so pale and stricken, so weak and helpless as if the world had been cut from beneath her feet.

"Jim," she said slowly, "I just talked to a man on the phone."

"I know," said Jim, who didn't feel at all surprised.

"He told me some horrible things about you. He said he was Dr. Bright and that he'd just talked to you and you were on your way up here."

"That's right," said Jim.

He pushed past Gladys, went into the bedroom, took a small bag down from a closet shelf, and lifting a false bottom, extracted a .45 automatic pistol, which he slipped into his coat pocket, then he turned and started back into the living room. Gladys tried to bar his way but he brushed her aside.

"Jim," she cried, "why did that man call me? Why did he tell me those horrible things about you? Why should you have a girl at the beach? I don't understand at all."

She was pale and shaking, but Jim looked at her unmoved, crossed the living room hurriedly, and went out slamming the door.

Gladys took several steps after him, holding out her arms feebly, then she stumbled, fell to her knees, and buried her face in the cushions on the divan. This sudden reversal of everything was too much for her: she could not get herself together. If only Jim had said something, tried to console her, lied to her, even, she might have borne up under the shock. But he'd stalked in and out of the apartment, silent and implacable, like a figure in a dream: a Jim she didn't know, couldn't imagine: a grim, relentless Jim immovably bent on some unimaginable end.

"I'll never see him again," she said. "Never again."

XIII

Jim hurried down the street afraid that Doc might get away. He had only one thought in his mind: to eliminate Doc! Nothing made any impression on him: neither the hot California sunshine, nor the roar of traffic, nor the people hurrying along this busy side street: nothing! He was completely insulated from the outside world. "Of course he'll lam," he kept telling himself; "I'll miss him sure."

But when he flung open the door of the bar there was Doc with a drink in his hand and his foot on the rail, trading jokes with the bartender, his hat at a jaunty angle, and a sardonic smile on his tight-lipped mouth.

Jim hesitated briefly. This was it, finally: the thing itself: a play that had to be completed. Jim drew his gun.

The bartender looked toward Jim, then his face turned green and he dove down behind the bar. The glass fell from Doc's hand. He was taken completely by surprise. But he was game. He whirled suddenly, made a dive toward the far wall, to throw Jim's aim off, and shoving his hand into his pocket, fired twice through the cloth, the bullets going wild and breaking the glass high above Jim's head.

Jim took careful aim and fired three times. Doc lunged forward, hit mortally, made a grab at the wall, missed, then turned slowly, took a few backward steps, leaned on a table for a moment, as if in deadly weariness, then suddenly his knees buckled, and he sank slowly, staring at Jim with blank, unseeing eyes: finally he fell full length on his face.

Jim glanced down at him, feeling nothing at all, neither pity, remorse, nor satisfaction, then he turned, ran out of the bar, and hurried across the street into the Marwood Arms garage. One glance told him that he'd never get his car out in time to make a getaway: the garage was jammed, the cars three deep. His Cadillac was back against the wall.

The garageman came toward him, smiling.

"Your car, Mr. Lloyd?"

"No, Joe," said Jim. "I've changed my mind."

He went out quickly, and turned into the alley behind the hotel. Already the hue and cry had started. The little bartender was standing in the middle of the street, bawling hysterically.

"A guy's been shot! A guy's been shot!"

XIV

Gladys came around slowly. It was as if she had been startled from a deep sleep and couldn't manage to get fully awake. She stayed with her face buried in the cushions of the divan, trying to make herself believe that she'd had a horrible dream and that in a little while she'd be laughing at her present disquietude.

A commotion in the street below finally brought her around. She could hear voices, a lot of voices, and the irritated blasting of auto horns; and then, cutting through the confused hubbub, a police car siren wailed frantically, louder and louder as it passed the hotel and turned the corner: then it stopped, leaving a strange silence.

Gladys got slowly to her feet and went to the window. Below her a crowd was milling excitedly in front of a little bar, and a pale man, hatless and in a white apron, was trying to keep them from getting in. Two burly cops swung out of the squad car and, heedlessly pushing people out of the way, went inside with the bartender. Another cop came on the run and took up his place in front of the door, waving everybody back.

Gladys watched listlessly for a moment, then she turned away. The commotion below seemed unreal, as if it were happening on another planet. She went to the bar like a sleepwalker, poured herself a drink of straight bourbon, and tossed it down, coughing and shuddering violently, then she sat on the divan and stared at the carpet. She was entirely at sea: she didn't care whether she lived or died.

After a while she lay back and closed her eyes. Tears came and ran slowly down her cheeks; but she actually felt no emotion at all: she was numb.

XV

Shake started back in amazement when he opened the door and Jim came in. The big fellow didn't look quite as smooth and unruffled as usual. His tanned face had a greyish cast to it, his necktie was awry, and his eyes had a strange, almost haunted, expression.

"What ... what happened, Mr. Farrar?" Shake faltered.

"Doc and I had a little trouble."

"I knew it," cried Shake. "I knew he'd never be satisfied till he ..." Shake stopped suddenly, stunned by a premonition. "Doc! Is he dead?"

"Very dead," said Jim, sinking into a chair, taking off his hat, and wiping his forehead which was cold and clammy.

"Cops kill him?"

"No. I did."

Shake put out a hand to steady himself, then he fell down into a chair and sat staring at the big fellow, trying to make himself realize that it had actually happened at last. For months he'd known that Doc would end on a slab in the morgue. But he'd never had any idea the big fellow would be the one to let him have it. Mr. Farrar wasn't that kind. He was a smooth operator who stayed out of trouble and let the strongarm guys and junkies kill each other off and run into jams with suckers and the law.

"You didn't," said Shake, completely bewildered.

"I did," Jim insisted. "He asked for it. When I wouldn't pay off he told my wife about Tony, my girl. It was a rat trick and he got what was coming to him."

Shake nodded slowly.

"Yes, Mr. Farrar—he did."

"Look, Shake," said Jim. "I'm in a jam. I've only got a couple hundred bucks on me and I couldn't get my car out of the hotel garage—it was parked back of two other cars...."

"Just a minute though, Mr. Farrar," Shake put in, showing more alertness than Jim had ever seen him show before. "Doc lives here with me off and on. The cops'll be sure to turn up here sooner or later, and maybe sooner. Anybody see you come in?"

"No," said Jim.

"Good. There's a room right down the hall in such bad shape that it can't be rented: plumbing's on the fritz, everything's wrong with it. A floating crap game uses it sometimes—that's all. I think the proprietor's okay, but we won't take no chances with him unless we have to. I'll put you back there right now."

"Swell," said Jim.

Shake got up and Jim followed him down the dark corridor of the rickety little hotel, and into a stuffy, boxlike room. The blinds were drawn and it was dark inside.

"This is it," said Shake, grinning apologetically. "It ain't much. But I guess you can stand it for a little while."

"Yeah," said Jim, sitting down wearily, and taking out his wallet. "Look, Shake. You go get me a U-Drive-It car. Also try to call Johnny at Santa Monica. And give this number a couple of rings. It's my beach number. If you get Johnny at either place, tell him I'll meet him at the Ship—to wait. I'm goddamned," said Jim jumping up, suddenly irritated, "if it's not enough to drive a guy crazy. If I don't want Johnny I can't get rid of him. If I need him I have to send out the militia."

"Now you take it easy, Mr. Farrar. I'll get out of here quick before the coppers show. I'll go out the back, and I'll come in that way. I may miss 'em even if they're looking for me. If anybody'd happen to come in here while I'm gone you tell 'em you're waiting for the other crapshooters—there's a game."

"Okay. And thanks, Shake. You got more on the ball than I thought."

Shake grinned feebly.

"It's sort of like old times. I been in plenty jams, Mr. Farrar. And I used to be pretty nimble. Course I ain't the man I was." He shook his head slowly, then went out, softly closing the door.

He crept down the back stairs and started across a dingy alley full of garbage cans and trash. With a sudden wrenching he thought of Doc. Things would never be the same again without him—but it was better in a way. Poor old Doc was out of his misery now. Shake felt no animosity toward Jim. Shake had been a racket man all his life; he believed in and lived according to their code. Doc had always been in a state of confusion. He could never make up his mind whether he was on the legit, or a crook. It was impossible to explain to him that you did certain things a certain way or you were in trouble. Doc had been guilty of the unforgivable—and so he'd been taken care of. It was only justice.

Shake nodded to himself as he emerged from the alley into a side street.

"Yep," he said, "Doc just wouldn't learn. He thought the world belonged to him."

XVI

From time to time Jim glanced at his watch. Shake had been gone nearly two hours and he was beginning to wonder if he hadn't better take a chance by himself. It wasn't that he didn't trust the old con man: Shake had always had the reputation of being one hundred per cent right: he might bungle things but he wouldn't put the finger on you. No, he wasn't worried about a double-cross. But the coppers might have got their hands on Shake.

Jim paced up and down impatiently for a moment, then he went over to the window, pushed the blind aside and stood looking out into the dingy, narrow street. Dirty-faced Mexican and Italian kids were running up and down, yelling. An occasional car, taking a short cut, honked its way between the grimy brick buildings, avoiding the kids, fat old women, and commission-house trucks, which were backed up to the curb. Beyond the slum area, loomed the big buildings of downtown Los Angeles, looking a little misty in the early evening.

Pictures began to flash before Jim's eyes: Gladys, stricken and helpless, holding out her hands to him; Doc ducking for the wall, trying his last conniving trick, before the lead caught up with him, the greenish-faced little man in the white apron standing in the middle of the busy side street, hysterically yelling his lungs out.

Jim jogged himself back to the present with a quick shake of his head. No use crying over spilt milk. He had things to do. It wasn't a first-degree rap: Doc had started the shooting. Of course Jim's witness, the little bartender, had been down behind the bar when the shooting occurred, but with the right kind of handling he might be persuaded to give a good account of himself in the witness chair.

"Providing I want to stand trial," said Jim, and then suddenly there rushed over him such a feeling of despair that he groaned aloud and bent forward slightly as if in pain. The world looked black and hopeless. He thought about the long fight with the law he'd have to make, months in jail, endless wrangles with lawyers, fixers, and front men; and then after all that agony—maybe a conviction, and a stiff stretch: even up to twenty years. Jim recoiled, and stood cursing Doc, and trying to fight down useless regrets. If he'd never told Pop Gruber where he'd be: if Pop had ignored Doc: if Johnny had ignored Pop: if he'd ignored Johnny— the futile procession of "ifs" lengthened out interminably.

Jim pulled himself up short. "I've got to find Johnny," he said aloud, decisively, trying to talk down his feeling of hopelessness. "And I got to get my money." He glanced down into the street, thinking for a moment that he saw Shake, then he let the blind fall back into place. "Let's see," he mused, "how much dough have I got at the beach? Between fifty and sixty grand...."

At the sound of a guarded footstep in the hall, he turned. There was a soft knock at the door, and Shake's voice muttered: "It's me, Mr. Farrar."

Jim opened the door.

"What happened to you, Shake?"

"God, I'm glad you stayed," said Shake, looking hot and exhausted. "I was afraid you'd think I'd sold you out or something. I was back an hour ago, and damned near ran into a couple of harness bulls, looking for me. They stayed around till just now. I was hiding back in a ware shed."

"Got the car?" Shake nodded. "Good," said Jim. "Say—did you locate Johnny?"

"No. He checked out of the hotel, and nobody answered at the beach."

"He what?"

"That's what they told me. He was gone all morning, then he came and checked out."

"That's damned funny," said Jim, staring.

"Come on, Mr. Farrar. We better be going."

"You're not going, Shake," said Jim. "You've done your part. Thanks a million."

Shake was very lonesome. He wanted to go along with the big fellow in spite of the danger. With Windy in San Francisco and Doc dead he had nobody. True he had the books he'd always dreamed of and the leisure to read them and nobody to bother him: but at night he couldn't sleep from loneliness. Dreams are fine, Shake had discovered, if you don't realize them.

"I could be a big help. I'm just rusting here, Mr. Farrar. If you're figuring on going to Mexico, I know all the angles."

"Mexico's my best bet. I want to hole up till I can get things organized and locate Johnny. He's got to put the wheels in motion for me. Maybe he can make a decent deal with the D.A. If so I could come in and give myself up. But they're not dragging me in till I know what's what."

"Yeah," said Shake, eagerly, "you got it right. Mexico's the place to hole up. I know a guy in Bellamy, Arizona, who'll look after you and get you across the border without any trouble at all. And on top of that he can get you any kind of credentials you want."

Jim studied Shake, who looked pale and agitated. His dewlap was trembling with emotion.

"What's your angle, Shake? You're clear; not wanted. Why put your neck in a noose?"

Shake lowered his eyes and shifted in embarrassment. "Well—I'm just sort of dying on the vine, sitting around here. I haven't been in action so long I ..."

"All right, Shake.... Let's go."

A broad smile spread over Shake's fat, pale face.

"I figure I'll just lock up my room and blow," he said; "if I get back—fine. If not—it won't matter to nobody one way or another."

XVII

The sun had set and a beautiful summer evening was closing down as they neared the ocean. Shake was driving. When they reached a big suburb, where the houses were widely spaced and the traffic was light, Jim told him to pull over to the curb and park. Shake obeyed, then sat glancing at Jim, who took out his gun, wiped it clean, and leaning out of the car, tossed it down a manhole grating.

"That's that," said Jim, as Shake started off. "I was hoping that I'd never have to use that heater."

They drove along in silence for a long time. Shake sat thinking calmly about Doc: poor crazy Doc: Always jumpy and irritable and sore at the world, and hating everybody.... In the old days Doc had had his points: he'd been lively and witty and full of very funny sardonic comments on everything. What an eye for sham he'd had: nothing took him in. Shake sighed deeply. He was going to miss Doc: he'd never forget him.

At a curve in the road they came to the top of a hill and before them was the sea, glistening faintly under a soft lavender-blue mist in the fading evening glow. A slim silver new moon seemed to float above the sea, light as a feather. The dimmed-out shoreline showed a few vague and distant points of light.

"Pretty, ain't it?" Shake observed, and Jim nodded.

It was night when they got to Jim's beach house. Two sailors from the Coast Guard were patrolling the road, with rifles slung across their shoulders. Jim spoke to them and they answered with distant politeness.

"I never been down here before," said Shake as the sailors went on. "Brother—this is something. You can't see your hand before your face."

They got out and groped their way around the house and Jim fumbled with his key at the front door. As he was opening the door, he noticed that a big car was parked a few feet down the road, and suddenly he remembered that night he'd surprised Tony. But there wasn't a light showing any place in the house, and when he stepped into the pitch-black living room it was so still that the ticking of a clock seemed to fill it with sound. Jim was positive there was no one in the house: there was a feeling of abandonment in the atmosphere.

He switched on a light.

"Nice place you got here, Mr. Farrar," said Shake, respectfully.

"Yeah," Jim replied, absently; then he hurried into the bedroom and

turned on the lights. Tony had gone, that was obvious at a glance. All
her toilet articles had disappeared from the dressing table. He opened
the closet; it was empty except for a lot of forlorn-looking coat hangers.

"Well, I'll be damned," said Jim with a grim laugh. "She sure picked
the right time to blow."

He went back into the living room.

"Mr. Farrar," said Shake, "I thought I heard somebody prowling around
outside."

"Probably the Coast Guard guys on their way back. You stay here,
Shake. I got to go down to the locker room."

Jim hurried down the narrow stairway and with a key he took from
his wallet; he started to open one of the locker doors, but instead he
stopped and stared: it was already unlocked and slightly ajar. He flung
it back violently and, kneeling down, lifted out a small, tin strongbox,
shaking it as he stood up. There was something in it all right; but it
didn't seem heavy enough. It had also been unlocked. Jim raised the lid
and his heart contracted. All his money was gone. There was nothing in
the box but a sealed envelope.

He went over to the unshaded bulb which hung from the ceiling by a
cord, and was the only light in the room, and holding the envelope up
he stared at it. It was addressed to him in a handwriting he knew;
Johnny's. He tore it open and read the enclosure:

Jim:
I'll probably hang myself for this later. But I've gone south with all
your dough, figuring you don't need it now. I got drunk one night and
told Tony about it. You can write the rest. I'm sorry I turned out to be
such a rat. I'm surprised at myself. Tony's with me—and in that respect
I guess I'm doing you a favor.
J.

Jim began to laugh; he leaned against the wall and laughed for a long
time. This was the limit. Johnny and Tony. Who could have imagined
such a combination?

Suddenly he realized that what he was laughing at wasn't funny. He
pulled himself up with an effort, knowing that he was on the verge of
hysteria. He had no lawyer and no dough. Why lam for Mexico now?
What was the point in it?

Through a fog he heard Shake calling to him. He hurried to the foot of
the stairs.

"Yeah?" he shouted.

"You better come up here, Mr. Farrar. It was a dame prowling around.
She's waiting on the porch. I wouldn't let her in."

Tony!

Jim compressed his lips and came up the stairs three at a time.

"She says she seen you come in and she's got to talk to you. I told her,
I said, 'Listen, sister...'"

Jim rushed to the door and flung it open, then he started back. It was Gladys. She was holding out her hands to him. "Jim! Jim!" she said.

He caught her just as she started to fall and carried her to the big divan. Shake stared at him open-mouthed.

"It's my wife," said Jim. "Get her a drink. Whiskey. Right in there."

"No kidding," cried Shake, staring overcome. He'd heard the truth about Jim and the million-dollar sucker from Doc, who'd finally broken down and told him.

Jim began to unfasten Gladys's clothes. Coming to himself, Shake made a dash for the whiskey, stumbling and nearly falling in his haste.

XVIII

Gladys didn't come around fully for some time. But both Jim and Shake breathed easier when she began to move her hands about, and they both smiled with relief when she opened her eyes—even if she did close them again at once.

Finally Gladys spoke:

"Where's that girl?"

Embarrassed, Shake cleared his throat and turned away.

"She's gone," said Jim. "For good."

"Why did you have her here, Jim? I can't understand that at all."

Shake moved farther off and became intensely interested in a picture on the wall.

"I knew her before I met you," said Jim, rather curtly, Shake thought. "Anyway—what does it matter now?"

"At least," said Gladys weakly, "I'm glad you knew her before."

Shake turned.

"Mr. Farrar, maybe I better step outside for a minute."

"Go in the bedroom, Shake, and shut the door. Make yourself comfortable."

"Yes, sir. Thanks."

Shake hurried out, sighing with relief, and when the bedroom door closed behind him he addressed his image in the dressing table mirror: "He talks to her just like she was anybody—a woman with all that dough! I just can't understand it. Funny fellow, Mr. Farrar is. I wish I knew how he feels inside. Not like me—that's a cinch." Shake studied his pale, flabby countenance for a moment, then he shrugged, turned away, and sat down on the bed. "I never was much on looks," he mused, "even at my best. I guess I'm the quiet, homey type." He giggled briefly at his own wit, then he began to look around him, sniffing. "Brother!" he exclaimed. "I'd sure like to meet the babe that stunk this place up. Certainly smells expensive. Sort of oriental, like the stuff Cleopatra must've used—way back in the Middle Ages." Shake sat with his hands on his knees, thinking about how beautiful the Nile Queen must have looked in those far-off days he'd read about so many times in books he'd picked up in various penitentiary libraries. Shake loved to fall into daydreams and pretend that he was living in what he referred to as "old history days": especially when he was at peace—as he was at the moment: owing to the fact that he had attached himself to Jim. All his life Shake had been attaching himself to somebody, always with unpleasant or disastrous results. But, as he was very simple and of an optimistic nature, he kept trying. Jim was the best yet, even if he was in a jam.

Gladys felt so much better now that she was sitting up. She and Jim looked at each other in silence for a long time. She hardly knew him. He had dropped all pretense and looked like a different man: a strange male, handsome, remote, impersonal. At the moment it was impossible for her to imagine that they'd ever been close. Suddenly she thought about that night in Mexico: they'd had champagne and she was feeling very carefree and gay: they'd gone out on the balcony to listen to the music which drifted up from the cantina across the street: beyond the town the mountains loomed, black and huge under the starry sky.

"What are you thinking about?" asked Jim, made a little uneasy by the long silence.

"I was thinking about that night on the balcony of the Mexican hotel. You probably don't even remember."

"I remember."

Gladys glanced at him, noting his set, unsmiling face and the harsh lines about his mouth. When she'd first heard that he was suspected of killing the strange little doctor, it had seemed fantastic to her; especially so as she'd got the information from Mr. Evans, who was silly and flighty, like an old maid. It was utterly incredible that the Jim Lloyd she knew could even contemplate such a thing—let alone do it. Now she understood. She had seen behind the smooth mask of lazy good nature.

She took a folded-up newspaper from her pocket and handed it to Jim. The front page was filled with war news and garbled accounts of the confused doings of the Washington bureaucrats. The stuff about the killing was on the second page. Doc had been identified, his record unearthed. But Jim was referred to as James Lloyd, wealthy oil man. It was conjectured that he'd been swindled by Doc, the con man, and had taken his revenge. Jim read the account carelessly and threw the paper aside.

"Your name is not really Lloyd, is it, Jim?" asked Gladys.

"No," said Jim. "I've used a lot of them, but my real name is James Driscoll. Most people think my name is Farrar."

"You married me for my money in cold blood, didn't you, Jim?"

"Yes."

"That's what the little doctor told me. But I didn't pay any attention to him till he mentioned the girl—Toby."

"Tony."

"That's right. What happened to her?"

"She left."

The color had come back into Gladys's face. She felt much better, but she was so confused by Jim's blunt answers that she could think of nothing to say, and there was a long pause. Gladys took out her compact and tidied her hair, glancing into the little mirror. Jim watched her absently, trying to figure out just what it was best to do. Mexico was the safest place to jump to, considering that Shake knew the ropes, but he needed a stake and needed it bad. If it came to the worst, he could always hit Shake, who certainly must have quite a hunk of his cut left. But he hated to do it. Shake was broken down and one of the boys: he'd never yet played a guy in the profession for a sucker.

"How did you get here?" Jim asked suddenly.

Gladys glanced at him quickly.

"The little doctor told me just where to come. I thought you might be here. First, I tried to get in; then I waited and waited."

"I don't mean that. Did you drive?"

"Of course."

"In what?"

"Your car."

Jim leaped up, hurried across the room, and flung open the bedroom door. Shake was lying on the bed, luxuriously smoking a cigarette, and smiling to himself. Jim thought he looked like a silly fool. But Shake was happy; he was thinking about how it must have been in the "old history days."

"Shake!"

The con man sat up, open-mouthed, jerked back so suddenly to reality by Jim's curt tone that he was a little confused. "Yeah, Mr. Farrar. I was just ..."

"My car's outside. Take it down the road and ditch it some place. Then call up the U-Drive-It joint: tell them you want to keep the car all night. Make it good so we won't have 'em reporting the car to the coppers as missing."

"Okay, Mr. Farrar."

When Shake had gone, Gladys said:

"I never thought about the car."

"It's all right."

Jim turned and paced up and down restlessly.

"I can't tell you how all at sea I feel," said Gladys. "You seem like a complete stranger."

"I am," said Jim curtly.

Gladys looked at him, then she compressed her lips and spoke so determinedly, that Jim stared at her in surprise.

"No, you're not. You're married to me."

"What do you mean, Gladys?"

"I mean I'm going to stay with you. Have you any money?"

Jim sat down, studying his wife, puzzled. "Wait a minute. You haven't got any idea what you're letting yourself in for. I'm wanted for murder. If you help me or go around with me—with full knowledge: which they can prove—you're an accessory. It's a felony. They can send you up."

"To me those are just so many words."

Jim groaned.

"You've got to be sensible, Gladys."

"Why?"

"Look. You're a nice respectable woman. I'm what's known as a racket man. No future for you. Nothing but trouble."

"You didn't answer my question," said Gladys, ignoring his remarks. "Have you any money?"

"No. Not much."

"I gathered up everything I could get my hands on. I thought you might need it. I've got over fifteen hundred dollars in my handbag and jewelry worth at least thirty thousand."

"You shouldn't be running around alone at night with …" Jim paused and swore briefly, then he held out his hand. "Give it to me."

Gladys picked up her handbag and held it out to him. He took it from her, stripped it of the money and jewelry, which he stuffed into his pocket, then he handed it back to her.

"Now, look," he said. "I'm hitting for Mexico with Shake. We'll drop you off near a bus stop. When you get back report the car as stolen. If the cops question you, tell them you were out looking for me. You went in some place to phone and somebody copped the car."

"No," said Gladys, stubbornly, "I'm going with you."

"You're crazy," cried Jim, standing off and studying Gladys, wondering if maybe she wasn't a little batty after all. Was this any way for a well-brought-up woman to act?

"That is possible."

"But I don't get it."

"It's very simple. I love you, Jim."

"Yeah, yeah," said Jim, impatiently. "So you love me. But what's that? There's a time for everything, and this is just no time for love."

Gladys got up and came toward him.

"You'll never understand, Jim. I know that now. But I just can't live without you. I don't care what you've done."

Bewildered, Jim took her in his arms and mechanically kissed her and stroked her hair. "I've seen some crazy dames in my time," he told himself, "but …" He stood shaking his head.

"Gladys," he said wearily, "I'm going to have to go all over this again. You've just never been up against things like I have. You don't know what you're running into. They're bound to catch up with me some day; they'll take you, too. And you'll have to do a stretch in some damned dirty women's prison. My God—be reasonable. Do what I say. Then you'll be safe."

"No," said Gladys with complete finality.

Jim drew away from her and ran his hand across his eyes. The strain was beginning to tell on him. He sat down suddenly and stared morosely at the carpet.

"Okay. I'm just as nuts as you are if I take you along. But—okay."

Gladys glanced at him, then sat down on the divan opposite him.

"Jim," she said softly, "there's a question I want to ask you. It worries me. You don't have to answer if you don't want to."

Jim looked up.

"Yeah?"

"It's about Doctor Bright." She glanced at Jim anxiously, afraid he'd react in some violent manner. She expected him at least to wince away from the thought of the little dead doctor.

"What about him?" Jim asked indifferently.

Gladys paused for a moment, trying to find words for what she wanted to say.

"I've been worrying ever since I heard about it—although at first I couldn't believe it. I mean, I've been worrying about its effect on you—your feelings. I...." Gladys faltered badly, then came to a full stop.

"You mean you figure I might go nuts with remorse?"

"Well ..." Gladys began hesitantly.

But Jim burst out laughing.

"Don't worry about that. He asked for it and he got it. Usually, in this business, a rat doesn't live to be forty-five. Doc just rode his luck to a fall."

"I see," said Gladys, staring at Jim, trying to grasp his meaning. And suddenly she realized that a great abyss separated them: he could never really understand her; she could never really understand him. It was a sad and somewhat terrifying thing to contemplate, and yet, actually, it made no real difference to her.

Jim had got up again and was pacing the floor when Shake came back. The con man entered hat in hand, smiling apologetically, and avoiding Gladys's eyes out of embarrassment.

"I took care of everything, Mr. Farrar," he said. "I found a good spot for the car. There's a joint down the road: roadhouse, dancing place, drive-in: you know. And it's packed. What a crowd. So I parked there—got a ticket, everything. If nobody comes for the car before twelve, the parking guys won't think nothing of it. They'll just go home. It's better than leaving it on the road."

"Nice work," said Jim.

"I even got a hitch back," said Shake, grinning, feeling very proud because the big fellow was praising him. "I also took care of the U-Drive-It guy. All set."

"Fine."

Gladys said nothing. She sat staring at Shake. The man must be a criminal, like Jim; but he looked even less like one. He had a very kind face and a soft manner. You'd trust him on sight.

"Let's get started," said Jim, abruptly. "My wife's going with us."

Shake stared, completely flabbergasted.

"You mean, she ...!" He was unable to go on.

"Yes," said Jim. "I can't talk her out of it."

Shake didn't know what to say. He stood shaking his head helplessly. This was going to make it tougher, much tougher. Every cop in the country would be looking for her.

"I don't know, ma'am," he said. "This is no picnic."

Jim had Shake pull up at an important intersection of a remote Los Angeles suburb. They'd been on their way for nearly an hour. Jim was riding in front with Shake, letting Gladys have the whole back seat to herself. He intended to travel five or six hundred miles before daylight, he and Shake spelling each other at the wheel, and he wanted Gladys to be able to relax as much as possible. He'd given her a worn old top coat he'd had at the beach and a couple of blankets he'd taken off Tony's bed. It got cold at night, driving through the desert.

He turned.

"Gladys—listen. There's a bus stop right over there and it's still early. This is your last chance. From here on we roll: no stops. Think it over."

"It's no use, Jim."

Gladys wrapped herself up in the overcoat and settled back.

"Okay."

Before they started off, Jim bought the second edition of a morning paper, and lit the overhead light to read it.

"Go ahead," he said to Shake.

Jim made a sudden movement and Shake glanced at it.

"Anything wrong?"

"No. Just keep driving."

They'd identified him. Some smart guy on the bunco squad had figured it out. Jim read his description, smiling to himself ironically.

"James Lloyd, alias Jim Farrar, alias Reed Wallace, alias James Driscoll. Forty years old. Six feet tall and weighing about a hundred and eighty-five pounds. Fair complexion, tanned. Grayish-brown hair, curly. Well-dressed and supposed to be handsome ..."

"Supposed to be, is right," thought Jim.

"... he is of an athletic build and very strong. He looks like a prosperous man of affairs, and has a polite manner. He stays at the best hotels and is a big tipper. When last seen he was wearing a brown tweed suit, a tan shirt, dark brown tie, and light brown pork-pie hat..."

"Not bad," thought Jim, "not bad at all."

He switched off the overhead light.

"What's in the paper, Jim?" asked Gladys.

"You can read it later. I'll save it." Then he turned to Shake. "When we get out in the country, pull up a side road. I'm going to change my clothes and ditch this outfit."

"Okay," said Shake.

XIX

Jim was driving now with the accelerator almost to the floor. Gladys was lying down in the back seat, wrapped up in the coat and the blankets, sleeping like a child. The strain of the last few hours had finally overcome her. She was completely exhausted.

Occasionally Shake, who was sitting beside Jim, dozing intermittently, glanced at the big fellow, noting how grim and set his face looked in the pale glow from the dash. The con man would shake his head slowly from side to side. He'd seen some funny ones in his day, but this was the funniest of all: the sucker lamming with the one who'd thrown the chisel. It just didn't make any kind of sense.

It was a beautiful clear night. A white moon had risen slowly above the peaks of the big, distant mountains, and the desert floor was flooded with moonlight, looking bluish-white and eerie. Black clumps of mesquite and greasewood flashed past the speeding car and made Shake feel a little dizzy when he glanced out the window. The black deserted road with its sharp white line rushed at them ceaselessly, straight as a railroad track for miles, then taking erratic turns, which caused Jim to throw the wheel over suddenly. At times Shake grew cold with fear; he hadn't ridden at this speed for years: but the sight of Jim's big-knuckled, capable hands grasping the wheel reassured him. The big fellow knew what he was doing: he was a good guy to tie to.

"This friend of yours," Jim said, speaking out of the side of his mouth, never taking his eyes from the road, "can he get us a car?"

"He can get you anything," said Shake with a nervous giggle. "And he ain't too hungry for dough: not like some guys, I mean. You see, I done him a good turn in stir once; and he's not the kind of guy who forgets. The good turn cost me a jolt in solitary—so it was worth something. Boy, I'll never forget that." Shake sat thinking about those interminable black days, that feeling of being buried alive and abandoned to your fate. "Solitary's sure hell," he observed.

"I guess it is," said Jim. "I don't know anything about it personally. I know it made a lunatic out of Fargo. Course he was kind of crazy to start with."

"You cooled him off once, didn't you?"

"Yeah," said Jim, indifferently. "Look, Shake. Your friend's got to get somebody to drive this car back to Phoenix and ditch it."

"Don't you worry, Mr. Farrar. I'll take care of everything."

There was a long pause. The car topped a rise in the desert floor and for a moment they could see the flat, moonlit wasteland stretched out before them for miles, then the car dipped down and as they crossed a deep draw nothing was visible but the starry sky and the clumps of mesquite along the borders of the road. At last they came out onto the flat again. Ahead of them, half blinded by the headlights, a coyote crossed the road leisurely, staring at them, its eyes glowing red. Jim slowed down a little to keep from hitting it.

"I'd sure hate to be that coyote," said Shake, shivering slightly. "Out here in this Godforsaken place all alone."

"Oh, I don't know," said Jim, and Shake glanced at him, expecting him to laugh, but he didn't. There was a long pause, then Jim said: "Take a look at the missus. See if she's all right."

Shake turned and looked, then he smiled. "Sleeping like a baby— sound as can be."

"She must be worn out," said Jim. "She doesn't even sleep good in bed."

There was another long pause, then Shake spoke.

"This friend of mine, he'll get us across the border with no trouble at all. There's a pretty good-sized town about a hundred miles or so from the border where some guys I know have hid out in the last few years. None of them ever had any trouble. Harry—that's my friend—he looks after them A-one if they're right. He knows all about you, Mr. Farrar— who doesn't? He'll be tickled to death to see you."

"Pretty good-sized town, eh? I hope so. Those little Mexican whistle stops are something for the book. A guy might just as well be in stir."

"Yeah." Shake paused for a moment, then glanced at Jim. "Say—ain't you been at it quite a spell? Want me to take it?"

"Okay."

He pulled up at the side of the road and they changed places. The stopping of the car woke Gladys. She sat up and stared around her wildly. She couldn't figure out where she was. All about her was nothing but silent moonlit desert, looking like a vast landscape on a dead planet.

"Jim!" she called. "Where are you?"

"I'm right here, honey. How you making out?"

"Fine. But please come back here with me."

"You'll rest better if I stay up here."

"No, I won't." There was a plaintive note in her voice that gave Jim a strange feeling: it was like a kid calling out in the dark.

He got into the back seat with her. He put his arm around her and she snuggled down and put her head on his shoulder. "Is it much farther?" she asked, sleepily.

Jim laughed.

"Quite a bit. Just relax."

Gladys closed her eyes and in a moment went back to sleep, sighing contentedly.

"We're doing fine, Mr. Farrar," said Shake after a while. "I know that little town up ahead."

"Good," said Jim, wanting a cigarette badly, but refraining for fear he'd disturb Gladys.

As he sat there thinking and watching the desert rush by, it suddenly occurred to him that this was an insane thing he was doing. Why had he brought Gladys along?

"Nice going," he told himself. "You must be losing your grip. You should've made her stay in L.A. It's no good for her and no good for you."

He shook his head in irritation. Damn it—what was happening to him? He wanted a cigarette and he was going to have one. Moving gently, he slipped his hand into his pocket. Gladys stirred and murmured in her sleep. He froze.

"Oh, well," he thought, "I can have one later."

XX

It was siesta time and the Mexican town was as empty of movement as a vacant moving picture set, which it resembled. In fact, even in the cool of the early evening, when the citizens crowded the plazas, San Gorgonio looked not unlike something you'd expect to see on a movie lot. It was a big town but with a primitive Mexican character; thousands of adobe houses were jammed together along the narrow, crooked streets; at night, oil lamps burned in the windows; and in the main plaza stood a huge, decaying old cathedral, with worn steps leading up to it, and high overhead a notched and corroded belfry in which was a huge bell, whose iron clangor filled the town on Sundays and stirred to sluggish activity the torpid black buzzards which roosted on the cathedral roof.

The sun was beating down with what seemed like a purposeful ferocity. Heat glanced off the white buildings, the sunlight was dazzling, and when a brief breeze stirred it was like a breath from a furnace.

Jim was sitting alone in a big cantina drinking a bottle of very good cold beer. He just couldn't get into the habit of sleeping in the afternoon. Gladys had begged him to try it, and he had; but with bad results. He'd turned and tossed on the hot sheets, sweating like a bull, and getting more and more irritated. It was no use. He had to sleep at night. Anyway the heat didn't bother him as long as he went about his activities as usual, ignoring it. Both Shake and Gladys had got so that they looked forward to siesta time: Shake, because he was just naturally lazy and trifling and preferred sleeping to anything else; Gladys, because she was nervous and rundown and needed as much rest as she could get.

Jim groaned inwardly, thinking about Gladys. Day by day it became more apparent to him that this couldn't last: the strain on Gladys would soon be more than she could bear. Nothing in her life had prepared her for such a situation as this: and besides, she was of a delicate nature, very high-strung and sensitive. Without courage, she might have turned into one of those boring, nervous invalids: too good for this world. But Gladys fought her nature savagely, and the more Jim was with her the more respect he had for her: At times she irritated him by her over-solicitousness and by her desire to be with him constantly; but after all, these were minor matters. Gladys was strictly okay.

Jim, who was not introspective by nature, and seldom gave a thought to anything except self-aggrandizement in one form or another, would often try to figure out just how he felt about Gladys. But he always gave it up ultimately as a bad job. He just didn't know. It was a new experience for him. He'd never met a woman anything like her. All the women he'd known were almost as promiscuous as himself, or on the chisel. You knew what you were doing. But with Gladys a new element had entered into his life, upsetting all his preconceived notions. The thought of applying the word "love" to what he felt never occurred to him: that overworked word had been bandied about so much that it had become practically meaningless. He'd heard too many cheap broads drivel on about love: most of them cheating on one guy or another. It reminded him of a dame he used to take around once in a while in Florida: she was married to a nice guy who gave her everything; but she two-timed him with any good-looking fellow who would take the trouble to make a pass at her; then she used to disgust Jim by getting sentimental over some silly movie and crying when things weren't going too well for the young screen lovers.

Mush! Silly, cheap, meaningless mush!

No—that wasn't the way he felt about Gladys. And as for the sex angle—well, in that respect women weren't too different. What really puzzled Jim most was, that for the first time in his life he felt acutely responsible for someone else's welfare. That was it. He'd got so he thought about Gladys first and himself next. But why?

Jim started on his second bottle of beer, and relit his cigar, which had gone out. It was almost impossible to realize that things could get into such a muddle in so short a time. One minute he'd been on top of the heap: married to a million bucks, a respected citizen—at least around the Marwood—and with a very sharp lawyer, who could look out for him, and an extremely handsome and lively broad stashed. Bang: just like that! And it was all over.

"Maybe the boys were right," he mused; "yeah; maybe I just don't give a damn anymore."

He thought about Tony and Johnny for a moment, then dismissed them from his mind. Why worry about that now? Anyway—he knew the answer. Johnny was no rat and no pushover. Tony had just been too much for him, and to Jim that was understandable. If Gladys hadn't come along, he himself would have been as far overboard about Tony as Johnny was.

"The damned little Irish fool," said Jim without bitterness, "will he be sorry!"

A few minutes later Shake showed up, looking for him. Jim winced slightly. Poor old Shake was such a bore, always drooling on about the past. He had on a wrinkled tropical suit and sweat was dripping off his chin. He sat down wearily across from Jim and leaned his elbows on the table.

"Hi, Shake."

"Hello, Mr. Farrar. I didn't sleep so good today. Anyway—a damned bellboy woke me up with a special-delivery letter. Bad news."

"Yeah? What?"

"The heat's on in L.A. You're wanted for kidnapping now, too; on account of the missus. Course nobody can figure she went with you on her own hook. I still don't understand it myself."

"What about Lonergan?"

"He says: nix. He can't make no deal with the D.A. at the moment— and he wants some more money. Lonergan, I mean."

"Damn! I've seen some hungry guys in my day: but lawyers get all the marbles!"

"He says we've got to lay low. It would be murder to come in now."

"We've got to get in pretty soon. Gladys can't stand much more of this. I wish she'd listen to reason and go in with you. Then I could stay here and everything'd be okay."

"Yeah," said Shake, thoughtfully.

"Don't say anything to her about this," Jim admonished, sharply.

Shake was hurt. His loose mouth dropped.

"Why—Mr. Farrar. You know me better than that."

Jim went out on the balcony for a breath of fresh air. San Gorgonio was over three thousand feet up and at night a cool fresh wind always blew from the east. Below him the streets were brightly lighted, battered old cars were driving about the plaza, and music was drifting out of the open doors of the many cantinas. The sky was clear and starry; the air dry and crisp. In the bright moonlight Jim could see the buzzards sleeping all in a row, with their heads under their wings, on the edge of the cathedral roof.

Suddenly he thought about Santa Cruz and that other night on the balcony when Gladys, who meant nothing to him then, felt romantically inclined and he wanted to make wisecracks, but refrained.

Here he was on the balcony alone: but the town below him might just as well be Santa Cruz, the lights looked the same, the mountains loomed just as high beyond the town, the same music rose from the street. It was as if a scene was being repeated, but with ironic overtones now, just to show the meaningless of all scenes, of all life—everything.

Jim turned away, terribly depressed. Gladys was calling him from the bed. He was so worried about her he couldn't think of anything else. She looked white and exhausted. But he knew better now than to argue with her about going back to Los Angeles with Shake. It would do no good. She'd merely get so thoroughly upset by the argument that she wouldn't be able to sleep the whole night.

"Yes, honey," he said.

"You're not happy, are you?"

"Well ..."

"I know you're not. It's this town. It's the monotony. It's me."

"No, it's not."

"I've certainly caused you a lot of trouble, Jim."

"Oh, not so much."

Gladys lay staring at the ceiling listening absently to the music. Jim sat down wearily in a chair beside the bed.

"Aren't you going to get undressed, Jim?" asked Gladys, turning.

Jim hesitated.

"Oh, I guess so." He got up yawning and began to unbutton his shirt.

Gladys turned her face away. She was crying but he pretended not to see. Boy, she was really in bad shape; her nerves all shot; something just had to be done.

He quickly threw on his pajamas, switched off the light, and got into bed. Gladys turned to him and he held her in his arms till she fell asleep. Gradually he eased her away from him and got her into a comfortable position; then he sighed, rolled over on his back, and lay staring at the dim reflection of the streetlights on the ceiling. The music sounded sad and faraway.

"I'll bet I don't sleep a wink," Jim said, and in a minute was asleep.

But he woke up with a start some time later, feeling very depressed and nervous. He'd had the old dream again, and it had run true to form with scarcely a variation. Jim lay swearing and trying to get himself in hand. Was it a prophecy? There was nothing fantastic or impossible about it—it could happen. And for a long time he lay rigid, struggling against the conviction that it *would* happen, that it was a dead certainty.

But gradually he calmed himself, got into a more comfortable position, and was just drifting into sleep, when Gladys woke him up, shaking. She was having a nervous chill, her teeth were chattering, and she was cold as ice. Scared, Jim jumped out of bed, filled a hot water bottle and rushed back with it, stumbling in his haste. He switched on the light and stood looking down at Gladys. Her face was deathly pale; she stared up at him, smiling weakly.

"What a woman you've got on your hands, Jim," she said.

"It's this damn foreign country and no decent doctors and all the worry and strain ..."

"No. It's just me. I'm a silly, useless woman."

Jim grinned, meaning it; and bending down he began to stroke Gladys's forehead.

"You'll be all right. Keep a stiff upper lip. Maybe we'll get good news soon, then we can go back to L.A."

"We'll wait till we do," said Gladys determinedly.

"Sure, sure," said Jim.

Shake woke him early next morning. He'd just got another special-delivery letter. Jim shut the door of the bedroom carefully—Gladys had finally got to sleep—and took Shake over by the windows in the sitting room.

"Keep your voice down," he whispered.

"The heat's really on, Jim," said Shake, sadly. "Lonergan says no deal will be possible for at least a couple of months—if ever. There's a big reward out for you; and the police department's being goosed by the Mayor because the papers're playing it up. It might even be better for us to move on to another town."

"Shake," said Jim, "we're leaving for L.A. today. This is killing the missus."

"But, Mr. Farrar—my God! We'll get nabbed."

"You stay here if you feel that way."

"Why? I ain't wanted."

"If you're caught with me it will be bad."

"Yeah," said Shake, meditatively, "but it's you I'm worrying about. It's hot in town."

"I don't want to argue," said Jim.

"Okay—I'll go."

"After a while, I'll wake the missus. Then you give her the good news. Con her. We're supposed to go in; everything's set."

Shake stood shaking his big head from side to side. This was bad, very bad. But he'd seen it coming.

XXI

San Gorgonio was soon left behind and they were winding down a mountain road, Shake driving with what Jim thought was undue caution. Gladys looked and felt much better: the "good news" had bucked her up wonderfully. Jim was sitting in the back seat with her, holding her hand. He felt very calm and tranquil now that he'd made up his mind what to do.

"It's beautiful here," said Gladys, looking out at the heavily wooded country they were passing through. "Jim—see that stream? Doesn't it look cool and fresh?"

Jim glanced out the window indifferently. Nature meant little or nothing to him: he couldn't understand why people raved about scenery: just a lot of dirt, trees, and rocks. Give him a city, particularly at night, with all the lights on and things stirring. Anybody that wanted the country could have it.

"Yeah," he said.

Gladys glanced at him, then looked again.

"Jim," she said, "you look so funny this way. Take your hat off and let me see."

Jim obliged. In order to make the play seem more legitimate, he'd disguised himself by shaving off his mustache and getting a German haircut—which Shake annoyed him by repeatedly calling an "Oshkosh, by gosh," haircut, then laughing as if he'd said something very funny. He looked leaner, much harder, more virile, and older.

"With your dark glasses on and your hat off, I'd hardly know you," said Gladys. "You look like a German officer or something like that."

Jim put his hat back on and turned to Gladys.

"Look, honey, I want to explain everything to you so you won't get mixed up and cause a fuss. I'm wanted for kidnapping you. That's silly of course; but until you turn up who's going to know different? All right. So Shake takes you back to the Marwood and you tell Evans you left suddenly because you were so upset, and you've been looking for me all over the country. That story doesn't sound too good, I know. But pay the bill and you'll have Evans on your side. I'll bet he's been sweating blood over that grand or so we owe." Jim laughed.

"But, Jim...."

"Let me finish, honey. When you turn up, the heat will be off me on the kidnapping charge. Then all that's left will be a manslaughter rap; I'll stand trial for that, and with any kind of luck I'll beat it. Then we're set."

"But you'll be in jail."

"Not long. I'll be out on bail."

"I hope you know what you're doing, Jim," said Gladys, looking at him anxiously.

"Of course I know what I'm doing." He put his arm around Gladys. "I only ask you to do one thing: cooperate. Otherwise you'll just make it tough on me."

"I'll do whatever you say, Jim."

"Shake's got his instructions. He's clear so you don't have worry about him. The law doesn't want him for anything."

They rode for a long time in silence.

"But suppose something goes wrong?" Gladys demanded suddenly.

Jim spoke to her soothingly.

"Nothing can go wrong, honey. Stop worrying."

They spent the night at a little auto court. Neither Gladys or Jim could sleep but each pretended to be asleep to keep from disturbing the other. Finally in the middle of the night, Jim couldn't stand it any longer and lit a cigarette. Gladys turned toward him instantly.

"You awake, darling?"

"I just woke up," lied Jim. "Sorry to bother you but ..."

"I don't mind at all."

There was a long silence. In the darkness all that Gladys could see was the red glow of the cigarette which dimly lit up Jim's face when he puffed on it.

"I wish I could stay with you, Jim," said Gladys, finally. "I just can't stand the thought of...." She broke off, and fought for control of her emotions. She had a feeling something would go wrong and that she'd never see him again. But of a sudden a comforting thought occurred to her: that's exactly the way she'd felt that day in the Marwood when Jim had left her to settle accounts with the little doctor. Such feelings didn't mean much; they were merely fears.

"Everything's going to be all right," said Jim soothingly.

He crushed out his cigarette.

"I must seem like an awful woman to you, Jim. Nothing but trouble. Nothing but complaints."

"You're a wonderful woman, Gladys," said Jim, his voice trembling with emotion. Then he caught himself up short, ashamed of himself for speaking in such a way.

Gladys was surprised by the tone of his voice, and deeply pleased. He'd never spoken that way to her before. She settled herself into his arms and in a few minutes was asleep. Jim held her until he was so cramped he couldn't stand it any longer, then he slowly and carefully extricated himself from her. She slept on. He lay in the darkness staring up at the ceiling.

He wished he could sleep. He didn't want to be jittery the next day: it was going to be tough enough as it was. He turned over on his right side and after a long time managed to get to sleep.

Sometime later he groaned, then his eyes opened and he lay, half awake, sweating clammily. That damned dream again: and more terrifying than ever before. This time, old as Jim-Rodney was, he was being led to the scaffold for a particularly shocking sex murder. He could see the white horrified faces of the spectators ...

"No," cried Jim, confused and so agitated that he was shaking the bed. "It wasn't me. How could I have ...?"

In another moment he was fully awake and hot with shame. He glanced at Gladys to see if his cry of fear had disturbed her, but she was sleeping peacefully.

"Pretty soon," said Jim. "No more of that. I don't know who arranges what happens to people, and I don't know if that's what they got arranged for me—funny, I'd dream it all the time—but if it is, they're going to get one hell of a big surprise."

A few minutes later he was sleeping peacefully.

XXII

Shake started to drive off half a dozen times, but Gladys always checked him. She just couldn't force herself to go and leave Jim alone.

"Please, honey," Jim said finally, "go ahead. You're holding things up. I'll see you in a day or two. Now don't worry."

Gladys clung to him and kissed him repeatedly, and when Shake, who was crying too, drove off, Jim caught a last glimpse of Gladys's pale, tearful face pressed to the window. He felt terrible. All his resolution deserted him for a moment. He wanted to grab a taxi and catch up with Gladys. They could lam back to Mexico. What the hell! Anything was better than this. But he got hold of himself finally and, turning abruptly, went into the Ship Cafe. The bartender glanced at him quickly, then lowered his eyes in a way that puzzled Jim. Had he recognized him? It was possible. Anyway, it was no great matter. According to Johnny, the big Irishman was a right guy; not the kind who yells copper.

"Bourbon and soda," said Jim. "Will you take it over to a table? I'm going to make a phone call."

"You bet I will, sir," said the bartender with impersonal politeness, but as soon as Jim had disappeared into a public phone booth at the rear of the place, the bartender hurried to the house phone and nervously made a call.

Jim had a little trouble getting Miss Evans at the Marwood Arms. She was terribly confused at first. "This is Mr. Lloyd," said Jim.

"Who? Who? Not the Mr. Lloyd who ...?"

"That's me. Now listen. I understand my wife will be at the Marwood in a half hour or so. Please look after her. She's going to need you."

"Yes, Mr. Lloyd. I'll ... I'll do what I can." Miss Evans sounded scared to death.

"Remember that night I didn't show up till very late? And you looked after her? That's what I mean."

"Yes, Mr. Lloyd. You can trust me."

"Thanks a million," said Jim and hung up. Jim made another phone call, which took time, then he sat down at the table where the bartender had put his drink. He was surprised how calm, almost indifferent, he felt. That proved something to him. He was doing the right thing: the thing, in one form or another, he'd been intending to do ever since he'd gone to pieces in Florida. He drank his drink and had the bartender bring him another one.

As the minutes passed Jim grew more and more contented. From time to time he glanced at his watch, but without impatience, and after a while he lit a cigar and ordered another drink. He had a feeling that the bartender was watching him, and he glanced at the big Irishman ironically every once in a while, but it didn't really matter, now. He began to sip his third drink. Suddenly he became alert. The front door was opening.... But he immediately relaxed.

A little spindly man wearing glasses came in with a big, loose-mouthed, blonde broad. They sat at the bar. She called the guy with her "daddy" in a sugary voice and kept glancing back at Jim, who was hoping they'd drink their drinks and get out: which they did—chiefly because "daddy," in spite of being near-sighted, began to notice that his blonde friend was going on the make for Jim.

As they went out Jim grunted to himself:

"No wonder Gladys threw me so at first. That's the kind of babies I'm used to—only difference is, mine were better looking."

It was getting a little stuffy in the place so Jim opened the window near him. It was a beautiful day. The sun was shining in an almost cloudless blue sky, and a strong, cool wind was blowing in from the sea, bringing the pleasant odor of salt water and seaweed. Gulls were flying over the far-away beach, their parrot-like cries sounding faintly above the noise of the surf. Far out, the sunlight danced on the bluish-green water where a trim-looking Coast Guard boat was moving swiftly south, toward San Pedro.

Jim watched the boat lazily, then he turned suddenly and almost started off his chair. Johnny had just come in the front door, looking white and shaky. The bartender glanced at him, then jerked a thumb in Jim's direction. Now Jim understood; the bartender had been tipped off to watch for him and give Johnny a ring. But what was Johnny's idea, walking in on him like this?

The little lawyer hesitated for a long time, then, as Jim gave no sign, he walked slowly to the table and sat down. The bartender, keeping an eye on Jim, hurried over with a straight whiskey.

"Thanks," said Johnny, looking up gratefully. "I need it."

The bartender winked and went back behind the bar and immediately became absorbed in a newspaper. Johnny tossed his drink down, shuddering. Still Jim said nothing. Johnny's arrival was so unexpected and so inopportune that Jim didn't quite know what to do or say. Strangely enough, he felt no animosity toward Johnny.

"Jim," said the little lawyer, "I've been trying to find you ever since you sent Doc over."

"Why?"

"Why!" cried Johnny, his jitteriness showing now in irritability. "He asks me why. I'm your lawyer—is that right? And I've got your dough."

"You're crazy ... that's all that's the matter with you."

"You almost got it right. I *was* crazy. But I woke up."

"Where's Tony?"

"Last I heard she was at the Biltmore. Jim, as soon as I read about the shooting, I took a powder on Tony—the little bum! Honest to God, Jim, I can't believe it happened. Me running out on you like that—taking your dough." Johnny put his hands over his face and sobbed. Jim saw tears trickling down between his fingers.

"Oh, stop acting like a slob," said Jim curtly. "It took guts to walk in here like this—now you spoil it."

Johnny made a great effort to control himself.

"I haven't slept two hours straight for over three weeks," said Johnny, "and I'm shot. What's all this about kidnapping that woman?"

"I took her with me. She wanted to go. We've been holing up in Mexico."

"What are you doing here? Things are hotter than a two-dollar pistol."

"She couldn't stand it."

"She couldn't stand...." Johnny cried, outraged, and unable to continue for a moment. "Wait a minute.... Who's crazy?"

"Look, Johnny. Do me a favor. Get out of here. I got business to take care of and I don't want you gumming up the works."

"Not until we've talked things over. I walked in here in the first place figuring I might get a slug—so you see what a swell chance you got to scare me out now."

Jim shifted about impatiently.

"We got nothing to talk over. Everything's set. So scram!"

"I hear that Lonergan's handling things for you. Is that right?"

"Yes."

"Look, Jim, what's the matter with you? He couldn't fix a horse race in Mexico."

"He's the only guy I could get hold of at the time."

"Not that I could do you any good right now—nobody could. But with this dough and a couple of breaks, maybe I could later. Get back to Mexico. Lay low. Let me look after things. We might eventually get a fix with the court: if you be a good guy and come in of your own free will—you know, that old angle. Some judge might even let you plead guilty to manslaughter."

"Do what? I'll plead guilty to nothing. You think I'm going to do time—at my age? I'd come out an old man."

"But good God, Jim; this is serious. I know you never did time. I know you've beaten every rap that's come up; never even had to stand trial. But this is different. This is murder. You can't go around shooting people—and then buy up a judge. Be sensible."

"You think I'm a cinch to be convicted?"

"Naturally."

"That's what I thought."

Johnny studied Jim, who sat staring at his empty glass. "Say, what have you done to yourself?" Johnny demanded. "I thought Clancy'd made a mistake when I first came in the front door. Disguise, eh?"

"More or less. Look, Johnny. Beat it, will you? I got a date. You're just wasting your breath. I'm not going to hide out, and go running all over hell and back from the law, and I'm not going to stand trial. So figure it out."

"I don't get it."

"Well, take the problem home with you. Sit down quietly and work on it."

Suddenly Johnny glanced at Jim shrewdly and Jim could see the little lawyer had an inkling.

"And I always thought you were kidding," said Johnny.

"About what?"

"About being tired. I remember the first day we hit town. You were in awful shape. I just thought you'd been drinking too much."

"I haven't been the same since I left Florida. And I'll never get back to what I was. Not a chance. So now will you go home and let me alone?"

Johnny looked at Jim steadily for a long time, then he turned away, made a quick movement and came up with a small, blunt automatic. Jim glanced at the bartender; Johnny's back was to him—he'd noticed nothing.

"You're going to march out of here and come home with me. If anybody shoots you—it'll be me."

Jim sat very still for quite a while, staring at Johnny, whose eyes began to waver. In a moment Jim reached over and took the gun out of his hand.

"Johnny, do me a favor. Go home. Time's getting short."

Johnny was appalled by what he felt sure was going to happen.

"But Jim—think it over. Besides—this is no way to do it. Good God, Jim...."

"I've been thinking it over for months," said Jim. "And this is it."

Just as Jim finished speaking two burly Los Angeles policemen came in the front door. Johnny turned and looked at them, then he cried:

"Here he is. Right back here."

Clutching the table, he kept himself between Jim and the cops.

"Okay, Lloyd," called one of the cops who had a bull neck and a beefy red face. "Get on your feet. You got a date downtown."

All of a sudden Jim lost his nerve. Maybe Johnny's hysteria affected him or maybe the strain of the Mexican interlude had snapped his willpower, or maybe it was nothing more than the animal fear of death, strong in a man as healthy as himself. He got shakily to his feet, his face pale, his heart pounding.

The world had shrunken to the size of a third-rate cocktail bar and there was nothing in it but himself and two cops. Everything about him seemed nightmarishly unreal but startlingly distinct. He saw the reflection of the blue sky in the bar mirror: a gull flew across it. He noticed what kind of buttons the cops had on their blue coats; and he saw that one of the cops was chewing a toothpick, the end of which was slightly frayed.

Every nerve in his body wanted to give up and get it over with. But suddenly he thought of Tom Rodney, that disgusting, filthy old man with cataracts on his eyes, drooling as he talked. Then he got a flash of himself: it was a cold, cloudy, gray day; the prison doors opened and he came out, weak from confinement and prison fare: his hair white, his teeth gone, spectacles on his nose, dressed in prison hand-me-downs, and with five dollars in his pocket. He'd be the sport of dirty-faced kids on the streets, fat greasy women who stunk would think they were too good for him; if he was lucky he'd get a job selling papers; if not, he'd be panhandling on the street: how about a dime, mister—I haven't eaten a thing today. Sleeping in lousy flophouses; taking handouts at missions for down-and-outs—providing he'd attend services; being pulled in for vagrancy by big tough cops who didn't give a goddam how they handled a guy who had nothing on him they could mooch ... NO!

With a sudden movement, Jim flung Johnny out of the way and drew his gun. The cops were so taken by surprise that they backed off, their faces going white, and fumbled for their guns, the holster flaps giving them trouble.

Johnny, propelled by the powerful push, had hit the bar and fallen to the floor. He had just got to his knees when Jim fired. The bullet went wide, very wide; and smashed the section of glass in the mirror nearest the door. The cops were still fumbling. Jim fired again. This time it went high, ricocheted, and imbedded itself in the bar with a sharp, splitting sound.

Then both cops fired at once. Jim dropped his gun and staggered forward two steps. One of the cops fired again.

"That's enough, you big bum!" yelled Johnny in a frenzy. He started after the cops, but Clancy caught him from behind and held him.

The cops still pale, stood looking down at Jim, who had fallen on his face and was dying, moving his head slowly from side to side. Both cops took out their handkerchiefs, pushed back their caps, and mopped their brows.

"Good thing he was a lousy shot," said the bull-necked one, with a sickly grin.

Johnny sneered at them.

"He could've shot your buttons off if he'd wanted to."

The cops looked at each other, then the one with the toothpick in his mouth said:

"What's eating you, mister? You turned him in, didn't you?"

"Not me. I'm his lawyer."

"Oh," said the cop, "a lawyer. Okay, mister." Then he turned. "Better call the Coroner, Chuck. It won't be long now."

Jim moved his head more and more slowly. He was back in San Gorgonio. It was sunset; in the west the sky was a fiery red, the streets were still hot, but a cool breeze was starting to blow from the east. He and Gladys were having dinner in the flagged patio of the hotel, where a fountain played, and a sad-faced Mexican youth strummed a guitar and a sad-faced girl sang plaintively of unrequited love. Gladys said:

"I saw this place in my dreams years ago. Honestly, Jim...."

... Johnny turned away and, leaning on the bar, burst into tears. Jim's head had stopped moving.

The cop with the toothpick in his mouth went up to the bar, still mopping his face.

"My God, it's hot," he said to Clancy. "How about a nice tall one—on the house."

XXIII

It was Saturday afternoon and the dingy little Los Angeles barroom was crowded. The mechanical piano had been going since one o'clock, playing over and over again the same old tunes. Outside a heavy January rain was lashing at the streets and driving people into doorways.

Shake, in a showy new suit, was sitting in a booth, holding forth to a couple of seedy-looking moochers, who were listening to him politely— after all this fat guy was buying them drink after drink!

"... and I'm the only one who really knows the inside, see? I was in on it from start to finish. It was one of them big things that went sour. Everybody took a beating one way or another. It was sort of like fate had stepped in and said they oughtn't to do this, these people, and they're going to suffer for it." Shake, half-tight, was getting a little fancy and the moochers glanced at each other as if to say: Oh, well. It's his dough. "The big fellow got killed down in Santa Monica—you probably read about that."

"Yeah," said one of the moochers, "I remember that." Then he lifted his empty glass and studied it carefully.

"How about another?" said Shake.

"Well...."

Shake called the waiter.

"All around again," he said, grinning. Then he turned back to his "friends." "The big fellow'd shot Doc a few weeks before."

"Yeah," said the moocher, "I remember."

"Well," said Shake, warming to his subject, "Doyle, the lawyer, got to drinking and went to pieces—he's in a sanitarium right now, taking a cure. Windy's in clink up in Frisco. Course it didn't have nothing to do with this caper—but that's beside the point. I'm the only one who didn't take it on the chin. Even poor old Pop Gruber kicked off—and I'm damned if I know who got his money."

The waiter came with the drinks and Shake gave him a good-sized tip.

"Here's looking at you, Mr. Thomas," said one of the moochers. "It's damn seldom a guy meets a gentleman like yourself."

Shake grinned, feeling like a man of affairs. Then he turned and pointed.

"Pop used to always sit in that booth right over there when he'd drop in for a drink after he got through uptown."

One of the moochers lifted his glass in the direction of the booth Shake had indicated.

"To old Pop," he said.

"That rich dame," one of the moochers put in, "what about her? She didn't take no beating. Even if she did—what would it matter? Give me a million and I'll take all the beatings anybody can hand out."

"I don't know about her," said Shake. "But she was a fine woman—a lady. She claimed the big fellow's body—give him quite a burial."

"She must've been a mighty funny woman," said one of the moochers, shaking his head judiciously, "falling for a guy who treated her like that."

Shake sighed. Suddenly he had a drunken desire to cry and, getting up abruptly, he started for the men's room. On the way he turned.

"Will you gentlemen excuse me?" he said. "Order up another round if you like."

The moochers looked at each other and shrugged as if to say: Why not?

THE END

Tomorrow's Another Day

W. R. BURNETT

To WHITNEY,
MRS. TRAMMELWAITE,
and MR. SCOUF

Life is neither a spectacle nor a feast; it is a predicament.
SANTAYANA

BOOK ONE

Ray Cooper was the kind of man nobody ever looks at twice. People who were introduced to him seldom remembered him. He seemed to go about in a cloud of anonymity. He was of average height and build; his clothes were neither smart, bizarre, nor untidy. He had brownish hair, brownish eyes, and a moderately healthy complexion. The only thing the least bit unusual about him were his glasses, very thick-lensed, making his eyes look remote and a trifle sad.

Ray was forty-eight, and an ex-sportswriter of considerable note. For half a lifetime he had been a heavy drinker and some years ago had spent several months in a sanatorium. Now he drank nothing but beer and was in fairly good physical condition, except for his teeth, which he was having pulled one by one.

He was sitting in a booth in the bar of Benny Hayt's Turf Café, alternately studying a *Racing Form* and staring out the window into Warehouse Square, deserted now except for an occasional belated car that would burst through the intersection of Motley and Pulaski Streets as if in a hurry to get out of this part of town. Ray could see the dim boulevard lights of Motley Street stretching off toward the South Road Bridge and the total darkness of the open country. It was a June night. A faint lake mist made haloes around each lamp. Clouds of june bugs were dashing themselves at every light they could find, and piles of dead ones cluttered the sidewalks. Ray always felt a little uneasy at the Turf Café. Beyond it the slums of a huge city pulsated in the darkness.

Not more than a dozen people were scattered about the bar. A polite but stubborn drunk was arguing mildly with the head bartender, a sad, tough-looking little Irishman, who after a moment glanced over at Ray and shrugged resignedly, as if to say: "See what I got to put up with?"

Ray took a sip from his glass of beer, then impatiently folded up his *Racing Form* and stuffed it into his coat pocket. No use trying to pick winners tonight. In the first place, he was too nervous, couldn't concentrate; in the second place, when Lonnie got through upstairs they might not have any money to bet with. Ray was getting old and knew it. This rackety, hand-to-mouth existence was all right when you were young, but there came a time when you wanted a little security; you wanted to relax and be your age. After all, Lonnie was only thirty-two, still young. Skirting disaster by a hair was his idea of a good time. Ray groaned, thinking about all the money that had run through Lonnie's fingers since he'd known him—over half a million, sure. And what did he have to show for it? A big, twenty-year-old beach house, falling apart, a couple of Cadillacs, and a wardrobe a movie star might envy.

The two years in the army hadn't changed Lonnie a bit—at least not so you could notice. Of course he'd come back limping and used to sit and swear at his gimpy ankle by the hour. But he even "cussed optimistically." Pinky Ryan, Lonnie's cook and general servant, had made that crack, and no truer words were ever spoken. Adversity of whatever kind seemed only to encourage Lonnie; he never learned.

Take his "wound." Most men would have been embarrassed by it and would have invented all sorts of lies. Not Lonnie. He told with gusto how, on leave in Italy, they'd all got drunk and stolen two jeeps, and how he'd been thrown from one, which hit a bump, and had been run over by the other. It wasn't only that he didn't want people to think he was a hero. It was just that it was the sort of silly, purposeless episode which seemed to delight him.

When Lonnie first came back from Europe, Ray, as a veteran of World War I who had seen some active service, wanted to swap reminiscences. But Lonnie shied off, and his attitude was so marked Ray came to understand that either he was completely indifferent or—what was probably nearer the truth—he was anxious to forget all about what he'd gone through. Aside from the episode of his "wound," a jumble of comical stories about guys in his outfit, and an occasional vague reference to Kasserine Pass as being "pretty rugged" he had practically nothing to say about his two years in the army. And Ray respected his desire for silence on the subject.

Ray winced slightly, thinking about the big game upstairs. Lonnie was in tough company, playing with men who had real money, while Lonnie was on the ragged edge. One exceptionally bad night, and goodbye beach house, Cadillacs, and whatever small reserve he had. Suddenly Ray wanted to get up and pace the floor. The thought of the future made him feel panicky. He was now as dependent on Lonnie as he'd been on his own father when he was a boy. Gradually he calmed himself, lit a cigarette, and took a little book out of his pocket, propped it up before him, and began to read. It was Suetonius' *Lives of the Twelve Caesars*. Ray was hipped on Roman history. It soothed and relaxed him. He'd even tried to write a novel dealing with the Augustan Age; but it had proved to be too much for him, although every once in a while at night when he couldn't sleep he'd get the dogeared manuscript out and glance through it. To him it seemed pretty good and he was secretly proud of himself.

He glanced up. Somebody was speaking to him—Benny Hayt.

"What's that, Benny?" he demanded. "Didn't hear you."

"All the time you are reading books, Mr. Cooper," said Benny somberly. "Why do you read books? That is all nonsense, Ray."

The old newspaperman noticed the "Mr. Cooper" and the "Ray" and smiled to himself. Poor Benny was as uneasy socially as he seemed to be every other way. His instinct was to call everybody "Mister." He was from the slums of Naples and born of parents who could neither read nor write; he felt inferior. At times he over-compensated for this feeling by being overfamiliar and even rude to everybody. Benny had a good business and was a member of a big gambling syndicate, which included, besides himself, Jack Pool, one of the most successful gamblers in the country, and Mr. W. W. Keller, a rich Lake City businessman and realtor, who had instigated the big Oxford Park real estate development, which had made a dozen fortunes for men in the know. But all this did not cure Benny of his uneasiness. Deep inside him he was still a bewildered and frightened immigrant. He had even changed his name to no purpose.

Benny was about fifty, a short, stocky, dark Neapolitan. His face was fat and pitted. He had kinky black hair, which he tried to plaster down, and under his heavy blue chin a dewlap trembled. In the old days he'd made a fortune out of bootlegging and had become a power politically. Things had changed, but Benny still had plenty of money. He almost always looked either somber or surly. At rare intervals he smiled, showing strong white teeth and looking like a mischievous kid. He had the reputation of being tricky and vindictive.

Ray made some offhand comment about reading, then he asked how the game was coming. Benny raised his palms and shrugged violently.

"To me it makes no difference. Let them play, the fools. I take my rake-off."

"Yeah," said Ray, "you're on the right end all right." He hesitated, decided to say nothing further about the game. No news was good news.

"Your boss," said Benny, eying him somberly, "he's doing pretty fair. Run of luck." He chuckled without his somber expression changing. "You better bust up this game, I think."

"Doing that well, is he?" Ray's pulses began to jump.

Benny sat down opposite Ray, put his chin on his hands, and stared sadly out the window into Warehouse Square.

"Yeah. He's going pretty fair. Sam Ballard's taking a beating—but good."

Ray grimaced.

"It's always the guy you don't want to take a beating who does."

"Money's money," said Benny. "If he don't want to lose, he shouldn't gamble. Mr. Pool's inching along—the Greek, I mean."

Ray smothered a smile. The thought of Benny calling the elegant Mr. Pool—born Ajax Macropoulos—"the Greek" to his face was one for the book.

"Rank's a smart operator," Benny went on; "he don't get hurt much one way or another. Gregg's a big gambler over at the track—owns a lot of beetles; he's losing some. And that Coster fellow—I never seen him before. He's a big boy from downtown—he came with the Greek. He owns a department store."

"Yeah," said Ray, "Karr-Dean Company. We won't cry about him."

"I don't cry over nobody," said Benny sadly, "not even my mother, if she'd lose her wad in a stud game. Nobody makes you play."

He turned to a waiter who was passing.

"Eddie, bring me a glass of soda water—put ice in. It's hot tonight. And another beer for Mr. Cooper—on the house."

"Okay, Mr. Hayt," said the waiter, hurrying off.

"Thanks, Benny," said Ray.

Benny ignored him and stared out the window.

"Look at them damn fool bugs beating their heads against the light. Wonder what their idea is?"

"You got me," said Ray, thinking that maybe all life was like that, but recoiling from the thought.

The little Irish bartender, Gordy, wouldn't trust anybody to wait on the big boys upstairs. He took care of them himself. This time when he entered with the tray, they were not playing. Some were seated, some were standing, smoking. Mr. Ballard, looking strained and pale, was pacing the floor. Gordy threw him a sympathetic glance; he knew he was taking an awful beating. Ballard was A-one in his book. He put down the tray. Jack Pool made a move toward his pocket, but Lonnie Drew already had a big bill out and tossed it on the table.

"Thanks, Gordy," he said, smiling. The smile, Gordy reflected, that threw so many dames into a dither—or so he heard.

"Much obliged, Mr. Drew," said Gordy, glancing again at Ballard, then going out and closing the door softly behind him.

Lonnie turned and, rubbing his chin reflectively, studied Ballard. Lonnie was a tall young man, slightly over six feet two, and weighing nearly a hundred and ninety pounds, though he didn't look it. He was long-legged and his build seemed slight and graceful, partly because of his expensive, well-cut clothes. His sun-faded blond hair was thick and curly; his face gave an appearance of delicacy till you noticed the solid, projecting chin. His blue eyes, surrounded by sun-wrinkles, were mild and observant. He had an almost boyish air in comparison with the dark, hairy, sophisticated, and elegant Greek, who sat nearby, sipping a liqueur and glancing up at him ironically from time to time.

Rank, a city politician and a tough, quiet little man, was chewing on a frayed cigar and riffling a stack of chips. Gregg, the horse owner, who hadn't removed his sweat-stained Stetson hat all evening and who looked lean, sunburnt, and fit, was staring at his glass of straight bourbon as if he couldn't make up his mind whether to drink it or not. And Coster, the big businessman from downtown, tall, heavy, well-fed-looking, with a pleasant smile, too perfect false teeth, and pince-nez, was looking out of the window, from which he could see an ugly reach of Pulaski Street and a few scattered neon signs.

It was nearly midnight. The game had been going since mid-afternoon.

"Well, what do you say, Lonnie?" Ballard demanded. "I'm in to my ears, and I've got no more cash."

"We play always for cash," said Pool smoothly, staring at his carefully manicured nails.

"But that restaurant of mine—it's worth a lot of money. Anybody can tell you that."

Nobody said anything. Ballard looked about him anxiously.

"It's not up to me," said Coster, as if somebody had accused him of something. "This is my first time."

"Yes," said Pool, "Mr. Coster is my guest. I'm very embarrassed. He was looking for a big game. I told him this was the biggest in the Midwest. Now we are wrangling over cash."

Lonnie glanced at the Greek with distaste. He had never liked this smooth, conniving, handsome, perfumed, over-barbered gambler, even in the old days when he'd been head bellboy in the Erie Hotel and the Greek had been—well, pretty much what he was today. A big tipper, but a man who liked to yell at and embarrass the help; a man who complained about the food, the service, everything. A man who would do you an ill turn merely to show his superiority to you. The dislike was mutual. The Greek could never forget that Lonnie had once been in a very inferior position. He thought that Lonnie was getting far too big for his pants.

Ballard turned to the others.

"How do you fellows feel?"

Gregg merely shrugged, then tossed down his drink. Rank raised his eyebrows.

"With cash it's simpler," he said.

"Yes," seconded the Greek, "with cash it's always simpler."

"He said that," snapped Lonnie, feeling antagonistic and throwing a look at Pool, who smiled, showing his slightly pointed but dazzlingly white teeth.

"I was merely reiterating."

"Oh, well," said Ballard, and reached for his hat. He looked pale and sick.

Lonnie felt a sudden stab of pity.

"Look, Sam," he said, "I'll lend you some dough. I hate playing against my own money, but—"

Ballard's thin, pale face brightened.

"Damn nice of you, Lonnie. But—not without security. I'll put up the restaurant against your loan."

The Greek smiled to himself with satisfaction. Lonnie was breaking his luck—he'd seldom known it to fail. A reuben, that's what he was, letting pity interfere in a matter like this! The Greek felt immensely superior to most other men; their lives were all complicated and snarled up with sentiment, pity—such things. It was very droll.

They began to play. After the third card both the Greek and Coster tossed their hands in. Coster smiled happily.

"For ten years I've been looking for a game like this. Excellent!"

"I'm so glad that you are pleased, Mr. Coster," said Pool.

"And all on account of a beautiful girl," laughed Coster. "Things have the strangest way of working out at times."

Lonnie glanced up at Coster and Pool as they looked at each other and smiled. He was curious. What was Coster talking about? What beautiful girl?

"Has Jack, here, run into another doll?" he inquired.

Pool's mouth tightened slightly. He did not like to have this ex-bellboy so familiar with him.

"Yes," said Coster, laughing, "a delicious, delightful doll. One of the models in my store. He sends her huge bunches of flowers every day. All the other girls are so envious—" He laughed a little fatuously; the drinks he'd had were beginning to tell on him.

Pool threw him a veiled glance, but said nothing.

"And," Coster went on, laughing heartily, "I don't think our Casanova is doing quite as well as he expected."

"Oh, I expect nothing," said Pool. "Her company is enough."

Lonnie laughed briefly. Who did the Greek think he was kidding with his polite manner? All he did was chase dames; a procession of them had passed through the hotel in the old days. And he was mean with them, and stingy. An all-around bad guy.

"She's quite a girl," said Coster. "I'd be after her myself if I wasn't a worn-out old married man. My son discovered her in a little place called New Vienna, about a hundred miles from here. The most beautiful girl I've ever seen—really; built to display clothes, and—"

"Cards!" Rank cut in sharply, glancing at Coster.

"Pardon me, gentlemen," said Coster, coming to himself. "I'm afraid I talk too much."

"Oh, no," said Pool, smiling. "Who could help talking about so charming a girl?"

"A grand I'm right," said Lonnie.

The others quietly threw in their hands.

It was nearly three a.m. The café was dark except for a night-light behind the bar, and the chairs were stacked on the tables. A big, shuffling Negro was mopping the floor, humming sadly to himself. Gordy, the head bartender, and Ray were sitting behind the bar on camp chairs, eating sandwiches and drinking coffee out of a small tin pail.

Ray was very tired. There was actually no reason why he should wait for Lonnie, but here he sat. He would hardly admit to himself that he didn't like to go home alone to the big, rambling old house on the beach where the lake lapped monotonously at the shore all night long and the whistles of the freighters far out sounded mournful in the stillness. Besides, he was anxious to hear how the game had come out. He'd got a few reports from Benny, but now Benny was sleeping peacefully in a room behind the bar; they could hear him snoring.

Gordy jerked his thumb.

"I wish I could tear it off like that."

"Have trouble sleeping?" asked Ray.

"I don't get two hours a night. Between six and eight I sleep a little. That's why I stick around so late."

"That's tough."

"Yeah. I used to take a lot of that junk. But—what the hell! I felt dopey all day." He stared at his sandwich for a moment. "It's been ever since that wife of mine kicked off. I never knew a guy could feel so lousy over a thing like that. I wasn't even nice to her most of the time. More coffee?"

Ray took the pail and tipped it up quickly to hide his embarrassment. He felt sorry for Gordy and didn't know what to say.

While he was drinking, somebody began to bang on the door. The big Negro went over and tried to wave the man away, but he kept banging. Irritated, Gordy jumped up, went to the door, and peered out; then he grinned and unlocked the door, calling over his shoulder to Ray: "It's Mr. Drew's boy with the car."

Ray sighed with relief. The game was over. Lonnie must have phoned from upstairs. Ray rose and went to meet Lonnie's chauffeur, a slender little Chicago Czech, named Willy Fiala, who was grinning and slapping Gordy on the back.

"Hello, kid," said Willy, always as cheerful as Lonnie; in fact, he aped his boss in everything, or tried to. "Hawz about a little after-hours drink? They always taste better."

"All locked up."

"Fine thing!" He turned to Ray. "Boss ain't down yet, huh? Called me half an hour ago."

As he spoke, the door that led to the room upstairs opened and Lonnie came out alone.

"You still here, Ray? Hello, Willy. Let's go." He noticed the bartender. "Thanks for the service, Gordy. I guess it brought me luck."

"Thank *you*, Mr. Drew, for all them tips."

Ray looked at Lonnie with interest, very anxious to hear about the game.

"I know, I know," said Lonnie, glancing at Ray. "You can relax. We're in the dough."

"Oh, boy!" cried Willy, rubbing his hands energetically.

Pinky, the cook, had a snack ready for them, and Ray and Lonnie ate it in the narrow little breakfast room, which was hardly more than a butler's pantry. Willy and Pinky stayed in the kitchen—but with the door open so they wouldn't miss anything. Ray wasn't hungry, owing to the sandwich he'd eaten, but he pecked at the food to keep Lonnie company. Lonnie was hungry as a wolf, as he always was after a long gambling session, and kept stowing the food away and asking for more till Pinky finally said:

"Boss, if you ain't careful you'll bust."

"It's my hollow leg," said Lonnie.

Finally he stopped eating, leaned back comfortably, and lit a cigarette to go with his last cup of coffee.

"It seems," he said to Ray, "we're in the restaurant business."

"How do you mean?"

"I won over fifteen thousand cash, and Sam Ballard's restaurant."

"My God!"

"Holy jumping—!" cried Willy in the kitchen, and Pinky dropped a pan.

"The Lake Shore Inn's quite a place," said Ray. "What are you going to do with it?"

"Run it," said Lonnie calmly. "What else? Sam's going to manage it for me."

Ray groaned.

"Is that sense, Lonnie? He just lost it, gambling. How can you trust a man like that?"

"You don't understand, Ray. You talk about writing books, but you ought to learn about people first. As long as Sam's working for me he'll be okay. Losing his own place is something else again."

Ray sat shaking his head and staring out the window at the many winking lights of Bass Island. The moon was up and there was a pale, jewel-like shimmer on the water. The window was open and a fresh, cool breeze was blowing in from the lake, stirring the curtains.

"Besides," said Lonnie, "I've had my eyes on that blonde babe who worked there for some time." He laughed. In the kitchen Willy and Pinky laughed, too. "You know—the hostess. Her name's Annette, I think."

"Do you have to own the place to get an in with the hostess?"

Lonnie got up and yawned and stretched.

"It helps," he said. "Now hit the hay."

Ray envied him. Lonnie would throw off his clothes, get into bed, drop off in a second, and sleep like the dead—till somebody shook him awake. It was great to be like that.

"By the way," said Lonnie, turning, "the Greek got a slight pasting tonight. He dropped about five grand. The guy from downtown won about that—what's his name? —Coster. All in the family, I guess. The Greek's on the make for one of his models. Beautiful kid, I understand. Maybe I should go take a look."

"What about Annette, the hostess?" Ray demanded, slightly irritated.

"What do you want me to do—confine myself?" asked Lonnie.

Pinky and Willy roared. Ray ran his hand over his face wearily, said nothing.

"Say," said Lonnie, "see anything in the *Form* tonight? You had time enough to pick a three-horse parlay."

"Bad card every place."

"Yes. Monday's usually beetle day. I want to bet that Flying Fast horse at Aqueduct on Thursday, though. Call Joe in St. Louis. We'll bet a grand across and he can lay it off any way he pleases."

Ray nodded. No use to argue. Personally he didn't think much of the horse.

"Gregg—the guy there tonight—is going to give me one for Saturday
if I don't bet it at the track. He's got a couple pretty fair horses now."

Lonnie yawned and stretched again. He turned and was just starting
for the bedroom when somebody began to bang on the front door. Lonnie
and Ray exchanged a look. It was past four a.m.

"You don't suppose it got out you won a lot of dough, and some of the
boys—" Ray began.

"Would they knock?" asked Lonnie, shrugging.

He turned, went quickly down the hall, punched on the porch light,
and unlatched the front door. Willy came in behind him hurriedly and
stood at the far end of the hall with a gun in his pocket. Lonnie opened
the front door. A tall, fashionably dressed woman, whose face was partly
in the shadows, was standing on the lower step.

"Well—!" exclaimed Lonnie, smiling.

"Are you Mr. Drew?" asked the woman; she spoke thickly and swayed
slightly. Lonnie realized she was very drunk.

"Yes," said Lonnie. "Won't you come in?"

"Don't be funny," the woman said. "I've had about enough of men like
you."

"Well, I'll never have enough of women like *you*," said Lonnie, "but
maybe I shouldn't point."

"Oh, a wise guy," said the woman. "Let me tell you something, wise
guy—"

A man sitting in a car in front of the house called: "Wanda!"

"Be quiet, you loud-mouthed bastard!" cried the woman violently;
then she turned back to Lonnie. "It's my brother."

"There seems to be some doubt about it. Say, Wanda, won't you come
in and have a drink? I think you need one."

The woman boiled inwardly for a moment, then she cried:

"All I want out of you, mister, is—tell that Greek to come out and face
me like a man!"

"What Greek?"

"Don't give me that. He came home with you. Somebody told me so."

"Oh, you mean Jack Pool. He didn't come home with me."

"I don't believe it."

Lonnie stood aside.

"Why don't you come in and search the house? He might be hiding in
my bedroom. Shall we go see?"

Willy began to giggle. Ray and Pinky were both behind him now,
listening.

The woman stood perfectly still for a moment as if she couldn't make
up her mind whether to slug Lonnie or not. The man in the car called:
"Wanda!" insistently.

She burst into a sudden fury, turned her back on Lonnie, ran down
the steps, stumbling twice, and when she got to the car, she began to
belabor the driver with her purse. The man ducked and temporized for

a minute or so, then he got out of the car, hit the woman a blow that made Lonnie wince, put her in the back seat, and started down the steps.

Lonnie waited, tense. The man appeared. He was tall and heavily built, with slanted blue eyes and high cheekbones.

"That's my sister," he said mildly. "I've about had a bellyful for one night. Pool ain't here, is he?"

"No," said Lonnie.

"The kid thinks Pool's been giving her the runaround. Personally, I think he's been goddamn nice to her. But once in a while she gets drunk; then she acts like this. I put up with it just as long as I can." He reached out his hand toward Lonnie. "My name's Joe Pavlovsky, pal. Sorry about this."

They shook hands and the man turned and went back up the steps. Lonnie shut the door, then stood looking at the others. They all burst out laughing at once.

"Maybe that will teach Jack to leave Polish dames alone. She was quite a dish!"

"You can have her," said Ray.

Lonnie yawned and stretched, then he turned and went into the bedroom.

"Good night," he called, shutting the door.

Willy stood shaking his head in admiration.

"What a line, what a line!" he mused; then he threw back his head and laughed, a high-pitched whinny that set Ray's nerves on edge.

"Good night, boys," said Ray, and went downstairs to his big bedroom on the lower level of the hillside beach house.

Ray lay in his bed, his head propped up on two pillows, reading the early edition of the *Morning Journal* and sighing with contentment. For the moment he felt safe, and free from the little nagging worries that ordinarily plagued him. Of course, the haven he'd found, after many years of searching, was a very precarious one, but it was better than bucking the world alone—much better!

Ray had no relatives; his parents had died years ago. And as for friends, a man makes very few close ones jumping about the country from paper to paper. Besides, most men his age were married and had kids. A single man had very little in common with the head of a family; he was out of it, that's all.

Ray's life had been a succession of disappointments and disasters, culminating in the sanatorium hiatus. Shortly after he was released as cured, he met Lonnie one afternoon at the Lakeland Racetrack. An old newspaper handicapper, Gil Smith, introduced them. Lonnie had been taking a bad beating, but, to Ray's surprise, was laughing about it, apparently not the least bit disturbed. Ray had minutely studied the *Form* the night before and had found what to him looked like a sleeper in the eighth race. After a slight hesitation he told Lonnie about it, but warned him that he was strictly an armchair handicapper and knew nothing about the stable's intentions or the actual condition of the horse. Lonnie said: "You can't be any more wrong than I've been today," and bet two hundred across the board on the horse—six hundred in all. The horse won in a driving finish at odds of seven to one.

Ray had been with Lonnie ever since and had gradually taken on many duties, the least of which was handicapping; he bought the food and supplies, helped Pinky plan the meals, paid the bills when they were paid at all, and generally looked after the running of the house. He kept Lonnie company when Lonnie wanted him along and minded his own business when he didn't. He occasionally had rows with Willy and Pinky, who were always getting out of line. And when Lonnie wanted to make a big bet, up in the thousands, he placed the money by telephone with various Midwest bookmakers, who could then do what they wanted with it, lay it off or let it ride. In Midwest betting circles Lonnie's word was as good as a bond. He had almost unlimited credit with hundreds of bookies from Cleveland to Louisville and from Pittsburgh to Kansas City. He had never welched in his life; he paid his losses no matter how much it hurt.

To Ray, Lonnie was a phenomenon. Born of a Cockney father and an Irish-American mother, Lonnie had been brought up in the slums of Brooklyn. He had practically no formal education and yet he could get by almost anywhere. He was never out of countenance, never seemed to suffer from a feeling of awkwardness or inferiority.

Lonnie's father had always hated America, but stuck it out until his son was sixteen and already earning his living; then he deserted his family and went back to the Pennyfields he'd been dreaming of all these years. Lonnie's mother died soon after and Lonnie was on his own.

At eighteen he was in Lake City, head bellboy in the swanky Erie Hotel. Here he picked up his ideas of how a man should live. He was an expert with the dice and from time to time won sums that seemed fantastic to the other bellboys. Finally he was discharged for insubordination. He was twenty years old. Since then he'd never worked at a steady job.

Ray shook his head, thinking about Lonnie. He envied him his lack of fear in the face of such a tough and complex world. Lonnie seemed to enjoy the combat.

Ray threw his paper on the floor, turned off the light, and lay looking out the window. Dawn was showing palely beyond the dark mass of Bass Island, which lay on the glassy water as if floating, one of the Enchanted Isles, bathed in lavender mist. Far off to the south in the industrial district a factory whistle blasted loudly.

Ray composed himself to sleep.

2

It was a hot July evening. The setting of the sun had brought no relief, as a lukewarm offshore breeze was blowing. People were sweaty and irritable.

Ray sat in the little office of the Lake Shore Inn in his shirtsleeves, his hair rumpled and his shoes off, staring irritably at a huge ledger. He had a new job now—checking Sam Ballard's books for Lonnie. In fact, he'd suggested it himself, as Lonnie was no one to pay any attention to the niggling details of running a business. He was content to take Sam's word for it.

As he worked, Ray could hear the noises from the kitchen: the rattle of dishes, the clink of silver, and the strained voices of the help. Although it was early yet, the restaurant was almost full. As it was Saturday, the bar had been jammed since mid-afternoon.

The door opened and Ray glanced up. It was Sam Ballard in his double-breasted, black serge suit and his starched collar. He looked cool and unruffled.

"How do you stand it?" Ray demanded irritably.

Sam stared blankly.

"Oh, the clothes, you mean. Heat doesn't bother me. Never did. But in the winter I'm cold all the time. I'll take summer. Books balance?"

"Pretty much. Small item I can't locate. Nothing important."

"Glad you're taking over. Lonnie wouldn't look at the books. And then somebody could say I gypped him." Sam chuckled. "The best thing that ever happened to me was when I lost this restaurant."

Ray looked at him in amazement.

"What are you talking about, Sam?"

"Now I don't worry," said Sam, "and I have some fun. I've got a good job, and none of the headaches I used to have. If the place loses money, it loses money. Anyway, how can a guy worry with Lonnie around?"

"I do his worrying," said Ray, a little annoyed.

"Well, *he* won't do it; that's a mortal," said Sam, laughing again.

George, the headwaiter, a solemn-looking Italian, opened the door and came in.

"Mr. Ballard—"

"Yes, George."

"Mr. Pool called for a reservation—three. I'm having booth number one set for him. Is that right?"

Sam nodded. George went out.

"Lonnie coming in for dinner tonight?" asked Sam.

"I think so. Pinky's on the warpath because Lonnie eats out so much now. He thinks it has something to do with his cooking." Ray smiled mirthlessly and wiped his face with a wilted-looking white handkerchief.

At eight o'clock Lonnie was sitting in the office, drinking a long Tom Collins and smoking a cigar. He seemed restless to Ray, who was lying on the couch glancing idly through a *Racing Form*.

It was cooler. The wind had shifted and was now blowing from the lake. All the office windows were open and there was a clean, pleasant odor of deep, fresh water in the room.

"Smell the lake?" said Ray. "Nice, eh?"

Lonnie ignored the question and sat turning his glass in his hand.

"I've been out trying to do a little business today," he said finally.

"I was wondering where you'd got to. I spent the afternoon balancing the books."

"Everything okay?"

Ray nodded. Lonnie smiled at him.

"See? I told you."

"Sure, Lonnie. But business is business." Ray slapped the *Form* irritably and pretended to study it.

After a long silence Lonnie said:

"I'm looking for a buyer for the inn."

Ray turned, annoyed.

"Why? Does a legitimate business scare you? You may need it later."

"It's not my racket, and it bothers me."

"I didn't think anything bothered you."

"You need a drink, Ray. The heat's got you."

He pressed a buzzer under the desk and in a moment a waiter looked in.

"Tall, cold beer for Mr. Cooper," said Lonnie, smiling at the waiter, who nodded and went out. "Yes," Lonnie went on, "it makes me feel funny to own a place like this. I might get interested; then I'd be tied down. Look at Sam. He's been tied down for years. You can't go away—do anything. Pretty soon the business owns you. No, thanks."

Ray turned and studied Lonnie.

"Well, I never expected to hear you talk like that. You are scared of something, aren't you?"

"Call it what you like. I don't feel natural. Of course, I'm not giving it away. I want my price."

The waiter came in with the beer, followed by Sam, who was smiling in a way that puzzled Lonnie. The waiter gave Ray his beer and went out.

"What's bothering you, Sam?" asked Lonnie. "You've got a very strange look on your kisser."

"Your friend Jack Pool just came in," said Sam, "with this Coster fellow—you know, the downtown tycoon."

"So—?"

"You should see the doll with him! I took a look and said to myself: 'No, it's not real.' Then I took another look, and still I don't believe it!"

"Sam!" said Lonnie. "At your age!"

"I can look, can't I? —and remember!"

"You're breaking my heart." Lonnie got up abruptly. "I think I'll go get a cigar." He turned. "Say, what do you hear from Annette?"

"Haven't heard a word since she went on her vacation. Maybe she caught herself a soldier and got married."

"I hope so," said Lonnie. "She's a very possessive type."

"You should know."

"Look, fellows," said Lonnie, "I'll break down. I never got to first base with Annette."

"I heard different."

"So did I," Ray put in.

"You heard wrong. I date her one night. Things are going fine, so I don't rush it—too much, I mean. The next date she wants me to come up to her apartment. I think to myself: things are going great. But when I get there she's in an apron and she's cooked me up a nice big meal. She did everything but put out my slippers. I pass."

Ray laughed, and glanced at Sam.

"Can't blame a girl for trying."

"Somehow my interest died, as they say in the movies." Lonnie looked from one to the other. "So now you know." Winking, he went out.

Sam sat down and lit a cigar, puffed on it reflectively, then said:

"I never saw a guy so cagy. He shies off before there's anything to shy at—like a two-year-old filly first time at post."

"Yeah," said Ray. "I'd like to see the woman that could marry him."

Lonnie crossed the restaurant, without looking to right or left, and went to the cashier's counter, near the bar.

"Hello Irma," he said. "Give me one of those Coronas."

Irma was middle-aged and all business. She had worked for Sam Ballard nearly five years and didn't quite approve of the new boss. She got out the cigar box without a change of expression or a word and offered it to Lonnie, who selected a cigar, bit off the end, and lit up. Irma put the box back and turned to her work. Lonnie leaned on the counter and glanced about the restaurant. Suddenly his pulses gave a jump. He'd seen the girl! She was sitting between Jack Pool and Coster in the front booth. She was talking animatedly and the men were laughing. She had thick, curly dark hair which fell in a long bob to her shoulders; as she turned her head under the lights, Lonnie noticed that the hair had glints of red in it. She was about twenty-one or two and her face was of a delicate, patrician beauty so distinct and unusual that Lonnie stared openly. She was slender and looked extremely smart in her fashionable clothes; Lonnie judged that she must be tall. Of a sudden she looked up and their eyes met. For the first time in his mature life Lonnie felt embarrassed. He glanced quickly away and turned to Irma.

"Looks like our friend Mr. Pool has got a winner this time."

"Just another glamour girl—a clotheshorse," said Irma sourly. "And what I think of a girl who'd run around with that wolf—!"

"He seems to do all right."

"With that type—yes. All they're looking for is money."

"Is that all?" said Lonnie. "Think of that!"

He turned away, crossed the restaurant, waved at Pool, who nodded grudgingly, ignored the girl, and went back into the office.

"Well?" said Sam.

Lonnie seemed a little disturbed—not quite his usual smooth self. Both Sam and Ray studied him. He sat down at the desk, opposite Sam, and picked up the house phone.

"Let me speak to George." There was a long pause. Lonnie began to whistle out of key. Ray and Sam exchanged a glance. "George? Lonnie. I'll eat in the office tonight. No hurry." He hung up and started whistling again.

"What did you think of the doll?" asked Sam impatiently. "You went out to get a look, didn't you?"

"Very nice number," said Lonnie indifferently.

Sam looked puzzled.

"Oh, well," he said, "maybe it's just that I'm getting old."

It was about nine o'clock. Lonnie had finished his dinner long ago, and Sam kept glancing at him, wondering why he was hanging around, doing nothing, not even reading the *Racing Form* or a newspaper. He was sitting with his feet up on the desk, blowing smoke rings and languidly spearing them with his forefinger. From time to time he made some uninteresting comment about nothing in particular. Ray had gone home. Sam was beginning to feel uncomfortable.

"Something on your mind?" he asked finally.

"Who? Me? No."

There was a long silence. In the middle of it George came in with a check for Sam to okay. Sam glanced at the check, then said:

"What's the matter, George? Pool's checks are always good here. Don't embarrass him like that."

George flushed painfully. He was one of the best headwaiters in the business and knew it. He just didn't make mistakes. Drawing himself up, he said:

"Please excuse me, Mr. Ballard. But Mr. Pool hasn't been here since the new management."

Sam glanced at him shrewdly.

"Quite right, George. My mistake."

George bowed and went out.

"Touchy so-and-so," said Sam, "but quite an asset to a place like this."

"Pool and his girlfriend are leaving, I guess," said Lonnie conversationally.

He'd been making dull remarks like that all evening.

Sam merely looked at him. After a long pause Sam spoke.

"What's eating you, Lonnie? You make me nervous."

Lonnie got up.

"I don't know," he said. "Maybe it's the weather. I think I'll go home and take a swim. It's nice in the water on a night like this."

"You can have it."

"I swam almost to Bass Island one night."

"You what?"

"Bright moonlight. Willy went along with a rowboat."

"You're crazy," said Sam, appalled at the thought. Imagine a guy out in that dark water, miles from shore! He shuddered inwardly, unable to conceive of a man voluntarily doing such a thing.

Just as Lonnie opened his mouth to speak, there was a sharp knock at the door interrupting him, and George came in, followed by Joe Greer, who had charge of parking the cars for the restaurant. They both looked very worried.

Lonnie glanced at them.

"What's the matter, boys?"

"We've got trouble," George began, but Joe cut in impatiently.

"There's a dame outside, Mr. Drew. She's loaded to the ears and she's got one of them things in her purse—a rod. She—"

"What's her beef?" Lonnie demanded, glancing from George to Joe.

"She's gunning for Mr. Pool and his girlfriend. Camp's out there with her now and so is the colored girl from the ladies' room. They—"

"She's been telling everyone around the place," George put in. "It's very embarrassing."

"The Polack!" said Lonnie. He turned to George. "What about Pool? Did you tell him?"

"No," said George. "I thought I'd better tell you first. Mr. Pool is getting ready to leave."

"Call the police, Sam. And you, Joe, keep the dame busy out front," said Lonnie; then he turned abruptly and went out.

"First serious beef we've ever had in this place," said Sam reflectively.

Lonnie hurried across the restaurant. Pool was helping the girl on with her coat; Coster was standing by with his hat in his hand, fatuously beaming. Pool turned and looked at Lonnie penetratingly, trying to read his intentions in his eyes.

"Hello, Jack," said Lonnie. "Very glad to see you here. How are you, Mr. Coster?" He glanced at the girl, who was smiling slightly as if she wanted to be included but was too polite to say anything. Yes, she was tall, and with long, beautiful legs. Also long black eyelashes which made faint shadows on her cheeks. And she looked so natural and fresh and un-made-up.

"My name's Drew," said Lonnie. "I own this place. I hope the food was satisfactory."

"Oh, very," she said.

"This is Miss O'Donnell," said the Greek, his lips tight. "And now you'll excuse us, won't you, Lonnie?"

Lonnie put his hand on Pool's arm.

"I wish you'd all come in my office for a drink. I'd appreciate it."

Puzzled, the Greek studied Lonnie from under lowered lids. At that moment a commotion just outside the vestibule caused everybody to turn, a commotion dominated by a loud, angry feminine voice.

The Greek started slightly, then controlled himself.

"Why shouldn't we all have a drink? —except that Miss O'Donnell doesn't drink," he said smoothly, escorting her at once toward Lonnie's office, "but I know she won't mind."

The girl sensed that something was up and looked quickly from Lonnie to the Greek. This delighted Lonnie, who told himself: "She's no cluck, this girl!" He walked beside her, smiling. Coster followed, swinging his hat, utterly oblivious.

Lonnie opened the door, and the girl went in, followed by Pool and Coster. Sam looked at them with surprise, then glanced at Lonnie.

"Everything okay?" he asked.

"Certainly, Sam," said Lonnie. "Why not?"

Sam rubbed his chin, nodded vaguely to everybody, turned and went out, closing the door behind him.

After Lonnie ordered the drinks over the house phone, there was an embarrassed pause. Pool seemed on edge and sat trying to listen to the outside sounds without seeming to. Coster looked about him placidly, noting the sporting prints on the walls. Miss O'Donnell could hardly contain herself; she was full of curiosity; she wanted to know what was going on and hoped it was exciting, but she decided for the moment not to inquire.

"Quite a place you won, Mr. Drew," said Coster, laughing heartily. "Well, that's one way of going into business."

"What do you mean, Mr. Coster?" asked Miss O'Donnell.

"He won this place—in a poker game. I was there."

Miss O'Donnell looked at Lonnie.

"He's joking, of course."

"No," said Lonnie, for some reason or other feeling embarrassed and wishing that Coster hadn't brought up the subject, "I won it, all right."

"How fantastic!" exclaimed Miss O'Donnell. "Do you just go around winning things—Mr. Drew?"

"Sometimes I lose."

"How sad that must make you feel!"

Lonnie glanced at the girl. What was the idea? Was she trying to rib him?

"I don't feel much, one way or another," he said aggressively. "I've been at it too long."

"Oh! Easy come, easy go," said Miss O'Donnell. "I see."

Lonnie was beginning to dislike her. Where did she get that superior pose? Why didn't she climb down off her high horse? Being a model wasn't so much, was it? It was the men flocking around, probably, flattering her, making her think she was the most beautiful girl in town—not that she wasn't! Lonnie averted his face. This dame was *too* good-looking.

A police car siren began to moan in the distance. They sat listening as it came closer and closer.

"It seems to be coming here," said Miss O'Donnell. "How exciting! Maybe the police are going to raid your place, Mr. Drew!"

"Why should they?"

"I don't know. But it's a very interesting idea."

Lonnie rubbed his hand over his face, genuinely puzzled by this girl. Her cheeks were flushed and her eyes shining; she looked about fifteen at the moment, very eager and excited.

Just as the waiter came with the drinks, the police car stopped in front of the inn with a loud squealing of brakes; the siren ground to a stop. The waiter was very nervous and his hands shook as he handed round the drinks.

"What's happening?" Miss O'Donnell asked the waiter suddenly.

The waiter stammered, glanced apprehensively at Lonnie.

"I don't—I don't know, miss. Little trouble in the parking lot, I think."

"Yes," said Coster, coming to life, "what *is* happening?"

The Greek shrugged and sipped his liqueur.

"How should I know?"

Miss O'Donnell turned her bright, intelligent eyes on Pool.

"It has something to do with you, Mr. Pool. I'm sure of that."

The Greek smiled indulgently.

"You're guessing."

Lonnie was heartened at the way she called the Greek "Mr. Pool"—no familiarity there. On the other hand, the Greek's manner of looking at the girl annoyed him extremely. It was a sort of refined leer! The Greek's large, dark eyes, heavy-lidded, liquid, and sensual, had always annoyed him—they were even rather effeminate. He wanted to say to the girl: "Look, honey, this is not the kind of guy for you. He's had more women than you've had dresses. And he'll have many, many more, in spite of all you can do." Lonnie got up abruptly, annoyed with himself. What the hell was he thinking of!

There was a knock at the door. Lonnie opened it. A squad car policeman stepped in.

"Hello, Mr. Drew," he said. "Sorry to bother you. But what do we do with this broad?"

"Just see that she gets home. No charges."

The copper grinned, and glanced at Pool, then at Miss O'Donnell, who was straining her ears.

"Okay, Mr. Drew," said the copper; then he looked about him again and went out.

"Well—!" exclaimed Coster, glancing from the Greek to Lonnie. "What's all the mystery?"

"Nothing very serious," said Lonnie. "Some woman got a little drunk and insisted on making a disturbance. I was afraid she was going to force her way into the restaurant, so I brought you all in here."

"Very thoughtful of you," said Coster. "I can't stand the sight of a drunken, disorderly woman."

"Yes," said Miss O'Donnell, "very thoughtful, wasn't it, Mr. Pool?"

The Greek gave her one of his indulgent smiles.

"Sometimes, little girl," he said, setting Lonnie's teeth on edge, "you are too smart. Much too smart."

"That's what I keep telling them at the office," said Miss O'Donnell, "but nobody believes me."

"You don't need to be smart," said Coster—"a girl that looks like you." The Greek finished his drink and got up.

"Shall we?" he asked of the girl and Coster, who both got up. "Many thanks for the hospitality, Lonnie. We'll come back often."

"Yes," said Miss O'Donnell, "and next time please arrange some more excitement. I like it."

She offered her hand to Lonnie. It was strong, firm, and cool. He pressed it quickly and let it go. Their eyes met. Her smile was very pleasant and friendly. Lonnie smiled back, but lowered his eyes, momentarily out of countenance and furious with himself for feeling as he did.

As soon as the door closed behind them he began to pace the floor. When Sam came in he found him in a state: his face was flushed and he was talking to himself.

"Hello," said Sam.

Lonnie ignored the greeting.

"Can you imagine a girl like that running around with a no-good, low-life Greek? What's she thinking about? Don't she know he's a chiseling, woman-chasing …"

"Look who's talking," Sam observed.

"Well," said Lonnie, "I'm ten years younger, and I don't paint my toenails and douse myself with perfumery and I don't leer at dames. At least I don't think I do."

"But you *do*," said Sam. "I used to see you leering at Annette."

"That does it," said Lonnie. "Goodbye." He went out, banging the door.

3

Ray was sitting in a booth at the Turf Café, studying a *Racing Form*, sipping a beer, and waiting for Lonnie, who was upstairs playing stud. It was an impromptu game, not one of the big ones, and Ray wasn't much worried about it. They had come in for a drink after a show. The Greek was sitting in a booth with Benny Hayt, sipping a liqueur. They all sat down and talked. Later Gregg, the horseman, showed up with a couple of his friends and after a drink or two suggested some stud.

It was nearly midnight. As it was a Saturday, a rowdy crowd filled the bar, and Gordy, the bartender, was having a little more trouble than usual. There were a lot of outlanders working in the various defense plants of Lake City and either they hadn't learned yet that the Turf Café wasn't a healthy spot to throw your weight around in or they didn't care. After a while Benny appeared from a back room, leaned on the bar, and sadly observed to the crowd that if they didn't slow down on the rough stuff he'd toss them out in the gutter. Benny's manner intimidated most of them, but several of the patrons jeered.

Benny shrugged and touched a buzzer under the bar. Grinning, Ducky Flanagan came in from the back room. He was a huge Irishman who'd fought heavyweight around town for years; he had a broken nose, a scarred and swollen brow, and cauliflower ear. With his friends he was gentle as a lamb, like many prizefighters; but when action was needed at the Turf, he was the man for it.

Ray looked on quietly from his well-protected booth. Ordinarily he was opposed to violence, but swaggering, bragging, and quarrelsomeness irritated him to such an extent that at the moment he was hoping that Ducky would flatten one of these loudmouthed fools.

Ducky rubbed his chin and glanced mildly across the bar at the customers.

"How about it, friends?" he said. "Let's take it a little easy, eh, friends? All everybody wants to do is to have a little fun. Am I right?"

A big lanky man jeered and called:

"Aw, get back in your cage, ape. You ain't so tough."

Ducky came round the end of the bar, grinning. The lanky man stood his ground. Suddenly Ducky dove low, seized the man about the legs, jackknifed him across his shoulder, and started to carry him to the front door. The man dropped his beer glass on the floor, where it smashed, and began to kick and yell. Just at this moment the door that led to the gambling-room upstairs opened and Pool and Lonnie came out.

Ray noticed them and got up. The Greek, who hated violence and considered it a form of stupidity, recoiled slightly, wincing. Lonnie, apparently preoccupied, paid little attention to the struggle and came immediately to Ray's booth.

"Let's get out of here," he said.

"Put me down, put me down," cried the man, comically kicking his legs. "I'll behave."

Benny burst out laughing. Ducky gently set the man on his feet, then stood in front of him, shaking his forefinger at him.

"Now you be good, see? Be nice," he said; then he grinned, winked at the man, and went back behind the bar.

The patrons crowded round the man, all laughing, all good-natured again; then they surged to the bar. Benny was handing out free beer.

Lonnie and Ray were halfway to the door when the Greek caught up with them.

"Lonnie," he said, "funny thing. I forgot to thank you for the way you handled that little business at the inn."

"Forget it."

"No," said the Greek, "I won't forget it. It might have been very embarrassing."

"I'd pay her off and let her go if I were you," said Lonnie.

The Greek didn't like this remark. He bit his lip, stared at the floor.

Lonnie started out and Ray followed him.

"Anyway, thanks," called the Greek.

Lonnie nodded without turning. He and Ray went out. It was a warm, moist night. Mist blurred the vast dimly lit vista of Pulaski Street. It had rained earlier and the asphalt was wet and shining, mirroring the tall light poles.

Near the curb Lonnie stumbled. He stopped, raised his right leg, and gripped his ankle, swearing.

"I told you you weren't ready to drive yet," said Ray. "I wanted you to let Willy."

"Okay," said Lonnie, irritably. "You drive."

He went round the side of the car and got in the passenger seat, smiling ironically. He knew that Ray didn't see well and hated to drive, especially on a wet night, when a car was likely to skid. Ray got in and slammed the door.

"If you'd only listen to me—" he began, but Lonnie cut him off.

"Never mind that. I've got to start driving again some time. I'm tired of babying my leg."

They drove in silence for quite a while through the deserted, dark, shining streets of the warehouse district, then Ray turned off into Keller Road and they saw before them, glimmering faintly through the mist, the clustered neon signs of Oxford Circle and the tall arc lights in among the trees of Oxford Park.

"I dropped ten G's tonight," said Lonnie suddenly.

"What!" cried Ray, and in his excitement jammed on the brakes. The car skidded in the streetcar tracks, went out of control, narrowly missed the concrete rampart of a safety-zone, then glanced lightly off a high curb and righted itself.

Ray's heart was pumping wildly and his vision was blurred. Finally he got himself in hand.

"I didn't like the angle of that last billiard," said Lonnie. "You can do better than that. What you need is a little chalk on your cue."

Ray burned in silence.

When they drove up to the house, all the floodlights were on and the place was lit up as if for a Christmas party. As soon as the car stopped, Willy appeared, looking a little wild.

"Boss," he said, "that dame's here."

"What dame?"

"The Polack!"

"What's she doing here? Is she drunk?"

"No, she's okay. Her brother's with her. I told her we didn't know when you'd be here, but she said she was going to wait."

"What does she want? I don't feel like arguing with a dame tonight."

"You got me. But her brother brought you a whole case of imported Scotch. A present, he said."

"Where did he get a case of Scotch?" Lonnie jumped out of the car in his excitement, turned his ankle again, and sat down on the low wall in front of the house to rub it, swearing.

Ray helped him down the steps. Willy opened the door. Wanda and her brother were sitting stiffly on straight chairs in the hall. They both got up.

"Hello," said Lonnie. "Say, thanks for the Scotch."

The brother flushed slightly.

"Don't mention it, pal."

Wanda was sober and quiet-looking. She didn't seem as tall as she had the night she'd come to the door drunk and furious. Her face looked both refined and coarse, a strange combination. She had high cheekbones, like her brother, a low broad forehead, blond hair, probably dyed, and very dark eyes and eyebrows.

"How do you do, Mr. Drew?" she said, speaking with strained formality. "I hope you don't mind us waiting like this."

"You see—we wanted to talk to you," put in the brother.

"Let's go in the living room," said Lonnie. "I want to sit down. My leg's bothering me."

"You were in the army, weren't you?" asked Wanda politely as they went into the living room. Lonnie nodded. "Were you wounded?"

Lonnie explained about his "wound" and they all laughed. When they were seated Ray looked in.

"Got some work to do," he said. "Good night, everybody." He went out quickly.

Lonnie was going to call him back, then changed his mind. Ray probably needed a drink after that skidding act he'd put on.

"First," said the brother, "we want to thank you for not making any charge against Wanda. The police were very nice to her."

"Yes," said Wanda, "I might have lost my job. They are very strict at Karr-Dean."

Lonnie's face brightened.

"Oh, you work there."

"Yes. Model."

"Do you know Miss O'Donnell?"

Brother and sister exchanged a quick glance, then Wanda laughed, a rather vulgar laugh, and immediately seemed more like the dame Lonnie remembered.

"That's funny. She was asking me about you—all about you."

Lonnie sat up very straight.

"Why?"

"She thinks you're very attractive."

Lonnie felt himself flushing and quickly lit a cigarette to hide his agitation.

"Did she say so?"

"Yes," said Wanda. "You see, I took her aside and told her all about Jack. He's so crazy about this girl that he doesn't know what he is doing. The fool—he asked her to marry him."

"Is she going to?"

Wanda shook her head.

"Not now. Maybe she wasn't even before I talked to her, I don't know. She seems like a pretty smart little girl—I like her. Isn't it funny? Before, I wanted to scratch her eyes out."

"Wanda's always shooting off her mouth," said her brother indulgently, "but she never really does anything."

"I've been going with Jack for two years. He took me every place. All of a sudden I couldn't even get him on the phone. Then I hear the gossip around the shop. I almost went nuts. Now I don't care. I've been a fool long enough."

"She's trying to get a job in New York," explained the brother. "She wants to get away from Lake City."

"Well, I'm glad everything is working out so well," said Lonnie.

"She finally got wise to herself. Guys get tired of dames, especially guys like Pool. Wanda's no school kid. She's been around. Pool was pretty much on the level with her."

"Joe's smart," said Wanda. "Maybe now I'll listen to him." She smiled at her brother.

"If the kid can get located in New York, I'll pull up and go with her. You see, pal, we never been separated."

Lonnie studied the pair of them, wondering. It was a type of relationship outside his experience. There was a short silence.

"The only thing I didn't like about the whole deal," said the brother, "was Wanda trying to queer it for Jack with the O'Donnell dame. But that's done."

"He had *something* coming."

"That's where I disagree. But—"The brother glanced at Lonnie, noting his preoccupation. "Well, we just wanted to thank you."

They all got up and Lonnie shook hands with both of them.

"Many thanks for the Scotch," said Lonnie. "And I'm going to be a gent. I'm not even going to ask where you got it."

The brother grinned self-consciously.

Ray had finally got himself settled down. The trouble with the car had unnerved him, but after a warm shower and a bottle of cold beer he had begun to feel better. Now he was lying in bed reading a volume of Mommsen's *Roman History* and enjoying the cool breeze from the lake, which was blowing in through the open windows, bellying the curtains. The night was quiet and serene. Crickets chirped in the tall grass at the side of the house, and moths tapped gently at the window screens, attracted by his reading light. Suddenly Ray remembered that Lonnie had said he'd lost ten thousand dollars, and sat straight up in bed. The book fell from his hand and he stared at the wall, all nerves again.

Upstairs Lonnie began to sing loudly. His range was small and he jumped from key to key, setting Ray's teeth on edge.

"I'm an old cowhand,
From the Rio Grande ..."

sang Lonnie, making the walls vibrate.

Ray bore it for a moment, then he bounded out of bed and hurried upstairs.

"I want to talk to that Brooklyn cowhand," he grumbled.

He knocked at Lonnie's bedroom door, then went in. Lonnie was sitting on the edge of his bed in red-and-white striped pajamas, soaking his right foot in a tub of steaming-hot water, balancing a tall highball glass, and singing at the top of his voice.

Ray looked at him in silence. In a moment Lonnie stopped singing. "What's your trouble?" he demanded.

"What about that ten grand?"

"Well, what about it? Forget it. Ancient history. You should know all about that—you read enough books on it."

"Why, you're higher than a kite!" cried Ray; then he began to laugh. "You're crazy," he concluded.

"This is good Scotch," said Lonnie. "That big Polack knows good Scotch when he sees it. I wonder where he stole it."

"What happened with Wanda?"

Just as Lonnie was going to reply, Willy came in with a teakettle. Willy was loaded, too.

"Hi ya, Ray, old boy!" he said, and began to pour water from the teakettle into the foot-tub.

Lonnie let out a yell and went straight up into the air, grabbing his right foot and dropping his highball glass.

"What's the matter?" asked Willy, staring. "Is it too hot?"

Lonnie merely looked at him. Ray leaned against the wall, helpless with laughter.

4

Miss O'Donnell started slightly when she saw Lonnie standing on the corner of Motley Street and Ashland Boulevard. He was holding a newspaper in front of him, but he wasn't reading it. As she approached, he lowered the paper, smiled, and touched his hat.

"Hello, Miss O'Donnell," he said. "How are you this evening?"

"Oh, I'm all right."

"Probably worn out from the fashion show."

She stopped and studied his face. There was an expression on it she didn't quite like—something resembling a smirk.

"As a matter of fact, yes. But how did you know?"

"Read about it in the paper this morning. I looked in for a few minutes, but there were too many fat dames sitting around."

"You looked in!" She began to laugh. "What ever for?"

"To see you."

"Did you see me?"

"Yes. You were modeling a black-lace negligee."

"That's when you *would* look in."

"I like you better this way."

She was wearing a smartly tailored suit and a brown, snap-brim hat with a feather in it.

"Thanks."

"We shouldn't be standing around like this," said Lonnie. "I've got to get you off your feet. How about the Palm Bar at the Erie? Or is that too close to home?"

"Mr. Drew," she said, drawing out her words, "there is something about your manner I don't like. In the first place, why should we go any place at all? In the second place, I'm not in the habit of going to bars except with my closest friends. In the third place, why shouldn't I go to the Erie Hotel or any other hotel if I feel like it? Goodbye. So nice to have seen you."

She turned away abruptly and started across Motley Street just as the light changed. Cars whizzed past, one coming very close to her. She was forced back to the curb. Lonnie caught up with her.

"Look, Miss O'Donnell," he said, taking her arm, "I was only kidding. Why don't you have dinner with me? Or maybe you've got an engagement. Just say so." He was torn between annoyance at her manner and desire for her company. What a hoity-toity babe!

"I have no engagement," she said, looking straight ahead. "I seldom go out. I'm on my way home to get a little rest."

"Are you going to walk?"

"I always walk."

"You mean nobody ever meets you?"

"I don't encourage it."

The light changed. She started briskly across the street. Lonnie was furious. The hell with you, he thought, and hurried back to his parked car, where he had a huge bunch of flowers and a box of candy. He got in and drove off, gritting his teeth.

But the nearer he got to the inn, the calmer he became.

"It was that crack about the Erie Hotel that did it. I didn't mean because the Greek lived there—I meant because it was right across from Karr-Dean. But I couldn't say so." Suddenly he burst out laughing. "What a going-over I got!" It kept getting funnier and funnier.

He turned in at the inn, parked his car, and went into the bar, where he drank three quick highballs before Sam found out he was there. George strolled over and inquired politely about his health, then Sam came hurrying from the office. He had a telegram in his hand.

"Came a few minutes ago," he said, handing it to Lonnie, who tore it open, glanced at it carelessly, then stuffed it into his pocket.

His luck was bad, very bad, and things were running in threes as usual. First, he'd dropped ten G's in a stud game—a pickup game at that. Second, he'd swung and he'd missed as far as Miss O'Donnell was concerned. Third, the buyer he'd had all hopped up about the inn had backed down at the last minute—it was in the telegram.

"What's on your mind, Lonnie?" Sam inquired. "You look a little flushed."

"Sam, you think you know something about the brush-off."

Sam raised his eyebrows.

"In this business I have to."

"You're just a boy, just a boy." Lonnie reached for a fresh highball. Sam noted the gesture and began to understand the flush.

"I'm willing to learn."

"It's an art—something you're born with, Sam. Don't worry your pretty little head about it."

A few minutes later Jack Pool came in and sat down next to Lonnie at the bar. Lonnie turned.

"Stepping out tonight, Jack?"

The Greek glanced at Lonnie wearily.

"What's the joke?"

"No joke. I've got a nice box of candy and some flowers in the car. You're welcome to them."

The Greek smiled faintly.

"That's a little out of my line."

"Corny, you mean?"

"Well—!" The Greek spoke evasively, then he turned to the bartender. "A double Martini, please."

"What do you suggest?"

"I make no suggestions."

Lonnie ordered another highball.

"Jack," he said, "that certainly was a beautiful girl you had in here the other night."

The Greek shrugged.

"No kidding," Lonnie went on, "I've never seen a more beautiful girl in my life. Know her very well?"

The Greek hesitated; his lips tightened, he got a little pale. Finally he turned to Lonnie and spoke with icy politeness.

"Maybe you are joking—maybe you've had one too many highballs. We'll say it's that. But please do not pry into my private business. It is something that annoys me very much."

Lonnie came to himself with a start. He'd been acting like a fool all day. The Greek was right.

"Sorry Jack," he said. Then he got up and went out. The Greek turned and looked after him.

"Stupid oaf!" he exclaimed under his breath.

The bartender brought him his cocktail. He drank it hurriedly, hesitated for a moment, then went to a pay telephone and called Miss O'Donnell. She was a long time in answering.

"Hello, Maureen," said the Greek.

"Oh, it's you, Mr. Pool."

"Why do you insist on calling me Mr. Pool, Maureen?"

"It's a very nice name. Look, I just got out of the tub; the window's open and there's a breeze blowing."

"I'll call you back in half an hour."

"Please don't. I'm going right to bed."

"This early?"

"Do you mind?"

The Greek restrained with great difficulty the biting recriminatory words he wanted to utter.

"Not at all. Good night. Pleasant dreams."

He went back to the bar and ordered another double Martini. "This is not really happening to *me*," he told himself. "It couldn't be."

It was four a.m. when Pinky woke Ray. He'd been asleep about an hour and he felt groggy and jittery at being waked up so suddenly. Pinky had on a dirty undershirt and sawed-off dungarees, and his pale-red hair was standing up all over his round head.

"Now what?" Ray demanded.

"The boss—he's drunk as a lord. I'm sure worried about him. He came home about half an hour ago and began yelling around because he couldn't find Willy. I went up to see what was the matter and he gave me a box of candy and a bunch of flowers!"

"What!" cried Ray, getting hastily out of bed, putting on his slippers, and throwing on a bathrobe.

"Yeah," said Pinky. "And now Willy's home. Willy's a little tight, too. The boss has got his trunks on and he says he's going to swim to Bass Island and call on Mr. Keller, and Willy's got to go along with the rowboat. And Willy's all for it."

Ray started out. Pinky followed him, still talking.

"Yeah, and the boss says he wants to call on Mr. Keller so he can get into society and be somebody and not be a bum all his life."

"He *must* be drunk," said Ray.

They found Lonnie in the kitchen. He had on a pair of red trunks and a stiff straw hat. He was stinking drunk. Willy was opening a fresh bottle of Scotch.

"Glad you're home, Lonnie," said Ray. "I found a couple of sleepers in the *Form* and I want to talk to you about them."

Ray sat down unconcernedly and took the *Racing Form* out of his bathrobe pocket.

"Remember Sir Knight? They've lowered him and he's going seven furlongs. Looks like a good thing."

"Horses, horses, horses," sang Lonnie.

Willy giggled loudly and almost dropped the bottle.

"The other one owes us money," said Ray. "Flying Fast. He's lowered, too. Of course he won't be the price of the other horse. But—"

"Flying Backwards—that's what he ought to be called, the goat!" said Lonnie. "I'm through betting on horses and being a bum. I'm going to get some place, see? That's why I want to talk to Keller. He'll give me a right steer, you can bet on that."

Ray and Pinky exchanged a glance. Willy had finally got the bottle open and was now stumbling around looking for glasses.

"I'll take a drink, Willy," said Ray. "Get me a water glass. I want a real slug."

Lonnie turned and looked at Ray foggily for a moment, then his eyes cleared.

"No hard liquor for you, Ray. It damn near killed you once. What's the matter with you?"

Ray congratulated himself silently on his inspiration.

"I'm tired of never getting drunk," he said. "You seem to be enjoying it. I think I'll have some fun for once."

"Put that stuff away," yelled Lonnie.

Willy turned and stared blankly.

"You heard me," Lonnie insisted loudly and belligerently. "That stuff's poison to old Ray."

Willy shrugged meekly and put the bottle away. Lonnie sat down at the table and put his arm across Ray's shoulder.

"You leave that stuff alone, pal," he said. "It's poison to you."

"Well, if you say so. You're the boss. Now how about taking a look at these horses, Lonnie. Maybe we can make a little dough."

They got him to bed a little before five. As soon as his head hit the pillow he was snoring.

In the kitchen Pinky turned on Willy.

"What do you mean, egging him on? Good thing Ray was here."

"Ray's a goddamn old woman," said Willy bitterly.

Pinky slapped Willy hard.

"Don't you never say that when I'm around."

Willy stared at Pinky in astonishment, holding his face; then he sat down at the kitchen table and began to cry.

Ray couldn't sleep. It was broad daylight. He lay looking out the window at Bass Island, dark-green and beautiful on the pale-blue water. It was so clear that he could see the white houses on the shore and an American flag flying from a pole at the Keller pier.

He was worried about Lonnie. It wasn't like him to get so drunk. As a matter of fact, Lonnie was hardly a drinking man at all; he seemed to have no need for it; he was a social drinker only, as a rule.

Ray shook his head slowly, wondering. Then he got up to get a cigarette.

5

It was a rainy Sunday evening. Things were very slow at the Lake Shore Inn. Most of the waiters were standing about, staring into space; the bartenders were polishing glasses and wishing it was closing time; and George, the headwaiter, who usually talked to no one except in the line of duty, had condescended to hold a conversation with Irma at the cashier's counter. Outside, a stiff wind from the lake whipped the tops of the tall oak and elm trees and blew the rain against the big front windows of the restaurant.

In the office Lonnie and Gregg, the horseman, were playing gin rummy for a hundred dollars a game, and Sam and Ray were looking on. Sam was itching to get into the game, but was waiting to be asked. After all, he was supposed to be working.

Lonnie went down with nine. Gregg tossed in his hand with a slight grimace. Lonnie penciled in a mark for another game and began to shuffle the cards. Gregg sat watching the rain running down the windowpanes.

"Off track sure for Monday," he said, "and I got a couple of fast-track horses going. It beats all."

Lonnie grunted and dealt the cards. Gregg picked up his hand, grimaced at it, then refused the draw. Lonnie picked up a card and went down with nine again. Gregg raised his eyes to the ceiling.

"How much do I owe?" he asked.

"Eight hundred," said Lonnie.

"This is getting boring. How about one for five hundred?"

"Why not make it eight?"

"Why, you're a gentleman after my own heart," said Gregg. Then he turned to Ray and Sam. "Isn't he a gentleman, now?"

"That's one way of looking at it," said Sam.

Lonnie shrugged.

"I'm tired of the game. If Gregg wins we're even and we can quit."

"Quit right now, Lonnie, if you want to," said Gregg. "Don't worry about me."

Lonnie shrugged and lit a cigarette. Gregg shuffled, dealt the cards, and went down with ten on the third draw.

"That's that," said Lonnie, yawning and throwing down his hand.

Ray and Sam exchanged a glance, then turned away. George knocked and came in.

"Excuse me, Mr. Ballard," he said, "young Mr. Keller and his sister are here. They have a guest. I put them in the first booth. I thought perhaps you'd like to come out and say hello to them."

"Thanks, George."

"On a night like this the bluebloods show up," said Lonnie with a laugh. "Go bow low, Sam. We might have to touch the old man someday."

Sam smiled and followed George out.

Ray went over in a corner to read the paper, and Lonnie and Gregg began to talk languidly of horse racing, then of gambling in general. Ray had never heard Lonnie sound so bored and indifferent, and from time to time he glanced up at him. Lonnie's face looked drawn. He'd light a cigarette, take a few puffs, throw it away, then light another one. Even Gregg began to notice Lonnie's boredom. He got up.

"Think I'll go eat," he said.

Lonnie merely waved indifferently. Gregg went out. Lonnie yawned loudly and widely, almost dislocating his jaw.

"You need a tonic," said Ray, glancing up. "Or maybe a shot of B-1."

"Thinking I might take a jaunt to New York," said Lonnie. "I understand the Greek left last night."

"I didn't know you were that friendly with Pool," said Ray, studying him, trying to sound him out.

"It's got nothing to do with him—except that he gave me the idea. Tough getting a hotel room, though. I understand they only let you stay one night."

"You can always sleep in the gutter."

"You meet a nice class of people that way."

"Now I *know* you need a tonic."

Lonnie rose and began to pace the floor.

"I got a tip," he said, "that the Greek took an awful pasting on a boat race that slipped. The horse ran fourth at long odds and the Greek had him across. I think maybe it was a syndicate bet: Keller and Benny, too. The Greek went East, I guess, to dig up a big bankroll."

"That's why you better hold on to the restaurant," said Ray. "It might come in handy."

"I'll hold on till I get my price."

Sam came back in, smiling.

"Everything's lovely. They all ordered *petite marmite* and we're cooking it special. Jack Pool's girlfriend's with them."

"Not the Polack?" exclaimed Lonnie, turning so suddenly that his bad ankle gave way and he almost fell.

Ray and Sam exchanged a puzzled glance.

"No," said Sam. "Little bright-eyes with the long dark hair. My dream girl."

"What's she doing with the Kellers, for God's sake?" Lonnie demanded savagely.

Ray glanced at Lonnie, bewildered. What in hell had got into the guy lately?

Sam looked at Lonnie in mild surprise.

"Why not? Is there a law or something?"

"This I've got to see," said Lonnie, and went out abruptly.

"Say, what's wrong with him?" asked Sam.

Ray shook his head slowly.

"I don't know. But whatever it is, it's serious."

Lonnie walked across the restaurant, looking neither right nor left, and stopped at the cashier's counter.

"A Corona, Irma."

The cashier got out the box and held it for him till he selected one; then she put it back and said:

"Every time she comes in, you come out."

"What's that—a song title?"

"Don't kid me, please, Mr. Drew. I've been around too long."

Lonnie turned.

"Oh, you mean her." Then he smiled and bowed slightly. Miss O'Donnell was speaking to him, smiling very pleasantly. Lonnie felt so uplifted that it scared him. All his life he'd felt nothing but the most casual emotions; he'd always been master of the situation. This was different, very different. He'd heard about guys running away from things. He'd always jeered at the idea. His instinct was to rush in, get it over with. Now he understood.

"I'll go back in the office—ignore her," he told himself. Instead he walked over to their booth and stood smiling, and glancing from Miss O'Donnell to the two Keller kids. Toby, the boy, was seventeen—chunky, sandy-haired, freckled, and ugly. His sister, Jean, twenty-one or two, was also sandy-haired and freckled, rather pleasant-looking in a somewhat boyish way, and she had an air that was lacking in her brother.

Miss O'Donnell introduced them to Lonnie, who acknowledged it, then said:

"I've met your father a couple of times. Very nice man."

Brother and sister exchanged a glance, then laughed.

"He doesn't know Pop," said Toby, and they laughed again.

Lonnie was a little bewildered and glanced at Miss O'Donnell, who smiled.

"Don't pay any attention to them. They're always joking, especially about their father. Won't you sit down, Mr. Drew?"

Lonnie hesitated, cleared his throat, and looked at his watch. Miss O'Donnell watched him from under lowered lids, smiling slightly.

"It's a busy night for me," said Lonnie, "but I can sit for a few minutes." He sat down.

"Very nice of you," said Miss O'Donnell, "to give us a few minutes of your time."

Lonnie glanced at her, wondering. But she was smiling at him calmly.

"We were just talking about Mary's life," said Jean, "and Toby and I have decided that she leads the most interesting one of anybody we know."

"Mary?"

"Her," said Toby, pointing at Miss O'Donnell. "Maybe you think her name is Maureen, but it's really Mary. For that matter, her name's not even O'Donnell—it's Donnell. Mary Donnell."

"Giving away my trade secrets—fine thing!"

"When we were in school together," said Jean, "Mary always said she'd lead an interesting life, and she's kept her word. All the other girls wanted to marry rich men and settle down. Even I did."

"You're telling *us*," Toby put in.

"Oh," said Lonnie, completely bewildered, addressing Jean Keller, "did you and—and Miss Donnell go to school together?"

"Yes. She was the most beautiful girl in the school. I was the ugliest. That is what drew us together."

"Don't you believe it," said Toby. "Mary always had more boys hanging around her than she knew what to do with. Sis got the overflow."

They all laughed and Lonnie joined in, not because he felt like laughing, but because he felt awkward, ill at ease.

"Shall I tell him all about your interesting life, Mary?" Toby demanded.

"I don't mind. But it might bore him. I understand he leads a very interesting life himself."

"Running a restaurant?" cried Toby, his voice cracking slightly. Then he caught himself. "Oh, sure. That probably is very interesting."

Mary Donnell burst out laughing, and Lonnie shifted and flushed.

"Oh, I do other things. Like playing marbles for keeps," said Lonnie, trying hard.

It got a laugh, much to his relief, and Toby turned and studied him for the first time.

"Gambling, you mean?"

"In a small way."

"Jeeps!" cried Toby. "Everybody Mary knows is a gambler. Take Mr. Pool, for instance. Of course, he's a professional gambler; that's different. When Pop found out Mary was going around with Mr. Pool, he almost blew a fuse. He thought it was awful."

"Mary's always doing awful things," said Jean. "But it's all in the spirit of good clean fun."

"How do you feel about professional gamblers, Mr. Drew?" asked Mary, smiling innocently.

"I can take them or leave them. Taking them is more fun."

They all looked at him. Then Toby got it. He laughed raucously.

"Toby!" admonished Jean. "I wish your voice would make up its mind which way it's going."

"That's a nice crack, Mr. Drew," Toby conceded when he'd stopped laughing. "I must remember that. Is it original?"

"More or less." Lonnie was beginning to feel a little at ease. He puffed calmly on his cigar. "Let's hear some more about Mary's life."

"Well," said Jean, "she had a chance to go on the stage in New York in a girl show, but her father got so upset over it that he made her quit school and come home. Then she ran away, but her uncle went after her and brought her home again. She went to State for a year and was elected the prettiest girl on the campus, in spite of the fact she was a freshman. Then Lloyd Coster discovered her, and his father gave her a job. She makes more money than any two models in Lake City."

"The end," said Mary. "It doesn't sound very interesting to me. Does it to you, Mr. Drew?"

"Well—it's too sketchy," said Lonnie. "And I can't read between the lines."

"There's plenty there, too, I'll bet!" Toby said to Lonnie, man to man. "My aunt says Mr. Pool is one of the most wicked-looking persons she's ever seen."

"Toby!" Jean exclaimed.

There was a brief silence, then Lonnie got up.

"I think I see your food coming. I hope you enjoy it. Very glad to have met you all."

He turned and hurried toward the office. He wanted to get away and think things over. They'd be in the restaurant for quite a while; he could always go back.

"Wasn't that a little abrupt?" asked Jean. "My, he's handsome!"

"Does he really gamble?" asked Toby. "Or was he kidding?"

"I really don't know," said Mary, looking pensively off after Lonnie.

Jean winked at Toby.

"I think Mary likes him. She insisted on eating here. We could just as well have eaten at home."

"I find him very amusing," said Mary, but there was something a little unnatural in the way she made this calm statement and both Toby and Jean turned and looked at her.

Lonnie had told George to keep him posted in regard to Mary and her friends. As soon as they got ready to leave, he was to be notified. He was sitting in the office, reading a newspaper. Ray and Sam were checking over the account of the day's receipts and occasionally glancing over at Lonnie, trying to interpret his long, persistent silence.

The house phone rang. Lonnie grabbed it with such violence that both Sam and Ray started.

"Okay," said Lonnie. "Thanks." Then he got up hurriedly and went out.

"It's getting me down," said Ray.

"It's probably a dame."

"I never saw him act that way over a dame."

Toby was helping Mary on with her coat. Lonnie came up smiling.

"Leaving?"

"Yes," said Jean. "The food was delicious."

"I wish you didn't have to go all the way into town with me, Toby," said Mary. "It's not late. I'll be all right."

"Jeeps, no!" said Toby. "The old man would bite my head off."

"What's the trouble?" asked Lonnie.

"Well," said Toby, "Mary brought her car and we have ours. We're going to follow her home—see that she gets there safe."

"Doesn't that sound silly?" Mary asked of Lonnie.

"No," he said, "it doesn't. It's a long dark ride into town."

"You see?" demanded Toby of Mary.

"Wait a minute," said Lonnie. "I've got to go downtown myself. I can follow you in."

He glanced from one to the other. Jean was looking at Mary with a rather strange expression, he thought.

"If you're going in anyway," said Mary, "of course—"

They left it that way.

Lonnie had a little trouble following Mary into town. It had started to rain again, making the visibility poor; besides, his right ankle and foot were bothering him, and when he pressed too heavily on the accelerator, pains shot up his leg. The wind had died and the rain was falling straight down now, a steady, gentle rain. All the streets were shining like black glass.

He caught up with her at an intersection near town. As they waited for the light to change, she smiled and said:

"The boulevard lights start here. I'll be all right now."

Lonnie shook his head.

"I might as well go all the way."

She shrugged slightly. She looked so beautiful and so incongruous driving her battered old Ford coupe that Lonnie just sat there staring. She noticed the intentness of the stare and smiled rather shyly, he thought. They were so preoccupied that they missed the light, and a car behind them honked wildly. They both drove off, laughing.

In a few minutes Mary parked in front of an old apartment building on the near West Side, just off Ashland Boulevard and the downtown section, and Lonnie parked behind her, got out quickly, and opened her car door for her.

"Thanks so much," said Mary. "It really wasn't necessary. But the Kellers are so conventional."

"They didn't sound very conventional to me," said Lonnie. "Or maybe I don't know what the word means." As he spoke, he quickly took off his topcoat and threw it around her. "Hurry. You'll get wet."

They ran up the walk to the shelter of the deep entryway of the apartment building. As they mounted the last step Lonnie stumbled and almost fell.

"Sorry," he said, very much annoyed. He didn't want Mary to think he was an oaf.

"It's slippery," said Mary, looking at him with veiled surprise. There was something so graceful about his appearance that his awkwardness puzzled her.

"No," said Lonnie, "it's my gimp. I was in the army for nearly two years."

"You were wounded?" asked Mary with marked interest.

Much to his own surprise, Lonnie for the first time wanted to lie about his injured leg. He hesitated, then told her the truth. Mary laughed.

"It got me out, anyway," said Lonnie, a little ruffled by her laughter.

"You didn't like it in the army?"

"No. Does anybody? I didn't mind getting shot at so much. But in the army you don't belong to yourself any longer. They own you! That I didn't like."

"I see what you mean," said Mary thoughtfully. There was a brief pause. "I really should go in now."

"Yes. It's cold and damp. You might catch cold."

She offered her hand. He pressed it gently, not wanting her to go, but not quite knowing what to do to prevent it. He felt unsure, ill at ease, far from his usual self-confident self. Mary withdrew her hand.

"I'd like to ask you in for a drink," she said. "After all, it was a long drive for you. But that's impossible. I share my apartment, and—" Her voice trailed off.

Lonnie laughed, feeling much better.

"I was going to suggest that we might drop over to the Erie or some place," he said, "but the last time I made a suggestion like that—"

"What was the matter with you that day? I was furious with you. You smirked at me as if I were a pickup you'd never seen before."

"Maybe I was a little jittery," said Lonnie. "How about it—shall we go someplace?"

"Well—" Mary temporized. "For a few minutes."

Things were a little slow at Salini's. There were scarcely a dozen people in the huge combination bar and café. Lonnie and Mary were sitting in a booth. He had a highball before him and she was drinking tea.

"The Kellers are trying to be very nice to me," she was explaining. "But it gets rather boring at times. Mr. Keller thinks I'm a lost woman, or something like that." She laughed and put her head on one side, and her thick dark hair, with its glints of red, moved across her shoulder and slid round to the front. She put it back with such a graceful, charming gesture that Lonnie stared at her in open admiration, knowing himself to be lost, resisting it feebly, and not having the slightest idea, at the moment, what to do about it.

He'd never met a person like her; in fact, he'd never even conceived of such a one. It wasn't only that she was the most beautiful girl he'd ever seen that made him seem to himself tongue-tied and awkward. There was something in her manner that threw him off, put him on the defensive, dampened his usual high spirits, and made him feel young, inexperienced, and gauche—a sort of gentle superiority, a thinly veiled satirical approach to things and people. He had an uneasy feeling that inwardly she was laughing at him, that he amused her as a pet monkey amused people.

"You see," she was saying, "Mr. Keller knew my father and my uncle. He also knows Mr. Coster, who was responsible for my coming to Lake City. He does his best to see that I live the kind of life he thinks is correct."

"Very nice of him," said Lonnie, not quite liking her tone.

"I suppose he means well. But I'm just not suited to the Keller type of life. Parties all the time—and always the same self-sufficient people, the same little group."

"Jack Pool's no improvement," Lonnie interposed, annoyed.

She glanced at him sharply, then smiled.

"You mustn't try to take Mr. Keller's place," she said sweetly. "One is enough. Besides, why should you object to Mr. Pool?"

Lonnie started to reply to this exceedingly awkward question several times, but hesitated, compressing his lips. Mary said nothing; she merely watched his struggle. Finally he said weakly:

"He's old enough to be your father. The Greek's at least forty-two."

"I must say," said Mary, taking a sip from her teacup, "that's a very feeble objection."

Lonnie flushed.

"You're right. I shouldn't have said anything in the first place. Forget it."

"No, we won't forget it. Because I want you to understand about Mr. Pool. He is a very persistent man. He almost forced Mr. Coster to introduce him. He has a huge account at Karr-Dean. Business, you know. He's been charming to me—nothing the slightest bit out of the way. Except lately—" She hesitated.

"Yes?" prompted Lonnie, eagerly.

Mary looked at him for a long time.

"Isn't it funny that I should talk to you like this? I don't understand it at all. I've hardly spoken a word to you before, and here I am talking to you as if—as if you were my brother."

"Wait a minute!" exclaimed Lonnie, annoyed. "This is the first time in my life any girl has ever said anything like that to me. Sorry! I'm not the brother type."

"Oh, don't be silly," said Mary with a touch of temper, and Lonnie looked at her in surprise. For a brief moment he'd caught a glimpse of a Mary he didn't know existed. A flash and it was gone. But he'd noticed how her eyes had darkened and narrowed and he felt a sultry power that he couldn't imagine existing in such a delicate-looking girl.

"Nothing silly about that," said Lonnie, doggedly. "I resent it, that's all."

"Anyway, I didn't mean it," said Mary indifferently. "It was a stupid thing to say. But I intended it as a compliment."

Lonnie's heart stirred painfully. He flushed and looked about him in embarrassment, then he leaned toward Mary and said in a low voice:

"You're the most beautiful girl I've ever seen in my life. I've been acting like a fool ever since the first day I saw you."

Mary looked at him fixedly for a long time.

"Why do you suppose I ate at the Lake Shore Inn tonight?"

"It was handy for the Kellers."

"No. I insisted. I wanted to see you. I thought perhaps you might not ask me for a date again after the way I acted."

"I would have, though."

"I know that now, but—" Mary hesitated briefly, then smiled. "You see, I talked to Wanda Pavlovsky about you. And she's very attractive and scheming and sophisticated and all that sort of thing. And she had ideas about you—I'm certain she did."

"No, she didn't. I got her out of a jam."

"Yes, I know. Even so."

Lonnie pondered.

"I talked to her about you," he said finally. "She came down to the beach one night to see me."

Mary stared at him intently.

"What happened?"

"Nothing. Her brother was with her. They brought me a case of Scotch."

"Well, that's a new approach."

"Has she gone to New York yet?"

"Of course not. That was all talk."

Lonnie studied her face carefully. Why was Mary so upset? Could she possibly be jealous? Lonnie rejected the thought. It seemed inconceivable.

"She told me that you'd thought of marrying Jack Pool," probed Lonnie.

"*He* thought of it—I didn't. I wouldn't consider it." There was a brief silence. Mary leaned toward him. "Wanda said you invited her into your bedroom, and you'd never seen her before."

Lonnie started and flushed.

"I was ribbing her. She was so drunk she didn't know her name. Anyway, her brother was with her."

"She didn't tell *me* so."

"Say, what is this?" Lonnie demanded. "Am I a little boy and you the teacher?"

"Oh, men!" Mary exclaimed. "If a girl looks at them they go all to pieces."

"You should know."

"Yes, I *do* know," she said angrily. "And that's why I have so little respect for them. Even Mr. Coster—silly old man!"

"You mean he's been making passes at you?"

"Very polite ones—all in the spirit of fun, of course."

Lonnie thought for a moment, not quite liking the turn the conversation had taken.

"Yes," he said finally, "I guess you must know a lot about it. Older men probably started throwing passes at you as soon as you left home."

"Yes," said Mary, "as soon as I started working."

She had been staring into her teacup as she spoke. Now she looked up at Lonnie, and although she was smiling, he thought he sensed a certain unhappiness in her expression and a certain wariness in regard to himself. This bothered him. He did not want her to think of him as just a man—any man; he wanted her to put him in a class all by himself.

For her part, Mary was wondering if she hadn't been a little precipitate in admitting that she'd used dinner at the inn merely as a pretext to see him. After all, what did she know about this tall, blond, cocky young man? Her instincts told her that he was a decent fellow at heart and that she could trust him. But it was so easy to be wrong. And hadn't Wanda insisted that Lonnie wasn't as nice as he looked and that he had quite a reputation as a chaser?

They drove home in silence, both preoccupied. Lonnie was trying to think of something to say that would put Mary entirely at ease. And Mary was trying to think of something to say that would efface the wrong impression she felt she'd created. What had possessed her to be so outspoken? If Lonnie knew her better he couldn't possibly misunderstand. But as it was—!

Lonnie walked with her to the entryway. There was a dim night-light burning now and the big outer hall was full of shadows. It had stopped raining, but the tall trees in front of the apartment house were still dripping, and water was running musically through the drainpipes.

"It's late, isn't it?" said Mary. "We must have sat there longer than I thought. I'll be dopey tomorrow. I need so much sleep."

"I need hardly any," said Lonnie absently. Then: "Will it be all right if I meet you tomorrow night?"

"I'd rather you wouldn't."

"Why?"

"I have a certain feeling about it. I don't like meeting people on corners."

"I'm not just 'people,' I hope. Anyway, I don't have to meet you on a corner. Suppose I come here after you? We'll have dinner—see a show—whatever you like."

Mary thought it over.

"All right. Meet me here at seven."

Lonnie grinned happily, slipped his arm around her, and was going to kiss her, but she drew back and looked at him calmly.

"Why are you in such a hurry, Lonnie?"

Nonplussed, he withdrew his arm.

"I'm in no particular hurry."

"Well, then—!"

Lonnie laughed, took her hand, and stood pressing it gently. What a wonderful kid! —clever and with a will of her own, but so sweet and charming and lovely that he felt nothing but tenderness for her at this moment. Also he felt strong and protective.

"If you ever have any trouble with Jack Pool, let me know," he said masterfully.

There was a short silence. Mary laughed and pulled her hand away.

"My hero!" she exclaimed. Then: "Why should I have any trouble with him? He's a perfectly reasonable man."

Lonnie was stung.

"That's just what he isn't!"

"Anyway," said Mary, "I think it's very silly of you to take an attitude like that. Suppose I said: 'If you have any trouble with Wanda, let me know.'"

"The hell with Wanda! I hardly know the girl."

"You may—if you're not careful."

"Just forget I said anything, if that's the way you feel about it. I was only—" Lonnie broke off. Damned if he was going to try to justify himself. He felt very much ruffled.

There was a long pause. They stood several feet apart, staring at each other.

"Well—good night," said Mary, and, turning, she went in hurriedly. Lonnie heard the big front door close.

He walked slowly back to his car, lost in thought.

Ray came in the house hurriedly. Pinky was in the hall and jerked his thumb toward the back of the house, then shrugged. Ray went out into the kitchen. Lonnie was sitting in the breakfast room with his hat on, eating ham and eggs.

"Well?" he demanded, turning.

"I almost got shot by the watchman," said Ray, "but I finally got the books. They're in the car. Too heavy for me to carry in."

"Willy," called Lonnie, "go help Pinky carry in the ledgers. Put them on the kitchen table."

Looking bewildered, Willy went out.

"Fine time of night to start figuring," said Ray. "Sam will think we don't trust him. Probably the watchman's called him up by now."

"I'm not going to worry about that," said Lonnie, shoveling food into his mouth.

"If I'm not too inquisitive," said Ray, "what the hell is this all about?"

"I'll tell you." Lonnie waved a fork. "I'm going to figure how to cut expenses and increase profits."

Ray stared.

"Why not let Sam—?"

"No. I'm going to do it myself. It's time I paid a little attention to business."

"Well, I'll be goddamned," said Ray. Then he rose and got himself a bottle of beer. "Look, Lonnie; let me in on this. What's going on?"

Lonnie turned.

"I'm thinking about getting married."

Ray sat down heavily, ignoring his beer. Willy and Pinky stamped into the kitchen and began to put the heavy ledgers down with thumps that shook the rickety old house.

"Be with you in a minute, boys," said Lonnie.

6

"Here comes the car!" yelled Pinky, running back into the house and colliding with Willy, who had just decided to come out. They were having a bitter argument when Ray opened the hall door and called to them.

"You both better get back in the kitchen."

Willy started away, but Pinky took Ray by the arm. "Is he really thinking about marrying this tomato, Ray?"

"I guess so," said Ray, nodding his head solemnly. "He's sure in a dither."

"He was in a dither about that Claudia babe," said Pinky hopefully.

Willy had come back to get an earful. He broke in. "Yeah. He sure was—for a while."

"Then," said Pinky, "he had to leave town to get rid of her."

"This sounds different," said Ray. "More serious."

"You mean he's really asked her to get hitched?" Pinky demanded.

"No, I don't think so. But he's going to. You know him. Once he gets an idea in his head—!" Ray glanced at Willy and Pinky. They both looked so sad and apprehensive that he couldn't keep from laughing. "Anyway, what do you guys care?"

"I don't want no dame bossing me around," said Pinky loftily. "I'll quit first."

"Me, too," Willy chimed in. "That's one reason I always liked to work for Lonnie. No dame to boss you around. Dames are a lot bossier than men."

"Here they come," said Ray. "Beat it."

Pinky and Willy rushed out, banging the hall door behind them, just as the front door opened. Ray's mouth sagged when he saw Mary. She had on a yellow sweater, a plain tan skirt, short socks, and flat-heeled shoes. She had tied a bright yellow silk scarf over her hair. She looked very young. Ray had never seen such an attractive girl before.

"This is my friend Ray Cooper I've been telling you about," said Lonnie.

"Hello, Ray," said Mary, smiling and offering her hand, which Ray held longer than was necessary.

"This is Mary Donnell," said Lonnie.

"How are you, Mary? It's a pleasure to see you here."

Lonnie glanced at Ray with some irritation. Did he have to act so awkward and silly?

"Is lunch ready?" he cut in.

"I think so. I'll go see." Ray smiled at Mary so softly and indulgently that Lonnie was reminded of the Greek and grimaced slightly. As soon as Ray had gone, Lonnie said:

"He's a nice old character. Let's go in the living room."

Mary glanced up at him, wondering why he was acting in such an unnatural manner. Then she looked about her at the house, noting how worn the rugs were and how much everything needed cleaning. There was a large, intricate cobweb just over the living room door, and a beam of light, striking down from the high hall window, mercilessly revealed the dustiness of the hall table and all the articles on it.

She followed Lonnie into the living room. The floor creaked ominously as they walked over to the huge windows that overlooked the lake and a long sweep of Half Moon Beach.

"Nice view," said Lonnie.

"Yes, beautiful. Oh, I can see the Keller place on the island. Did you build this house, Lonnie?"

"Me? It's twenty years old. I bought it cheap from a fellow who lost all his money in a crap game. I had it before the war. Pinky and Willy lived here while I was in the service. Ray was here awhile, too."

"You've got quite a retinue, then."

"Oh, they come in handy. After the war I want to get a big motorboat. Take cruises. Do you like boats, Mary?"

"Of course."

But she was paying little attention. She was surreptitiously looking about her. The living room, if anything, was dustier, more neglected, than the hall. It even smelled dusty.

"With a big motorboat I could take trips to Buffalo and over to Canada. I could go clear to Duluth if I wanted to...."

Lonnie was interrupted by the opening of a door. Willy popped in. He looked a little embarrassed. He had on a white coat that was much too large for him, and his blue-black hair was standing on end. Mary turned to look at him. His eyes got bigger and bigger.

"Lunch's ready, Mr. Drew," he said in a loud, unnatural voice. Then he popped back into the dining room.

Mary struggled to keep her face straight.

"That was Willy," said Lonnie. "He's another character. One of his brothers was a bad boy around Chicago in the old days. But Willy's all right. He used to be a taxi driver. He's a Czech."

"Very interesting," said Mary.

"Let's go eat."

Mary and Lonnie had eaten and were now out on the beach, sitting in deck chairs. Ray was having his lunch in the breakfast room, and Pinky and Willy were washing the dishes.

"If he don't marry her, he's crazy," said Pinky.

Willy merely whistled, loud and shrill.

"I thought you wouldn't work for a woman," called Ray.

"I'd work for *her*," said Pinky.

Willy whistled again. "You said it," he exclaimed. "Where did the boss dig her up?"

"I don't know. He never tells me anything," replied Ray, "unless it's something I know already or don't want to hear."

"Well, I always thought he'd be a sucker to marry," said Pinky. "A guy like him. But not since I seen this one. So it don't work out. He's had the fun."

"Yeah," said Willy, "that's right."

"He's going to settle down, he says," said Ray.

Pinky and Willy laughed jeeringly.

"You like the house?" asked Lonnie.

"Very much," said Mary. "It's nice living on the beach in the summer."

"I live here the year round. Of course, I could always take an apartment in town if it got too cold. But it hasn't yet. Anyway, I like it in the winter. Sometimes the lake freezes solid and you can drive over to Bass Island."

"Really? Isn't it dangerous?"

"I never heard of anybody falling through. Ever ride on an ice-boat?"

"No."

"Well, you've got a thrill coming. You go so fast you can't get your breath. And when you turn—well—!"

Mary smiled at him. He took her hand and held it.

"Look, honey," he said in an unnaturally solemn voice "why don't we get married?"

Mary lowered her eyes.

"I've been thinking about it."

Lonnie grinned.

"Well?"

"It might not work."

"Sure. But it might. It's at least an even money bet."

"I'm very jealous."

"So am I."

"I don't like a lot of people around."

"That's easy."

"I sleep ten hours a day."

"That leaves fourteen. Maybe I can see enough of you in fourteen hours."

"I hope not."

She withdrew her hand and sat staring off across the lake, which was pale-blue and covered with silver ripples where the water was open. Near Bass Island it deepened to dark-green and the white houses along the lake shore were reflected upside down in it.

"I'm a pretty impossible person in some ways, Lonnie."

"You mean you've got a temper? I know that already."

"I have a violent temper. And I don't get along with people as well as I should. And I have very few friends; only one really close one—Jean Keller; and—"

Lonnie broke in impatiently.

"Sounds to me like you're just making excuses."

"Besides," Mary went on, "if I was in my right mind I wouldn't marry a man like you in a hundred years."

"What's wrong with me?"

"Nothing. As far as you're concerned. But—well, if I marry, I want to stay married and have a home—all that sort of thing."

Lonnie looked at her and laughed.

"You surprise me. Irma, the cashier at the inn, said you were just another glamour girl. Do glamour girls want to be married and have homes?"

"I can't help my looks. And they're very deceiving—please take my word for it."

"I think you're just scared."

"*I'm* not. But *you* ought to be."

Lonnie studied her face for a moment, then laughed. "Did I tell you I'd quit gambling?"

"No."

"Did I tell you I was managing the inn now? Really working?"

"No."

"Well, it's true."

Mary rose.

"I'd like to go home, please."

"Why?" Lonnie demanded, jumping up. "I thought we were going to have dinner at the inn and—"

"I've changed my mind. I just want to go home and sit in my room and not see anybody till tomorrow."

Lonnie stared at her for a moment, then he shook his head and took her arm. They walked silently back to the house.

Ray had never imagined that Lonnie could be so distracted and jittery. He kept looking at him out of the corner of his eye as they rode into town in the phaeton. Willy was driving and they were in the back seat.

Lonnie was sitting slumped, with his hat pulled down almost to his nose, chewing violently on a ragged-looking cigar. He had the marriage license in his inside coat pocket and every once in a while he reached in and fingered it to see if it was safe. His face looked drawn.

"Ray," he said, "do you figure I'm making a mistake?"

Ray shook his head.

"Don't ask me that one. It's too hard to answer."

"I'm pretty sure she thinks *she's* making one. You see," he went on, "she's from awful nice people. She's got a good education. I'm just another guy from Brooklyn."

"Nothing wrong with you, Lonnie."

"Last night I was telling her about the old man, and also about when I used to work at the Erie as a bellboy. She winced. I'm not kidding."

"You probably imagined it."

"Well, why wouldn't she? I'm not much catch for her—if you look at it a certain way."

"Don't look at it that way."

"Oh, hell!" snapped Lonnie, and with a gesture of disgust threw the cigar butt out the window.

Lonnie found Mary looking pale and drawn. She was dressed to go out, but she showed no inclination to do so. It was a gray summer day, and the big old living room of her apartment was dim and shadowy. Lonnie stood with his topcoat collar turned up and his hat in his hand, looking at her.

"What's wrong, Mary?"

She didn't answer, turned her back on him, took a few steps away from him, pacing, then turned again and looked out the window.

"Would it embarrass you too much if I didn't?" she asked, avoiding his eyes.

"You mean you want to forget the whole thing?"

"I'll never forget it."

"I see," said Lonnie, turning his hat round and round.

"It's just not the way I wanted it to be at all," said Mary. "Can't you understand that?"

"Maybe. I never had any idea of getting married myself till I met you. In fact, I used to make cracks about guys who did."

"That's part of what I mean. You'd be satisfied if we didn't get married. Just as long as—"

"Did I ever say so?"

"No. But that's the kind of man you are."

"Look," said Lonnie, "I went to a lot of trouble to—" Suddenly he lost his temper. The nerve of this dame! He turned and went out, slamming the door.

His heart beat painfully; he felt so upset and depressed that he wanted to yell or do something violent. But as he walked down the dark old hallway toward the stairs, he suddenly realized that he also felt a certain amount of relief. He could relax now and be himself. It was the first experience of this kind he'd ever had, and it would be the last.

He walked slowly down the stairs. It was going to be a little embarrassing, facing Ray and Willy and Pinky, but—that would soon wear off. Just as he reached the bottom, he heard high heels clacking loudly behind him. His heart gave a bound. He turned. Mary was running down the stairs after him, her coat flying and her dress swirling back from her long, beautifully shaped legs.

At the bottom she paused and took his arm.

"Still want to?" she asked.

"Yes," said Lonnie.

And they walked out arm in arm to the car.

Ray and Willy and Pinky were sitting around the breakfast room table, eating cheese and crackers and drinking beer. They seemed a little solemn. Now that the excitement of the marriage was over, they had all begun to realize that in the nature of things the future couldn't be like the past: an era had closed. Things might be better for them or worse, but it wouldn't be the same. They all felt vaguely apprehensive.

Willy sighed.

"He should've let me drive."

"Rainbow Beach's only forty-five miles," said Ray. "I know. But his leg's bothering him."

"You think he wants you along on his honeymoon?" said Pinky, opening a new bottle of beer. "If he didn't take Ray, you got a swell chance of going."

They all drank silently. Ray rose to get some more cheese.

"I'm glad he got old Sam located," he said, unwrapping the cheese and cutting it. "That worried me." As a matter of fact, it worried Ray more than he would admit. Sam had been the first to go because of the new setup. Who would be next?

"Pretty tough, Sam having to leave the inn," said Willy dolefully.

"He's got a good job at Salini's," Pinky put in. "Anyway, he shouldn't've lost the inn, gambling."

"Don't go moral on me," said Willy. "You of all people."

"What do you mean?"

"I mean," said Willy, "that Lonnie can't even have a colored cleaning woman around the house."

Pinky jumped up, red in the face.

"That's a lie, you damn little hunky. You take that back." He reached for Willy, but Ray dropped the cheese knife and intervened.

"Cut it out, you guys," he said. "Remember that last fight you had?"

Ray pushed Pinky back into his chair.

"That wasn't no fight," said Pinky. "I hit Willy, and Willy hit the floor."

"I don't know about that, but you broke over a dozen dishes. And you're both lucky you didn't get fired."

Willy poured himself another glass of beer and pretended to drink it calmly, but he kept glancing warily at Pinky, who had a violent Irish temper and was given to outbreaks.

"Well, he shouldn't talk like that," grumbled Pinky.

"All I know is what Ella Lou told me," said Willy. "She complained to Lonnie about you. Maybe she lied."

"I was drunk," said Pinky. "I was just kidding around. She got the wrong idea."

"All right, all right," said Ray, sitting down. "Drop it."

They ate and drank in silence for a long time. Finally Willy said:

"I'd tell you guys something except I'm afraid to open my kisser around here. I might lose some teeth." He threw a reproachful look at Pinky. "It's about the boss. And you understand—it's only talk."

"Tell *us*—that's okay," said Pinky. "But don't tell nobody else—whatever it is." He turned to Ray. "This guy talks too much."

"Never mind," said Ray, placatingly. "What is it, Willy?"

"I ran into Joe Pacini last night. He works for Benny Hayt. He—uh—he told me—you understand, guys, it sounds silly—but he told me Lonnie married the Greek's girl."

Ray and Pinky stared blankly at Willy, who cringed slightly, not knowing what to expect. Neither Pinky nor Ray moved.

"Yeah," Willy went on recklessly, as if he couldn't restrain himself, "that's what he told me. The Greek's in New York, and Benny says to Joe: 'Brother, when the Greek gets back he sure is going to be sore as hell.' And when the Greek really gets sore, he's a dangerous character."

Pinky laughed uncertainly and turned to Ray, who was running his hand over his face absently, lost in thought.

The two men seemed so stunned and helpless that Willy took heart.

"Yeah," he said, "my brother used to know the Greek in the old days in Chi. He owned a tough joint on the near North Side for quite a while. He was strictly a guy to watch—smooth but bad."

"Don't repeat that to anybody," said Ray finally. "It doesn't make sense to me."

"Not that girl," Pinky put in. "She's got class wrote all over her. Course the Greek likes good-looking broads—but he ends up with ones like that Polack, not them refined dames."

"Anyway, that's what he said," Willy concluded, pleased at the sensation he had caused.

The conversation languished. They all sat staring into space, worrying about the future. Finally Ray got up and stretched.

"I'm going downstairs. Now, you boys behave yourselves—no fighting or I'll tell Lonnie when he gets back. Good night," he said, and went out.

Willy glanced a little apprehensively at Pinky, now that they were alone together. But Pinky paid no attention to him. He was lost in thought. Finally he asked:

"This Pacini guy—does he generally know what he's talking about?"

"He's like that with Benny," said Willy, holding up two fingers.

"This time he's got his dates mixed!" Pinky yawned and got up. "At least, I'll bet a month's pay."

"I won't take the bet," said Willy. "I'm only repeating what I—"

But Pinky was already going out the door. Willy sat waiting. As soon as he heard Pinky unlock the door to their sleeping quarters over the garage, he went into the breakfast room and got out a bottle of Scotch he had pilfered and hidden. Humming softly, he poured a stiff drink.

"Now, one's all you get," he admonished himself. "You got to make this last, because if you cop another one, they'll miss it."

In the big lower-level bedroom Ray was settling himself to read. It was a warm night. Through his window he could see the far-off, winking lights of Bass Island. The whistle of a freighter moaned sadly in the distance.

Ray lowered his book and glanced about him at this haven he'd found after over forty years of searching. Lonnie wouldn't let him down. Of course, the new mistress would probably want to run the house, though she didn't look the type, and Lonnie had given up gambling, or so he said. "Oh," said Ray, "he'll find something for me to do. We've been friends for so long."

He forced himself to read, and in a little while he was back many centuries. Rome was in a turmoil. Spartacus was leading a revolt of slaves and gladiators. It was growing almost to the proportions of a civil war....

The phone rang insistently. Ray grunted with irritation and waited. In a moment Willy stuck his head in the door.

"It's Mr. W. W. Keller," he said.

Ray sat up straight.

"I told him Lonnie wasn't here. He says he'll talk to you."

Ray got up and hurried to the extension in the hall. Willy walked slowly away from him, hardly moving, trying to get an earful.

"Yes, Mr. Keller."

"Is this Ray Cooper?"

"Yes."

"What do you know about this marriage?"

"What marriage?"

"Your boss, Cooper, and a Miss O'Donnell."

"You'll have to wait till Lonnie comes back, Mr. Keller. He'll be gone about a week."

Keller hesitated, then hung up. He was obviously fuming. Ray looked about him in bewilderment, scratching his head.

"What's it his business?" he asked nobody in particular.

Willy whistled dolefully.

"This is getting to be something," he said.

The Greek felt irritable and bored. He'd had a bumpy ride from Pittsburgh, where he'd been taken off the New York plane owing to a priority and forced to spend two days.

He sat in the creaking, rickety taxi, staring listlessly out at the almost deserted streets of the warehouse district.

"This cab," said the driver, breaking a silence that had lasted nearly half an hour, "it's just going to fall to pieces on me some day. We can't even get parts anymore."

The Greek made no comment. The driver glanced into the rearview mirror to get a glimpse of him. Was he dead?

"Yes, sir," the driver went on, "it's getting so I hate to go out in this thing. It's dangerous."

The Greek cleared his throat, but said nothing. The driver shrugged and lapsed into silence. He was bored and lonesome. Who did this guy think he was, anyway? Did he figure that he was better than somebody? Come to think of it, he hadn't liked the looks of the guy when he picked him up at the airport. Too slick, and then he'd smelled perfume on him—the kind dames use. Oh, well.

When the Greek came into the Turf Café, Benny, who'd been sitting alone in one of the booths, got up quickly to meet him. But the Greek waved him back.

"Phone call to make," he said. "Be with you in a minute."

The Greek got some change at the bar and disappeared into one of the booths. Benny was disappointed. He'd been waiting for this moment, and he hated to put it off a fraction of a second. He wanted to see the Greek's face when he heard about Miss O'Donnell. The Greek was so irritatingly superior; he'd been so successful in everything for years without one lapse. This was going to hurt.

In a few minutes the Greek left the phone and came over to Benny's booth. He was hard-eyed and looked irritable.

"Sit down, Mr. Pool," said Benny. "I got something I want to tell you." The Greek glanced at him, then sat down. "This Miss O'Donnell—"

The Greek cut in.

"What about her? Anything happen to her? I've been trying to get her on the phone."

"She's married," said Benny after a pause, timing it perfectly, he thought.

The Greek started slightly, made a move to rise, and then changed his mind. His face slowly turned a greenish white.

"I thought you'd like to know," said Benny.

"Yes. Certainly. Who did she marry?"

"Lonnie Drew."

The Greek was reaching for his cigarette case, but his hand stopped halfway.

"Lonnie! Are you sure?"

"Positive."

The Greek sat for a long time staring—so long that Benny began to grow more and more uneasy. He was afraid the Greek might have a stroke or something like that. Of course, he knew that the Greek thought pretty much of the girl—at least he'd heard so—and he also knew that he didn't like Lonnie Drew. But he wasn't at all prepared for a reaction like this. The Greek just couldn't seem to get himself together.

Finally the color began to come back into his face. Benny sighed with relief.

"Would you like a drink, Mr. Pool?" he asked.

"Yes. Thanks," said the Greek, politely. "Brandy."

BOOK TWO

Late August. The rich people of Lake City who had been able to get away for the summer were returning, opening their houses for the fall and winter seasons, and displaying their heavy tans in the clubs and swank restaurants. Some of them, owing to the war, were apologetic about having left, and many of them made excuses, claiming ill health or business. Some were merely defiant.

On Saturday nights now there were crowds at the Erie Pompeian Room and the Palm Bar, at Salini's and the Lake Shore Inn—for the moment the most fashionable spots in town. The gatherings were very mixed—not like the old days, as some Lake City people were always pointing out. Members of the old moneyed aristocracy mingled more and more openly with newcomers from downstate—with soldiers, sailors, and marines, with aircraft and munitions workers, and with the hordes of trainers and owners of horses who were pouring back into Lake City for the fall race meeting, which opened in September.

Everybody complained about the food, the liquor, and the service— but they kept coming back. There was something feverish about the atmosphere of these clubs, restaurants, and bars, and every month of the war it increased. Women, who had been moderate drinkers before, now got very drunk in public and made scenes. Every night, but particularly Saturday nights, there were verbal battles between drunken patrons, and sometimes actual brawls which had to be broken up. Bouncers, very polite, unobtrusive fellows, but nevertheless real bouncers, were employed now in the smartest places. The hysteria of the patrons communicated itself to the help. And all the managers of restaurants, clubs, and bars were in constant hot water, trying to deal with exactions that had nothing whatever to do with the ever-present labor trouble, a serious problem in itself. Lonnie was in the thick of it.

He had changed so much in the last few months that he was an almost continuous subject of conversation among those who had known him before his marriage. He worked long hours; he stuck to business. And when he was through, he went home and stayed there. He was never seen around the late spots anymore; he never turned up at Price's or at the Turf Café when there was a big game on; he was short with the city grifters, who used to consider him an easy touch and in some cases a meal ticket; and he seemed to pay no attention to women whatever.

He'd even got rid of Annette, who came back from her vacation full of health and energy and immediately set out to capture Lonnie in spite of the fact that he'd just been married. Annette was a very handsome blonde girl—a dish, as all the boys said—and she just couldn't understand Lonnie's attitude. If he'd explained to her that he'd just been married and was out of circulation for the moment, with the implication: "Stick around, babe," or if he'd seemed to be restraining himself with difficulty—and Annette gave him plenty of opportunities to restrain himself—she wouldn't have been so bewildered. But it gradually became clear to her that he was absolutely, blankly indifferent. She was hurt and furious. "She married him while I was gone," she confided to Irma. "If I'd been here ..." Irma merely grunted. Finally her conduct became so noticeable that Lonnie fired her.

Even Ray tried to intercede for her, but Lonnie merely told him to mind his own business.

Sometimes, studying Lonnie when he wasn't looking, Ray would shake his head, remembering the past. Now nobody had to worry about Lonnie. In fact, he worried about everybody else. He wanted to take all the responsibility, see to everything. He never mentioned gambling, except from time to time to make a curt comment about what a sucker so-and-so was for throwing his money away. Bookies from all over the state were always getting Ray on the phone to ask in plaintive voices what was the matter with their old pal Lonnie Drew? Lee Jacks even called from far-away Natchez. Right guys, they explained, were few and far between, and Lonnie had been one of the rightest.

At times when Ray was reading alone in his room, he'd get to thinking about the past, remembering the money Lonnie had spent, his many women, his recklessness, which extended from driving a car to gambling, his utter disregard of the future, his philosophy: "Stop worrying! Everything'll be all right." Such thoughts made Ray a little uneasy.

For the first time in his life he felt secure—felt that there was a steady hand on the rudder of the ship to which he'd entrusted his safety. And the hand wasn't Lonnie's—it was Mary Drew's. That girl! So beautiful, so delicate-looking, but with a will of iron. If it had all been up to her, he wouldn't have had a worry in the world. But she was acting through Lonnie, who was the instrument, and an instrument that could get out of order, go haywire, blow higher than a kite.

It was one of the most amazing reversals that Ray had ever seen. Everything had changed, from Lonnie's personal appearance to the conduct of his life. The house wasn't the same place at all: it had been cleaned, repaired, and redecorated, inside and out. It was beautiful to look at now. Pinky was a new man, happy, polite, and reasonable; Willy was an almost model servant; he'd even stopped stealing things after Mary had caught him twice and shamed him.

There was only one trouble: money was short, very short. Financially speaking, Lonnie had married at a bad time. Not long before, he'd dropped ten thousand dollars in a stud game; previous to that he'd lost nearly four thousand betting with the bookies. The inn was doing a land-office business, but the overhead was tremendous and getting worse in spite of all the Government controls.

Lonnie was frank with Mary in regard to everything except money, one thing she knew little about. She'd had no training at all of a financial nature. Her parents, both of whom had inherited a little, were vague in money matters. There had always seemed to be enough and so Mary had never been stinted; whatever she had wanted she got. Suddenly there wasn't any more and Mary was forced to think seriously about her future. Considering everything, she'd done well, but she'd never saved a penny in her life and merely thought of money as something you exchanged for something else; she never thought of it in terms of security. So she took Lonnie's word for the financial end. When she wanted to redecorate and refurnish, he told her to go ahead, it was okay. She turned the bills over to him and he paid them or stalled until he could comfortably do so.

Lonnie had but one source of income now—the inn. No more windfalls, no more small fortunes won in a single evening at the stud table. He had to make money with the restaurant—plenty of money, or else! Added to this strain were the many, endlessly ramifying worries of a small businessman in wartime. Besides, it was all new to Lonnie. At times Ray thought he looked a little harried, but he seldom complained.

Lonnie's new life was the talk of the gambling circles, and one night, much to everybody's surprise, Mr. W. W. Keller came to the inn to see him. Keller was an arrogant-looking little red-haired man about fifty years old. He had very broad shoulders, walked like a man half his years; and his small, gray-green eyes were very expressive and penetrating. Lonnie had exchanged greetings with him once or twice, and that was all.

They sat in Lonnie's office, smoking. Keller puzzled Lonnie by talking about the weather, the fall race meeting, and business. Lonnie knew that Keller was no man to pay a casual call. Everything he did had a purpose.

"Lonnie," he said finally, "I've been hearing great things about you."

"Is that so?"

"Yes. And I came here to tell you that I think it's fine."

"What do you mean, Mr. Keller?"

"I mean buckling down like this and making something of yourself. I was mad as hell when you married the kid—Mary. She's a wonderful girl. Never had a chance. Her parents—if you'll pardon me—are a couple of well-meaning damn fools."

"I've never met them. We haven't got around to going to New Vienna."

"Stay away from them," said Keller, gesturing with his cigar. "Keep things the way they are. You're doing fine."

"Thanks, Mr. Keller."

"Chickens come home to roost," said Keller. "As you know, I've associated with a lot of bums in my time, including men like Jack Pool and Benny Hayt. I tried to keep them in a separate compartment, if you know what I mean. Frankly, I love to gamble. I got to backing the Greek and Benny. We made a lot of money, and I had a lot of fun. But what happens? My daughter's best friend starts running around with Jack Pool. It was as if somebody had kicked me in the face. Of course, I blame a lot of it on that damned old woman of a Les Coster. Even so—" He hesitated, then puffed on his cigar. "Then she married *you*. I was fit to be tied. I consulted about getting it annulled. But—well, I did you an injustice, Lonnie. And that," he said, laughing, "is my story."

"I'm glad you feel this way, Mr. Keller," said Lonnie, a little annoyed, but also greatly pleased. "I decided it was time for me to settle down. I'm no kid any longer."

"Quite right. And stick to it." Keller got up. "I was just driving past," he said, "so I thought I'd stop in and get this off my chest." Lonnie walked to the door with him, anxious for him to leave so that he could call Mary and tell her all about it.

"Let you in on a secret," said Keller, "that may interest you. I've dropped out of the syndicate. No more of that for me."

Lonnie stared incredulously, unable to believe his ears. What a blow to the Greek and Benny!

"Yes," said Keller, "I want no more contact with such men after such a close squeeze. It sort of taught me a lesson."

"Well," said Lonnie, laughing uncertainly, "this will surely cause an uproar."

"Oh, they'll worry along without me. I understand the Greek's got a New York bunch backing him now. Or at least he says so."

When Keller had gone, Lonnie stood staring for a long time, thinking about the past and how gamblers all over the Midwest always used to be talking about the Big Three: Keller, Pool, and Hayt. In the world he'd frequented in the old days, this was a sensation comparable in the field of politics to the defection of a President. And it would have important repercussions. Benny and Jack would now be regarded with different eyes. Keller's money and respectability had given them a luster and an importance that now would be a thing of the past. Their credit would be definitely affected, because the reputation of neither, before the advent of Keller, had been very savory. They had never been considered "completely right." Lonnie shook his head, marveling. Then he suddenly came to himself and hurried to the phone.

He was glad to hear Mary's voice, as he always was, it sounded so light and pleasant and warm. He told her about Keller.

"Yes, darling, I know."

Lonnie swore to himself humorously. Damn it! She always *knew*.

"*How* did you know, Einstein?" he demanded.

"Jean called. They're coming to dinner—she and Toby. Toby thinks you're wonderful, and he's been furious with his father. Toby thinks you're a wit, so you'd better get out your joke-book and study it before you come home."

"What time do we eat?"

"Ten. Is that all right? The pressure should be off you by that time."

"Fine. I may have to come back, though."

"Oh, Lonnie!"

"Well, I'll see. But somebody has to be around here all the time. It's always something."

"You work too hard, darling."

Lonnie laughed.

"That's something I never expected to hear applied to me."

"Are you sorry?" asked Mary, immediately on the defensive. "Do you want to go back to horses and blondes? If so, please say so."

"Mary, I hope you're kidding."

"I am—in a way. But sometimes I worry, and you know it."

"I love you, baby."

"I love you, Lonnie. I love you so much that if you get bored, you may have a blonde if you like. But just one—a small one."

"I don't love you that much, darling. One false move out of you, and I start shooting."

They both laughed. When he'd hung up, Lonnie lit a cigar and sat down at his desk. Things were quiet for a moment. He leaned back in his chair and yawned luxuriously. In a few short hours, he'd be home in that now beautiful dining room, candles on the table, well-cooked, carefully selected food, Willy serving as if he'd spent years as a waiter at the Ritz, and an air, an atmosphere, about the whole thing—well, it was great, that's all. Mary never stopped amazing him. She was a homemaker, and the many ramifications of it took most of her time and energy.

There was only one trouble with Mary. She was violently, at times fantastically jealous. This was very flattering to Lonnie, but also a little irksome, especially as there was nothing for her to be jealous about. Other women hardly existed as far as he was concerned. Mary satisfied

him in every way. But he could never seem to convince her of this fact.
They had many quarrels, and when he spoke sharply to her, she reacted
with a violence that astonished and dismayed him. Her eyes turned
black as pitch, she seemed to grow in stature, and there was something
so formidable looking about her that Lonnie would draw back, staring.
It usually ended in a laugh; but on several occasions Mary locked herself
in the bedroom and wouldn't talk to him for hours. This was all due,
Lonnie finally came to understand, to her possessiveness. She wanted
him all to herself. She didn't want him even thinking about any other
woman. Lately she had grown calmer, and when they went out in public,
she did not immediately bristle at the sight of an attractive girl and
imagine that Lonnie was staring at her.

"Oh, well," said Lonnie, "I'm just as jealous as she is, only I conceal it
better."

It was a small matter, anyway. The important thing was that they
were extremely well suited to each other and very, very happy.

Dinner was over and Pinky and Willy were just finishing the dishes.
Ray was sitting on a corner of the kitchen table, smoking a cigarette
and watching them.

"Things sure went off well," said Willy. "We'll show them bluebloods."

"The old man'll be over for dinner next," said Pinky. "Mark my word."

Ray restrained a smile of amusement and went on smoking. Not so
long ago Pinky and Willy had been slovenly, bickering and impossible.
Nobody would have put up with them but Lonnie. Now they were
bragging about themselves for being so efficient. That little girl surely
had a touch.

"The missus wanted me to eat dinner with them," said Ray, "but I
wouldn't."

"Why?" Pinky demanded, turning.

"I think it's better that way. Then I never get in their hair."

"Good idea," said Willy. "Say, that kid, he's full of hell, ain't he? The
boss practically had him rolling on the floor, laughing. I almost busted
out myself a couple of times."

"Don't let me catch you," Pinky threatened.

"Take it easy," said Willy. "I said 'almost.' You think I want to embarrass
the missus?"

There was a brief silence. Willy put the last dish away. Pinky hung up
the dish towels.

"You guys like it this way, don't you?" asked Ray.

"Sure," said Pinky. "Why not? We do good work and we get appreciated."

"We get good dough, too," seconded Willy. "Better than we used to get.
And besides we get regular days off. When Lonnie was running things,
you never knew whether you was going or coming. Ask for a day off and
he'd get sore. Any time he called and couldn't find you he raised hell.
When you didn't want to get off, he'd always tell you you could have the
day off. Now we know when."

"Yeah," said Pinky. "And if we want to find out what to do, we ask. In the old days Lonnie'd just say: 'Figure it out for yourself, you bum. What am I paying you for?'"

Ray laughed. What they said was very true. They wanted and needed a boss. Now they had one. Ray was just getting ready to speak when the hall door opened and Mary came in. He got to his feet and smiled. Pinky and Willy turned and looked at her respectfully.

"Boys," she said, "you did wonders tonight. I want to thank you."

"Glad it went off so well, Mrs. Drew," said Pinky.

"Yeah," said Willy.

"Even the Cherries Jubilee lit up this time," laughed Mary.

"Yes, ma'am," said Pinky. "I finally figured it out."

"Did you get plenty to eat, Ray?" she asked, turning.

"Yes, thanks. Plenty. The boys took good care of me."

"Fine." Mary smiled at them all again, then turned and went out.

There was a long silence. Willy took off his soiled house coat and hung it in the closet. Then he lit a cigarette and leaned back against the table, smoking with marked enjoyment. Pinky joined him.

"There's one thing I still don't get," said Willy, "between ourselves. Why did she ever go around with that Greek?"

Pinky glanced at Willy, then at Ray, wondering how he'd take it.

"That," said Ray, "I'll never know."

They all exchanged puzzled glances. Finally Willy shrugged and put out his cigarette.

"I better see about ice in case they want some highballs."

In a little while Ray went down to his room and read the evening paper. He had some time to kill, as Lonnie wanted him to wait and go back to the restaurant with him.

The Greek was sitting in a booth at the Turf Café with a slender blonde and a small Italian named Gus, who looked comically pathetic in spite of his obviously expensive clothes and a huge diamond ring he wore on his little finger and displayed at every opportunity. Gus, a former Chicago racket man, was about forty-eight years old and had a reputation for being merciless in his business dealings, but a sucker for women, especially blondes. He'd served time in Juliet and Atlanta in the old days, but for over ten years he hadn't had a rumble of any kind. He'd been a very hard man to convict in court because the juries always ended by feeling sorry for him, in spite of his ugly record. Even the judges who sentenced him addressed him sympathetically. He talked in a low weak voice, he seemed in ill health, and he looked so small and harmless.

The Greek and Gus talked to the blonde desultorily for a few minutes, then she excused herself and went to the powder room. Gus followed her with his eyes.

"Nice kid!"

"Very attractive," said the Greek. "She likes you. I can tell."

"She a girlfriend of yours, Jack?"

"No. I've had her out to dinner once or twice."

"Maybe I can cut in then?"

"Why not?"

Gus smoothed his lank, greasy-looking black hair and stared off across the café.

"I think I'll go talk to Benny a minute," he said, "while the kid's away. We got some unfinished business."

The Greek nodded politely and Gus got up and shambled over to Benny's office behind the bar.

The Greek ordered a brandy and sat sipping it meditatively. He hadn't been feeling well lately. In fact, for the first time in his life he'd gone to see a doctor. His symptoms, as he explained them, were so vague and contradictory that the doctor had proceeded to run every test known to medical science. The Greek was sorry that he'd brought the whole matter up. The doctor had found nothing wrong with him. The Greek paid the bill, grumbling—it was a very large one, including innumerable X-rays, and so forth—and ever since, he had gone about talking against doctors, much to the surprise of the people who knew him well. Ordinarily the Greek wasn't one to talk—about anything. He usually contented himself with answering the questions directed at him; that is, if he considered them worth answering. It began to get about that the Greek was slipping, not the man he used to be.

"First," Joe Pacini, a surly gossip, would say, "this dame he was carrying a torch for took the well-known powder. Then Keller give him the brush. What does he do about it? He don't do nothing." Joe would laugh unpleasantly. "Now I ask you, pal: does that sound like the Greek?"

Even Benny was taking a slightly different tone with him. Men began to study him sharply, looking him over for flaws. But externally at least the Greek was unchanged. He was still irreproachably dressed; he was still as careful about his nails, his hair, and his face as an aging beauty; he still had that sleek, slender, man-about-town look, that dark, shining, almost gigolo-like air; and he was still seen about town with one good-looking and fashionably dressed girl after another. "He's got a front," the boys said, "a great one. But ..."

After a few minutes the blonde came back to the table. The Greek rose politely till she was seated; then he sat down beside her, looked about him for a moment, and said:

"Give a little, will you, honey? He's beginning to wonder."

The blonde smiled wearily.

"How did I know he was going to look like this? He looks like Jimmy Savo after he'd been out in the rain for a while."

"You don't have to marry him. Turn it on a little. He doesn't understand subtlety."

"Now I know what they mean by a fate worse than death."

The Greek's dark eyes flashed, then he veiled them. "Honey," he said, "I do not feel very humorous tonight. It would be simple for me to interest him in another blonde."

"Slow it down a little, Jack. What makes you so touchy lately? I'll do my best."

"All right," said the Greek, "but without jokes."

He ordered another brandy for himself and a Martini for the girl. Just as the drinks arrived, Gus came out of Benny's office and walked toward them, his face lighting up at the sight of the blonde.

"What's his last name again?" she whispered to the Greek. "I didn't get it."

"Borgia. Gus Borgia."

"Nice pretty name. Didn't the Borgias used to poison people back in ancient times?"

The Greek merely looked at her.

"None of his family, I presume," the blonde added, innocently.

Gus shambled up, grinning.

"We were beginning to wonder what had happened to you, Gus," said the blonde. "Or should I keep on calling you Mr. Borgia?"

"Gus suits me fine," said the little man, sitting down very close to the blonde and running his eyes over her with such frankness that the Greek turned and glanced off across the café.

Lonnie walked up and down nervously waiting for Ray to finish checking the books for August. It was a beautiful late-summer night, warm and mild. All the windows were open: the lawn sprinklers had been going most of the afternoon and now the wind was carrying the pungent odor of damp, new-cut grass mingled with the clean, pleasant smell of deep fresh water from the lake. It was Saturday and the restaurant and bar were jammed with a drunken, noisy crowd. The hubbub irritated Lonnie and he was anxious to get home to his big quiet living room, which overlooked the lake. Mary would be waiting, looking beautiful and fresh and young as usual, in one of her pretty negligees, her dark hair down her back or tied up like a schoolgirl's with a ribbon.

"Right to the cent," said Ray, taking off his thick-lensed glasses and wiping them carefully.

"I was afraid of that," said Lonnie.

"What do you mean?"

"Didn't you notice the take?"

"Of course."

"It's not enough. I'm going to end up behind the eight ball at this rate."

"You'll never go broke taking a profit."

"I mean I can't live on it. We've got to find some other way to make money."

"Now wait a minute, Lonnie," Ray began, apprehensively.

"I don't mean gambling. Something legitimate. Something where I can get my hands on a big hunk at once. I'll be on the edge in a month or two and then I'll spend the rest of my life chiseling out dimes. Maybe I'll make it and maybe I won't."

"Come on, Lonnie, let's go home. You're tired."

"All right," said Lonnie, suddenly docile.

"On second thought," said Ray, "maybe I better stay. It's a big night."

"For once let's forget it."

They went out. The place was packed. They were standing three deep at the bar. George came over to Lonnie.

"Excuse me, Mr. Drew, would you mind speaking to Mr. Pool? He has booth one and has been asking about you. I told him you were busy."

"Okay," said Lonnie, glancing at Ray.

The Greek got up, smiling politely, when he saw Lonnie coming toward him. There was a blonde girl in the booth with him, and a strange-looking, dark-faced little man who seemed too small for his clothes, like a comic whose head will suddenly disappear down inside his collar.

"Well, Lonnie," said the Greek, offering his hand, "how are you?"

They shook hands briefly.

"Fine," said Lonnie, "and you?"

"Fair. This is Rita Anderson, and Mr. Borgia. Lonnie Drew." The Greek bowed with a gesture, smiling.

Lonnie nodded, acknowledging the introductions. Then: "Food okay?"

"Perfect," said the Greek. "Really, the only decent restaurant in town. Won't you join us?"

"Sorry. I'm in a hurry. But thanks. Enjoy yourselves."

He walked to the door where Ray was waiting for him. "The Greek wants to be friends, I guess. Or maybe he's got an angle."

"He usually has," said Ray.

On the way home Lonnie observed:

"The little fellow with him—the Greek said his name was Borgia. Couldn't be Gus Borgia."

"You mean the old Chicago racket guy?"

"Yeah. He was a rough customer in the old days. I've heard Benny talk about him. He had a lot of fellows knocked off—or so they say."

"Not that little man!" Ray protested.

"If it's Gus—which it probably isn't—he's got a lot of money. He's been operating around Detroit." There was a long silence. Lonnie laughed finally. "I don't know what would ever make me think that silly-looking little character was Gus Borgia."

2

September, usually a mild month in Lake City, came in with cold lake winds and heavy rains. In ordinary times it was hard enough to heat the old beach house. Now, because of the fuel shortage, it was virtually impossible. When Lonnie bought the house he had intended to have the old-style coal furnaces torn out and unit heat installed, but he just hadn't got around to it. When he was in funds, he never thought of it; and when he thought of it, he was never in funds.

Not that it bothered him in the slightest. Half of the time, in the coldest weather, he'd forget to wear an overcoat. But Mary was of a more delicate constitution. Several times when he came home after work she met him at the door wearing a heavy coat. She laughed it off as a joke, tut it began to worry Lonnie.

He had a talk with Willy, who tended the furnace.

"First place," said Willy, "we ain't got enough coal. Second place, the damned old furnaces won't work good. They're all rusted and the flue-controls stick, and I got to be always fooling with them. The missus is cold all the time."

One night at dinner he brought the subject up jokingly just to see what Mary's reaction would be. She laughed and said:

"All I need is a mink coat—that will keep me warm."

"Go buy one," said Lonnie.

"You mean it? Are we doing that well?"

"We sure are," said Lonnie.

"They've got several beauties at Karr-Dean," cried Mary, delighted. "I've already looked at them. One especially. But it's very expensive, Lonnie. Three thousand dollars with tax."

Lonnie winced inwardly, but said:

"Is that all? Get it."

Excited as a kid, Mary got up and ran round the table to kiss him. Lonnie was such a wonderful husband and she'd had such doubts of him! She felt so ashamed of herself that she went out of her way to pet and wait on him the rest of the evening.

Lonnie was so preoccupied, however, that he hardly noticed the attentions she was lavishing on him. He felt disgusted. In the old days three thousand dollars meant nothing to him at all. He'd lose it one day and win it back the next. Now he was caught in a financial web he couldn't untangle. He had got to the place where he was worrying about hundreds instead of thousands, and no relief in sight. A sudden expenditure of three thousand dollars would put such a burden on his budget that it would take him at least six months to absorb it. Nevertheless, he wanted Mary to have the coat. Damn this penny-pinching!

The next day he talked it over with Ray, who winced openly.

"That'll break us, Lonnie."

"We're broke now."

"Not exactly. Look, Lonnie, why not keep on being practical? Forget the coat. Spend a little money to have the furnaces fixed."

"The hell with that," said Lonnie. "You can't get anything done now. Besides, the weather'll clear soon. I never saw a September like this in Lake City before in my life."

Ray argued a little further, but he realized that it was no use.

A few nights later Mary had what she called an "unveiling." When

Lonnie got home, Willy opened the door and, smiling mysteriously, told him to go into the living room. Lonnie hurried in. Mary in her beautiful new mink coat was waiting for him. As soon as she saw him, she began to "model" it, walking up and down, grotesquely exaggerating the steps and postures she'd learned at Karr-Dean.

She looked overpoweringly beautiful in spite of the clowning—so beautiful, in fact, that Lonnie could only stand and stare, his heart beating unevenly.

"I got it for a little less," she said. "Mr. Coster was very nice about it. And we don't have to pay it all at once, darling. A thousand down and the rest when they catch us."

"Oh, turning out to be a business woman!"

"I've always been—sort of."

"Sort of is right," said Lonnie, laughing, and hugging her until she made him stop, afraid he'd injure the coat.

However, the weather got worse instead of better. Bitter winds blew steadily across the lake from the northeast, and at night howled round the rickety old frame house, which creaked, groaned, and vibrated.

Mary came down finally with a bad cold. She seemed in such distress that Lonnie was frantic with worry and immediately called a doctor, a reassuring-looking big man of about fifty with iron-gray hair and a coarse, healthy red face. The contrast between Mary and the doctor was so glaring that Lonnie grew more and more uneasy. With the husky doctor bending over her, she looked so frail and delicate lying there— like a beautiful, over precocious child.

The doctor didn't mince words with Lonnie in the hall afterwards.

"She has a bad cold," he said. "Nothing alarming about that. But this place," he went on with an abrupt gesture, "is not good for her. Too drafty, too cold, too damp. And the weather right now is impossible."

"You mean she's got to go South?"

"No," said the doctor. "But if I were you, I'd get her away from the water. Find a house or an apartment in town—if you can. If you can't, try a hotel. And keep her there all winter. She appears to be in good health, aside from the cold, but she is delicately made and probably not too strong."

After the doctor had gone, Lonnie stood pondering what he had said; then he decided to talk it over with Mary. It was the only sensible thing to do.

She agreed at once.

"The first day I saw this house," she said, "I wondered. I can't stand dampness, and I get very cold in the winter."

"Why didn't you say something, darling?"

"I did. But you didn't seem to understand. So—"

"Sorry I'm so stupid."

After a long and protracted search Lonnie managed to find a seven-room apartment in a big apartment hotel, the Brookmeade. The rent was exorbitant, but he ignored that angle of it. They took Pinky with them. He was to "live in" at the apartment and do all the work. Willy and Ray stayed on at the beach house.

Mary recovered quickly and in a little while was deep in the congenial task of "fixing up" her new place. When Lonnie came home at night, he'd find her in excellent spirits and she'd take him by the hand and lead him about the apartment, showing him all the changes she had made.

The apartment was on the seventh floor and they had a wonderful view of the city: it lay all around them, sprawling and immense. At night lights winked to the far horizons.

But Lonnie was worried about money and found it harder and harder to enjoy anything, although he put on a very deceptive front for Mary's benefit.

He and Ray had long talks about it. Finally one night Ray said:

"Look, Lonnie, I'll give you my frank opinion. You're not being fair to Mary."

"How do you mean?"

"She's got no idea what a snarl your affairs are in. If she had, she'd help. You know her."

"I don't want any help from anybody," said Lonnie sharply. "If I can't make enough money so we can live decently, then I'm a jerk. And I might as well find it out, give up the whole thing, and get a job selling papers. That girl could have married money. Why should I stint her?"

"I disagree with you entirely," said Ray, "but—"

"You mean she'd want to help—she'd be happier that way?"

"Yes."

"Maybe. But eventually she'd begin to wonder what kind of a man I was. I don't want anybody—least of all her—to be making excuses for me."

"It's hopeless," said Ray.

Lonnie banged his hand on the desk.

"I've got to find a new way to make money."

One Saturday, after a particularly harassing day, Lonnie was sitting at the bar drinking a highball and staring into space. From time to time Mack, the bartender, glanced at him. The boss was changing—no doubt about it. He was losing that don't-give-a-damn air he'd always had. Mack shook his head gently and turned away.

Somebody touched Lonnie on the shoulder and a pleasant feminine voice inquired:

"How's my old pal?"

Lonnie turned. It was Annette, looking prettier than ever. There was a tall aviator with her.

"Hello, Annette."

"This is Captain Strader."

The men shook hands.

"I used to work for Mr. Drew," Annette explained, "till he fired me for being too diligent—in the line of duty."

The aviator laughed uncomprehendingly.

"How's the old married man?" asked Annette. "Unhappy as hell, I hope."

"Oh, come now," said the aviator, "you don't mean that."

"Always clowning," said Annette. "You know me. But he does look a little peaked. And he's got lines I never noticed before."

"That comes from listening to my customers' jokes," said Lonnie with an effort.

They seemed so carefree and irresponsible, the two of them! Annette was hanging on to the aviator's arm, looking up at him, and he was grinning down at her. They were out for a time, that's all. They weren't worrying about labor trouble, OPA rulings, deficits, and coal furnaces. They were out on the town, and the hell with tomorrow!

Lonnie got to his feet and glanced at his watch.

"I've got to leave," he said. "It's been nice seeing you." He turned to Mack. "Drinks on the house for Annette and the Captain."

When he'd gone, Annette said:

"How did you like that 'It's been nice seeing you' routine? He used to be one of the biggest bums in town."

"Well, he certainly doesn't look it," said the Captain.

"The little woman has whipped him into shape," said Annette with a laugh which wasn't exactly pleasant.

However, the Captain noticed nothing. He was having a wonderful time and for the moment loved everybody.

All the way home Lonnie felt depressed and bitter. He couldn't rouse himself. It was raining hard again and visibility was poor. The persistent bad weather seemed like an added affront. He drove recklessly over the shining, slippery pavements, taking chances, narrowly averting a crash at an intersection, and swearing viciously at a taxi-driver who yelled at him.

But when he got home the candles were lit in the dining room, Mary looked beautiful in her plain, tight-fitting, black dress; there was a fire leaping on the hearth, and the apartment seemed so cozy, so livable, so much a refuge from the rainy, blustering night—from the world, for that matter—that Lonnie felt a sudden pang and silently took Mary in his arms and kissed her gently and repeatedly. She drew back to look at him.

"Well," she said, laughing, "what is this?"

"Nothing, honey. I'm so glad to see you. I missed you today."

"I miss you every day. Sometimes I think the hours will never roll past."

Pinky had cooked sole Marguery from a recipe Mary had found in a French cookbook. It was delicious. Lonnie grew more and more expansive, and after a brandy with his coffee he announced:

"Ah, this is the life!"

Mary put her head on one side and looked at him, smiling. And her long dark bob, with its glints of red, slid round and she put it back with the same graceful, charming gesture Lonnie had noticed and admired that night, months ago, at Salini's.

"Don't you ever hanker after your life of gilded sin?" laughed Mary. "Not even one tiny little bit?"

"No," said Lonnie emphatically. "Not even a slight hanker."

A few nights later when Lonnie came in the restaurant, he saw the Greek sitting at the bar with a new girl—a brunette with long dark hair somewhat like Mary's, a pretty fair-looking kid, at least from a distance. Lonnie smiled to himself and thought: "It's just one after another with that guy, and he must be over forty. Time he was slowing down a little!"

He went toward the office, but George intercepted him.

"Good evening, Mr. Drew."

"Hello, George."

"Mr. Pool's been asking about you. I think he wants to see you."

Lonnie hesitated, a little puzzled. The Greek had been very pleasant and friendly with him of late. More so even than in the old days. Wasn't that a little strange? Lonnie decided to go on into his office, take care of a few routine business matters, and then come out later. But as he turned, the Greek looked around, saw him, and smiled.

"Hello, Lonnie," he called.

Lonnie nodded, waved a hand in acknowledgment of the greeting, then walked to the bar. The Greek's new girl had turned and was lazily observing him now. Lonnie decided that she looked better from a distance. Although her hair was very attractive, her nose turned up and her large blue eyes were too prominent and almost expressionless: and there was about her an affected air of languor and boredom. Strictly from the wrong side of the tracks, Lonnie decided, and overdoing the "sophisticate" business. She handled a long cigarette holder with a sort of awkward daintiness and sat with her chin in her hand and her elbow on the bar, trying hard to look glamorous.

"Hello, Jack," said Lonnie. "George said you wanted to see me."

"Well, not exactly," smiled the Greek. "Just wanted to buy a drink. This is Miss Kallen. Lonnie Drew, darling. He owns the place."

"Hello," said Miss Kallen without a change of expression.

"Likewise," said Lonnie, annoyed by the act.

The Greek noted Lonnie's expression and, lowering his eyes, smiled to himself. No subtlety about this fellow; all on the surface—a man you could read like a book.

"What will it be, Lonnie?" he asked.

"Bourbon and soda. But I ought to buy the drinks in my own place."

"Not at all," said the Greek, smiling. "And you, darling?"

"Another Martini," said Miss Kallen; then she turned to Mack, the bartender. "And, please, less vermouth and an extra dash of bitters. Not too much bitters now. Just an extra dash."

"Yes, ma'am," said Mack, compressing his lips. Telling him how to mix a Martini, this dame! Who the hell did she think she was?

"Where do you keep yourself?" the Greek asked. "I never see you around anymore, Lonnie."

"We don't go out much. I work pretty long hours."

The Greek turned to Miss Kallen, who was watching Mack mix her drink.

"He's only been married a month or so, and he seems to be taking it seriously. My best to your charming wife, Lonnie."

"Oh, these overly-married men," said Miss Kallen. "At times they're very tiresome. Not you of course, Mr. Drew." She turned quickly to Mack. "Only an extra dash now, remember!"

Mack's neck got red, but he made no comment.

"Things are moving along nice for me," said the Greek. "Maybe I'll drop around and talk to you someday soon. Something you might be interested in."

"I doubt it, Jack. I've got my hands full here with this place."

"Well, don't worry about it. Nothing definite yet."

Mack brought their drinks. Miss Kallen lifted her glass at once and sipped it critically.

"Enough bitters, miss?" asked Mack, ironically deferential.

Lonnie and the Greek turned to look at Miss Kallen. She was daintily tasting the Martini, trying to decide if it suited her obviously very fastidious palate.

"Um, well—" she considered. "Perhaps just a trifle too heavy—but it will do. Thank you so much."

The Greek turned to Lonnie.

"Anyway," he said, "I can drop in now and then, and we can have a drink together. We miss you in the stud games. They're getting dull. Gregg took a beating at the track, and he makes us put a limit on the game now. Rank's having trouble with his wife and beefs all the time." The Greek sighed as if for the old days and sipped his drink.

"Drop in any time you like," said Lonnie. "I'm generally here in the evenings and till pretty late."

"Doesn't it get rather confining, this sort of thing?" asked Miss Kallen languidly.

"Sort of," said Lonnie. "But at least I know where my next meal's coming from." The Greek smiled slightly at this sally, but Miss Kallen looked blank. "The restaurant, you know," Lonnie prompted.

"Oh, I see," said Miss Kallen, smiling as if it were an effort. "Funny—but not very."

"Mitzi's a little hard to impress," said the Greek enjoying himself. "Aren't you, darling?"

Miss Kallen stifled a yawn.

"*You* say so. But—well, after New York, Lake City seems a little—" She waved her hand languidly and left the sentence unfinished.

Lonnie bought a drink, then after a few more minutes of desultory conversation he excused himself and went to his office, wondering if the Greek enjoyed being irritated by the supercilious Miss Kallen. "Maybe that's just her public manner," thought Lonnie. "Maybe in private she acts more like what she looks like." He laughed shortly and sat down at his desk.

The Greek puzzled him. What was going through his mind? And what sort of "something" was he talking about that might be of interest? Lonnie sat thinking for a long time, then he roused himself and began to run through the papers George and Luigi, the head chef, had left on his desk.

3

Ray came into the office, took off his slicker (it was raining again), and hung it in the closet; then he removed his sodden hat and put it carefully on a chair. Lonnie sat with his feet up, watching him.

Ray took off his suit coat and struggled out of a heavy V-neck sweater.

"I got here just as quick as I could, Lonnie," he said, kicking off his overshoes. "Willy put the sedan in the shop. It's got a bad knock. I told him it was probably the rotten gas, but he wouldn't listen. So I had to drive over myself in the wreck." The "wreck" was Mary's battered old Ford coupe.

"When you locate yourself in the middle of those clothes," said Lonnie with a laugh, "grab a chair and sit down."

"It's this lousy weather," said Ray, defensively. "Everybody's got a cold, and I understand there's a lot of flu around. That damned old house is as drafty as a barn." He put his suit coat back on and sat down. "What are you so cheerful about?"

"The Greek's coming over. He's got a proposition."

"The Greek? He's making *you* a proposition? Wait a minute!"

Lonnie nodded, grinning cheerfully.

"And a legitimate one, he says. I don't have to put up a cent, and he guarantees me at least ten thousand dollars."

"What kind of guarantee? I don't trust that guy. God knows *you* shouldn't."

"You mean about Mary. Look, let's not kid ourselves. To us Mary's a miracle. To the Greek she was probably just another beauty. He's had plenty of 'em in his day."

"Yeah, but you made him look like such a chump."

"That's water under the bridge. Anyway, we can listen, can't we? Just think what ten G's would mean to us right now."

"Is Mary in on this?"

Lonnie cleared his throat and looked off across the room uncomfortably, rubbing his chin.

"Not so far. She might worry."

"She might talk you out of it, you mean."

"Look, Ray, we don't even know what the proposition is yet. Did you take a look at the bank account at the end of last month?"

"Yes."

"And the books?"

Ray nodded.

"Well—?"

"I know, Lonnie," said Ray. "But you've got a good business here. It's just that you won't even try to live within your income. Mink coats. Seven-room apartments. A beach house. And that grocery bill!"

"In other words, we operated at a loss of over a thousand dollars last month."

"Counting everything, yes. But the business made money—plenty of money for any reasonable guy. I still think you ought to let Mary in on it. Her allowance is far too big and—"

"No," said Lonnie. "I'll figure it out some way."

"And grow gray doing it. Or else go back to gambling."

Lonnie opened his mouth to speak, but a knock at the door interrupted him.

"Come in," he called.

George, the head waiter, opened the door. The Greek was standing behind him.

"Mr. Pool is here," said George.

Lonnie got up.

"Come in, Jack. You know Ray Cooper."

George bowed and went out, closing the door. The Greek came forward with a wide, pleasant smile that showed his slightly pointed but beautifully white teeth.

"Mr. Cooper," said the Greek, inclining his head. Then he shook hands with Lonnie.

"Sit down, Jack," said Lonnie. "How about a drink?"

"No, thanks," said the Greek. "I've stopped drinking for the time being. A doctor told me to."

He took off his well-cut dark topcoat and put it carefully over the back of a chair; then he sat down opposite Lonnie, who had returned to his swivel chair behind the desk.

"What little you told me about the proposition on the phone sounded all right, Jack," said Lonnie. "Let's hear some more."

The Greek glanced questioningly at Ray.

"And Mr. Cooper—?" he inquired.

"It's okay," said Lonnie. "He knows all my business."

The Greek shrugged slightly as if he didn't approve, then he lit a long cigarette which gave off a pungent, exotic odor.

"We expect to engineer the biggest coup that's ever been pulled off in the Midwest. We've got the money, and we've got the horse. But we need help."

Lonnie glanced at Ray.

"You mean you need help placing the money so it won't make too big a splash. Is that it?"

"That's it. We've talked it over—the syndicate, I mean—and as far as we can see, you're the only man around here who could possibly handle a proposition like this. You know every bookie in the Midwest. You've had plenty of experience spreading money out—"

"That's right," said Lonnie.

"And you're risking nothing. Win, lose, or draw, you get your commission. Ten thousand dollars, providing you get all the money up."

"How much money?"

"A hundred G's."

Lonnie whistled and glanced at Ray, who was sitting with his mouth open.

"That will take some figuring—a hunk like that," said Lonnie. "That's a tough order. To carry out right, I mean."

"Precisely," said the Greek. "That's why we're willing to pay such a commission."

"What's the horse?" asked Ray.

"He belongs to Ed Gregg," said the Greek. "He can run on any kind of track and he hasn't won a race in three months. He's had a bad hoof."

"You mean Saladin?"

"That's the horse."

The Greek took a pamphlet out of his pocket and handed it to Ray.

"You, I believe, are the handicapper?" he asked. Ray nodded. "Here's the condition-book. Look it over. Meanwhile," he went on, turning to Lonnie, "what do you think about it? Could you handle it?"

"I never handled one this big. But I brought one off once for nearly fifty G's. Yes, I guess I could handle it. But I want to think it over. This is nothing to take snap judgment on. It means a lot of work and thought."

Ray looked up from the condition-book.

"Offhand I'd say there were two horses in this race who outfigure Saladin; that is, providing they're in shape and trying."

"We're afraid of three," said the Greek, "and we'll take care of them. Gregg's already talked to two of the owners."

"Sometimes these big ones slip," said Lonnie, "as you probably know."

"Yes," said the Greek, "I know. I just had one slip recently. But the whole thing was so badly managed—well, this is different. In the first place, we've got a real horse going for us this time. Saladin worked six furlongs—a secret work—in twelve flat, breezing."

Ray whistled.

"Besides," said the Greek, "that's not your worry, Lonnie. You get your money no matter what happens."

There was a long silence.

"I'll think it over," said Lonnie.

"Look," said the Greek, "how can you turn us down on this? I'll give you a thousand dollars cash right now part payment."

"No," said Lonnie, "let me think it over tonight. Call You tomorrow."

The Greek smiled and shrugged.

"I don't know why you should hesitate. But—" He rose and picked up his coat.

"I've got a business to run," said Lonnie. "I'm up to my ears right now."

When the Greek had gone, Lonnie and Ray sat for a long time in silence, both a little awed by the magnitude of the proposed coup.

"Keller must have gone back in," said Lonnie finally. "Where would they get that kind of money?"

"Pool said it was a syndicate bet."

"Must be. What do you think, Ray? I'm looking for the catch and I can't find it."

"I figured there must be one before I heard the proposition. Now I don't know. I guess they just *need* you."

"Yes. And the Greek's no one to let a grudge stand in the way of making a little money." Lonnie sat shaking his head. "I don't know," he added uncertainly.

"It would be a tough one to handle. I don't think anybody could handle it but you, Lonnie." Ray sat staring across the room, thinking of ways and means. Suddenly he said: "Why don't we just forget it? You want to stay out of that game, don't you?"

"I intend to," said Lonnie. "No more of that for me. But this is different. It costs me nothing but work and time. I'll have an expense account, that's a cinch."

"Mary's not going to like this."

Lonnie whirled around in his chair to face Ray. "What do you mean? She's not going to hear anything about it, understand? She'd just worry."

Lonnie was sitting in the living room of the apartment with Mary, listening to the radio and staring moodily at the floor, lost in thought. Finally he came to, feeling Mary's eyes on him, and glanced up quickly. Mary looked away.

"Nice program," she said.

"Swell," said Lonnie, smiling, and in a moment was lost in thought again.

Mary got up and shut off the radio.

"What's the matter?" asked Lonnie.

She came over, sat on the arm of his chair, and began to stroke his hair.

"Are you bored, Lonnie?"

"Me?" he cried, turning and looking at her in genuine astonishment. "I should say not!"

"You hardly said a word all through dinner. And since we've been in here you've been staring at one spot on the carpet so long that I'm surprised you can see at all. Lonnie, you worry me sometimes."

"What are you talking about?"

"I'm afraid you're not very happy."

"I never was happier in my life."

"Sometimes," Mary went on, "I feel that you're living this way just because you know I like it, when you'd rather be out getting drunk, chasing blondes, and gambling."

"You can't do all three at once," said Lonnie, lightly; "at least I never could. Maybe I'm just the backward type."

He pulled her down on his lap and kissed her.

"Nevertheless," she said, drawing back, "I know you're not always frank with me. You're afraid I'll worry, or you're afraid you'll hurt my feelings, or—"

"Will you stop it?" he cried, kissing her again. "It's all imagination."

"Well, I certainly must have a very strong one then."

"To put it mildly, yes."

She felt better now. She kissed him and patted his face. "If you ever do want to go gamble and get drunk, please tell me—"

"You left out the blondes," Lonnie put in.

"Because," said Mary, going right on, "I couldn't bear to have you straining yourself being a good little boy just on my account."

"I've got an idea," said Lonnie. "Let's run over to Salini's. I'll have a couple of drinks, and we'll loaf around for a while."

"Maybe we can get the same booth where—you know." She jumped up, delighted with the idea.

When she left to get her coat, Lonnie rose and stood staring at the same spot on the carpet. Some instinct warned him that he ought to reject the deal. But, on the other hand, if there was a sleeper of any kind in it, he couldn't find it. Besides, if Keller had returned to the fold . . .

Mary danced gaily back into the room, wearing her beautiful new mink coat.

"That's a lovely hunk of fur you've got on your back, ma'am," said Lonnie.

"Yes," said Mary, "and just think: ten more payments and it's mine!"

They went out laughing, arm in arm.

Ray was surprised at the excitement he felt now that the decision had been made. He'd done his best to talk Lonnie out of going into the deal. First, because he didn't trust the Greek. Second, because he was afraid Lonnie, after engineering such a coup, would never be content to go back to running a restaurant. Third, because he was positive that at some stage of the game Mary, who was very sharp and observant, would catch on that something important was happening and insist on being let in on it. But all his words were of no avail. Lonnie simply would not listen.

"My conscience is clear," Ray told himself. "Now I can forget about it and pitch in."

They were all sitting in the back room at the Turf Café: Lonnie, the Greek, Benny Hayt, Ed Gregg, and Ray. From time to time Ray wondered vaguely why Mr. Keller didn't show up, but he was too interested in the proceedings to give it much thought.

"He was intended for a great horse, Lonnie," Ed Gregg was saying. "I was all set to run him in the Kentucky Derby when he went wrong. As a four-year-old he was in and out on account of that bad hoof. Even so I won three pretty fair stake races with him. He's game as a pebble. Now all of a sudden he seems to regain his best form, just like that. And nobody knows it but us." Gregg looked about him, grinned, and took a sip from his highball.

"Besides," said the Greek, "the only three horses we're worried about aren't going to try."

"We'll win by eight," said Gregg emphatically.

Benny sighed and rubbed his face uneasily.

"Only thing that worries me," he said, "is all this money pouring in. It's going to look bad."

"That's my job," said Lonnie. "I can plant it from New York City to New Orleans. A thousand here, a thousand there. Nothing to it. Ray here is the best man there is on the handle. We've turned some big ones in our time, eh, Ray?"

Ray nodded, noting that Lonnie seemed more like himself than he had for months. His blue eyes were twinkling, and he looked both eager and relaxed. He was like an old racehorse that hadn't been to post for years and suddenly hears the roar of the crowd and the bugle calling him to the track.

"If we get stuck," said Lonnie, "we can even bet a few thousand at the track. With the kind of handle they're getting, it wouldn't make much of a dent."

"No," said the Greek, "and it might be a good idea."

"Okay by me," said Gregg.

"Well—" said Benny, dubiously, "I don't know. I've seen 'em go so wrong. And if this one goes wrong brother!"

"How can it go wrong?" the Greek cut in hastily, throwing a sharp look at Benny.

"It better not, that's all."

There was something in his tone that made Gregg, Ray, and Lonnie turn to look at him. The Greek laughed.

"Benny's feeling a little low. Don't pay any attention to him."

Gregg got up slowly, yawning.

"I've had my say, boys. Now I'm going home and hit the kip. These morning workouts get me up mighty early."

When Gregg had gone, Benny got up, looked about him vaguely, stared into space as if he had something very weighty on his mind; then he said:

"No use two of us talking dough. I'll leave it to Jack. Think I'll go downstairs and see how things're going. Ducky's got the flu and I can't trust any of them other so-and-sos to keep things straight."

He nodded vaguely and went out. The Greek laughed.

"Benny's like an old woman," he said. "Maybe in the old days he was tough, but he's certainly got over it. Notice his hands shaking? He'll worry himself into an early grave. This one's just a little too big for him."

"What's he got to worry about?" asked Lonnie. "All he has to do is sit back and collect."

"Precisely," said the Greek. "But—" He shrugged. "Some men are like that. Now, about the money. We're going to turn it over to you, and you handle it however you please." Ray and Lonnie exchanged a glance. "We don't want anybody to have any idea where the money's coming from. We could deposit it to your account, but there are finks in a bank same as any place else."

"You mean you're going to turn it over to me in cash?" asked Lonnie.

"Why not? We all trust you, Lonnie."

Lonnie pondered. He was certain now that Keller was in on it and just didn't want his name to appear in any way. Otherwise it was very doubtful if Benny and the Greek would trust him with a hundred thousand dollars cash, in spite of his reputation. The same thought was running through Ray's mind and he felt relieved. After all, the Greek and Benny were a couple of wolves—very dangerous. But Keller was just an ordinary decent rich man.

"The money will be delivered to your office tomorrow evening. I know you've got a good safe."

"The best. Sam put out some real dough for it."

"Naturally," said the Greek. "When he was in the chips he always operated on a cash basis. I saw him count forty thousand dollars out of that safe one night."

"Poor Sam," said Lonnie. "When he went, he went fast."

The Greek shrugged as if to say that's the way of the world and continued:

"I'll deliver the money myself. Of course I'll have somebody with me. Ducky if he's feeling better. We'll count it, and that will be that."

"Fine," said Lonnie.

"Oh, yes," added the Greek. "I'm bringing you five thousand in cash for yourself. You get the other five after you've placed the money."

"What about an expense account? It's going to cost plenty to get this money up. No reason why I should stand it."

"We'll leave that to you—any legitimate expense, you understand."

"I won't pad it."

"We're sure of that," said the Greek, smiling pleasantly, "or you wouldn't be handling our money." He glanced from Ray to Lonnie. "Everything set?"

They both nodded.

On the way back to the restaurant Lonnie drove in silence for a long time. Ray smoked leisurely and stared out at the crowded streets of the downtown district. It was theater time. The boulevard lights were burning brightly in the clear air, and crowds were pouring in under the marquees. Lake City had changed greatly since the war. At night the sidewalks were jammed to capacity, traffic moved at a snail's pace and got into almost inextricable snarls at the main intersections, and there was a feverish, abandoned atmosphere he'd never noticed in the old days. Lake City at night looked like a boomtown, full of reckless strangers with money to spend.

"It's a cinch," said Lonnie as he turned off into a side street to avoid the traffic, "that Keller's in on this."

"I think you're right," said Ray. "Everything points to it."

"I'm going to make some real dough out of the deal," said Lonnie. "I'm going in with the play."

"What?" cried Ray, starting up. "For God's sake, Lonnie!"

"I'll save out a stake, don't worry. But this is too good to pass up. The way I'm operating now—small scale, I mean—I might be able to set myself for years."

"Or wreck yourself for good. I thought you were off gambling."

Lonnie laughed.

"Do you call this gambling?"

Lonnie and Mary had been to a movie and were now having a late snack at Salini's. Lonnie was in high spirits, and Mary, who was very sensitive to his moods—in fact, too sensitive for her own good—was in high spirits also. They talked about the picture they'd seen and Lonnie laughed so loudly remembering one of the gags that people turned to look at him.

"Lonnie!" admonished Mary. "They'll think you're drunk. What has got into you?"

"I feel great."

"It makes me happy to see you like this," said Mary. "You should take more time off. You work too hard."

"I don't do anything but order people around."

"But—such long hours. You were beginning to look a little drawn. How much do you weigh?"

"Haven't weighed lately."

"Well, when we get home I'm going to weigh you, and if you've lost weight, you're going to eat more. I don't want you all skin and bones."

"You're no Kate Smith yourself. Stop worrying about me. No, don't stop," laughed Lonnie, and squeezed Mary's hand under the table.

Sam Ballard dropped over to see them. He looked very neat and smart in his dinner coat.

"Hello, people," he said. "Did you hear the news? I'm going to open a new place for Salini. About a mile from you, Lonnie."

"Oh, competition, eh?" said Lonnie, grinning.

"It won't bother you any. You've got more than you can handle now. Or so I hear."

"That's right."

"Everything satisfactory?"

"Not like the inn," said Lonnie, laughing, "but it'll do."

Sam smiled, bowed, and left them.

"He's such a nice old man," said Mary. "Sometimes at night I worry about him. How could you take his restaurant that way, Lonnie?"

Lonnie hesitated.

"It's hard to make you understand. I was risking my own money. What's the difference?"

"Well," said Mary, "all the same I'm glad he's got a good job."

As they were leaving, a man in the crowded vestibule touched Lonnie's arm. He turned. It was Mr. Borgia with Rita, the blonde. They were such an incongruous couple that Mary stared at them, then glanced at Lonnie.

"How do you do, Mr. Drew?" said the blonde, smiling sweetly. "How are you?"

"Good evening, Mr. Drew," said the grotesque little Mr. Borgia, eying Mary eagerly.

Lonnie spoke to them and hurried Mary out. As they were walking toward the parking lot, Mary said:

"Why don't you introduce me to your friends? Are you ashamed of me?"

Lonnie glanced at her, then burst out laughing.

"You panic me with your remarks," he said.

"Such people!" Mary shuddered slightly.

"They're friends of your pal the Greek," said Lonnie, giving her a satirical look. "He brought them to the inn."

Mary ignored him.

"What is the little man made up for?" she demanded. "And the way he stared at me! And the girl—she must be at least a foot taller. And what was she wearing for hair? Really, Lonnie, you know the strangest people."

He turned to stare at her.

"*I* know the strangest—" Then he realized she was laughing at him. He seized her arm and shook her gently.

"Sometimes," he said, "I think you are too smart for your britches."

They walked into the parking lot with their arms around each other.

Both Ray and Lonnie were a little nervous and kept glancing at the office clock. The Greek was due with the money any minute now. Half an hour ago he had talked to Lonnie on the phone and they had decided it would be best for the Greek to drive around behind the restaurant and park near Lonnie's office, which had an outside door opening out on a little cement walk. Lonnie never had used this outside door and he found it so hard to open that Ray had to help him with it.

All day long Ray and Lonnie had been making lists of bookies. The key spots were easy, but there weren't enough of them to absorb that much money without a kickback of some kind. Theoretically they had been able to place a little over half the money. They still had quite a problem on their hands, but with that much disposed of they felt sure that they could eventually solve it without too much difficulty.

It was a pleasant warm night. A series of eccentric storms had passed over the Midwest, centering mostly in the region of the Great Lakes, and the weather had been so bad that even the oldest inhabitants claimed that they hadn't seen anything to equal it in fifty years. Now the weather, as if to balance matters, had moderated to such an extent that many people were going about without topcoats, and that afternoon Lonnie had seen a bunch of kids swimming at the beach as if it were midsummer. A gentle wind was blowing in from the lake. The moon was up, and from the office windows you could see the lake, flat as a pavement and bright with moonlight.

"How about Jacks at Natchez?" asked Lonnie, looking up suddenly.

"He can't absorb over a G. Two at most," said Ray, glancing up from his own list.

"Every little bit helps."

They heard a car driving slowly round the corner of the restaurant and they both sat with pencils poised, listening. Lonnie threw a look at the clock. The car continued, going slower and slower; then it stopped.

"That's it," said Lonnie; then he turned to Ray. "Have you got the new combination handy?" He had had the combination on the safe changed that afternoon.

"In my billfold," said Ray, getting up. "Why?"

"Just wanted to be sure."

A car door slammed, then another. After a moment there was a knock at the door. Lonnie walked over quickly and opened it. The Greek, carrying a briefcase, came in, followed by Ducky Flanagan, who looked very solemn and rather pale. The men all glanced at each other and nodded. The Greek put the briefcase on the desk and began to take off his topcoat. He also looked a little pale.

"Ducky," he said, "go out and get yourself a drink at the bar. I'll let you know when I'm ready."

"Okay, Mr. Pool," said Ducky. "I sure need one rock-and-rye." He turned to Ray and Lonnie. "I got up out of bed to help Mr. Pool with this business. I been sick as hell. First time I ever took down in my life." Ducky shook his big round head in complete bewilderment.

"All right, Ducky," said the Greek, obviously on edge.

Ducky nodded and went out into the restaurant, shutting the door behind him softly.

"I've got a sore throat myself," said the Greek, "and all the way over here that big gorilla keeps coughing—coughing."

He put his coat carefully across the back of a chair, sat down at the desk, and opened the briefcase with a key. Then he began to take out stacks of new bills in wrappers.

"Better start counting," he said, "because I've got a receipt here I want you to sign—purely as a matter of form, of course."

"Sure," said Lonnie. Then he sat down and carefully counted the money, which was mostly in large bills. When he had finished, he turned to Ray: "Now you count it."

Ray sat down at the desk with shaking hands and slowly riffled the bills, wetting his thumb methodically from time to time like a file clerk leafing through a pile of correspondence.

"A hundred and five thousand dollars, I make," he said, looking up.

"Right," said Lonnie.

The Greek shoved the receipt at Lonnie and took out a fountain pen, which he held poised.

"Satisfied, gentlemen?" he inquired. "If not, speak now. Want to count it again?"

Lonnie merely shook his head and, taking the pen from the Greek, signed the receipt with a flourish.

"Well," said the Greek, getting up, "so far so good." He pushed the briefcase across the desk toward Lonnie. "I'll make you a present of this. It's a nice one and I've got no more use for it."

"Thanks," said Lonnie.

"Now I think I'll go out and join Ducky in a rock-and-rye. My doctor says I mustn't drink, but I don't think he knows what he's talking about."

"Why not have it here in the office?" asked Lonnie. "I'll order it for you."

"No, thanks," said the Greek, picking up his coat. "In the first place, you men have got a lot of business to look after. Besides, I've got three phone calls I want to make."

"Suit yourself."

The Greek walked to the door and turned.

"Good luck, boys. If this one works out, none of us will have to worry for quite a while."

Lonnie hesitated, then said:

"I was a little surprised at Mr. Keller getting back in the game. He came in here one day and told me he was all washed up."

"Keller?" The Greek raised his eyebrows and looked from Ray to Lonnie. "Keller's got nothing to do with this."

Lonnie controlled a start and averted his eyes from Ray.

"I was just guessing," he said. "I figured with this kind of money—"

The Greek smiled a rather superior smile.

"Keller's not the only man with a bankroll in the Midwest. Gus Borgia's in with Benny and me now." He looked from Lonnie to Ray. "Maybe you'll come out and join me in a drink later."

"Sure, sure," said Lonnie hurriedly.

The Greek went out. Ray whistled with feeling and agitatedly lit a cigarette.

"That little guy *was* Gus Borgia," exclaimed Lonnie. "How do you like that?"

"I *don't* like it. Lonnie, if you're smart you'll back out of this right now. Give the Greek his dough and get your receipt. I thought that if Keller—"

"So did I."

Lonnie stood staring at the wall, unable to make up his mind what to do. All day long he'd been very happy, thinking about that nice big nest egg he was going to have in his kick in a week: maybe fifty G's, depending on what odds the horse paid. It was tough to throw it all away just like that! On the other hand, it wasn't good sense to get mixed up in a precarious deal with a guy like Gus Borgia. Some very tough boys had been deathly afraid of him in the old days, or so he'd heard. He stood looking down at the stack after stack of wrapped up, big denomination bills lying on the desk.

"I don't know, Ray," he said, uncertainly. "What can go wrong?"

"It's bad business," said Ray, worried by Lonnie's indecision. "I—"

Ray was interrupted by a loud crash as the outside door flew open, propelled by a violent kick. He and Lonnie turned. Two short, stocky men came in quickly, carrying heavy automatic pistols. One of them kicked the door shut behind him. They were well dressed in business clothes, one in blue serge, the other in light gray. Both had decorative handkerchiefs in their breast pockets. The one in blue serge was pale; the one in gray was swarthy and looked very dark and foreign, like a Syrian.

"Hello, fellows," said the swarthy one, grinning. "We just come in to collect some dough. I hope we don't have to shoot nobody to get it."

He backed Ray and Lonnie into a corner. They were so shocked and dumbfounded that they stood staring with their mouths open. Then he talked to the man behind him without turning.

"There it is on the desk, kid. And if I ain't mistaken I seen a briefcase. Load it and let's get the hell out." He grinned again at Lonnie and Ray, but his eyes were hard and merciless. "Just be good boys. It won't hurt a bit—like the dentist says—unless you jump. How about it, kid?"

"Keep your pants on," said the one in blue serge, stuffing money into the briefcase hastily and looking about him to see if he was missing any of it.

"Nice weather we're having, ain't it, boys?" asked the Syrian conversationally, still grinning. "I hope to God it don't rain no more, because I was beginning to grow web feet. How is it, kid?"

"With you in a minute."

Ray was shaking all over; it was like a nightmare to him. But Lonnie was beginning to recover.

"You must have had a tip on this one," he said, smiling slightly.

"Either that, pal," said the Syrian, "or we're just plain lucky. Yep, just lucky. We walk in and there it is all spread out for us."

"All right, boy," said the one in blue serge. "We're loaded."

They began to back to the door, both with guns leveled, the one in blue serge carrying the briefcase under his arm.

"Now be nice little boys and stay in that corner," said the Syrian, as he reached behind him for the doorknob. "Nobody's going to get hurt unless he asks for it."

He tugged at the door, couldn't open it. He began to get nervous; his gun wavered.

"Take it easy," said Lonnie. "The door sticks."

"Open the door, goddamn it!" the Syrian yelled at the man in blue serge. "I'll look after these guys."

The one in blue serge put up his gun and pulled at the door. The Syrian began to get pale. Lonnie was afraid he'd shoot without meaning to.

"Relax, now, relax," he said. "You'll get out." Finally the door came open. The men rushed out into the night, slamming it behind them.

"Good God!" cried Ray, deathly pale, and fainted and fell sideways before Lonnie could catch him.

Ray came around slowly. The first thing he noticed was a fiery taste in his mouth; then he realized that he was lying on a couch and wondered how he'd got there. Suddenly it all came back to him. He jumped up off the couch and looked about him wildly. Lonnie was sitting on the corner of the desk, smoking a cigar. He seemed a little pale, but calm.

"Did you call the police?" cried Ray frantically. "What's going on? Why are you sitting there? You're ruined, Lonnie. You know that, don't you?"

"Be quiet," said Lonnie. "Sit down and compose yourself. I'm thinking."

"He's thinking! Lonnie, for God's sake! Get this thing on record. Call the police right away." Lonnie didn't move. "I'll call them." He reached for the phone, but Lonnie pushed him back.

"Take another drink of that brandy," he said, pointing to the bottle on the desk. "And then sit down and stay put. The Greek'll be back in a minute. I've got to think this thing out."

Ray stared, and slowly, vaguely, he began to understand that there was more to this stick-up than he had at first realized. He took a stiff drink of brandy, shuddered violently, then sat down.

"Anything strike you funny about this?" asked Lonnie, pouring himself a drink.

"Come to think of it," Ray replied slowly, "yes. In the first place it was too pat."

"Much too pat."

"Yes. But what's the idea? It's not very healthy to go around robbing Gus Borgia—or I wouldn't think it would be."

"They didn't rob Gus. They robbed *me*. Don't forget I signed a receipt."

"Good God!"

Lonnie laughed ruefully.

"That briefcase the Greek was so anxious to give me really came in handy, didn't it?"

Ray stared for a moment like a man who'd just been hit with a club and was getting ready to fall.

"The Greek! He—"

"It looks like it," said Lonnie. "I guess Mary stuck in his craw worse than I thought. He fixed me good. And to top it off, he gets away with a hundred and five G's, most of it belonging to his pals, Benny and Gus Borgia."

"You better call the police, Lonnie. Get it on the books or you're cooked."

Lonnie slowly shook his head.

"I'm cooked any way you look at it unless I can figure an angle."

Ray stared at Lonnie, beginning to understand. A feeling of panic was growing on him. He reached for the bottle and took another stiff drink.

"God, this is awful! What are we going to do, Lonnie?"

"It's me, not you. You got nothing to worry about."

"The hell I haven't," said Ray simply.

Lonnie glanced at him and smiled.

"There's one thing about that Greek," he said. "He thinks he's the only smart guy around. He took months working on this and to him it looks foolproof."

"What do you mean? Got an idea?"

"No. But nothing's foolproof."

Ray's face fell.

"I thought maybe you had an idea."

"I'll get one, don't worry. This guy has really annoyed me!"

"To put it mildly."

Ray was trying to be sarcastic. But he'd already begun to look at Lonnie with admiration. The trouble was he was too used to Lonnie, too well acquainted with his weaknesses to be much impressed with him as a general thing. He was apt to forget that Lonnie had the gall of the devil, was afraid of nothing—in fact, rather inclined to rush into danger; was a very ugly enemy and an excellent manipulator; maybe not so subtle and evasive as the Greek, but certainly as smart. Ray began to feel better. A fool would have immediately called the police, made a hullabaloo, and ruined himself in the eyes of everybody, not to mention making a deadly enemy of Gus Borgia. Ray admitted ruefully to himself that that was probably what *he* would have done. A violent man, with enough intelligence to figure at all, would by now have the Greek by the throat—might even kill him. That would only make matters worse. A fearful man would already be on the lam. Lonnie, apparently undisturbed by thoughts of consequences, was calmly trying to work an angle, not only to save himself—which would have been anybody's concern—but so that he could pay off the Greek with interest.

"Jack is a cinch to come back," said Lonnie. "He's probably sitting at the bar right now wondering why we haven't run out yelling. In a little while he'll begin to think maybe the thing went haywire, because he's dead certain I'll yell copper. Now remember, Ray, when he comes back we'll just be sitting here talking. As far as he's concerned, the money's in the safe. That'll be the first jolt. Of course, he'll hear from his boys later. But even so he's going to be mighty uneasy."

"This takes nerve," said Ray, shaking his head.

"Sure," said Lonnie, "and I figure I got more than the Greek." Suddenly Lonnie gave a jump, snapped his fingers, and cried out: "I've got it."

Ray, whose nerves were jangled to the point where he could hardly hold himself together, started half off his chair. Just as he was asking

Lonnie for an explanation, there was a knock at the door.

Lonnie held up his hand in a warning gesture, then he called: "Come in."

The door opened and the Greek came in, followed by Ducky Flanagan, who was coughing violently, his face almost purple. The Greek looked too calm and composed if anything.

"The rock-and-rye didn't do you much good, I see," said Lonnie.

"No, Mr. Drew, it sure didn't," moaned Ducky.

"I got tired waiting for you," said the Greek, smiling pleasantly. "Anyway, it's time I went home."

"We got to talking. Sorry," said Lonnie.

The Greek threw a quick glance around the office. "Money's all put away, I see," he said, laughing, making a joke of it.

"You bet," grinned Lonnie. "Right in the safe."

A shadow crossed the Greek's face and was gone. He spoke to Ducky over his shoulder.

"Come on. Let's go. And when we get in the car, turn your face the other way when you want to cough."

"Sure, Mr. Pool. I'm sorry."

The Greek tried to open the outside door, but it stuck. He tried it again, then he turned and looked at Lonnie. "Is it locked?"

"I don't think so," said Lonnie carelessly. "It's hard to open."

Ducky grabbed hold of it, eager to show his strength, jerked at it violently—and the knob came off in his hand.

The Greek groaned and turned away.

"I guess we'll go out through the restaurant," he said, trying to smile and appear calm.

He opened the inside door and went out quickly. Ducky followed him to the doorway, then stood looking down stupidly at the doorknob in his big hairy paw. He was embarrassed and speechless. Suddenly he handed the doorknob to Lonnie and rushed out.

Lonnie burst out laughing and slammed the door shut behind them.

"The Greek's really worried," he said, "and boiling. He'll be doing worse than that when I get through with him."

"He's guilty, all right," said Ray. "He's not such a poker-face as he thinks. What have you got up your sleeve, Lonnie?"

"Sit down, Ray," he said, "and relax. I want to go back over the whole business." Ray sat down, even if he couldn't relax, and he tried to give Lonnie his undivided attention, but little fears kept creeping into his mind, fears he tried unsuccessfully to shrug off. Lonnie was up against a bad bunch and Ray remembered the old gag: "A guy can get killed around here" with a shudder. "The Greek wanted to get me," Lonnie was saying, "and he figured out a good angle. Not only would he get *me*, but he'd grab maybe seventy-five G's on the side. Perfect! But he made his first mistake by being so sure I'd yell copper. What made him think I would? Who'd believe me? Not Gus Borgia. He's too cagy. You hand a guy a hundred G's and right away a couple of strangers walk in and grab it. Would you believe it? Of course not. And the police wouldn't have believed it either. They'd've started grilling me right away, figuring I arranged the whole deal."

"Sure," said Ray. "But as far as I can see, you've only got one other out."

"What's that?"

"Why," said Ray, "to beat it—lam."

"Ruined for good, eh? And what happens to Mary? Does she lam, too? No, Ray. You underestimate me. Look, nobody can prove I haven't got the money except the Greek and he'll keep his big yap shut, you can bet on that. We've got two weeks' grace."

"Yeah. But after that?"

"Hold tight to your chair, son, because now I'm really going to throw you a curve. I'm going to bet the money on credit!"

"What?" cried Ray, jumping to his feet. "Good God, Lonnie—!"

"Yep. I got plenty of credit, and for once—I'm going to use it."

"Suppose the horse loses. You'll owe every bookie in the Midwest. Then you *will* have to lam!"

"He's not going to lose. It's the nearest thing to a cinch in racing history."

"Wait a minute, now," said Ray, rubbing his hand across his eyes. "You're going too fast for me. Wait, Lonnie. All right, say you get it up on credit, and say the horse wins. You'll still be a hundred G's out, the amount of the original bet. Not having put up anything except markers, the bookies will take a hundred G's out of whatever you win."

"That's right," said Lonnie. "I'm going to run short."

"Plenty short—even, as I say, if the horse wins. If he loses—"

"Forget about him losing. Anyway, if he loses I'll be clear with the syndicate."

"But the bookies—!"

"All right, all right," said Lonnie, waving Ray to silence with impatient gestures. "Now about that shortage. There's a way to handle it. I can tell the syndicate that there was such a huge amount up that the bookies wouldn't pay track odds—we'll never get better than three to one, you know."

"They might check."

"Yes, they might. But if I turn over to them, say, three hundred G's, they're not going to kick too much. It's quite a coup!"

"Too many ifs, Lonnie."

"However," said Lonnie, ignoring Ray's remark, "I don't like to work the shortage angle that way. It might look like a big gyp."

"Then you're licked."

"Maybe not. You're forgetting something, Ray. I'm not only trying to get out of a bad hole. I'm going to fix the Greek's clock, so it won't run so good anymore."

Ray suddenly had to sit down. He was having that nightmare feeling again. He hesitated, then took another stiff drink.

"I'm getting drunk, Lonnie," he said, shuddering; "but tonight—I just don't give a damn!"

Lonnie snapped his fingers, too intent on his problem to be concerned about Ray. Picking up a pencil, he wrote something on a card, slipped the card into his coat pocket, glanced at his watch, and stood up.

"I told Mary I'd be home early tonight, so I'm on my way."

Ray nodded wearily.

"This has been quite an evening!"

"Yeah," said Lonnie. "Now grab yourself a good sleep tonight—"

"You must be kidding!"

"—get up bright and early, and keep working on those lists. It's going to be tougher than ever now."

Ray sat staring at Lonnie.

"I'll be damned," he said rather thickly, "if you don't look happy about the whole thing."

"In a way, I am," said Lonnie, going to the door. "I hate guys who think they're smarter than everybody else. Goodbye."

He went out. Ray shook his head apprehensively. Now that his spirits were no longer buoyed up by Lonnie's optimistic presence, he began to see things more realistically. It was hopeless, hopeless! Lonnie would end up completely discredited, or shot. He reached for the bottle, paused, picked it up, held it for a moment staring at it, sighed, hesitated, then locked it carefully in a desk drawer.

"No time to start that, you fool!" he admonished himself. "All Lonnie needs now is for you to go on one of those two-week benders like you used to do in the old days."

Lonnie's mind was too full of projects for him to sleep; but if Mary suspected he wasn't sleeping she'd worry and begin to talk about his working too hard, so he lay without moving, staring up at the faint patterns of light on the ceiling. It was very late. Occasionally a lone taxi hooted in the street below, and at long intervals a surface car went clanging past. Beside him Mary was breathing gently. Forgetting the Greek for a moment, he began to think how pleasant it was to be lying there in the darkness, close to Mary. Images of the past rose before him: dames he'd known, wild parties he'd gone to, weekends in Chicago and New York.... He rejected these images contemptuously. He'd just been marking time, waiting for Mary to come along.

"Why aren't you sleeping?" Mary asked suddenly.

Lonnie jumped and then sat up.

"For that matter, why aren't *you* sleeping?" he demanded, startled and slightly irritated.

"I was playing possum," said Mary, "wondering how long you'd lie there staring at the ceiling. What's wrong, Lonnie?"

"Nothing's wrong."

"Oh yes there is. You didn't eat all your chocolate pie at dinner, and any time that happens—"

"I wasn't so hungry tonight."

"You see? There is something wrong. When you're not hungry—"

"Oh, for God's sake," said Lonnie. "You make me sound like a pig."

"Well, as far as appetite goes—"

"Besides I had a sandwich with Ray this afternoon. A big one."

"What kind?" Mary asked quickly.

"Well, a—a—"

"Please stop lying, Lonnie."

"Do you think I've got nothing to do but go around remembering what kind of a sandwich I had?"

Mary said nothing.

"Do you?" he insisted.

"You're probably getting to the blonde stage again," said Mary. "If so, please say so. Because—"

Lonnie grabbed her suddenly and began to kiss her. She struggled, pushed at him, turned this way and that, and even kicked at him with her little bare feet. Finally she lay still.

"Lonnie!"

Sometime later they were sitting at a corner of the big dining room table, eating scrambled-egg sandwiches and drinking chocolate. Mary had her long dark hair back over her ears and no makeup on. She looked very young and fresh and schoolgirlish, especially as now the faint freckles high up on her cheeks were visible.

"... The trouble with me is," said Mary between bites, "I've got nothing to think about but you. You've got the restaurant and making money to occupy your thoughts." She shook her head slightly. "I never had any idea this would ever happen to me. Not this way, at least."

"Are you kicking?"

"Of course not," said Mary. "I never knew anybody could be so happy. But—sometimes I know you get very irritated with me because I'm always worrying about you. How can I help it? I think about you all day long, Lonnie—wondering what you're doing, if you've seen a pretty girl and wish you weren't married. Things like that. I get furious with myself. I try to be indifferent. One time when I was trying to be very indifferent, you got worried about me and asked me if I was ill."

They both laughed.

"I'm afraid you're not the indifferent type," said Lonnie.

"Worse luck. Until I met you, though, Lonnie, I was always so sure of myself. I never got ruffled about anything. I always, in a way, had the upper hand. But you got me all mixed up."

"I suppose you think *I* wasn't all mixed up! I was the guy who was never going to get married, remember? The second time I saw you I wanted to marry you, and it made me mad as hell."

Mary laughed.

"Oh, how I hated you that day you tried to pick me up on the corner!"

"What a beautiful brush!"

"Yes. But that night I couldn't sleep and I got more and more irritated with myself. Mr. Pool called me up, poor man, and I'm afraid I was very rude to him."

"I'm sorry to hear that!"

"Yes, I know you don't like him. But there was no reason for me to be so—well, that's over with, thank goodness! Then that night at the restaurant, the night Wanda was drunk and caused the disturbance. In the office I wasn't myself at all. I felt so unnatural, and you irritated me so."

"And you kept making fun of me."

They both laughed.

"Love me, Lonnie?"

"More than anything in the world, honey."

She studied his face for a long time.

"But if you ever don't anymore—please—"

"Wait a minute," said Lonnie. "Are we going to start all over again? I thought—"

She jumped up suddenly, mischievously pulled his hair, then ran out of the room. He leaped after her, dashed into the living room in pursuit, crying: "Wait till I get you, young lady," wrenched his ankle as he tried to avoid an ottoman, and fell flat on his face. Mary turned quickly, surprised by the crash, and looked round for him. He had disappeared. She hurried back. Lonnie sat up, holding his ankle and emitting a long string of profanity that made Mary wince. She finally put her hands over her ears.

A few minutes later Lonnie was sitting in the bedroom with his foot in a tub of hot water.

"It's swelling fast," said Mary, kneeling beside him, bathing it. "You'll have to stay in bed tomorrow."

"Oh, no I won't."

"Please, Lonnie. Then I can wait on you."

"I'm too busy."

He spoke so sharply and with such irritation that Mary looked up at him in surprise.

"Lonnie—!"

"It hurts like hell," said Lonnie quickly, trying to cover up his unpleasantness.

She was immediately mollified.

"I'd better call a doctor. I never saw it swell like this before."

"It'll be all right in a little while. Lie down, darling. You'll be worn out tomorrow."

She ignored him and continued to bathe his ankle. Lonnie was groaning inwardly. Fine time for a thing like this to happen!

4

Joe Pavlovsky shifted his bulk about uneasily on a small straight chair in Lonnie's office.

"You get around a lot, Joe," Lonnie was saying, "places I'm never in. And there's something I'd like for you to find out for me. That is, if it's okay with you."

"Sure, Mr. Drew," said Joe, grinning. "Anything I can do for you any time—just speak up."

"By the way, how's your sister?"

"She's fine. Got a new job. She left Karr-Dean a couple weeks ago. She's over at Mandell's now. We often talk about you. Wanda thinks your missus is A-one."

"Didn't go to New York, then?"

"Naw. That was just one of her wild ideas." Joe grinned indulgently.

Lonnie handed him a cigar, took one himself, and they lit up.

"It's like this," said Lonnie, settling down to business. "We'll say that a big robbery has been pulled off. Maybe as high as a hundred thousand dollars." Joe lowered his cigar and whistled with feeling. "We'll just say that, you understand," Lonnie went on. Joe nodded. "We'll say that the robbery was committed by a couple of guys from Lake City— professionals. Now, Joe, it's pretty unlikely that a job like that could be pulled off without it getting around—among the guys in the know. Am I right?"

"Sure," said Joe. "Nobody's ever going to keep one like that from getting out. Guys are bound to brag—maybe to their dames, maybe to some other racket guys. Trouble with most birds is they can't learn to keep their big mouths shut."

"That's what I figured. I want you to find out about it for me."

Joe shifted uneasily and his chair groaned and creaked.

"I'd like to do you a favor," he said finally, "but—ain't that like finking?"

Lonnie smiled soothingly.

"The police have got nothing to do with this, Joe."

"I see. You just want to find out for yourself—personal."

"That's right. It's actually sort of a business matter."

Joe puffed on his cigar, rolled round in his chair, and crossed his legs.

"I never heard of no heist like that in Lake City," he said. "It ain't going to be hard to find out *something* about it."

"Joe, do you know Gus Borgia?"

Joe looked at Lonnie quickly and sharply with his hard, slanted blue eyes and spoke cautiously.

"Yeah. Why?"

"You might be doing him a big favor."

"Yeah? That wouldn't hurt me none."

"It's just a tip."

Joe smiled, more at ease.

"Come clean now, Mr. Drew," he said. "What is it you want to find out?"

"The names of the guys that pulled the robbery."

"Okay," said Joe, getting up, "as long as the law's got nothing to do with it."

"You got my word."

"Swell."

Lonnie reached for his billfold, but Joe warned him off with a gesture.

"No, no. This one is on the house. You was pretty nice to the kid sister and I don't forget things. All I ask is, put in a good word for me with Gus Borgia. That's better than dough in the bank."

When Joe had gone, Lonnie sat staring thoughtfully off across the room for a long time. Then he reached for the phone and called Mary.

"Hello, darling."

"Hello, Lonnie, dear. How's your ankle?"

"Feels a lot better. I can lace my shoe now."

"Don't forget what I told you—use your cane when you walk around."

"What are you doing? You were a long time getting to the phone."

"I'm a busy girl. Pinky's holding the man from the cleaners while I talk to you."

"Oh, go ahead then, honey."

"I'm sending your gray suit and your brown tweed suit and the ties you put out. Anything else?"

"No."

"The man from the cleaners is very good-looking. He reminds me of you."

"I'll have him shot tomorrow. I'd hurry home right now if it wasn't for my ankle. Oh, by the way, I'm going to be late tonight. You better eat something light about seven. Then we'll go to Salini's later."

There was silence at the other end.

"Hello. Hello," said Lonnie.

"Oh, I wish you were coming home, but— Don't forget now, Lonnie. Stay off that ankle."

Lonnie hung up, smiling. What a lucky guy he was to have a wife like Mary! He winced inwardly, thinking about some of the bums he'd gone around with in the old days.

When Ray came in, about eight o'clock, Lonnie was having dinner in booth one with Gus Borgia and Benny Hayt. Ray frowned slightly, nodded to them, then hurried on to the office. He was feeling very well pleased with himself, as he'd been up half the night working on Lonnie's betting problem and he felt sure that he'd worked out an almost foolproof system for distributing the money so that not too much of it would be placed in one spot and cause comment. He sat wondering why Lonnie was having dinner with Benny and Gus. It made him feel very uneasy.

Benny and Gus were working on huge steaks that Lonnie had had cut especially for them, and an attentive waiter kept filling up their wineglasses with champagne.

From time to time Gus grinned at Lonnie.

"Real scoffing," he said, indicating the food. "This makes Salini's look sick."

"Yeah," said Benny, smiling dolefully and stuffing his mouth full of French-fried zucchini. "Best food I've tasted since the war."

"I thought you both might like a nice dinner."

"How's that wife of yours?" Gus inquired. "She sure is a beautiful girl. Did you ever see her, Benny?"

"No," said Benny.

"This guy's got no right to be that lucky."

"What happened to Rita, Mr. Borgia?" asked Lonnie.

"Oh—one of them things." Gus sighed and stared sadly at his plate for a moment. Then he shook his head. "I don't know. She talks too much, and half the time I don't know what she's saying. Then she laughs, laughs. It got on my nerves. She left town the other day."

Benny and Lonnie exchanged a glance. They both knew that the Greek had used Rita as a come-on. Now that Gus was in the fold, Rita didn't have to worry with him any longer, and he'd been given the brush.

Lonnie had an idea.

"Excuse me, will you, fellows? Little matter I've got to look after. I'll be back in a minute."

When Lonnie had gone, Gus observed:

"Nice guy. Got class. And he's a smart so-and-so. Take my word for it."

"Sure, Gus."

"If he pulls this one off, he's tops in my book."

"He better pull it off."

Gus glanced up at Benny.

"What's bothering you?"

"Nothing, nothing."

"All I say is, it's a big one and a tough one. The Greek figured it out. But you notice he ain't pulling it off. Now what does that make him?"

"Smart, maybe."

Gus studied Benny with fork poised.

"Sometimes he's smart in a way I don't like," said Gus. "Someday he'll get so smart he'll figure himself right into a first-class jam." Gus spoke so bitterly that Benny began to prick up his ears.

"That so, Gus?"

"I'm saying so. He rubs me the wrong way, Benny, and you might as well know it. When I first settled in here, he was ringing my phone from morning till night. He was taking me out to dinner, he was introducing me to dames. Okay. So I go in. Now what happens? He's always busy."

Benny was surprised at Gus's attitude. You never knew about a guy. Who'd ever figure he'd be that touchy?

"He's been sick lately."

Gus grunted.

"It's the fumes from all that junk he sprays on him. He stinks like a New Orleans whore."

Benny laughed and reached for his glass. It was empty. The waiter rushed over and filled it.

"Me, too," said Gus. The waiter filled his glass and left. "Best service I've had since I was in San Francisco," said Gus expansively, "and the best goddamn dinner."

About half an hour later Benny, Gus, Ray, and Lonnie were sitting in the office sipping liqueurs and listening to a comedy radio program. Gus felt great and even smiled happily—something unusual for him. He kept laughing at the cracks of the radio comedian and winking at Lonnie. Ray looked on with a distinct feeling of trepidation.

The door opened and Wanda Pavlovsky came in. "Oh," she said, starting back, "I didn't know you were busy, Mr. Drew. I just dropped in to—"

Lonnie jumped up.

"That's all right, Wanda. We're just sitting around talking. How about joining us?"

She looked about her at the other men.

"Well—so long as I'm not interrupting anything." Lonnie glanced at Gus, who was on his feet, staring eagerly at Wanda.

At a little after ten Benny went home alone, and Gus and Wanda started out for a round of the nightspots. Gus was very much taken with the Polish girl, who said that she really ought to go home and get a good night's sleep, that she wasn't even dressed to go out, but if Mr. Borgia, who had such a way with him, insisted ...

Lonnie winked at Ray as soon as they were alone.

"The Greek's not so smart," he said.

"Will you stop congratulating yourself?" Ray demanded. "And sit down here and look over this plan?"

It was after eleven o'clock when Lonnie got to the Brookmeade. He was anxious to see Mary and he acted so impatient that the elevator boy kept looking at him out of the corner of his eye as the elevator climbed slowly upward. He'd intended to call Mary, but he'd been so busy he hadn't got around to it. What he couldn't understand was why she hadn't called him.

Pinky met him at the door with a scared face. "What's wrong with you?" Lonnie demanded. "Where's Mrs. Drew?"

"She's gone. She—she took a suitcase full of clothes and left."

"Why?"

"I don't know, I'm sure. And I don't want you to think it had anything to do with me. I—I—been so damned upset I—"

Lonnie grabbed Pinky by the arm.

"What did you do?"

"Me? I didn't do anything. All of a sudden I hear her walking up and down. And pretty soon I peek in. Her hair's going every which way and she looks so mad I'm scared. I never knew that a woman like the missus could look so mad. I thought maybe it was something you said to her over the phone and—"

"Over the phone! You mean it was that long ago?"

"Yes, sir. Right after the cleaning man left."

"Why the hell didn't you call me when she took the suitcase and went out?"

"Well, like I said. I thought maybe it was something between the two of you and none of my business."

"This is a hell of a note," said Lonnie, bewildered. "I don't get it."

He hadn't even taken his hat off. He walked around the living room, trying to figure out what to do. His ankle began to hurt him, so he sat down, but in a moment he jumped up and started to pace the floor again. Pinky stood near the door, looking on apprehensively. He was badly shaken and couldn't realize that this had really happened. Things were going along perfectly when all of a sudden—boom!—they blow up.

"Would you like a drink or something, boss?" he asked.

Lonnie turned and looked at Pinky strangely: Mary only gone a few hours and Pinky already starting to call him "boss" as in the old days. A sense of loss began to grow on him. He went quickly to the window and stood looking out so that Pinky couldn't see how panicky he was. Without Mary nothing seemed to mean anything at all.

"Did you hear me, boss?" Pinky insisted.

"Don't call me 'boss,' Pinky. You know Mrs. Drew doesn't like it."

"I'm sorry. It's because she's gone and—"

The phone rang. Pinky went to answer it, but Lonnie cut in front of him and grabbed up the receiver.

"Yes, Ray," said Lonnie, his face falling. "Talk up. I can't hear you."

"I've got to whisper. I'm afraid she'll hear me."

"Who?" cried Lonnie.

"The missus. She's here at the beach house and she's mighty upset about something. She's borrowed all our gas tickets and Willy's got the wreck over at the filling station now, filling it up for her. I think she's going home."

"Stall her. Do something. I'll be right there."

Lonnie brushed Pinky aside and went out. Pinky stood staring off across the room, shaking his head; then he began to whistle. He felt better. They'd just had a row, that's all, and Lonnie wouldn't admit it.

"If he's started chasing dames already," thought Pinky, "I hope she busts his head wide open with something."

Lonnie knocked on the bedroom door repeatedly, but got no answer. Then he tried to open it. It was locked.

"Mary," he called, "I know you're in there, so you might as well open the door."

"I'm not going to open the door until you go away. I'll stay in here all night if necessary."

"But what in hell is this all about?"

"And I'm not going to listen to any of your smart explanations. I've made up my mind. I'm going home and see my folks, then I'm going to New York. I just had a feeling things would turn out this way. That's why I almost didn't marry you."

"What are you talking about?"

There was a long pause. Suddenly Mary unlocked the door, opened it, and faced him. Her eyes were flashing, she looked much taller, and she seemed so formidable that Lonnie stared at her with a sort of awe.

"This!" she cried, slapping a card into his hand.

He glanced down at it, hardly able to make it out in the dim light. It read:

Pavlovsky
Call

Lonnie stared, looked up at Mary, who was regarding him fiercely, then he burst out laughing.

"Where did you get this?"

"In your gray suit. And I wasn't snooping. I was sending it to the cleaners."

"That means *Joe* Pavlovsky," said Lonnie, very much relieved. "I called him today on some business."

"Oh, really," said Mary. "Then why was it that Wanda turned up at the restaurant this evening?"

Lonnie cleared his throat, carefully rubbed his chin, and looked past Mary into the bedroom, avoiding her eyes. This was one for the book: circumstantial evidence!

"That's a hard one to answer, Mary."

"I thought it would be. You acted exactly as I thought you would. I knew you'd say it was her brother, so I made it my business to find out. Now do you give up, Mr. Lonnie Drew?"

"Yes," said Lonnie, "but not in the way you think. I've been holding out on you, Mary, and—"

"You don't need to tell me. I've been watching you lately. You're nervous as my aunt's tomcat. You pay no attention when I talk to you. You can't eat your dinner. You—"

"Mary, come in the living room," said Lonnie firmly. "You've just got to be told, that's all." Mary glanced at him, very much puzzled. "Hurry up. Don't stand there. I'll tell you the whole thing. But I want Ray with us. He'll bear me out."

"Ray!"

"Yes. He's in on it. And maybe he can help me explain it to you. I've been trying hard to keep this from you, Mary, but—"

Mary studied him, trying to read his expression. She felt very calm now. Some instinct told her that she'd been wrong and she had already begun to feel a little ashamed of herself.

A short time later Ray entered the living room. Mary was sitting on the big couch by the huge view-window; Lonnie was staring into the fire.

"Ray," said Lonnie, "we've got to tell Mary the whole thing. She's all mixed up."

Ray was taken aback.

"But, Lonnie—!"

"No buts about it. I'll start at the beginning and you prompt me if I get stuck. Some of it is going to be a little tough for her to understand, so we've got to make it plain."

They were both very much surprised by her reaction. She was neither angry, frightened, nor worried. She was exhilarated. Her color was high and her dark eyes were dancing with excitement.

"You understand," said Ray, "Lonnie's in quite a spot, Mary. He's in real danger."

Mary turned and smiled at Lonnie; then she went over and sat on his lap.

"I'm sorry, darling," she said. "But you must admit—"

"Sure. I admit it looked bad," said Lonnie, kissing her. "Otherwise do you think I'd have bothered you with all this stuff?"

"I still don't think she—" Ray began.

"Oh, yes I do," said Mary. "I understand very well. Of course, maybe not about the odds and—and the betting. But I can plainly see that Lonnie's in trouble." She kissed him. "But I'd rather have him in this kind of trouble than mixed up with Wanda Pavlovsky."

Lonnie and Ray exchanged a glance.

"Well," said Lonnie, "I'm glad it's all straightened out. Now we can go home."

"No, Lonnie," said Mary. "Let's stay here tonight. It's nice and warm now. Don't you think that would be fun?"

"Sure. Why not?"

Ray still felt uneasy about the whole thing, but he was glad to see them so happy and so absorbed in each other.

"Why don't I get Willy to fix a little snack?" he suggested. "You can eat right here in front of the fire."

"Grand idea," said Mary.

Later Mary turned to him in bed and asked:

"This little Mr. Borgia—you want to make him a friend of yours, is that right?"

"Yes," said Lonnie. "Why?"

"Don't you think I could work on him just as well as Wanda?"

"Now wait a minute, Mary," said Lonnie, sitting up.

"Not in the same way of course. Don't be silly. But couldn't I give a nice dinner for him? He can bring Wanda. And we'll have wonderful food and champagne. And I'll be very sweet to him and you can hold Wanda's hand under the table."

"Not bad. Not bad."

"I'll really go out of my way to make this a wonderful dinner, Lonnie. In no time at all we'll have him eating out of our hands."

Lonnie took her in his arms and began to stroke her hair gently. "You're quite a kid. Lucky day for me when I saw you."

She sat up abruptly. "I think I'll have guinea fowl, if I can get any. Clear mushroom soup with sherry. Perhaps baked Alaska—"

Lonnie pulled her back.

"Can't it wait till tomorrow?"

"But I've got to start planning, Lonnie."

"Sounds wonderful. Gus'll never have the heart to get me shot after he eats a dinner like that."

Mary hugged him suddenly.

"I'm scared in a way, Lonnie. If anything should happen to you, I wouldn't know what to do. But—it's so exciting. And I have such confidence in you, darling. Those other men—well, they haven't got a chance."

Lonnie wished it was that easy, but refrained from saying so.

"We'll pull it off, honey. Don't worry."

"But, Lonnie, Ray's right. I do wish you'd told me how much money we were spending and—and I wish I hadn't bought the coat. Please. You must tell me things."

The dinner was even better than Lonnie had expected. Willy and Pinky outdid themselves serving and the food was excellently cooked. Mary looked calm and beautiful in a dark dress and she kept up a continuous conversation with little Gus Borgia, who was so flattered he didn't know what to do with himself.

Wanda seemed perfectly at ease. But Gus was out of his element and suddenly became conscious of his table manners, dropped a fork, almost upset a wineglass, and finally dribbled his dessert down the front of his coat. He was as awkward as a boy at his first party, but he was having a great time.

Later they had coffee and brandy in the living room. Gus sighed with contentment and observed:

"You people sure know how to live. Now take me. I'm an old bachelor. I'm always knocking around from place to place. And I get into the strangest joints. Course it's getting worse all the time." He turned to Mary. "Mrs. Drew, where do you get servants like that?"

"She trained them herself," Lonnie explained.

"I'll be damned," said Gus, looking at Mary with a sort of awe. A kid like her, training grown men!

"The one with the black hair is Charley Fiala's brother," said Lonnie.

"No kidding!"

"He used to be a taxi-driver in Chi."

Gus laughed and finished his brandy.

"Imagine—Charley Fiala's brother. And this little lady here trained him. Mrs. Drew, you're a hundred per cent okay."

"Thank you, Mr. Borgia. Now how about some more brandy?"

"Maybe a little more. Thimbleful."

"Mary used to model with me at Karr-Dean, Gus," said Wanda. "She was our star."

"How come the guy who owns the store didn't marry her? He must be a sucker."

"Mary wasn't interested. Were you, Mary?"

"I'm afraid not. He was already married. More coffee, Mr. Borgia?"

"Yes. Hell, why should I stint myself? I'll probably lay awake all night, but if I do—I'll be thinking about this dinner and the little lady that figured it all out."

"Gus, you're a gentleman," said Wanda.

"I've been called a lot of things in my time," said Gus. "But never a gentleman." He laughed loudly and, reaching forward, slapped Lonnie on the knee.

Lonnie laughed appreciatively.

Hours later Gus had made no move to go home. He was sitting in a big armchair with a highball in his hand, talking about the old days in Chi, carefully editing it, of course, for Mary's benefit. Lonnie kept wanting to yawn and took drink after drink to keep himself awake. Wanda had long since given up and was now sitting with her legs stretched out, nodding from time to time. But Mary was sparkling as brightly as ever.

"You've certainly had a most interesting life, Mr. Borgia," said Mary. "It must have been wonderful."

"Oh, I don't know," said Gus pensively. "It's more fun telling about it than it was living it."

Wanda's head fell forward and she woke with a start. They all looked at her.

"Say," said Gus, "what time is it getting to be?" He glanced at his watch and almost dropped his highball. "Good God! It's nearly two. This evening has sure gone fast."

It took Gus nearly half an hour to thank Lonnie and Mary and to say goodnight. As soon as the door had shut behind him and Wanda, Mary kicked off her high-heeled shoes, flung herself down on the couch, and lay full-length.

"If he'd stayed another fifteen minutes I'd be stinking drunk," said Lonnie.

"Well," said Mary, "at least it was a success. But—poor Wanda!"

"Yeah. I guess that's what all dames say about Gus. Maybe that's what makes him look so sad and beaten."

"I thought he was very nice and polite—considering."

"He certainly thought you were wonderful. Well, I think we struck a good blow tonight."

"Oh, I'm so tired," said Mary. "I think I'll sleep right here."

Gus Borgia was sitting in booth one at the inn, waiting for Wanda. He was wearing a new double-breasted blue serge suit; he'd discarded the starched collar he always wore for a soft one, and he'd had his lank black hair, which was usually hanging about his forehead in a bang, cut shorter. He looked decidedly better and younger.

George and Leonard, the Austrian waiter, who handled booth one, were hovering about him, seeing that he had everything he wanted. Gus tipped as fantastically as he'd done in the Capone era in Chicago. Several nights before, he'd given George a fifty-dollar bill and Leonard a twenty. Things like that simply didn't happen anymore and the help needed no urgings from Lonnie to wait on Gus hand and foot.

In a little while the Greek came in and went to the bar. Mack grinned and immediately began to mix a double Martini. Although as immaculately turned out as usual, the Greek seemed nervous and jumpy. There were signs of strain in his face, and under his eyes were dark shadows of fatigue.

Gus noticed him, but gave no sign. Wanda had told him a few things about the Greek that had annoyed him excessively. From time to time Gus glanced in the direction of the bar, where the Greek sat with his chin in his hand staring gloomily into the bar mirror, but seeing nothing. Gus misinterpreted his stare and thought the Greek was admiring his handsome face in the glass.

"Loves himself, that guy," said Gus under his breath. "I can't stand a man who fights a mirror. A dame, yes!"

Mack put the Greek's drink in front of him. Shifting his position to sip it, the Greek caught a glimpse of Gus in the mirror. At that precise moment Gus was looking at him with distaste. The Greek noted the expression and turned. His aplomb deserted him. He grew pale. But in a moment he composed himself, smiled, nodded, and came over to booth one, carrying his drink.

"Hello, Gus," he said, smiling. "Didn't know you were here."

Gus nodded, studying him, making no effort to be friendly.

"Mind if I sit down?"

"No," said Gus. "A dame's coming here to meet me, but—"

"As soon as she comes, I'll leave," said the Greek, sitting down quickly. "Talked to Lonnie about the deal lately?"

Gus nodded.

"Everything's all right, I suppose."

"Why not?"

"Well—it's a big deal. Sometimes at night I get to thinking maybe Lonnie's not big enough for the job—might bungle it."

"You picked him."

"A man can be wrong, Gus. He seemed like the best available at the time."

"Why didn't *you* handle it?"

"It's a little out of my line."

Gus sipped a highball and looked past the Greek, who cleared his throat, hesitated, hastily lit a cigarette, then said:

"I understand you've been seeing a good deal of Lonnie."

"Yes," said Gus proudly, "him and his wife. Classy people. I was out there to dinner the other night. Best food I ever tasted."

"He's a smooth worker, Gus. Probably got an angle."

"Such as—?"

"He might be trying to get you in a good humor—just in case."

"Just in case what?"

"You never know."

"Look, Pool, I'm nearly fifty. I been around a long time. Don't tell me my business."

The Greek laughed.

"Gus, for God's sake," he said. "Who am I to tell you your business? It was merely a suggestion."

Gus studied the Greek for a moment, making him very uneasy.

"Of course," said Gus, "if you got some real information—"

"No, no. Just an idea." The Greek waved the whole thing aside with a languid gesture. "Forget it."

Gus saw Wanda coming and got up. The Greek glanced at Gus, thought for a moment that he was dismissing him, but, noticing finally that Gus was looking toward the front door, he turned, started slightly at the sight of Wanda, and got to his feet.

Wanda was out of breath from hurrying.

"Gus," she exclaimed, "I'm so sorry I'm late. But—" Then she turned as if just noticing the Greek. "Oh, hello," she said coldly.

"Hello, Wanda." The Greek smiled and bowed politely. "I was just leaving."

"I'm so sorry," said Wanda sarcastically, sitting down.

Gus grunted with amusement.

"See you around," he said to the Greek, really dismissing him now.

The Greek went back to the bar and ordered another double Martini.

That night he couldn't sleep even after taking a lukewarm shower and a sleeping tablet. He lay for hours in the darkness listening to the night sounds and trying to figure out what was going on. Gus's attitude worried him.

About three o'clock he sat up in bed, struck by a sudden thought.

"He's going to bet the money on credit," he told the walls. "Why didn't I think of that?"

He got up, threw on a bathrobe, and began to pace the floor. For a little while he felt completely demoralized, then he sat down and began to figure. But the longer he figured, the less sense it made. Even if the horse won, Lonnie'd be a hundred G's short, and how could anybody explain a shortage like that to Gus Borgia, who in the old days had had men shot for much less?

The Greek laughed to himself.

"Lonnie's trying to soften Gus up—that's obvious. But he'll never get away with it. Underneath, Gus is all business and wants what's coming to him to the penny."

The problem became more and more complex; its ramifications seemed to stretch off endlessly in all directions. The Greek finally forced himself to narrow it down to one simple item: he wanted to ruin Lonnie. That had been the motive behind the whole idea. The fact that he'd already made around seventy G's out of the transaction was pleasant, but merely incidental.

Every time the Greek thought about Mary and Lonnie he broke out into a cold sweat and was plagued by vicious, murderous desires, which horrified him. Violence was foreign to his subtle, evasive nature. Never in his life before had he been troubled by such impulses; consequently he feared that his defenses against them were weak.

Gradually he calmed himself and after another cigarette went back to bed.

"He's done," the Greek said aloud. "He's washed up. Finished. And he'll be lucky if he doesn't end up on a slab in the morgue."

He tried to compose himself to sleep, but after a while gave it up and lay staring at the ceiling. Another facet of the situation had occurred to him. If the horse won, he himself stood to make a considerable sum. But if this happened, Lonnie would be in a less precarious position. If the horse lost, the thing would be out of Gus's hands entirely, but Lonnie would owe every big bookmaker in the Midwest.

The Greek lay for a long time torn between his desire for more money and his passion to see Lonnie reduced to a cipher, if not actually killed.

He realized, knowing Gus, how dangerous it was to tamper in any way with the running of the race, but ...

Thursday night, and the race was to be run on Saturday. It was after one o'clock, a fire was burning brightly in the living room fireplace, Mary was lounging on the couch, trying to keep from falling asleep, and Ray and Lonnie were sitting at a table, working over a huge schedule which seemed to grow more and more complicated as time passed.

Finally Lonnie threw down his pencil and got up. His ankle was hurting him and he felt irritable and tense.

"Mary," he called, "for Lord's sake, why don't you go to bed?"

"No," said Mary drowsily, "I want to stay up till you're through."

"It may be a long time yet," said Ray wearily, taking off his glasses and wiping them. "We get it together in one place and it falls apart in another."

"I wish I could help."

Lonnie came over to the couch and kissed Mary lightly. "You've been a great help, honey. And you're a great girl. I hope we don't end up in the gutter."

"I'll take a chance," said Mary. "Of course, we can always go to New Vienna to live. I own a house there."

Lonnie turned to Ray.

"She's been holding out on us."

"It's a very small house. It only rents for forty-five a month furnished."

"Your furniture, too?"

"Yes. It's an old place my grandmother used to own."

"First time I ever heard of it."

"I let my folks keep the rent money, so I've never—"

"How would you like to live in New Vienna, Ray?" asked Lonnie.

"Sounds great."

They all laughed. Feeling better, Lonnie went back to the table and sat down.

"What did Gregg have to say tonight?" asked Ray.

"He thinks there's nothing to it. He worked the old horse seven furlongs in twenty-six and he was hard held all the way."

"He should walk in."

"That's what Gregg thinks."

Lonnie turned to look at Mary, then he nudged Ray, who glanced over at her. She was sitting up with her arms folded, sound asleep.

BOOK THREE

It was a mild fall night. Mary, Ray, and Lonnie had had a light meal at the inn and were now driving out Lake Shore Boulevard toward the Lakeland Racetrack. On their left was the lake, pale, vast, and empty under the stars; on their right were the massed, tall buildings of the downtown section. After they crossed the North Shore Viaduct, over the labyrinthine mazes of the railroad yards, they could see, far to the south, the fiery glow of the steel plant against the soft blue night sky.

"Fast track tomorrow," said Lonnie, looking out at the cloudless, starry sky. "Gregg says the old horse can run on anything, but according to the form his best races were over a fast track."

"Do you know," said Mary, "I've never seen a horse race? My father was always going when we still had some money. One winter we took a trip to New Orleans and my mother and father went to the track every day. But they left me in the hotel with my nurse. I was three years old. I was very much annoyed with them for that."

"At the age of three she was annoyed with her parents!" laughed Lonnie.

"Well, it's true," said Mary, turning to look at him. "I can still remember how lonely I was. I spent half my time staring out the hotel window. I remember one day it rained and the town was all misty and the roofs looked like pale silver—it made me very sad. When my parents came home they'd be laughing and happy and talking about the horses and the crowds. I almost hated them."

"That's no way to talk about your parents," said Lonnie, glancing at her, mildly shocked; and Ray turned away to hide a smile. He had never expected to hear Lonnie voicing such conventional sentiments.

Mary ignored Lonnie's remark.

"Maybe that's why I never went to horse races after I grew up," she said thoughtfully.

"There have been days," said Lonnie, "when I wish my parents had scared *me* away." He and Ray laughed.

Lonnie turned off the boulevard now and went down a narrow side road that led to the stable area of the Lakeland Track. Ahead of them loomed the tall bulk of the grandstand, dark now except for a few small scattered lights.

At the stable area gate a couple of watchmen flagged them down and came over to the car. Lonnie explained that he had an appointment with Owner Ed Gregg, but the watchmen shook their heads.

"No visitors," said one of them. "Owners, trainers, and employees only."

A man came round the end of a barn, walking fast. He passed under one of the eave-lights and Lonnie called to him. It was Ed Gregg. He hurried over to the car.

"Just coming to look for you," he said. "Mighty strict around here."

Gregg got into the car with them and they drove a short distance down the road and parked. Beyond was the huge stable area, housing thousands of horses and men and giving off a powerful odor of hay, leather, and liniment.

After Gregg had been introduced to Mary, he said: "Well, we're getting a fast track, and the old horse's in good shape, but—"

"But what?" asked Lonnie.

"Some finagling going on," said Gregg. "And I don't like it a bit. There's an old fellow here named Burt Crouse. He's got a gypsy stable—three horses. Two of them's entered in our race tomorrow and he's going to run them both."

"You mean he's got a chance? Why didn't we take care of him?"

"First place," said Gregg, "he hasn't got much of a chance. Second place, a man couldn't trust him. He's the kind of guy you *can't* take care of. In a pinch he'd accept money from everybody and then do what he darn well pleased."

"Well, if he hasn't got a chance—"

"It's like this," Gregg explained. "We're going a mile, which is about the old horse's limit since he was hurt. There's only one way he'll run. He gets out in front and stays there. If you try to run him from behind, he sulks. All right. Crouse has got an old sprinter, Gilt Armor. He can't run over six furlongs to save his life—but—he can run it around eleven, which is mighty fast for this race. Then Crouse has got a fair mile horse, Day Moon, that runs from behind. Begin to see what I mean?"

"Yes," said Lonnie.

"After all," Gregg went on, "this is no big handicap. The purse is only twelve hundred. But Crouse is really going for it and I'd like to know why. He's got no money to bet. And who would back him—a gyp like him?"

"Maybe he really figures he can win," said Lonnie. "Maybe he needs feed money."

"The way the race is stashed up, he might just get in with Day Moon. The three best horses outside of the old horse aren't even going to try. But how did Crouse know that? If they were all trying, he wouldn't have the chance of a snowball in hell." Gregg turned to Mary. "Excuse me, ma'am."

"You mean somebody's talked?" asked Lonnie.

"Looks like it."

There was a long pause.

"You see," Gregg went on, "if Gilt Armor takes the old horse six furlongs in eleven, the old horse may get a little late coming home, and with the others out of it Day Moon might nip him at the wire."

Lonnie considered for a moment, then asked: "Got any ideas?"

"No," said Gregg, "not a one. All that I can do is my best, me and the old horse. And we'll probably win, but it's going to be a tight fit."

"No use talking to Crouse, I don't suppose." Gregg shook his head emphatically.

"Not a chance. He's already bragging around he's going to win the race."

"I'll think it over," said Lonnie. "If there's any change in our plan, I'll send you a wire."

"Okay, Lonnie," said Gregg. "Don't get me wrong. I think we can win. But there's just a possibility—and this is such a big one—" He laughed uneasily. "I don't figure to sleep much tonight."

On the way home Mary said:

"Does that mean we're not going to win, Lonnie?"

"No, no," said Lonnie soothingly. "Gregg's just nervous. Naturally—it's a big responsibility."

Ray glanced at Lonnie, but made no comment.

They had a hard time persuading Mary to go to bed. She was very excited and nervous and kept talking about what a wonderful time they were going to have at the track the next day. Finally Lonnie picked her up, carried her into the bedroom, and sat her down on the bed.

"You've got to get some rest, honey," he said. "You haven't had a good night's sleep for over a week."

"How about you?"

"I don't need it the way you do. Since I've been married I've been getting more sleep than I ever got in my life before."

It was the wrong thing to say. Mary looked at him a little reproachfully; then she got up and went into the dressing room. Lonnie hesitated, then followed her. She was sitting at her dressing table, beginning to fix her hair for the night.

"You know you haven't been getting enough sleep," he insisted.

"I know," she said mildly.

"Well, then—?"

"I don't know what makes me so silly," said Mary. "Here I've been trying to help, and actually I've just been in the way. Haven't I, Lonnie?" She turned and looked up at him.

"How can you say a thing like that?" he demanded. "Don't you understand? Having you here is what makes it all fun."

Mary's face softened. Then her expression changed abruptly and her dark eyes flashed.

"And you stop talking about when you weren't married. I don't like it."

"I'm sorry," said Lonnie. "But I was only—"

Mary laughed and, jumping up, threw herself into his arms. He kissed her gently.

"I'm so happy, Lonnie," she said. "And you've been so wonderful to me, and sometimes I feel so useless—"

A little while later the house was quiet. Mary was sleeping peacefully, and in the living room Ray was sitting on the couch watching Lonnie pace the floor.

"You've got to call Gus," said Ray. "He should know about this."

"What he doesn't know won't hurt him."

"Yes. But good God, Lonnie—!"

"You're forgetting something, Ray. Gus might call the whole thing off. Then what?"

Ray stared.

"I never thought of that."

"Where would we be if he called the money back?"

Lonnie sat down and poured himself a drink.

"No," he went on, "we've been taking plenty of chances all along. One more won't kill us."

Ray looked at Lonnie with a mixture of impatience and awe. Lonnie was in his element!

The Greek was playing no-limit stud with Rank, Coster, a horseman named Crowley, and a stocky little Italian from Chicago, a friend of Gus's, called Diamond. The Greek seemed so detached and indifferent that Diamond kept glancing at him, wondering. After all, a guy could get killed in this game, financially speaking. Was it an act?

Diamond had heard a lot about the Greek, but had never met him before. He'd always been told that he was quite a boy. A great hand with the dames, a guy who lived on the fat of the land like a millionaire, and a no-limit plunger in any kind of gambling game. Diamond was unimpressed. To him the Greek looked like a tired character in spite of his perfect clothes, his immaculateness, the jaunty boutonniere. He was pale, had dark circles under his eyes, and didn't seem to have a word to say.

Diamond ran the Greek out of two pots in succession and chuckled to himself. "It ain't a guy's reputation," he mused; "it's what he does in action." Diamond began to ride his luck hard, delighted by the way things were going. In half an hour he beat the Greek out of nearly twelve thousand dollars.

Coster turned to the Greek.

"Lucky in love, I guess. Otherwise—"

The Greek's lips tightened, but he made no comment. "He must be, he must be," chuckled Diamond. "The cards are sure giving him a going-over."

Still the Greek said nothing. But he hated them all, the damned swine! Why couldn't they keep their mouths shut and play cards? Why did they have to keep talking, talking.... All of a sudden he felt so nervous that he couldn't stay on his chair any longer. He got up abruptly. They all turned to look at him.

"Deal me out this time," he said, and left the room.

The hall outside was dark and deserted. The Greek felt faint and leaned against the wall for support. He was wondering how long a man could go without sleep; it had been days now. He'd lost count.

A sudden surge of violent hatred for Lonnie shook him, and his heart began to pound. Panicky now, the Greek hurried down the stairs and out into the bar.

"Yes, Mr. Pool?" said Gordy, glancing up politely. Then he took a good look at the Greek. Something was wrong with him, that was a cinch.

"Straight bourbon," said the Greek, trying to appear calm.

"Yes, sir."

Gordy got it for him hurriedly and the Greek tossed it down, then leaned against the bar for a minute.

"You all right, sir?" asked Gordy.

"Yes," said the Greek, smiling weakly. "Had a touch of the flu lately, and I can't seem to throw it off."

His heart slowed down, he became calmer, and in a moment he sighed with relief.

The front door opened and Wanda came in wearing an enormous hat and a new mink coat, followed by Gus, then Benny. They all looked flushed and happy as if they'd dined and drunk well.

The Greek had got to the place where even the sight of happiness violently irritated him. Benny, Gus, and Wanda all began to talk at once. He turned his back on them and ordered another straight bourbon. Gordy handed it to him quickly. The Greek still looked so pale that Gordy was worried.

"Straight liquor, eh?" said a voice behind him. "You a little on edge, Jack?"

The Greek turned. Gus was regarding him ironically. He forced a smile.

"Slightly."

"Well, this time tomorrow night it'll all be over," said Gus. "And a couple days later we'll be cutting up a nice hunk of moola."

"I hope so," said the Greek.

"He hopes so!" laughed Gus, who'd had a little too much to drink, turning to the others. "This guy only *hopes* so. We *know* so, don't we, Benny?"

"We sure as hell do," said Benny, trying to sound as confident as Gus.

"With that boy Lonnie handling things, we're a lead-pipe cinch, a lock. Am I right?"

"You're always right, Gus," said Wanda, slapping him on the back.

The Greek moved away from them, looked about him uncomfortably, then bowed slightly.

"Will you excuse me? I'm in a game upstairs."

"Why, go ahead," said Gus. "Don't let us stop you."

When the Greek had gone, Wanda looked after him for a moment, then turned.

"What's on his mind? He seems a little solemn or something, doesn't he?"

"He always seems a little solemn or something," said Gus, making a face and shrugging.

It was after one o'clock and Ray was just leaving when the phone rang. Lonnie grabbed the receiver off the hook quickly so it wouldn't ring again and wake Mary, who as a rule was a very light sleeper.

"There's a call for you, Mr. Drew," said the girl on the Brookmeade switchboard. "A Mr. Augustus Borgia—" Lonnie smiled with amusement at the high-sounding name—"and," the girl went on, "there's a man just come in to see you. Wants to know if you'll come down."

"Who is he?"

"Name please?" he heard the girl say. "He says it's Joe, Mr. Drew."

"Tell him I'll be right down. Put the call on."

He covered the transmitter with his hand.

"Gus's on the phone," he said to Ray, "and Joe Pavlovsky's downstairs. Maybe he's got some news."

"I wish I knew what this was all about. I'd rest easier," said Ray.

"No, you wouldn't," laughed Lonnie, then he held up his hand for silence. "Hello, Mr. Borgia. How are you?"

"I'm fine. How about you, Lonnie?"

"Same here."

"Good. Well, I just called up to wish you luck with the thing—you know. As a matter of fact, I'm slightly loaded and I been sitting around here chewing the fat with Wanda and Benny, and we got to talking about you. Wanda says to give the missus her best, and that goes for me, too. Greatest little kid I ever seen."

"Thanks, Mr. Borgia."

"How did you like that 'Augustus' routine? I thought you'd get a kick out of it. My name's really Agostino, but what the hell! I'm a good American, and why should I go around with a tag like that?" Gus laughed. "One of my brothers—Louis—changed his name to Borg, and everybody thought he was a Swede, so he changed back. He says: 'I'd rather be taken for a guinea any day than a Swede.'"

Lonnie laughed appreciatively.

"Yeah," said Gus, "and he's right. Well, I won't keep you, boy. Just want to put a little bug in your ear. Pull this one off slick. You can do it. I'm settling in on Lake City for good. I can sure use a smart guy like yourself around here. Hey, wait a minute. Wanda wants to talk to you."

There was a pause. Lonnie turned to Ray and winked. He could hear a good-natured squabble going on at the other end of the line and Gus's voice came to him faintly: "Aw, hell. What you want to tell him that for? What does he care?"

Wanda got on the phone.

"Hello, Mr. Drew. This is Wanda. Just thought you'd like to know. Gus and I—we're going to get married."

"Well, I'll be damned," said Lonnie, genuinely startled. "Nice going."

"Yeah. I got him sold I can make him just as good a wife as Mary does you. Of course, maybe she'll have to give me some pointers—" Gus took the phone away from her.

"How about that, Lonnie? Okay for your missus to tell Wanda what's what?"

"Sure. Sure, Mr. Borgia. Congratulations."

"Ain't it hell? I get by for forty-eight years and now I take the plunge! It's all account of you and your missus, Lonnie, so it better be good."

"I'll see what I can do."

Ray stood listening, wondering what it was all about. Lonnie hung up, chuckling.

"Wanda hooked Gus," he said.

"What!"

"Yeah. They're going to get married."

The bedroom door opened and Mary peered in.

"Who's going to get married?"

Both Lonnie and Ray started.

"Little bright eyes," said Lonnie. "Never misses anything." He told her about Wanda and Gus.

Mary shuddered slightly.

"Poor Wanda!"

"Oh, I don't know," said Lonnie. "Gus must have around a million bucks."

"It's not enough," said Mary, and Ray laughed.

Lonnie snapped his fingers, remembering. He went over to Mary and kissed her lightly.

"Joe Pavlovsky's waiting for me down in the lobby," he said. "I'll be back in a few minutes."

"How does it happen that these Pavlovskys always come in bunches— like bananas?" Mary demanded.

"You go back to bed," said Lonnie. "You need sleep."

"If you say that again—!"

"But you do."

"I know, Lonnie, and I wish I didn't."

"You're just afraid you'll miss something."

She laughed, kissed him, and shut the door.

On the way down in the elevator Lonnie tried to explain to Ray about Mary.

"She's the strangest girl," he said. "A—a funny mixture, I mean. Half the time she seems like she's not grown up. But don't ever think she isn't. It's just a kind of manner, I guess. Because she's sharp as a tack. I'd hate to try to put one over on her."

"You did try, and look what happened."

"Yes, but I mean something serious."

Ray stared at him dumbfounded.

"You mean you don't think this is serious?"

"Not between Mary and me it isn't."

Ray shook his head; he was both envious and irritated.

They found Joe Pavlovsky sitting in the lobby reading a newspaper. He got up quickly. Ray stopped to say hello to him, but Lonnie said:

"See you tomorrow morning, bright and early, Ray."

"Sure," said Ray, looking from Joe to Lonnie. "Good night."

Ray went out reluctantly, looking over his shoulder. He was very apprehensive about tomorrow. It didn't seem possible that Lonnie could pull off such a coup—and on credit. Not only that; Lonnie was cooking up something for the Greek. Ray had a sudden desire to get to the seclusion of his bedroom. At best he felt inadequate to cope with the endless worries and fears of daily living. Lately things had taken on an almost nightmarish intensity. This he wanted to escape from, if only for a few hours. He'd brew himself some tea (he was getting so that he detested beer), put on his pajamas, get in bed, and lose himself as long as possible among the brutal intricacies of Roman history.

"Well, how we doing, Joe?" Lonnie was saying.

"Pretty good, Mr. Drew. I got the dope you wanted. The heist was pulled off by Lew Metz and Steve Abud. Lew's a local boy. Steve's a Syrian from Detroit. He's only been here for a little while. He used to work for Gus Borgia."

"What?" Lonnie stared at Joe.

"Yeah. That's right."

"We finally got a break," said Lonnie, rubbing his hands in satisfaction. "This is turning out a lot better than I thought it would."

"I don't know," said Joe. "It's mighty uneasy stuff. Lew Metz'd shoot a guy for fifty bucks. At least he would in the old days. Now he's on the big time, of course."

"Could you get in touch with these guys, Joe?"

Joe moved about uneasily in his chair and got a little red in the face.

"I could. But—"

Lonnie noticed the extreme reluctance. He changed his tactics.

"Have you talked to your sister lately?"

Joe glanced at him with surprise.

"I see her every day."

"Did you know she was going to marry Gus Borgia?"

Joe's mouth dropped open, he stared at Lonnie in amazement, then a wide grin spread over his heavy, tough-looking, high-cheekboned face.

"You kidding?"

"No. Gus told me so himself tonight."

Joe laughed delightedly.

"I knew that kid had the stuff!" he crowed. "I used to tell everybody: 'You watch that Wanda kid. She's got something on the ball besides curves. She's a cinch to make good in a big way.' Going to marry, Gus, eh? Not a bad guy to have for a brother-in-law." He looked up suddenly at Lonnie. "All thanks to you, too."

Lonnie waved this aside.

"Wanda had to do the work," he said.

Joe nodded thoughtfully, his face serious now.

"What do you want me to get in touch with these guys for?"

"Not much. When you talk to them just kind of hint that you're in with Gus—which, in a way, you are. But don't come right out with it. Understand?"

"Yeah. I think so."

"Tell them Gus wants to see them—about the middle of next week. Wednesday or Thursday. Keep in touch with me, Joe. I'll tell you when to bring them around."

"That ain't going to be hard to do," said Joe. "All the boys think Gus is the biggest thing there is. That all?"

"Yeah," said Lonnie, "only it's important as hell. If you run into any snags, let me know."

They got up. Lonnie offered his hand and Joe took it and pumped it diffidently; then he grinned.

"How do you like that about Wanda? I can't get over it."

"Good news, eh?"

"Sure is. You should see the coat Gus bought her. Over three G's— mink. I could see he had it bad. A guy's got to have it bad to lay out three G's for a coat. But I never figured he'd marry her."

Lonnie said goodnight, then went back to the elevator. On the way up, the elevator boy inquired:

"Wasn't that Joe Pavol I saw you talking to?"

"Yes. I think he used to fight under that name."

"He's the best heavyweight I ever saw around here. What's he doing now?"

"I don't know," said Lonnie, glancing at the kid. "Why?"

"Oh, I just wondered, Mr. Drew. Curiosity, I guess."

Lonnie suddenly realized that his suspicions were running away with him. Even he was getting jumpy. Maybe he *did* need some sleep after all.

When he opened the door, he saw Mary sitting on the couch, reading a magazine.

"I thought you were in bed."

"I couldn't sleep. Lonnie, I feel so strange when you're not here."

"I was right down in the lobby."

Mary jumped up suddenly and flung herself into his arms. He kissed her, then drew back to look at her, smiling. But her expression was so serious that his smile faded.

"Hey!" he exclaimed. "What is this?"

"I was reading in the magazine about a girl who ran away on the day she was supposed to be married. I almost did that."

"I know. You got very huffy with me that day and I walked out on you—but very slow and with my ears cocked."

"Just think," said Mary. "Wouldn't I have been a fool?"

"Oh, I don't know. You didn't do so well for yourself—considering." Mary hugged him.

"Nobody could do better."

Lonnie laughed, extremely pleased, but not wanting to show it.

"Your low ambitions surprise me. Even Wanda did better."

"Oh, poor Wanda," said Mary, thoughtfully. "Don't you feel kind of guilty? After all, it's your fault."

"Guilty!" cried Lonnie. "I was just talking to her brother. He's so tickled I thought he was going to bust."

"What is this between you and Joe?"

"Oh," said Lonnie, offhandedly, "he's just getting some racing information for me. Nothing very important."

"Don't want to tell me, do you?"

"Later," said Lonnie, kissing her. "It's too hard to explain."

They went into the bedroom arm in arm.

2

Since seven a.m. Lonnie and Ray had hardly been away from the telephone. They'd hired a downtown office for the weekend, and through the connivance of a minor Lake City telephone official they'd been able to get perfect long-distance service. Lonnie had known the official for a long time. Before the war he'd been in charge of phone service for all the bookmakers in town. In those days it had been more or less legitimate. Now it was strictly under-the-counter and the official had to be paid off; but Lonnie didn't mind—it went on the expense account.

It was nearly noon. Their office was on the tenth floor of the McKinlock Building. Below them, spread in a huge panorama, was Lake City with all its tiny houses clustered along the shores of the lake and spreading out southward fanwise as far as the eye could see. There was no wind and a pale grayish pall of smoke from the hundreds of war plants hung over the city. The sun was shining and the enormous expanse of water visible from the office windows was covered to the far horizon with silver ripples, which at times gave off flashes of light. Far out, a black ore-freighter was plowing slowly westward toward Duluth.

Lonnie sat down and poured himself a cup of coffee from a thermos jug and began to sip it.

"How are we, Ray?"

"Better than I ever thought we'd be. We've even got a little extra room. What a business the bookies must be doing!"

"Why not? The tracks themselves are breaking all betting records. We got room for ten G's more?"

Ray turned to look at him.

"Why?"

"That's for me—if we can place it."

"Take it easy, will you, Lonnie!"

"Look. If this one blows up, that's only a drop in the bucket. You know that."

"I guess you're right. But—" He reached for the phone. "I'll see what I can do."

They sat waiting for the call. Lonnie laughed.

"If the bookies get scared and start trying to lay it off, there'll be some fun."

Ray groaned and poured himself a cup of coffee.

It was nearly three o'clock when they drove into the parking lot at the Lakeland Racetrack. Post-time for their race, the Ashland Handicap, was four thirty. Mary looked beautiful in a new red hat and her mink coat, and Lonnie had also dressed for the occasion in a double-breasted gray flannel suit and a grayish tweed topcoat. Ray couldn't get over their attitude. It was as if they were on their way to a gay party. They were apparently without a care and Mary kept laughing at the remarks Lonnie was making. It was very strange. Lonnie was just naturally of a reckless disposition and enjoyed skirting disaster by a hair, and Mary had full confidence in Lonnie. She'd told Ray several times that he mustn't be so nervous: Lonnie would bring it off.

But Ray was terribly worried. His hands were cold as ice and he kept clearing his throat nervously.

The place was jammed. As they left the gate and started across the wide lawn toward the grandstand, a race was being run and they could hear the roar of the crowd.

"Listen," said Mary. "Sounds like a football game."

By the time they got into the box seats Gus had reserved for them, the race was over and the winner was prancing back to the winner's circle, the little jockey in pale-green silks standing up in the stirrups. A wave of applause and cheering ran over the grandstand.

"Must have been the favorite," said Lonnie. "Lot of happy people."

Mary saw Wanda and waved. She was sitting alone in a box in the next section.

"Gus'll be back in a minute," she called.

"Here he is right now," said Lonnie.

Gus and Benny were coming down the aisle from the mezzanine, both smiling, Gus happily, Benny sadly. They saw Lonnie and stopped in front of his box.

"We just had a winner," said Gus, showing a roll of bills. "Ed Gregg told me to get a few tickets on the horse that just won. He cantered."

"Nice going," said Lonnie.

Gus spoke to Mary.

"How's the little lady today? Nervous?"

"No," said Mary, calmly, "why should I be? We're sure to win."

"That's the spirit," said Gus, laughing. "You hear that, Benny?"

Benny tried to grin affably, but it was clear that his heart wasn't in it. He didn't have as much optimism in his nature as Gus; he always feared the worst.

"Seen Pool around any place?" Gus asked Lonnie. "I been calling him half the day."

"No," said Lonnie, "but he's probably over in the clubhouse with the swells. That's where he usually is."

"He's a sick man or something," said Gus reflectively. "He acts funny. Benny knows him well and he says he's changed so he's hardly like the same guy."

"That's right," said Benny dolefully.

Lonnie could hardly suppress a smile of satisfaction. At least he'd been right about one thing; his nerves were steadier than the Greek's.

When the horses came out for the next race Mary exclaimed at the sight of a beautiful chestnut filly with flaxen mane and tail.

"I'll bet she wins," said Mary. "Doesn't she look wonderful?"

"Yes," said Lonnie. "But handsome is as handsome does."

The filly's tail and mane were tied up with pink ribbons and her coat had been rubbed and polished until it was full of highlights in the bright sun. She danced along sideways, very proud of herself, as if she knew she was being admired.

"She makes the others look terrible," said Mary enthusiastically. "And doesn't the jockey look wonderful in pink?"

Lonnie burst out laughing and even Ray smiled wanly. Mary turned to look at them, puzzled.

"Well, he does," she insisted.

"That's Monk Curwen—that jockey," said Lonnie. "One of the toughest little apes in the business. I'll have to tell him he looks lovely in pink."

"What's so funny about that?"

"Nothing, darling. And in case you're interested, Monk's going to ride our horse. But what he's doing on this beetle I don't know. He usually has his pick of mounts."

"What's a beetle?" asked Mary.

"A goat," said Lonnie. "A—a—well, she hasn't got a chance, according to the *Form*, that little beauty. She must be out for exercise."

"Why are they running her if she hasn't got a chance?'"

"That has always been a mystery to me," said Lonnie. "Some stables get too high on their horses."

Mary glanced at him, then gave up. If he was going to talk in a jargon, there was no use pressing him. She looked at her program.

"Oh, her name's Bell Song. What a lovely name!"

"Yes," said Lonnie, "and she's twenty to one. And she'll probably get in at the end of the next race."

"I want to bet on her," said Mary firmly.

"I thought you were opposed to gambling," said Lonnie, winking at Ray.

"Did I ever say so?"

"No," said Lonnie, rubbing his chin, "you never did. Anyway, this wouldn't be gambling. You'd just be giving your money to the track. Why don't you hold it? Then you'll have it after the race."

Mary took two dollars out of her purse and handed it to Ray.

"Will you bet that for me on Bell Song? I don't know how you do it."

Ray smiled at Lonnie, left the box, and disappeared into the mezzanine. Gus came over to talk to them. When he found out that Mary had bet on Bell Song at twenty to one, he laughed and said:

"I was going to bet a couple of bucks on Black Prince, but I think I'll go along with the little lady."

"Take it easy, Mr. Borgia," said Lonnie. "Don't throw your money away like that."

Gus laughed.

"Two across just for fun," he said. "Maybe she's got something there."

When the horses broke from the gate, everybody in the grandstand jumped up and began to yell. Mary looked about her rather apprehensively for a moment, then she stood up too. Bell Song was in front. Monk Curwen had rushed her out of the gate at breakneck speed, and after the first few jumps she was ahead of the field and on the rail, winging.

"Well," said Lonnie, "they're trying, anyway. That's why Monk's in the saddle, I guess."

As they turned for home, three horses on the outside began knocking at Bell Song. Monk leaned far over, talked in her ear, and shook his whip at her. A big black gelding burst out of the pack and began running the leaders down one by one. His jockey was whipping and kicking.

"There goes your bet," said Lonnie.

But Monk coaxed and entreated, shaking his whip, and the big black gelding just didn't quite make it. Bell Song won by a head, staggering under the wire, spent.

"But—I won!" cried Mary, turning to Lonnie and staring at him with amazement. "I thought you said—"

Lonnie fell back into his chair and pulled his hat down over his eyes. Gus rushed over to the box and shook Mary's hand.

"Can you pick 'em!" he cried. "I was just going to bet two across for fun. But I bet fifty across instead." He waved the tickets delightedly. Then he noticed Lonnie's expression. He stared for a moment, then burst out laughing.

"I see the old man wouldn't listen."

When they flashed the prices on the tote-board, a gasp went up from the crowd. Bell Song paid $44.30 to win, $19.80 to place, and 511.40 to show.

"What do I get?" asked Mary.

Ray told her.

"I'll cash your ticket," he said, and left the box.

Mary sat down.

"What made you think she was such a—a beetle?" she demanded of Lonnie.

"I guess my crystal ball is out of order," said Lonnie.

After the fifth race had been run and won by an odds-on favorite, Lonnie began to get restless. The big one was coming up. He turned to look at Gus, who had been laughing lightheartedly all afternoon. He was chewing a pencil and staring at the track, lost in thought. Benny had his hat off and was carefully scratching his kinky black head. Lonnie turned. Ed Gregg was touching his arm.

"Can I see you a minute, Lonnie?"

"Sure." Lonnie excused himself and followed Gregg to the corridor that led to the mezzanine. Ray looked after them uneasily.

"Something's up," said Gregg, speaking in a low voice. "We've all been ordered to the steward's room. Jockeys, trainers, owners—everybody. Just thought you'd like to know."

"Nothing we can do about it now," said Lonnie, "no matter what it is. The money's all up."

"I know. I'm going to do my best to win this one, but— Soon as I find out what's up, I'll come back and tell you, and you can tell Gus if you want to."

"Okay, Ed."

Lonnie went back to the box. Ray looked at him inquiringly.

"Anything wrong?" asked Mary.

"No," said Lonnie casually. "Why?"

"Oh, we were just wondering."

In the steward's room the head steward, John O'Malley, a big red-faced Irishman, was talking to the assembled group of owners, trainers, and jockeys. Monk Curwen, in Gregg's gold and white silks, was lounging back against a table, glancing about him ironically. Gregg was nervously chewing on a ragged cigar and from time to time throwing a glance at old Burt Crouse, who looked grim.

"Boys," O'Malley was saying, "I'm not accusing anybody of anything, you understand; but a lot of ugly rumors have been going around about this race. I've been told a dozen times that it's a boater. Nobody seems to know who is supposed to win, but everybody seems to think there's more here than meets the eye. So far we've run off five races today, and not a soul has suggested that any of them were other than straight. Now why, boys, would there be such rumors about this one race on the card? See what I mean? Where there's smoke, maybe there's some fire. Any comments?"

He glanced about him mildly at the group. Nobody said a word.

"All right. I'm not expecting anybody to deny anything, because I'm not accusing anybody. I just want you all to know that we are going to take special pains to see that this is a true-run race. If there's one jockey in this race who gives any signs, even the slightest, that he's not trying for his life to win, I'll see that he gets the severest penalty it's in my power to inflict. Not only that—the first four horses will be given a saliva test. If they've got any junk in them, the trainers are in real trouble and I'll do my best to see that their licenses are taken away from them. Do I make myself clear?"

There were low murmurs of assent. Most of the jockeys stood staring at the floor, avoiding each other's eyes.

"Now I've had my say," said O'Malley, "and no hard feelings. We've been trying to run this track straight to the best of our ability. So far I think we've done a pretty fair job and we've got the confidence of the public. Let's keep it. All right, boys." He turned and went out.

Nobody made any comment. The men filed out slowly. Burt Crouse was almost purple in the face with fury. He stamped out, brushing jockeys out of his way. Gregg noticed this and smiled grimly. The old gypsy didn't have much chance now with all the owners trying.

There was no time for a conference of the horsemen implicated in the coup. Besides, it would have been too dangerous now. O'Malley was a tough man and he meant business. Gregg shook his head. At the moment he was wishing that he was back on his little Kentucky farm among the blue grass, sitting on the veranda, with a tall drink in his hand, listening to the birds chirping, and watching his yearlings cavorting in the paddocks. Racing was just one damn thing after another. You couldn't win! If you had a fast-track horse ready, it rained. If you were all set to go with a mudder, there was a drought. When you had plenty of racing, your horses were all crippled; during a lay-off they were all sound as a dollar. Gregg remembered the Florida horseman who had immortalized himself by jumping off a bridge, crying: "No more close finishes!" And now—on top of everything else—rumors were flying around that the Federal Government was getting ready to close all the tracks for the duration.

Gregg groaned inwardly, went back to the grandstand, took Lonnie aside, and told him what had happened. Lonnie whistled, then stood shaking his head.

"No use to tell Gus," he said. "We either win or we don't."

"I'll do my best with the old horse," said Gregg, "but he's going to have his hands full with Gilt Armor forcing the pace. Burt Crouse is mad as hell. He can't win now, but he can still run me in the ground."

"Which horse are you most afraid of?"

"Sea Hawk. Of course, he's not what he used to be. But he ran a mile at Arlington once in thirty-six and four fifths. Oh, well."

Lonnie stood lost in thought for a moment.

"Ed," he said finally, "there's something about the Crouse business I'd like to find out. It looks to me like he's been double-crossed. If we lose, forget it. But if we win, slip him a hundred dollars or so and see if he'll talk."

"All right, Lonnie. I'll try it."

Saladin, a big chestnut horse with a white blaze between his eyes, entered the paddock, accompanied not only by Gregg and Monk, the jockey, but by two strapping grooms, who kept talking to him in quiet voices. He stood over sixteen hands and had the strength of a locomotive. Although he was usually mild-mannered at the post, for some reason he hated the track paddocks and was always restive until the bugle sounded, announcing the race.

"What do we do now, Mr. Gregg?" asked Monk, sighing.

"Just what we intended. Take him out in front and keep him there. That's all the instructions I can give you, Monk. You've rode him before."

Monk grunted and looked about him at the other horses and men. Johnny Gonzalez had the mount on Gilt Armor, and his dark Mexican face contrasted strikingly with the white silks of the Crouse stable. Near him was spindly little Abe Kean, also in the Crouse white silks; he was riding the dark horse, Day Moon. Sea Hawk, a long-legged bay gelding, though more lightly weighted by the handicapper than Saladin, who had been a stake horse at one time, was the favorite, and at the moment his odds were two to one. Bunny Winch, one of the best stake riders in the Midwest, had the mount on him and was swaggering around the paddock in the pink and gold silks of the Miami Farms, rolling a cud of tobacco from cheek to cheek and grinning at the people who were jammed at the railings staring at the horses. There were four other horses in the paddock: Lone Star, a bay mare from Texas, who was conceded no chance at all; Ricardo, a three-year-old black gelding, lightly weighted, who had a lot of speed but seemed to show most of it in his workouts; Blue Flame, a gimpy old horse, seven, who every now and then ran a hard-hitting race, usually over an off track; and a four-year-old filly, Animate, flighty, post-shy, but with a turn of speed that at times seemed blinding. However, she was given to sulking and was a very poor racing tool.

Crouse passed Gregg and spoke out of the corner of his mouth:

"Somebody pulled a fast one."

"So it seems," said Gregg without looking up.

Far off, beyond the grandstand, a bugle sounded, blowing first call, summoning the horses to the track for the running of the sixth race, the Ashland Handicap at one mile.

Gregg gave Monk a leg up, and as the little jockey swung into the saddle Gregg said:

"Take him out in front—just like I said. Die there if you have to."

Monk nodded and saluted casually with his whip. The parade to the post started. A wave of excitement rose from the huge crowd in the grandstand, and the horses and their jockeys sensed it and reacted to it in their various ways. Saladin was quiet now; he knew the race was not far off; no more hanging around the paddock with strangers staring at him. Monk set his jaw. Abe Kean became paler and more gaunt-looking, and his mount, Day Moon, a sleepy-headed horse, woke up a little and nickered at the crowd. Sea Hawk pranced sideways, nervous as a cat; but his tough-faced little jockey, Bunny Winch, was as calm as if he were riding in the park; turning, he spat across the big gelding's shoulder for luck. Gilt Armor, in the number-one post position, with Johnny Gonzalez up, led the parade to the track; he raised his front feet like a high school horse, and Johnny kept eying the bandages on his front legs apprehensively. Animate, the skittish filly, was accompanied to the track by a Shetland pony, led by a groom; she wouldn't go any place without the mischievous, hammer-headed little pony, who was more trouble than she was.

In the grandstand people were standing up to see the horses come out on the track.

Ray crossed his fingers deep in his pocket and stared relentlessly at his program, though the print was swimming. Lonnie was smoking a cigar calmly. He had his arm across the back of Mary's chair and from time to time he gently patted her shoulder.

"Look," said Mary, "here they come." She stood up. "Ours is number two, isn't it? Oh, I see him. He's enormous, and he's a red color like Bell Song."

"Chestnut," said Lonnie.

"All right—chestnut. But that's a good omen, don't you think? I mean, because he's the same color as Bell Song."

Lonnie turned to Ray.

"She's beginning to talk like a typical woman horseplayer."

Ray managed a weak counterfeit smile. He wished that he was any place but here. He didn't even know if he could stand it. He felt like telling Lonnie that he had a bad headache and wanted to go to the men's lounge and lie down for a while. But he winced as he imagined the look he'd get. He thought longingly about his nice big bedroom there at the beach waiting for him; about his row after row of books that soothed him with their stories of stirring events of a far-off time— events you didn't have to sit through, but could read about in tranquility.

Lonnie looked over at Gus's box. Benny was sitting slumped down, staring uneasily at his program. Wanda was smoking a cigarette and looking about her calmly. Gus flung a cigar butt away from him violently, then stood up and began to go through all his pockets. He turned and said something to Wanda, who immediately began to look about her on the floor of the box. Finally Gus found his cigar case.

Nobody had seen anything of the Greek all afternoon. They were all beginning to wonder what had happened that could keep him away from the track on a day like this.

"He's getting awful jittery lately," Benny suggested. "Maybe he can't take it."

But just as the horses were nearing the starting gate, he appeared out of the mezzanine and went to Gus's box. He was wearing a tight-fitting double-breasted topcoat of some dark material and a black Homburg hat. He had a white boutonniere in his lapel, and he was carrying a cane.

"Look at Cholly Knickerbocker," said Lonnie, nudging Mary. "Your old soul mate."

"Doesn't he look a little pale?"

"He should," said Lonnie. "Besides, on him it looks good."

Gus said something to the Greek, who turned and smiled and bowed in the direction of Lonnie's box. Lonnie bowed too, ironically, and Mary nodded briefly with a little fixed smile.

The starter was having plenty of trouble. The filly, Animate, was holding up the race by her antics at the post. They would no sooner get her into her stall than she'd break through and they'd have to do it all over again. This happened four or five times. Then they tried backing her in, with no better results. Little by little her nervousness began to communicate itself to the other horses. Gilt Armor reared in the gate and almost caused an accident. Johnny Gonzalez was forced to dismount and get up again. Lone Star broke out prematurely and ran a sixteenth before her jockey could slow her down and turn her around.

The crowd was frantic and loud yells of both encouragement and protest came from the jammed grandstand. It was the big betting race of the day. A huge fortune had been wagered by the crowd, and most of it was on either Sea Hawk, odds-on favorite now, or Saladin, second choice at two to one.

"I thought we'd do a little better than that," said Lonnie, referring to the odds, "but if we win—"

He was interrupted by a roar so violent that the concussion of it almost knocked his hat from his head.

"*They're off!*"

Ray got up, but averted his eyes from the track. He still had his fingers crossed in his pocket, and he began to pray silently. Mary had Lonnie by the arm and she was squeezing with all her strength, but he noticed nothing. He stood with cigar poised, staring at the speeding horses.

Gilt Armor had beaten Saladin out of the gate and had now taken the track. Setting a burning pace, with the little Mexican kicking him forward, he took the first turn at a dizzy angle, opening up a lead of nearly two lengths. This bothered Monk Curwen because he could tell that the old horse, Saladin, didn't like it: he was blowing, fighting for his head. Monk heard thunder on his right and turned just in time to see Animate, the crazy little filly, go past him as if he were tied. In ten more jumps she had the lead and the old front-running sprinter, Gilt Armor, was already beginning to chuck it. If he was outpaced this soon, then why exert himself! He started slowly to drop back. Johnny Gonzalez whipped him fruitlessly.

Monk set out in pursuit of the filly, who was widening the gap at an alarming rate. Saladin seemed sluggish, not able to find his proper stride. He'd been bothered by Gilt Armor's taking the lead from him at the start and he seemed a little bewildered now, not quite himself. Monk began to talk to him softly, urging him on. It wasn't time for the whip yet, not by a long shot.

"What's he trying to do with that filly?" cried Lonnie. "You'd think they were going five furlongs."

"That's the old Bill Daly," said Ray. "She might stagger in."

"There goes Sea Hawk," said Lonnie. "What's the matter with Monk? If the Hawk's that close to him at this stage, he's beat."

"What do you mean—Sea Hawk?" cried Ray, beside himself with excitement. "There go all of them."

It was true. The whole pack was moving up on the back stretch with the exception of Gilt Armor, who was dropping out of it. Day Moon began to move up between horses and in a moment was running neck and neck with Sea Hawk.

"All right, big boy. Come on, big boy," Monk was coaxing. "Now we're going, big boy. Run for the oats, kid, run for the oats."

Saladin had found his stride, and he was running effortlessly now, all out, the way he liked to run. Slowly and methodically he was cutting down the lead of the wildly running filly, who was beginning to prick her ears at the heavy sound of approaching hoofs. As she turned into the back stretch she tried to quit and run out, but the jockey steadied her and kept her in forward motion, although he couldn't get her back on the rail. Saladin thundered up behind her, and in a few strides Monk had him on the rail and in the lead.

A great roar went up from the grandstand.

"He may make it," groaned Ray, shutting his eyes.

"From here on in it's tough," said Lonnie, glancing over at Gus's box.

Gus was chewing on a cigar and pounding the box railing. Wanda was yelling and waving her arms. Benny merely stared like a sleepwalker. But the Greek looked pale and shaken and kept wetting his lips as if they were parched.

Saladin was turning for home now, still running effortlessly. Monk kept him into the rail so no one could slip through on him and save enough ground to inch out the race. Monk began to hear thunder on his right and, without looking around, took to the whip. A tremendous roar shook the grandstand. Three horses, running as a team, were gaining on the leader, all the jockeys whipping and kicking. Sea Hawk was on the inside, Day Moon in the middle, and Blue Flame, running one of his good races, was on the outside.

"I can't look," said Ray. "They're running over him."

"Oh, goodness," cried Mary, "look at all those horses!"

"This is no race, it's a cavalry charge," cried Lonnie. "Keep him in there, Monk. Keep him in there."

The grandstand was a bedlam. Men were capering in the aisles, waving their programs, and yelling instructions at the jockeys.

They were close to home now and Saladin had begun to falter. In a moment all the other three horses were lapped on him. It was nothing but a blur to the people in the grandstand. Four horses were running neck and neck; the jockeys' heads were bobbing, their whips flashing, and huge clods of dirt were flying high, adding to the confusion.

As they neared the wire, Monk let out a rebel yell and hit the old horse a resounding blow with the whip. Then it was over.

But nobody knew what had happened—not even the jockeys. The people in the grandstand stared at one another in bewilderment. It was as if it had all occurred in a dream. They had seen a cloud of horses pass under the wire at precisely the same moment. A few half-hearted arguments started, but actually the huge crowd was stunned and did not cheer or applaud as the horses came back toward the judges' stand.

O'Malley was grinning.

"That was a horse race, wasn't it?" he said to one of the other officials. "I guess I better give the boys a talking-to before every race."

"Who won it?"

"How the hell do I know? With four heads on the post!"

A loud murmur went up from the crowd as "Photo Finish" was flashed on the tote board.

Monk rode back, confidently flourishing his whip, and saluted the crowd as he dismounted.

"What makes you think you win it?" demanded Bunny Winch, sourly. "I nipped you, son. I nipped you."

"What did you do—put your tongue out?" sneered Monk. "It's long enough."

Lonnie had begun to sweat. He took out his handkerchief and wiped his face. Ray was at the point where he was merely glad it was all over, no matter which way it went.

"Why don't they tell us who won?" exclaimed Mary. "This is terrible."

"They have to develop the picture," said Lonnie. "As far as I'm concerned, I don't know whether we ran first or fourth. But that Monk Curwen rode a great race. The old horse looked like he was beat sure, then he gave a jump."

"It all depends," said Ray, "on who was nodding when."

There was a sudden hush as the crowd became aware that the men in the judges' stand were studying the photo to determine the winner.

Gus was pacing up and down in front of his box, puffing violently on his cigar. Benny seemed in a state of collapse. The Greek was standing up, smoking a cigarette, looking very pale but dapper.

Finally the numbers were flashed up in the midst of a wild tumult in the stands.

Saladin had won.

3

They had finally managed to get Mary to bed. She kept insisting she was so excited that she couldn't possibly sleep, but a few minutes after her head touched the pillow she was breathing gently, dead to the world.

Lonnie went back to the living room and sat down wearily. He felt exhausted and his ankle was paining him. Ray looked pale and spent.

"Well," said Lonnie finally, "all we have to do now is wrap it up."

"Yes," agreed Ray, "that's all. It's only a little matter of explaining away a hundred G's to Gus Borgia."

"That Gus!" laughed Lonnie. "What a character! I thought we'd never get away from him."

"He certainly had a load on when we left."

"Don't worry. Wanda'll look after him."

"There I agree with you. She's beginning to mother him already."

Ray smiled wanly and Lonnie laughed. There was a long pause, then Ray got up.

"I think I'll head for the beach. I've been hanging around hoping—"

Lonnie looked up quickly.

"Hoping I'd talk, eh?" He shook his head. "I'm not even sure myself yet, so why should you worry about it?"

"I hope you're not counting too much on Gus's friendship. When it comes to money, he's all business, I hear."

"I know, I know." Lonnie got up impatiently, anxious now for Ray to be on his way.

But Ray stalled, lit a cigarette, glanced about the room aimlessly, very reluctant to leave.

"Jack Pool was looking better tonight," he said tentatively. "He even seemed to be having a good time."

"After four double Martinis," said Lonnie, yawning, "anybody's liable to have a good time."

"Do you suppose he's still got something up his sleeve?"

"If he has, he better produce."

The phone rang and Lonnie answered it. The switchboard girl informed him that Mr. Jack Pool was in the lobby and would like to see him. Lonnie hesitated for a moment, then said:

"Okay. I'll be right down." He turned to Ray. "Speaking of the Greek—"

"You mean he's downstairs?"

Lonnie nodded. Then he tiptoed over to the bedroom door, opened it a crack, and peered in. At the sight of Mary sleeping so peacefully, he smiled indulgently and softly closed the door.

On the way down in the elevator Ray asked:

"Do you suppose he wants to make a deal?"

Lonnie was lost in thought, smiling to himself. He turned.

"Who?"

Ray grimaced with impatience.

"The Greek!"

"Oh, him. How should I know? Say, did you ever see anything in your life like the way Mary took to racing? She's got sporting blood, that girl."

Ray merely nodded.

"And the way she's held up under all this trouble!" crowed Lonnie. "She's got what it takes."

"She thinks you're infallible, that's all."

Lonnie laughed.

"She did until I tried to tout her off Bell Song. I'll never forget the look she gave me after the race. She'll never feel the same about me again."

The elevator stopped and the boy opened the doors. The Greek was waiting, near the desk. He still looked dapper, but his boutonniere had wilted, and his hat was at a rakish angle, very unusual for him.

He smiled pleasantly when they came up to him. "Always together," he said, "like Damon and Pythias."

Lonnie glanced at him with but slightly veiled distaste, then turned to Ray.

"Call you tomorrow."

Ray hesitated, looked from one to the other, wanting to stay. But there was a certain finality in Lonnie's tone he couldn't disregard. He said goodnight and went out.

"Well, Jack—?"

The Greek glanced about him.

"Wouldn't it be more convenient for us to talk upstairs?"

Lonnie shook his head curtly.

"Mary's asleep. I don't want to disturb her."

The Greek smiled.

"That little lady—she's caused us all quite a lot of trouble, hasn't she? Like Helen of Troy."

"Say, what the hell is this?" Lonnie demanded. "First it's Damon and Pythias. Now it's Helen of Troy. You're a little loaded, aren't you, Jack?"

"Slightly," said the Greek, making an effort to recapture his usual manner. "At least let's sit down."

Lonnie nodded and the Greek selected a couple of chairs partially screened by a potted palm.

"I'm going to come right out in the open—" the Greek began.

But Lonnie cut in.

"That's a little unusual for you, isn't it, Jack?"

"Maybe. Maybe. Anyway, you need me and—shall we say I need you?"

"Go ahead and say it. In other words, you want to make a deal."

"Precisely."

"No, Jack. No deal. You made one, some time ago, and now I'm going to force you to like it."

The Greek hesitated, stared thoughtfully at his shoes for a moment, then:

"It would be so simple. You'd be solid with Gus, and the whole thing would be cleared up—and nobody hurt."

"Suppose the horse had lost?"

The Greek shrugged.

"That would have been very unfortunate."

"For me, especially. And you did your best, didn't you, Jack?" The Greek merely shrugged again. "Okay. So now you take the consequences."

The Greek glanced up and smiled shrewdly.

"But how about you? You're in no bed of roses yourself. If you'd listen to me it could all be worked out. No one the wiser."

"I'll take my bumps—you take yours. We'll be settling up Wednesday or Thursday."

The Greek studied Lonnie's face for a long time, then he rose.

"Well—I did my best, Lonnie. See you when we settle up."

He turned and walked to the door, swinging his cane.

"What gall!" exclaimed Lonnie, grimacing.

He found Mary sitting in the living room, waiting for him. He was both irritated and touched.

"Don't say it," said Mary, forestalling him. "I woke up and you weren't here and ..."

"Well, you're mighty calm about it."

"I called downstairs. The girl said you were in the lobby talking to Mr. Pool. What did he want?"

"Oh—nothing much. He's just worrying about the payoff."

Mary looked at him shrewdly.

"He's scared, isn't he?"

"Maybe. This is the first time I've ever seen the Greek loaded."

He sank down on the couch beside Mary and sighed. "I'm tired, for once."

"Too tired to talk?"

Lonnie turned and glanced at Mary in surprise. "Talk? What about?"

"Us."

Lonnie smiled wearily and put his arm around her. "Can't it wait until tomorrow?"

"No," said Mary, "I want to talk now while I'm feeling the way I am. By tomorrow, I might change my mind."

"Well, this sounds serious."

"It is. And important. It's mostly about you, Lonnie."

"Me?"

"Yes. It's that—well, this may sound awfully silly to you, but what I want more than anything else in the world, Lonnie, is for you to be happy." She turned her head away and laughed self-consciously. Lonnie hugged her gently, unable to speak for a moment, he was so surprised and touched by the tone of her voice. "Isn't it strange," Mary went on, "when you try to talk about serious things, it always sounds so sappy and as if you were putting on and didn't really mean it?"

"It didn't sound sappy to me," said Lonnie. "And while we're on the subject, that's just the way I feel about you."

"I thought so," said Mary. "That's one reason I wanted to talk to you. But I've been putting it off and putting it off. And then I woke up, and the apartment was so quiet, and I couldn't find you! Lonnie, if you ever left me I couldn't bear it."

Lonnie laughed.

"Don't worry your head about that."

There was a short pause and Mary stared at the floor thoughtfully.

"What I'm trying to say is I want you to do what you want to do. If you want to run a restaurant, run it. If you don't, give it up. I hate the thought of you doing things just to make me happy. And I won't have it!"

"Yes, ma'am," said Lonnie, grinning, very much pleased.

"Before all this other business came up, you were working so hard and at night sometimes you looked so sort of harassed and not like yourself. That's what I really mean. I want you to be yourself, Lonnie. That's what's important."

"I was never so happy in my life, honey," he said. "Maybe I'm changing. Stop worrying about me, will you?"

"No," said Mary, "never. If you're really changing, Lonnie, then I'm glad you've settled down. But sometimes at night, when you're sleeping, I lie there thinking about you being in the army for two solid years— never doing anything you really wanted to, lying in the mud, getting shot at, while we were all here safe and sound and having a good time."

"Oh, it wasn't so bad."

"What I mean is," said Mary, going on quickly, "you've earned the right to do as you please."

She seemed so excited that Lonnie spoke to her soothingly.

"Sure. Sure. I get the general idea, honey."

"I know you're laughing at me, but I can't help that—"

"I certainly am not," he protested, but Mary ignored his comment.

"If you want to gamble, gamble. As long as we're the way we are, I can be just as happy in a hotel. If we can afford nice things, fine. If we can't, it doesn't matter." She was nodding her head so emphatically that Lonnie could hardly keep from laughing. All the same, a great wave of tenderness swept over him and he pulled her head down on his shoulder and held her tight as if he was afraid she'd get away from him. Since his marriage Lonnie had never been conscious of any particular desire to gamble or to return to the rackety, feast-or-famine type of life he'd been leading prior to meeting Mary. Turning Mary's words over in his mind, he began to feel a great sense of relief, a sense of freedom. He had no intention of taking advantage of this freedom, but there it was, his for the asking, if he desired, or needed, it.

"Honey," he said, "you told me once that what you wanted was a home. That you wanted to settle down and live like other people and—"

"Yes," said Mary, disengaging herself and sitting up very straight, "I did. But what I want above everything else is for you to be happy."

She returned to his arms and they sat in silence for a long time, both perfectly contented. Suddenly an image leaped up before Lonnie: Mary the first time he'd seen her, with her long, thick, dark hair glinting red under the lights, talking animatedly, and so beautiful he could hardly believe his eyes. And Irma, the cashier, saying: "Just another glamour girl—a clotheshorse!"

Lonnie sighed with happiness. They sat on. The big room was very quiet except for the ticking of the clock. Street noises reached them faintly, seeming like a part of the silence. Finally he said:

"Mary, do you suppose there's anything in the icebox that I could—?"

She pulled away, turned, and looked at him with amazement.

"Lonnie! How you can think of eating after that huge dinner you put away tonight?" She shuddered delicately.

"Just a growing boy," said Lonnie, slightly embarrassed, but trying not to show it. "And what about my vitamins?"

Mary got up, laughing.

"Come on," she said, "let's go see."

In a little while Lonnie was eating cold fried chicken and potato salad and drinking a glass of beer. He felt expansive.

"That Greek!" he exclaimed. "What a guy! Slippery as an eel, and with plenty of nerve. I used to enjoy working on him in a stud game. You'd never get a flicker out of his eyes, but he'd squirm on his chair when you had him in trouble. I played with him so much I could almost read him like a book. I guess he could read me, too, but not so well. He thinks he's a lot smarter than he is. And he thinks I'm a lot dumber than I am. That's where he made his biggest mistake." Lonnie gnawed on a chicken leg, too intent on what he was saying to mind his table manners, and Mary winced slightly. "Stud's a great game," Lonnie went on. "If you want to know a guy, play stud with him. You can go around with a fellow ten years and not know much about him. Play stud with him once and you begin to get the hang of him. It's a wonderful game. Something different comes up every second. And, oh, can you get murdered!" Lonnie's eyes were shining with excitement. Mary smiled composedly for his benefit, but she felt inward qualms. Lonnie was just a born gambler. Fears for the future began to plague her, but she put them resolutely from her mind.

"You must teach me to play stud some time, Lonnie," she said, pouring out more beer for him.

Lonnie had just got to sleep when the phone rang, rousing him. Half awake, he hurried into the living room, stumbling in his haste and hurting his ankle. He swore briefly, then picked up the receiver.

The night clerk said:

"There's a man wants to talk to you, Mr. Drew. Won't give his name, but says it's very important."

"All right. Put him on."

"Hello," said the man, "is this you, Mr. Drew?" The voice was high-pitched and nasal, but tough, and vaguely familiar.

"Yes. What's the idea, calling this time of night?"

"Look, Mr. Drew, I understand you're a nice guy. Want to stay that way, don't you?"

"Come on. Speak up."

"Be wise, Mr. Drew, and talk business with that party who talked to you tonight. Otherwise—"

Suddenly Lonnie remembered the voice: it belonged to the pale fellow who wore the blue serge suit, the one who finally managed to get the office door open.

"This is Lew Metz, isn't it?"

Dead silence at the other end of the line.

"Come on, I know your voice. Look, Lew, take a tip from me. You're on the wrong side of the fence."

"This ain't Lew. But what are you talking about?"

"I'm talking about Joe Pavlovsky. Didn't he contact you in regard to Gus Borgia?"

"Could be, pal."

"All right. Ask your friend Steve Abud about Gus. He can tell you whether it's healthy to buck him."

"The hell you say!" There was marked surprise in Lew's voice.

"The man I talked to tonight's in a spot. Why should you pull his chestnuts out of the fire and maybe get yourself burnt?"

"I'll think it over."

"Swell. And if I were you, I'd listen to Joe Pavlovsky. He's going to be Gus Borgia's brother-in-law in a few days."

"Sounds good."

Lonnie hung up and hurried back to bed.

"What now?" asked Mary. "I could hardly make out a thing you were saying you talked so fast."

"It's nothing, nothing," said Lonnie, yawning widely and drifting back into sleep.

4

"The Greek wants to talk to me private downstairs," Gus said to Benny. "I don't know what about, but it must be something pretty important. What time is it?"

Benny looked at his watch.

"It's five minutes of two, Gus. Lonnie should be along any minute now with the dough. He'll come up the back stairs."

"Buzz the Greek and me when he comes." Gus started out of the gambling-room, but turned, and a wide grin spread over his ugly little face. "I still feel good about the way we pulled that one off."

Benny groaned.

"It was too close for me, and then on top of everything else I had to go and get stinking drunk. I haven't felt the same since."

Gus laughed and went out. Benny! He'd have a gripe if he died and went to heaven and became an angel. An impossible guy!

He found the Greek in a booth, waiting for him, and sat down without a word.

"Hello, Gus," said the Greek. "How are you today?"

Gus ignored the greeting.

"What's on your mind?"

The Greek shifted, glanced out the window, and lit a cigarette. Gus's attitude was discouraging; it was definitely irritable and unfriendly.

"Just got a tip and I thought you'd like to know about it. I understand Lonnie's got quite a big shortage and—"

"What do you mean—shortage?" Gus cut in savagely. "You mean the bookmakers welched?"

"I don't know the cause," said the Greek smoothly. "Somebody—not mentioning any names—gave me the tip. He says Lonnie's got a story all cooked up, but—"

Gus rubbed his chin and stared at the Greek so long that he became uneasy.

"Just thought you'd like to know."

"Jack," said Gus, "you hate Lonnie's guts since he married your girl, don't you? Okay. That's your privilege. But don't let it run away with you. What kind of silly goddamn story is this—Lonnie with a shortage! Why?"

"That I don't know," said the Greek. "And maybe the tip's no good. But I thought I ought to tell you."

Gordy came from behind the bar and hurried over to Gus's booth.

"Excuse me, Mr. Borgia, but you're wanted upstairs."

"Thanks," said Gus; then he got up. "Come on, Jack. Lonnie's here. We'll soon find out about this shortage."

They walked along side by side to the stairway door.

"Gus," said the Greek, "I'm not trying to tell you your business, but why don't you give Lonnie a chance to spill his story? Pretend everything's all right. Let him hang himself."

Gus glanced at him sideways.

"Sure. Sure. Why not?" But he was thinking it was probable that the Greek knew a hell of a lot more than he was telling and that it might be a good idea to be very cagy about the whole business.

When they entered the gambling-room, Lonnie and Ray were sitting at the table with Benny. Before them was a black briefcase.

"Hello, Mr. Borgia," said Lonnie. "Well, this is the day."

"So it seems, so it seems," said Gus, pulling up a chair. "Let's get down to business."

The Greek stood looking on, calmly smoking a cigarette. Lonnie ignored him and began taking papers out of the briefcase.

"Jack Pool gave me a better briefcase than this," said Lonnie, arranging the papers, "but some so-and-so ran off with it."

"Yeah?" said Gus, looking from one to the other. "How was that?"

"Well," said Lonnie, "he stole it off my desk in the office. Can you imagine a guy walking in and stealing a briefcase off your desk?"

Although he knew something was behind Lonnie's remarks, Gus couldn't figure out just what. He made no comment.

"Well, here we are," said Lonnie, indicating the stacked-up papers and tapping each pile as he mentioned what it was. "Here are certified checks. Plain checks. Postal money orders. Telegraph money orders. And here, I'm sorry to say, are some IOU's—about ten thousand dollars' worth. Some of the boys are asking for time, in other words."

"Ten thousand?" said Gus mildly, his face relaxing into a relieved smile. "Well, that ain't bad at all with this kind of dough." He looked about him complacently.

"You start checking, Benny," said Lonnie. "We'll get through quicker."

Gus grinned.

"Nice going, Lonnie. That's the biggest one I ever pulled in my life. Biggest one I ever heard of, for that matter."

"Yeah, it's a big one all right," said Lonnie. "There's only one trouble."

"What's that?" asked Gus quickly.

"I'm a hundred G's short."

Ray winced and lowered his eyes. The pencil flew out of Benny's hand and he had a coughing spell. Gus got slowly to his feet and stood with his mouth open, staring at Lonnie; then he turned and stared blankly at the Greek, who merely shrugged.

"In other words," said Lonnie calmly, "we're short the amount of the original bet."

Gus stammered, red in the face, then found his voice. "But—why, Lonnie, for Cryssake? Why?"

Lonnie smiled and raised his hand.

"If you'll just sit down, Mr. Borgia, and stop yelling at me, I'll tell you."

Gus sat down abruptly, took out a cigar, and began to chew on it.

"It better be good," he said.

"You remember a few minutes ago, Mr. Borgia, I told you somebody stole the briefcase Jack Pool gave me? Well, the money was in that briefcase."

"The hundred G's?" cried Gus.

"Yes," said Lonnie, "but it wasn't exactly what you might call pilfered. A couple of guys walked in with guns and stuck me up."

"When was this?" cried Gus, looking about him like a vicious trapped animal.

"About ten minutes after it was delivered to me by Jack Pool."

Benny groaned and started coughing again.

"Why didn't you tell somebody?" cried Gus. "Me, for instance?"

"Would you have believed it?"

"No, by God! And I never would have turned no hundred G's over to you if it hadn't been for Pool. He—" Gus stopped chewing on his cigar and turned to stare at the Greek.

"You don't believe that story about the stickup, do you, Gus?" asked the Greek smoothly.

"Not particularly. But answer me one thing, Jack. If you hate this guy's guts so, why did you insist on turning all that dough over to him? There's something here that ain't kosher and I'm going to find out what it is. And if I don't, somebody is going to get hurt, and I don't mean tapped on the chin."

"He always had an A-one reputation," said the Greek, "and we all agreed he was the right man to handle the deal."

"I didn't know a goddamn thing about it and you know it," cried Gus. "I was a stranger here then. You and Benny talked me into it."

There was a brief lull. In the midst of it Benny said in a stifled voice, tapping the pile of papers:

"It's all here, Gus—except the hundred G's."

Gus almost exploded again, but contented himself with a violent snort of disgust.

"That's right," said Lonnie. "You see, Mr. Borgia, if I'd've yelled copper you'd have been out a hundred G's. As it is, you've made a hundred G's—and that's not alfalfa!"

"Yes," said Gus, restraining himself with difficulty, "but if it hadn't been for this little mix-up we'd've made two hundred G's." He looked about him violently. "What do you guys take me for—a reuben? I come in here from Detroit with a bankroll and right away the wolves begin to gather. Look, boys, remember me? I'm Gus Borgia. People don't do things like that to me—not and live."

"What are you looking at me for?" stammered Benny. "I got nothing to do with it. If you're out, I'm out. And so's Mr. Pool—Jack," he added, correcting himself.

"Take it easy," said Gus, "and let me figure this out for myself. You guys got me to go into this deal—Lonnie didn't. Or maybe you're all working together, cutting me up. After all, I'm a stranger—I don't know the ropes!" Gus looked about him wildly.

"Just a minute," said Lonnie. "How do you think I won this dough, Gus?"

"My God!" cried Gus, slapping his forehead. "I never thought of that. Are you going to sit there and tell me you bet a hundred G's on credit?"

"A hundred and ten. I bet ten for myself."

"Now I've heard everything."

"If you don't believe me," said Lonnie, "call any big bookie in the Midwest, or practically in the United States. We had dough spread from New York City to St. Louis, and from New Orleans to Chicago.

Just pick one out and call him."

Gus calmed down and began to laugh.

"Suppose the horse lost?" he demanded.

"I'd've been in hock the rest of my life," said Lonnie, "or dead."

"You got guts, all right," said Gus; then he chewed thoughtfully on his cigar for so long that they all began to get more and more uneasy. "However, Lonnie," he went on finally, "you might have stashed my dough and had it to fall back on in case you lost."

The Greek smiled and turned away slightly. Things were going very nicely.

"You're certainly a tough guy to convince, Mr. Borgia," said Lonnie. After a pause he went on. "There's something else I didn't tell you that you ought to know. Somebody tried to louse up the race for us."

"How do you mean?"

"For Lord's sake, Mr. Borgia. You know a true-run race when you see one, don't you?"

Gus's mouth dropped open.

"Good God!" he cried. "I thought at the time it was a mighty close fit if we were paying off three owners, but—what happened?"

"First somebody hired Burt Crouse to try to beat us with his two horses, then the same guy double-crossed *him* and told the stewards the race was a boater." Lonnie went on to explain what had happened and Gus sat listening intently, from time to time darting a glance at Benny and the Greek. "And I can get you proof," Lonnie concluded.

"This is the goddamnedest tangle I ever seen," said Gus. "But we're still out a hundred G's, and that's what's really sticking in my craw."

"This is the way I look at it," said Lonnie. "Somebody was gunning for *me*, Mr. Borgia, not *you*. They heisted me for the hundred G's and they thought that would be the end of it, but when they found out I was betting on credit, they tried to scramble up the race."

Gus shook his head.

"I don't know, Lonnie. You certainly got yourself in an awful hole."

Lonnie turned to Ray.

"Go down and get my overcoat, will you, Ray? I left some letters in the pocket I want Gus to read."

Shaking, Ray got up and went out. He was panicky. As far as he could see, Lonnie hadn't made a dent in Gus Borgia. And this was it—the last card! If it didn't work, they were cooked.

"One thing I'll say about you, Lonnie," said Gus. "You got the gall of the devil, or you'd never pulled this one on me. Or maybe I'm getting old. Maybe I'm slipping. Maybe I ain't the guy I used to be. Maybe I ought to back to Chi, where people know me." He was working himself up into a rage, and Benny and the Greek began to look at him apprehensively.

But Lonnie was only mildly worried. He knew that while he hadn't got far with Gus, he'd at least planted a doubt in his mind.

They heard the sound of heavy footsteps mounting the stairs, and they all turned toward the door. Ray came in followed by Joe Pavlovsky, Steve Abud, and Lew Metz.

"Come on in, guys," said Lonnie, cheerfully. "Things are kind of mixed up here and I need a little help."

Gus jumped up, furious.

"What the hell is going on here?" he cried. "All I want is my dough that's coming to me and what happens? A bunch of apes walk in!" He lost control of his voice, and his face got so red they were afraid he'd have a stroke.

"Hello, boss," said Steve Abud timidly. "I didn't even know you was in town till Joe here told me."

Gus fumed and puffed, tried to speak and couldn't; then he turned suddenly to look at the Greek, who was deathly pale.

"What do you make of all this, Jack?" he demanded.

The Greek leaned against the wall for support and tried to unfasten his collar.

"We didn't know that was your money we heisted, boss," said Steve, weakly. "Honest to God we didn't."

Gus turned to him in a fury, seized him by the lapels, and shook him violently, yelling:

"Who hired you? Who hired you?"

Steve raised his arm slowly, shaking with fright, and pointed at the Greek.

Gus let out a yell, jerked a gun out of his pocket, and, moving with a swiftness uncanny in such a harmless-looking little man, hit the Greek over the head with the barrel. The Greek fell headlong with a loud moan. Lonnie jumped in behind Gus and caught his arm just in time to keep him from shooting the Greek on the floor. Gus was weak as a cat, surprisingly so, and Lonnie had no trouble at all subduing him.

"Times have changed, Gus," said Lonnie. "Times have changed."

"Yeah," said Gus, breathing heavily, but subsiding, "you got something there!"

After listening to Lew Metz and Steve Abud and also to Ed Gregg and Burt Crouse, who had been waiting in the hall, Gus finally got the whole story. He sat rubbing his chin and glancing from time to time at the Greek, who was sitting at the table with his head in his hands, moaning with pain, completely demoralized.

"Remember what I said about Jack?" Gus demanded, turning to Benny. "Didn't I say he'd outsmart himself some day?" Then he pointed at Lonnie with his cigar. "And there's another guy who'll outsmart himself if he ain't careful. However," Gus went on, "any time you want to work for me, young fellow, you got a job."

"Thanks, Gus," said Lonnie, flushed with victory. "I'll give it a little thought."

Gus grinned; then he turned to Steve.

"I got a job for you."

"Okay, Mr. Borgia—you bet," said Steve eagerly.

"Stick to Jack Pool till he digs up the rest of that money. And I mean *stick!*"

"Yes, *sir*," cried Steve, throwing a contemptuous glance at the Greek.

"And you and Lew can keep your share of the heist." Steve and his partner grinned happily.

When they got to the car, Lonnie was limping.

"My gimp again," he said. "Drive, will you, Ray?"

Ray was pale and shaking.

"Not me!" he groaned. "Let's take a cab."

Lonnie noticed for the first time the condition Ray was in.

"Sorry, Ray," he said. Then he laughed. "Things were pretty rugged for a while, weren't they?"

"That's a mild word. No more of that for me."

Lonnie laughed again. He was still flushed with victory and in high spirits.

"Slide in, Ray. I'll drive."

5

Lonnie and Mary were in their bedroom at the beach house, getting ready for dinner. All the windows were open and a gorgeous Indian-summer night was pouring in. Mary was already fully dressed, but she was still struggling with her hair, which she couldn't get fixed to suit her. Lonnie, in his shirtsleeves, was tying his tie. Mary turned to him.

"Shall I wear my hair up tonight? It looks simply awful this way."

Lonnie glanced over at her.

"It looks great to me no matter how you wear it."

"Oh, you're no help at all."

Lonnie grinned and went on with his tie. Mary turned back to the mirror and started to work on her hair again.

"There," said Lonnie, patting his tie, "that does it." Then he stood staring into the mirror. "How do you think I ought to wear *my* hair tonight, honey? Would bangs go with a blue necktie?" He pulled his hair down over his forehead.

Mary turned, slightly annoyed; then she burst out laughing.

"You feel good, don't you, Lonnie?"

"Sure."

"I'm glad things turned out so well. I always thought they would, but—all the same, it must be a great relief to you."

"Gus even offered me a job."

"Are you considering it?" Mary spoke lightly, but she was worried. A connection with Gus could lead, she was certain, to nothing but trouble.

"Oh, I don't know," said Lonnie thoughtfully. "I've got a pretty good business. And now I'm solvent."

"And please, Lonnie, let's stay that way. I mean about expenses. We spend too much money."

"Sure, sure," said Lonnie carelessly.

He put on his coat; then he began to fold a decorative handkerchief for his breast pocket.

"Ordinarily," he said, indicating the handkerchief, "I wouldn't wear one of these things—looks too much like the Greek. But tonight—well, it's a special occasion. I don't want to disgrace you in front of your friends."

"Lonnie! Mr. Keller's no more a friend of mine than he is of yours. And as for Toby and Jean—!"

A sudden thought struck Lonnie and he began to wonder. Turning, he looked at Mary for a long time. She noticed his scrutiny and became a little self-conscious, or so it seemed to him.

"How did you happen to ask the Kellers over to dinner tonight?" he inquired.

"Well, I ran into Mr. Keller downtown. He asked about you. And—you know how it is. One thing led to another." Lonnie turned away and lit a cigarette, still thoughtful. "As a matter of fact, Lonnie, I think he wants to talk business with you."

"I thought that was it."

"Do you object?"

"Of course not."

"Then I don't understand your expression. You look suspicious, as if you thought somebody was trying to put something over on you."

"Keller never does anything without a purpose. That's what I mean."

"Well, just so you don't think it's a conspiracy," said Mary firmly. "I've told you a dozen times I want you to do what you want to do."

"I know."

"Mr. Keller heard all about the coup—I think that's what you call it— and he was appalled. He said you must have the nerve of the devil and that you ought to be discouraged from doing things like that in the future. I told him you did what you pleased and I was perfectly satisfied."

Lonnie grinned and, coming over to Mary's dressing table, put his arm around her and kissed her.

"My hair! My lipstick!" cried Mary.

"Oh—sorry!" exclaimed Lonnie, drawing back. Then: "I'm glad you said that to Keller. But I'll bet he gave you a talking-to."

"He did. He said you ought to give up gambling for good. He told me he'd given it up, and he was an older man than you and had been at it longer."

"How do you like that!"

"And he also said that he thought the Government was going to close all the tracks and that all the bookies would have to go to work."

Lonnie laughed.

"God help us! I can just see that bunch of boys in a defense plant. We're not *that* bad off, are we?"

Lonnie laughed again, then he sobered and began to study Mary's profile. She sensed that he was looking at her, but she pretended to notice nothing and went on fixing her hair. All the same there *had* been a conspiracy—of a kind—and she felt decidedly guilty. Keller was a very strong-minded and authoritative man, hard to resist. He'd brushed her scruples aside. "Mary," he'd said, "you're like one of the family, and I'm not going to stand by and see your life all messed up. If I'd known the trouble Lonnie was in, I'd've lent him the money to pay his way out." She'd tried to explain that Lonnie had only gone into the deal because they'd been spending so much money, principally on her, and were in the red to such an extent that something had to be done. Keller brushed all this aside also. "There are other ways to get money," he said. "Businessmen can borrow. If they couldn't, nobody could stay in business, especially now." "But Lonnie's no businessman," she'd protested. "Oh, isn't he?" jeered Keller. "He's done mighty well with that restaurant. Better than Ballard, an old restaurant man, did. He just needs settling down, that's all. Once he gets out of his head the idea that the only way to make money is to gamble, he'll give us all a run for it." Then Keller had practically invited himself to dinner.

"Keller's one of those 'I'm telling you' guys," said Lonnie finally. "But he's all right. A smart man."

There was a long pause. Mary finished with her hair and got up.

"At least listen to him, Lonnie," she said, rather diffidently, he thought. "Then—do as you please."

Pinky stood with his ear pressed to the kitchen door, trying to hear what was going on in the dining room. But he could only catch a word or two, and after a minute he swore to himself and gave up. All the same, something was going on. "I guess I know what I'm talking about," he mused. "I said Old Man Keller'd be eating here." He lit a cigarette, leaned back against the sink, and began to hum "The Rose of Tralee" softly, singing a word here and there. He felt good.

Willy came in with the tray and put it down on the sink.

"Well—?" cried Pinky.

"I can't make out what it's all about," said Willy, shaking his head. "He talks too fast and, anyway, he makes me nervous. He looks right through you."

"It's something about business, ain't it?"

"Yeah, I guess so."

"I'll bet he's going to take the boss in with him. That's my prediction."

"Your prediction!" scoffed Willy. "Since when did you set up as a prophet?"

"I said Keller'd be eating here, didn't I?"

"Anyway," said Willy, ignoring Pinky's boasting, "it makes no difference. The boss won't go in with Keller. Why should he? A guy smart enough to pull off what he did, with fellows like Benny Hayt and Gus Borgia, is not going to waste his time running a business. He'll get rid of that restaurant just as soon as he can. Mark my word."

"Mark your word! You were never right in your whole no-account life. I say Keller wants to take the boss in with him, and I say the boss is going to go for it."

Willy reached into his pocket and fumbled frantically.

"I got twenty bucks says you're wrong. Put up or shut up."

"You got a bet," cried Pinky. "Lay your dough right here on the sink with mine."

Willy complied. There was a pause, then Pinky went to the kitchen door and listened.

"They're leaving the dining room," he said. "Now I won't be able to hear a damn thing."

"I'm sure going to enjoy spending that twenty bucks of yours," said Willy, grinning. "Velvet, that's what it is, velvet!"

Pinky grimaced, then drew back from the door. "Somebody's coming."

"It's probably Ray. He's sure had a big time tonight."

"Yeah. The missus just wouldn't take no for an answer that he eat with them."

"He ought to be able to give us the dope."

The door opened and Ray came in. His face was flushed from the wine he'd drunk at dinner and he looked so dressed up that he seemed almost like a stranger to Willy and Pinky.

"That was a fine dinner, Pinky," he said. "Mr. Keller can't stop talking about it." Pinky swelled out his chest and glanced contemptuously at Willy, whose lips tightened. "And, Willy, the missus is proud of the way you served." Willy grinned and strutted a little.

"Anybody can serve," said Pinky, annoyed. "It takes talent to cook."

They began to bicker, but Ray intervened.

"Not so loud, boys."

"Say," demanded Willy suddenly, "what's going on in there?"

"Plenty," said Ray. "Mr. Keller's branching out again. He wants Lonnie to go into the restaurant business with him."

Pinky laughed loudly and slapped his thigh in his excitement. Willy glanced uneasily at the money on the sink.

"The boss ain't going to, is he?" he asked in trepidation.

"I don't know," said Ray. "He'd be foolish not to. But you know him."

"He'll never do it," cried Willy.

Pinky nodded vigorously.

"It's a cinch. Don't forget—he's got the missus now."

"I certainly hope he does," said Ray, thoughtfully. "It's a great opportunity. Mr. Keller wants to take over the dining room and grill in the New Richmond Hotel, and another big place on the south shore. And he wants Lonnie to supervise all of them, including the one Lonnie's got now. Each place will have its own manager. It leaves Lonnie pretty free. But—I don't know."

There was a pause and they all stood lost in thought. Finally Ray came to himself and spoke.

"I'm going downstairs. I'm full as a tick. Maybe I'll lie down for a while. Lonnie wants me to go back to the apartment with them as soon as the Kellers leave, so keep me posted, Willy."

"You bet."

"I thought we were going to stay here all night. Damn it!" grumbled Pinky. "I brought my pajamas."

"The ones with the red and green awning stripes, I'll bet," jeered Willy. Ray laughed and went out.

"You see?" said Pinky. "What did I tell you?"

"He'll never go for it in this world!"

"How about another twenty?"

Willy carefully scratched his head and considered.

"If you're so sure," he said finally, "how about odds?"

"Okay. Twenty against fifteen. But you got to put it on the sink. I wouldn't trust you as far as a blind man could see you."

Willy hesitated.

"What's the matter?" jeered Pinky. "Lost your nerve?"

"I ain't got the cash."

"Then forget it. No tabs with me." Pinky rubbed his hand over his face and lit a cigarette. "He's a cinch to go in," he insisted. "Then pretty soon we'll probably buy a house on Ashland Boulevard or maybe Oxford Circle and then we can all be together again like in the old days." He turned and studied Willy. "Ain't you glad you stopped stealing Lonnie blind? You'd've been fired long ago."

"Yeah?" cried Willy, flaring. "And maybe it's a good thing you give up chasing the cleaning woman through the house. How would the missus like that?"

They began to quarrel bitterly. Pinky finally lost his temper. He grabbed up a dish and was just getting ready to heave it at Willy, who was cringing against the wall with his arms over his head like a terrified monkey, when the door opened and Lonnie came in.

"What the hell's going on here?" he cried. "Can't you bums settle down for one night?"

Pinky grinned self-consciously, lowered the dish, then put it carefully back on the sink.

"He's always annoying me," explained Pinky, jerking a thumb at Willy. "He's got a nasty tongue."

"Yours is not so sweet," said Lonnie, curtly. "I've been leaning on that buzzer for five minutes. You bums better watch your step."

Pinky and Willy sobered at once and exchanged a glance.

"What is it you want, boss—Mr. Drew?" stammered Willy.

"Rustle up some ice for the highballs. And make it snappy."

"Yes, sir."

Lonnie glanced past him at the sink.

"What's that money over there?"

Pinky and Willy looked at each other in embarrassment.

"It's a bet we got," said Pinky. Then he hesitated for a moment. "About you."

"Me?"

"Yes, boss—Mr. Drew. We heard—that is, we thought we heard—that maybe you're figuring on going in business with Mr. Keller. Willy bet me you wasn't."

Lonnie looked from one to the other, then his face relaxed.

"Willy," he said, "you lose. I hope at least you got odds."

"No," said Willy, shaking his head, "even."

Lonnie laughed. "Didn't your old lady ever warn you about gambling?" he inquired. Then he turned and went out, still laughing.

Pinky picked up the money, waved it at Willy, then stuffed it into his pocket with a flourish.

"When did I set up as a prophet, eh!" he crowed.

But Willy paid no attention to him. He fell down onto a kitchen chair and sat with his head in his hands. He seemed so despondent that Pinky began to glance at him.

"What's wrong with you?"

"I was going to step out tomorrow night. Now I'm strapped. Good-looking babe, too."

Pinky grimaced.

"Never mind the con. You ain't getting any of this dough back."

Pinky leaned against the sink and lit a cigarette, humming to himself. All of a sudden Willy jumped up and slapped his forehead.

"Oh, God! The ice!"

He began to rush around. Pinky folded his arms and watched Willy's frantic movements with detachment. In a moment, softly and sentimentally; he began to sing "The Rose of Tralee."

THE END

W. R. BURNETT BIBLIOGRAPHY
(1899-1982)

NOVELS
Little Caesar (Dial, 1929)
Iron Man (Dial, 1930)
Saint Johnson (Dial, 1930)
The Silver Eagle (Dial, 1931)
The Giant Swing (Harper, 1932)
Dark Hazard (Harper, 1933)
Goodbye to the Past (Harper, 1934)
The Goodhues of Sinking Creek
   (Raven's Head, 1934)
King Cole (Harper, 1936)
The Dark Command (Knopf, 1938)
High Sierra (Knopf, 1940)
The Quick Brown Fox (Knopf, 1942)
Nobody Lives Forever (Knopf, 1943)
Tomorrow's Another Day (Knopf,
   1945)
Romelle (Knopf, 1946)
The Asphalt Jungle (Knopf, 1949)
Stretch Dawson (Gold Medal, 1950)
Little Men, Big World (Knopf, 1951)
Vanity Row (Knopf, 1952)
Adobe Walls (Knopf, 1953)
Big Stan (as by John Monahan; Gold
   Medal, 1953)
Captain Lightfoot (Knopf, 1954)
It's Always Four O'Clock (as by
   James Updyke; Random, 1956)
Pale Moon (Knopf, 1956)
Underdog (Knopf, 1957)
Bitter Ground (Knopf, 1958)
Mi Amigo (Knopf, 1959)
Conant (Popular Library, 1961)
Round the Clock at Volari's (Gold
   Medal, 1961)
Sergeants 3 (Pocket, 1962)
The Goldseekers (Doubleday, 1962)
The Widow Barony (UK only;
   Macdonald, 1962)
The Abilene Samson (Pocket, 1963)
The Winning of Mickey Free
   (Bantam, 1965)
The Cool Man (Gold Medal, 1968)
Good-bye Chicago (St. Martin's,
   1981)

SHORT STORIES
Across the Aisle (*Collier's*, Apr 4,
   1936)
Between Rounds (*Collier's*, Aug 30,
   1930)
Captain Lightfoot (*Argosy*, UK, Nov,
   Dec 1954, Jan 1955)
Dr. Socrates (*Collier's*, Mar 23, 1935)
Dressing-Up (*Harper's*, Nov 1929;
   Ellery Queen's Mystery Magazine,
   June 1947)
First Blood (*Collier's*, Apr 23 1938)
Girl in a Million (*Redbook*, Jan 1938)
Head Waiter (*Cosmopolitan*, Sept
   1931)
High Sierra (*Five Star Western
   Stories*, July 1941)
The Hunted (*Liberty*, June 28 1930)
I Love Everybody (*Argosy*, UK, July
   1943)
Jail Breaker (*Collier's*, July 7, July
   14, July 21, Aug 4 1934)
Little David (*The Saturday Evening
   Post*, Feb 15 1947)
Mr. Litvinoff (*Collier's*, July 18 1931)
Nobody Lives Forever (*Collier's*, Oct
   9, Oct 16, Oct 23, Oct 30 1943)
Nobody's All Bad [Billy the Kid]
   (*Collier's*, Jun 7 1930; *Ellery
   Queen's Mystery Magazine*, Dec
   1953)
Protection (*Collier's*, May 9, May 23
   1931)
Racket Alley (*Collier's*, Dec 16 1950,
   Jan 6 1951)
Round Trip (*Harper's*, Aug 1929;
   Ellery Queen's Mystery Magazine,
   Dec 1950)
Suspect (Collier's, July 4 1936)
Throw Him Off the Track (*Argosy*,
   Dec 1952)
Traveling Light (*Collier's*, Dec 7
   1935; *Ellery Queen's Mystery
   Magazine*, Sep 1951)
Vanishing Act (*Manhunt*, Nov 1955;
   Mike Shayne Mystery Magazine,
   Aug 1964)

War Party (*Lilliput*, May 1954)
Youth Is Not Forever (*Redbook*, Feb
  1939)

ESSAYS
Whatever Happened to Baseball?
  (*Rogue*, June 1963, article)
The Roar of the Crowd (Potter, 1964)

SCREENPLAY CONTRIBUTIONS
The Finger Points (1931)
Beast of the City (1932)
Scarface: The Shame of a Nation
  (1932)
High Sierra (1941)
The Get-Away (1941)
This Gun for Hire (1942)
Wake Island (1942)
Crash Dive (1943)
Action in the North Atlantic (1943)
Background to Danger (1943)
San Antonio (1945)
Nobody Lives Forever (1946)
Belle Starr's Daughter (1949)

Vendetta (1950)
The Racket (1951)
Dangerous Mission (1954)
I Died a Thousand Times (1955)
Captain Lightfoot (1955)
Illegal (1955)
Short Cut to Hell (1957)
September Storm (1960)
Sergeants Three (1962)
The Great Escape (1963)

UNCREDITED SCREEN
CONTRIBUTIONS
Law and Order (1932)
The Whole Town's Talking (1935)
The Westerner (1940)
The Man I Love (1946)
The Walls of Jericho (1948)
The Asphalt Jungle (1950)
Night People (1954)
The Hangman (1959)
Four for Texas (1963)
Ice Station Zebra (1968)
Stiletto (1969)

Made in the USA
Columbia, SC
06 May 2024

34959780R00157